SPIES AMONG US

AN ALEX BOYD THRILLER

MEL HARRISON

AHA PUBLISHERS

Edited and Interior Design by AHA Publishers, an imprint of A Howard Activity, LLC

Cover design by Bob Hurley. BestImpressionsBookDesigns.com

Jaguar photo by jaguarment at wikimedia commons cc by 2.0 (desaturated).

PRINTED IN THE UNITED STATES OF AMERICA

ISBN: 979-8-9872226-1-4 (paperback)

Available for purchase on Amazon.com and TheWritersMall.com

ACKNOWLEDGMENTS

I want to thank my wife, Irene, for her ceaseless efforts to improve what I wrote. Her proof-reading, story line suggestions, and character critiques all helped to keep the novel focused and real. As a fellow career Foreign Service professional, Irene served with me around the world, sharing the same risks, frustrations, and exciting times.

My editor, Paula Howard, deserves an extraordinary thanks for reviewing my manuscript with a keen, professional eye. An excellent writer in her own right, she taught me how to write more effectively in order to capture the imagination of the reader.

Finally, I need mention that I drew upon open, unclassified sources for references to the tools of electronic espionage. I hope you find the novel exciting as much as I enjoyed writing it for you.

TABLE OF CONTENTS

ACRONYMS

DS – Diplomatic Security
DCM – US Embassy Deputy Chief of Mission RSO and Regional Security Officer
MI-5 – British Security Service (Domestic)
MI-6 – British Secret Intelligence Service (Foreign)
SAS – Special Air Service (British special forces elite regiment)
Spetsnaz – Russian Army equivalent to US Army Delta Force, US Navy SEALS
SVR – Russian Overseas Espionage Service, successor to the KGB

Major American Characters in US and London
Alex Boyd – Special Agent DS and RSO at US Embassy London
Dennis Hager – Under Secretary of State for Management
Charles Martin – Secretary of State
Jim Riley- Director Diplomatic Security, State Department
Rachel Smith – Political Counselor/US Embassy, Alex's wife
Wakefield Summers – Deputy Secretary of State
Archibald Watson, Assistant Secretary for Europe, State Department

US Embassy London
Anna Battles – CIA Station Chief
Roger Carpenter – FBI Legal Attaché
Erica Evans- Management Counselor
Gary Jones – Outgoing Regional Security Officer (RSO)
April Scott- Political Officer
Bainbridge Wellington - DCM, US Embassy, in London

United Kingdom
Geoffrey Carver – Assistant Director, MI-5
Gerald Davies - Assistant Commissioner Metropolitan Police, London (aka Scotland Yard)
Hilda Humphries Ph.D. - Professor at Oxford University
Lars Nilsson - Swedish boyfriend of April Scott (Dimitri Vasiliev)
Ray Penner - Commander, Special Branch, Metropolitan Police
Deidre Plummer – Public Affairs, Metropolitan Police
Sir Nigel Sharpton – Permanent Secretary, Foreign Office
Mark Thompson-Parker – Colonel, 22 SAS
Bill Turpin – Warrant Officer, 22 SAS
Josh Rosen – Inspector, Special Branch, Metropolitan Police

Russian Diplomats Washington DC
Andrei Balakin – Senior SVR official, Russian Embassy
Nickolai Petrov – SVR handler of senior American spy for Russia
Ludmilla Petrov – Wife of Nickolai, SVR officer, Russian Embassy

Russian Officials, Moscow
Anton Kuznetsov – Director SVR
Ilya Sokolov – Deputy Director for Operations SVR

Russian Assassins
Sergei – Sgt. in Russian Army, Spetsnaz
Viktor – Sgt. in Russian Army, Spetsnaz

1

THE RENDEZVOUS

Oxfordshire, England

April Scott paced in her Oxfordshire hotel room like a delicate bird trapped in a cage, occasionally readjusting her cream-colored blouse which had become tighter over the years. Her stomach was in knots from tension. Pausing by the antique mahogany cabinet, she pulled out a cigarette from the packet resting on top, lit it, and inhaled deeply. Smoking in the room was against hotel rules. *Screw it,* she thought, *I want one and I need one.*

A short glass of whiskey was sitting next to the Marlboro packet with a smidgen of liquid left. April grabbed it and polished it off, feeling the burn in her throat as she swallowed, then splashed more whiskey and water into the glass for a second time in the last thirty minutes.

Walking over to an open window, she inhaled deeply on her cigarette, then slowly blew smoke outside into the cool night air. She leaned back against the wall thinking about her impending rendezvous with Lars Nilsson, then realized her hand was trembling. With each additional puff, her eyes began tearing up. Reaching into the right pocket of her outdated plaid skirt, she clenched the small SD card she would pass on to him, something she had done on a few prior.

occasions during the last three months. April feared the secrets on the drive were perhaps all he cared about, but her heart yearned for his love and companionship. He had, after all, told her he loved her so many times.

Could it be true? Could he want both my love, as well as the information I've stolen? A tear ran down her cheek. *It is possible, isn't it?* She wanted to believe it.

April's leather purse lay on the bed. She walked across the room and picked it up. Her hand quivered slightly. *Why am I nervous?* In the outside leather compartment was her US Embassy-London ID card. She took out the color-coded card, which signified she held a top-secret security clearance, as did all other political officers in her section.

After staring at it, she made a fist, slowly bringing it up to her mouth, and bit into one of her fingers, as if pain could offset the treason she was committing. She knew exactly what she was doing and the pain didn't help.

"COME ON, get out of my way!" Lars Nilsson cursed the heavy traffic snarling the Oxford city by-pass. He shifted from 2nd to 3rd gear as he accelerated away from the pack on the A40, realizing he was already late to meet April. Instinctively, he reached out and touched the gift box on the passenger seat. *Hopefully, this necklace will make her forget my tardiness,* he thought. *I'm only ten minutes away.* His foot pressed harder on the accelerator as traffic picked up.

I'm only half looking forward to seeing her, he sighed, *but seeing her regularly is part of my assignment, and it's necessary.* The words rumbled around in his head. *Surprisingly, our sex is better than I expected even though her conversational skills are a trifle dull. She focuses more on everyday politics than I like; and a great beauty, she is not. Although she is passable.*

He shook his head and felt bad about his duplicity. April was a good woman and he had used her as if she didn't matter. *But she does matter, at least to me.* The truck in front of him pulled to the side, and he finally had open road ahead; his dark blue Volvo sedan lurched forward, and he thought he might not be so late after-all.

A few minutes later, Lars saw the sign for the country hotel and turned off the main road, followed the elm tree lined lane until he reached his rendezvous. The surrounding lawn was immaculate, and the plantings around the mid-nineteenth-century brick hotel were neatly trimmed and full of life. Large drops of rain began pounding the car as he parked in the gravel lot. He quickly pulled his expensive tan leather weekend bag out of the trunk and ran to the entrance.

To hell with the weather, he thought. He and April would spend the night at the hotel and eat dinner in its excellent restaurant. Tomorrow, he would drive her around the Cotswolds, visiting small villages, antique shops, and delighting in the charms of the English countryside before returning to spend a second night with her at this hotel. *Not a bad assignment, really.*

Lars loved the English countryside; in fact, he loved *everything* about England. He enjoyed its history, its fine dining at select locations, its charming pubs, and he treasured the bespoke tailoring of his suits and shirts. He even valued the freedom he enjoyed, although he could never speak of the latter back home. Next weekend would be much the same but at a different location. No doubt in the coming days in London, she would pressure him about seeing her every evening, and he would make time to see her a little extra, maybe once or twice. But as before, he would tell her that not only did owning his own electronics company demand long hours, but his business required a lot of travel to the continent, so he would be gone more often than she would like.

Sorry, my dear, but I have to earn a living.

He entered the hotel, already knowing which room she was in, and walked up the broad staircase with its dark wood banisters to the second floor. Taking a deep breath, he knocked three times on the door and waited for his "sweetheart" to answer.

April opened the door, Lars stepped into the room, and she wrapped her arms around his waist, then looked up at his face before kissing him tenderly. With his free hand, he reached behind to close the door, and dropped his bag on the floor. Finally, he returned her full embrace. When they separated, he saw she had been crying and made a mental note to be cautious with what he said tonight.

"How was your drive?" she asked.

"Tedious, too much traffic. I'm sorry I'm late." "Let me take your coat."

First, he reached into the pocket of his worsted wool blazer and handed her the rich looking green box with the necklace.

"What's this?" Her face brightened. Holding the box in her left hand, she pointed to the box's upscale logo with her right index finger. "You shouldn't have, Lars."

"Nonsense, you deserve it," he smiled.

She opened the gift and took a deep breath, then kissed him full on the mouth. Tossing the empty container onto the bed, she fastened the gold necklace around her neck. When she was done admiring her reflection in the mirror, he handed her his blue blazer and she hung it over the back of a chair. Then turning back to Lars, she rubbed her hands together nervously, and smiled.

Lars looked at her closely. *She's off tonight. Something is wrong.* Then he asked, "Is everything all right, darling?"

It was silent as a graveyard for an extended moment. She clasped her small hands together, resting them under her chin, while he waited patiently.

"I have something to ask you, but I'll wait until later."

As much as he wanted to know the problem right away, his instincts and training told him not to rush her. Let it play out. He sensed her fragility and knew she needed to be reassured that everything was going to be okay. Lars stepped forward and held her in his arms. The only sound was the rain pouring down onto the slate roof of the hotel.

"Would you like a drink?" she asked.

He nodded and she poured him a double whiskey, then they sat down in chairs facing each other. He admired the room's floral-patterned wallpaper adorned with prints of horseback riders in red coats. She, however, seemed to have a major concern on her mind and was oblivious to the decor.

Lars watched her carefully, concerned about her attitude. He knew she had insecurities about her age, thirty-eight years old and unmarried, as well as about her figure since she was few pounds overweight. He brushed back the loose blond hair hanging over his eyes and smiled at her, trying to reassure her that everything was fine. Lars knew he was attractive to women. Indeed, that was one reason he had been selected for this type of work.

"Shall we go downstairs to the restaurant now?" he asked.

She nodded, and they polished off their drinks.

Lars grabbed his jacket off the chair, slipped it on, and took her hand in his. They left the room for what he hoped would be an enjoyable meal. But, instinctively, he knew there was trouble on the horizon; he would have to use compassion and subtlety to deal with it.

∼

LARS AND APRIL sat at a table next to a tall window overlooking the majestic garden outside. Yellow ground level lights illuminated the outside and gave them a pleasant view of the garden and boxwoods lining a pathway. Inside the high-ceilinged dining room, dark wood paneling rose halfway up the walls. From the top of the paneling to the high ceiling, a muted red toile pattern of wallpaper displayed scenes of 17th century men and women of apparent wealth picnicking on lawns with servants in attendance. The large stone fireplace at the end of the room had a small blaze going, although this wasn't necessary since the temperature in early March wasn't that cold. Nevertheless, the crackling sound was pleasant, as was the aroma of burning wood.

He ordered steak au poivre with dauphine potatoes. She had rack of lamb with a mint sauce and asparagus with hollandaise. Lars examined the wine list and selected a full-bodied French Bordeaux. He had been to this restaurant before, although not with April, and loved the little things that gave it elegance: White linen tablecloths, the glass-enclosed candles burning in the center of each table, the crystal wine glasses, and fine bone china settings everywhere.

Throughout the evening repast, April spoke of inconsequential things. He felt she was just making small talk until she got to what was upsetting her. Occasionally, she mentioned something about British politics, but not in depth. Lars knew she was more intelligent than she was revealing this evening and assumed that something was keeping her from showing off. Several times he had to carry the conversation, so into their conversation, he wove snippets of news from the latest newspaper headlines and trivia from his latest travels to Warsaw, Prague, and Budapest. By the end of the meal, they had polished off the bottle of Bordeaux and both were feeling a pleasant buzz. Nevertheless, they were able to meander upstairs to their room without embarrassing themselves.

April collapsed into an overstuffed, cream-colored wing chair while Lars sat on the end of the bed, facing her. He waited for her to talk. She stared into his blue eyes before she cleared her throat.

"Lars . . . I want to be with you forever. I want to wake up every morning with you at my side. I want you to be my partner . . . for life." She looked for his reaction.

He smiled, anticipating there would be a "but," and waited. "But I'm not comfortable copying classified material from the Embassy so that your Swedish friends can be reassured that the US and NATO have Sweden's security in mind when they are dealing with Russia." She continued to lock eyes with him.

There it was, he thought. *Careful now . . .*

"Sweetheart, I appreciate that you have misgivings about passing on this information," he replied. "I can assure you that it's only to confirm what we believe already to be the case. It's like an insurance policy: We don't think we'll ever need it, but can we afford to take the risk?"

"I could go to *prison* for what I'm giving you, Lars. Surely, your foreign office is getting official assurances from Washington all the time. And besides, why do *you* have to get involved? You own an electronics company in London. You're not a Swedish government official."

"It's quite natural for governments to reach out to their private citizens for information," he countered. "I'm sure the US Government does the same with American businessmen abroad. And besides, the Swedish Government knows that I travel extensively and have a wide range of friends and contacts. It's only natural to make inquiries, don't you think?"

He watched her reaction closely and believed she was considering what he had said. Nevertheless, he needed to drive home his point and convince her that providing classified material was not that big a deal. "Look at it this way: The US and Swedish governments have the closest of relationships. Sensitive information is shared all the time. Sweden and the rest of NATO also have a joint interest in maintaining stability in northern Europe by deterring Russian aggression. It's just natural."

He casually crossed one leg over the other. April stood up and went into the bathroom. He heard water running, and when she came out, she was drying her face off with a towel.

"I'm sorry, Lars, I love you; I truly do. But I can't continue sneaking around my office copying secrets so your people can be 'reassured.' This has to stop, now!"

Her vehemence surprised him. "Maybe we should consider this tomorrow morning when we haven't been drinking," he said.

"No. I've decided. Moreover, I think we should take our relationship to the next level. I want to get married. There, I've said it. I want to get *married* to you!"

She dropped her towel onto the chair and walked across the room sitting down beside him on the bed. She put her arms around his shoulders and kissed him. He was nearly speechless and realized he wasn't prepared to come up with a clever reply.

"I love you too, April. But why not sleep on it, and when we have clear heads in the morning, we can discuss it further." He smiled at her but saw her face growing red with anger. She stood up abruptly.

"I *don't believe* you love me! And if that's the case, I think you should leave right *now*."*Oh, my god, does she mean it? Or is it the alcohol talking?* he wondered. His professional tradecraft had completely failed him tonight. *Perhaps it is best to regroup in the morning and take a new approach, maybe even tell her the truth of who I am.* However, he would have to consult with the others before taking that step.

"Okay, I won't force myself upon you," he managed. "If you want me to leave, I will. But please, April, let's talk about this in the morning. I love you, *too*." He tried kissing her on the cheek, but she pushed him away. Lars stared at her, then picked up his unopened weekend bag and left the room.

April lay on the bed sobbing for a long time, then drew a bath, stepped out of her clothes, and slid down into the hot soapy water to soak. As she lay there, she looked at her toiletry bag resting on the sink, remembering there were sharp razor blades inside.

Is my situation that hopeless? She couldn't decide and began crying again.

2

A QUESTION OF LOYALTY

A Firing Range in Washington, DC

"I see you're still a pretty good shot," Bill Stiles said to Alex Boyd, a senior special agent with the Diplomatic Security Service. As range instructor, he stood behind Alex in one of the ten firing lanes at the facility. "You scored 285 out of a maximum 300 points possible. Not bad for your first day back at the range." It was Alex's warm-up round with the DS 9 mm pistol.

"Thanks, buddy, but I should be able to do a lot better than 285. How about if I put the Glock aside and requalify with my former weapon, the Sig Sauer?"

"Everyone is supposed to make the transition to the Glock model 19. You know that."

"I know, but I just beat the qualification score with the Glock in the warm-up. So, how about it?"

"Well, I guess so, but only because I like you."

In the adjacent firing lane, Special Agent Linda Cantrell overheard them and called out. "Oh my God, enough of this bromance! Next, you guys will want to go out for a beer or something."

All three of them laughed easily. Alex had known Linda for five years and Bill Stiles for fifteen. The burley Stiles had joined DS after years as an Army warrant officer. He was a terrific instructor, especially with agents who were more challenged at the range, therefore, those who needed more help. Alex respected that quality. As for Cantrell, the solidly built Tennessee woman had grown up with weapons, loved to hunt, and had a well-earned reputation for being an excellent shot.

Glad to be active again, Alex took a moment to look around the range. At one end, shooters stood before their lanes where familiar metal partitions were between each position. Overhead wires carried the targets downrange and back on motorized pulleys, thereby altering the distance to the target. All side and rear walls were padded with ballistic absorbing material. And, of course, there was the ever-present smell of cordite in the air from spent ammunition. In the adjacent weapons cleaning room, the 'aroma' of Hoppes gun lubricating solution filled the nostrils. Often in a jovial mood, Bill Stiles would say: "I love the smell of Hoppes in the Morning," his homage to the movie, 'Apocalypse Now.'

Alex hadn't been to the shooting range since he had been shot in Cairo by a terrorist from Egyptian Islamic Jihad. An AK-47 bullet had gone through his left bicep and entered his body just under his armpit, causing so much damage that he had almost died. That was six months prior. Upon his return to active duty just two months ago, DS Director Jim Riley put him in an advisor position, reporting directly to Riley. Now that he was fit again, Alex was required to re-qualify with DS weapons. He had always been an extraordinary shooter, even getting perfect scores a few times, including on the night fire course. The question now, however, was whether he was still up to the task.

While Bill walked off to get a Sig Sauer model 228 from the weapons locker, Alex chatted with Linda and five other headquarters agents who were also here to requalify. All had served in embassies abroad and wanted Alex to give them first-hand details of the Cairo shootout. Before Alex could tell them much, Bill returned and handed the 9 mm Sig Sauer pistol and holster to Alex who loaded three magazines with thirteen rounds of semi-jacketed hollow-point. He was ready. Bill went into the control booth, turned on the microphone, and started the official qualification round.

"All agents, chamber a round, holster your weapon, and approach the firing line."

Alex knew the drill. First, they would fire from the three-yard line. So close that only a novice could miss the target. But most assassination attempts occurred at very close range, so agents had to be ready and capable of drawing fast and firing accurately to protect their VIP. Accidentally shooting by-standers was a tragedy to be avoided at all costs.

Then additional rounds of fire would take place from seven yards, fifteen yards, and finally at twenty-five yards. Targets were electronically controlled by the instructor so that each target would swivel to face the shooter, giving the agent only a short period of time to draw the gun and fire before the target swiveled back, making further shots worthless. Timing intervals varied from as little as three-seconds to fire off two shots at three yards, to longer intervals at greater distances, sometimes requiring a combat reload. At the twenty-five-yard distance, agents had to shoot a few bullets with their off-hand, meaning Alex would have to switch the pistol into his left hand for the final five shots.

Compared to the semi-annual training at the Diplomatic Security extensive outdoor range facility, located several hours away, this indoor requalification course was a piece of cake. Today, Alex only had to fire his pistol, the Remington pump shotgun with oo

buck ammunition, and the Heckler & Koch MP-5 9 mm submachine gun. However, at the outdoor range facility, the 5.56 M-4
carbine, and incorporated movement between targets, pop-up
targets, shooting from moving vehicles, and clearing a house with
mock terrorists and hostages was also added.

After a while, at the end of the pistol requalification course,
Alex had scored 292, an improvement from his earlier practice
round. Yet, he felt rusty. *If I had time, which I don't now,* he thought,
I'd ask Bill Stiles for a chance to shoot after everyone else is gone.

The opportune moment passed as the group moved on to the
MP-5 submachine gun exercise. That's when Alex was surprised.
Lifting his left hand to hold the front part of the weapon, called
the 'forearm,' he felt discomfort, a twinge of pain, under his left
armpit. The Egyptian surgeons who had operated on him had told
him he might feel this using certain arm positions for some time.
They simply had declined to say for how long. Now, this pain was
affecting his shooting accuracy, but was bearable. When Alex fired
the shotgun, the same thing happened.

Oh, well, he thought, *at least I've qualified.* He thanked Bill for
swapping the Glock for the Sig Sauer, and said he'd call to get in
more range time. Then, after shaking hands with the other agents,
Alex drove back to DS headquarters. He needed to review an
important Top-Secret report that Director Riley had given him for
a second time. The subject was espionage and concerned a high-
level State Department official.

∼

AS HE READ the detailed secret intelligence assessment, Alex felt
his blood pressure rise. He recognized it had the intricacies of a
John LeCarre spy novel. Bits and pieces fit together almost like a
jigsaw puzzle, yet didn't quite reveal every aspect of the case.
Although deeply concerned with the allegations, he realized not

everything he was reading was fully supported with hard evidence.

To Claudia Jacques credit, the analyst from Diplomatic Security who had drafted the report for Director James Riley, she had accurately noted the *lack* of irrefutable evidence for each allegation. Nevertheless, it was a damning notional indictment of Under Secretary of State for Management Dennis Hager.

Alex took off his black-framed reading glasses and pitched them onto his desk. He disliked wearing the new glasses, believing they made him look old, *Well, at least older than my forty years,* he thought. To the contrary, his wife, Rachel, said they gave him a "distinguished, professorial appearance," as she put it. Still, that wasn't necessarily a positive quality in his mind.

He had been a complete jock his entire life - tall, muscular, and still in possession of a full head of mostly dark hair except for a hint of grey at his temples. Not that he was against academic types, not at all, in fact, he was well-read and believed his analytical skills were excellent. It was just that he lived in a world of occasional violence, not stuffy academia. *"Looking like a professor just isn't my thing"* was how he justified it.

He picked up the intelligence assessment again and opened the folder. *It's clear why Jim asked me to review this long document,* he thought. Riley's instincts and professional experience had drawn him to the conclusion that U.S. Under Secretary Dennis Hager could be a spy working against the United States. Before he could re-read a specific section of importance, he heard a knock on his door. Alex looked up and saw Claudia Jacques in the open doorway. She was conservatively dressed in an attractive pants suit of grey tick-weave. A strand of pearls hung around her neck.

"Claudia! Come in," he smiled. Standing, he pointed to a chair in front of his desk. "Thanks for coming so quickly. I just wanted to go over a few points in the report before I see Riley."

"No problem, Alex." She looked around his office before sitting down.

"I admire your décor," she said. "Instead of all the cop memorabilia like most agents have like law enforcement plaques and police baseball caps, you've hung photos of places where you've served: Pakistan, Italy, France, Egypt, Argentina, and Tunisia. Very nice."

"Thanks. I figure everyone has plaques and hats. Those aren't memories, but these photos are, at least they are to me." Many of the photos showed Alex standing next to a tall, stunningly attractive woman, Rachel Smith, his wife.

"I see you've still got your State Department awards stacked on the floor in the corner. Are you ever going to put them up?"

"I haven't decided." "Why not?"

"I guess I feel a lot of my colleagues could have received these awards if they had been serving at the right post at the right time."

"I wouldn't be so sure. Not everyone rises to a challenge."

"Well, maybe you're right, Claudia. But a big factor in getting an award is sometimes based on how well your boss writes you up for the award nomination. That is, if he or she even *does* that."

"You're abnormally cynical today. What's up?"

Alex shrugged. "Maybe I just need another cup of coffee."

"I think it's because you don't tolerate all the bullshit in Washington very well." She spied another photo of Rachel set on the cadenza behind his desk. Rachel was standing in front of the Trevi fountain in Rome, laughing, about to toss a coin over her shoulder into the fountain for good luck. Seeing Claudia smiling, he asked, "What?"

"Rachel is the most beautiful woman I have ever met in person. You're a lucky guy."

"More than you realize." He had known Claudia for a few years. He liked and respected her; she worked in the DS Threat Analysis Office, handling both general threats in the European area, as well as all counter-intelligence threats worldwide. Now in her late thirties, she had been with DS for ten years.

"I heard you won't be with us much longer," he said. "That's right. I accepted a job offer from the CIA. It seems that finishing my Ph.D. last year in modern Russian history finally paid off."

"Congratulations, I'll miss you. You're a terrific analyst and a good friend."

"Thanks. But it's time to move on. Now, what can I tell you about my report?"

"To start, we both know that Under Secretary Hager and Director Riley hate each other. There's bad history between them based upon service at two embassies abroad, the last one when they both served as senior officers in the American Embassy in Moscow."

"Yeah, Hager, was the Management Counselor there, and was much too lax in countering the Russian threat of electronic and physical infiltration of the embassy. He and Riley clashed over everything: Access controls, wearing ID badges, and especially the non-fraternization policy with locals. When I was writing the report, Riley told me that Hager had the ambassador's ear. The ambassador thought Riley was too 'old school' regarding not trusting the Russians. It didn't end well."

Alex put his reading glasses back on and flipped to an earlier page in the report; it was the part when Hager had been a less senior Foreign Service officer and had served in the embassy's management section in Warsaw, Poland. By coincidence, Riley had been the RSO in Warsaw at that time.

"Tell me about Warsaw," Alex asked.

"It's pretty straight forward. Riley investigated Hager for receiving kickbacks from outside vendors on multiple embassy contracts. I read the original investigative case file, and the allegations couldn't be proven. Hager cleverly managed to distance himself from all paper trails. In the end, Riley could only nail a local Polish embassy employee for taking bribes. But the investigations left a bitter taste for everyone."

"Do you think Hager is dirty?"

"Possibly. He supervised the awarding of those contracts. Alternatively, he just might have been incompetent. But my guess is that he was smart enough to avoid direct accountability while pocketing some cash under the table."

Alex thumbed through additional pages in Claudia's report. While there were several items very critical of the now fifty-five-year-old Dennis Hager, the one that caught Alex's attention involved the two *verified* sexual affairs early in Hager's career in Buenos Aires, Argentina. Hager had been married to his first wife then, but in subsequent divorce proceedings, she alleged he was always flush with cash that he couldn't explain. *Was there a link between the money and the affairs?* Alex wondered. *Why would someone pay him money, unless it was for illegal activity? And what kind of activity?*

"I have almost twenty years' experience in Diplomatic Security," Alex said, "and I've seen a few marital affairs by embassy officers, but usually the officer is bleeding for money as a result, not the other way around. This case is bizarre; it should have been looked into further at the time."

"I agree. Unfortunately, the RSO had his hands filled with terrorism problems."

Alex had served in Buenos Aires on his first post abroad, but it was about a decade after Hager had departed the embassy. He vaguely recalled one employee saying Hager had a relationship with an Argentine woman of substantial wealth. Regarding the second affair, Alex's local investigator said Hager had been involved with a West German expatriate. *Hmm,* Alex thought, *what did these two women do for a living? Who were they, really?*

"Did we ever identify who the two women were? I asked," Alex said, "but because of the passage of time, no one could remember their names."

"There wasn't anything in the file to indicate who they were," Claudia replied. "I'd especially like to know about the West German."

"It was a long time ago," Alex sighed. "It seems that Dennis Hager's judgment and honesty are certainly questionable, but espionage? It's a big step from being a womanizer to being a traitor."

As Alex reached across his desk to grab a yellow highlighter, a stabbing pain in his left side made him grimace; he leaned back for a moment. *Shit, I keep forgetting the doctor told me that spot would be tender for several more months.* A 7.62 rifle bullet wound from a massive shootout with terrorists in Cairo six months earlier wasn't quite healed yet. He had been close to dead when the Egyptian surgeons had sliced him open to repair the damage. Now, he sat upright and breathed cautiously until the pain subsided.

I'm not getting old, dammit, just taking a breather, Alex thought and smiled. Fortunately, Claudia had been looking down at her notes and had missed Alex's reflex of pain. He didn't want it generally known that he was not back to one hundred percent fitness. No one needed to know.

"Here's the amazing thing about all of this," Claudia was saying. "Every time Dennis Hager returned to Washington in-between overseas assignments, he finagled himself into another significant special assistant job in one management office or another. He became the right-hand staffer to powerful people who helped Hager get promoted time and again."

"So, I noticed," Alex replied. "Now, as the Under Secretary for Management, he, once again, supervises Jim Riley. Poor Riley has to battle for resources and programs every week against opposition from that son-of-a-bitch."

Alex closed the file while rubbing his left side for a few

seconds and looked at his watch; he only had five minutes before his meeting with Riley. "Claudia, thank you for discussing your report," he said. "Let's have lunch before you move on to the CIA."

After she left, he stepped into the hallway toward the office coffee pot, again unhappy with the burned smell of the pungent dark liquid that had been sitting for a while. He filled his personal Virginia Cavaliers mug, sipped the bitterness, and walked into Director Jim Riley's office with the Hager file in hand. *I'm going to tell him what I think about all the allegations against Hager, even if he doesn't want to hear it.* Alex was determined that Riley heard his honest opinion.

3

THE OFFER

Washington DC

Riley lowered *The New York Times* onto his large Mahoney desk when he saw Alex enter. "Did you see *The Times* this morning?" he asked while stabbing the front page repeatedly with a finger loud enough to be heard in the next room.

"Nope, I barely got through the *Washington Post* sports section before Rachel wanted to talk about work issues."

"She didn't grab the paper first?"

"Nah, she read it online while getting ready for work. Nobody can multi-task better than she can. What's so important in *The Times?*"

"The God-damned Russians arrested one of their own senior SVR officers, claiming he was a CIA spy," he said. "This makes the second arrest this year of a CIA spy in Moscow and it's only *March*. Don't know why they don't just still call them KGB."

"What's Langley saying about the arrest?" Alex asked. "So far, there's no comment in the paper. In an hour, I'm going to an inter-agency meeting about this topic. Maybe I'll learn something there."

"I wonder who gave *The Times* that information." "Probably a viper who wants to poison the public's view of the Agency or has a personal axe to grind," Riley replied.

Alex looked at his boss and thought Jim Riley looked terrible. He had bags under his eyes, his facial skin looked less tight than a few months ago, and his complexion was pallid. Riley now walked with a slight stoop of his shoulders and seemed to have aged ten years since the new administration had taken over the White House in January. That's when new political appointees began being placed in every federal agency. Alex knew Riley still had a few years to go before mandatory retirement, but he was physically spiraling downward like a plane shot out of the sky.

"I gather you want to talk about this secret file on Dennis Hager," Alex said, raising the file with his right hand.

"Yes, I do. I value your perspective. What did you think about the report?" Riley asked.

Alex took a seat in the dark leather chair in front of Riley's desk. He knew this conversation was important; you didn't accuse the powerful Under Secretary of State for Management of treason unless you could back it up. Before speaking, Alex looked at the wall behind Riley's desk. It was covered with the usual accumulation of numerous government service awards for outstanding performance, plaques of appreciation from other agencies like the US Secret Service, and the US Marshals, and Riley's academic diplomas from Notre Dame and the National War College. Riley was a man of accomplishment and experience. His instincts had always been good in the past. Alex appreciated this man more than words could say.

"I thought it was well written and fairly well-documented, but if you want my opinion regarding whether to send it to the FBI for the purpose of opening an espionage investigation, I advise against it at this stage. Hager's policies are damaging to DS, but we can't say with confidence if that's because he's a spy."

"I already spoke with a senior contact at the FBI, informally, of course," Riley replied. "They agree there isn't enough evidence to officially open a case. They doubt the attorneys at the Justice Department will accept the report's suppositions linking Hager to espionage, at least not yet. Naturally, they claimed they weren't interested in the large cuts he's trying to make to Diplomatic Security. That's not very convincing since the FBI probably views any cuts to DS as an opportunity to fill the void and increase the number of their agents overseas."

"What did the FBI think about any potential links between the collapse of specific CIA intelligence operations and wherever Hager had served abroad?"

"They felt it was circumstantial," Riley replied. "I acknowledged that point and told them that was exactly *why* they should investigate further . . . to dig up concrete facts."

"And?"

"It wasn't worth their time without further predication. I guess they want the case handed to them in a gift box with a red bow attached. I don't know who's worse, that sneaky little shrimp Hager, or the bureaucrats in the FBI and at the Justice Department."

Alex noted the sarcasm and took a sip of coffee. "It's hard to stomach the fact that since Hager took over the Under Secretary job, he's already proposed serious cuts in RSO positions abroad, as well as downsizing most of our domestic operations. Shit, the White House only promoted him into the position three *months* ago. He's not wasting any time screwing Diplomatic Security."

"Yeah, tell me about it."

"Is there something you want me to do with this report?"

"I guess not. I just wanted your opinion. Consider the report FYI." As Riley seemed to sink deeper into his chair, Alex noticed again how pale his complexion seemed. When combined with his thinning grey hair, he appeared positively cadaverous.

"I know Hager hates me," Riley said, pausing before continuing, "and the feeling is mutual. But to destroy DS at a time when terrorism is growing just doesn't make sense, unless Hager's loyalties to the US are suspect. We've all known his judgment is terrible, but I feel his actions reflect something more than just bad judgment. Hell, at the weekly meetings of all the assistant secretaries, everyone asks me, '*What's going on, Jim? Why is Hager trying to destroy DS?*' I haven't found anyone in State who agrees with that son-of-a-bitch, or even likes him."

Alex reflected upon the views of the other assistant secretaries. They were fellow Foreign Service Officers, like Hager, and if *they* didn't like him or his policies, that meant a lot.

"What does the new Secretary of State think about this situation?"

"Damned if I know," Riley replied. "Nothing is final yet, so maybe Hager's crazy ideas haven't risen that high for approval. But DS is fighting for its life now."

"Is there anything I can do for you, Jim? You're the best director we've ever had, and you deserve our support. I'm sure I can rally the troops if you want a public relations campaign to push back against Hager. And you know we also have friends on Capitol Hill who can help."

"Thanks for the offer. I'll let you know when the time is right. But there is something else of importance I want from you."

"I'm all ears."

"Are you aware that John Simpson will be retiring soon for the private sector?"

"I've heard rumors."

Simpson was a deputy assistant secretary of State for Diplomatic Security, essentially Riley's number two, and his presumed eventual successor.

"Does he have a corporate offer in hand?" Alex asked. "No, but he'll hit mandatory retirement age in the winter, so he's already floated his resume to corporate headhunters. I'd like you to consider replacing Simpson. It would mean working in Washington for several years."

"Really?" Alex raised his eyebrows and leaned forward in his chair. "I'm sure there are a lot of others who would do a great job, Jim, guys or gals who really *like* being in Washington."

Riley smiled and stood up. He walked to the windows of his corner office and stared out at the Washington Monument and Lincoln Memorial for a few seconds, both hands in his pockets; then he turned back to Alex. "You've just mentioned one reason why I want *you* instead of the others. Of all the potential candidates, you're the only one who is most focused on the needs of the field, the needs of our regional security officers, and our engineering officers, as opposed to 'feeding the beast' of the bureaucracy in Washington. Since I've occupied the position of director, I can't tell you how many times a month one of our offices proposes some new 'over-the-top' report for RSOs to fill out. They think RSOs have nothing better to do than sit at his or her desk and write reports.

"You're not like that. You know RSOs need time to cultivate contacts with the cops and the Ministry of Interior. You recognize RSOs need to train the embassy Marines and local guard force. *Dammit!* RSOs need time to think about what's truly important, not just sit on their asses reporting another metric to Washington." Riley's voice had risen louder, and Alex noted his harsh criticism of the many contractors who now filled the ranks of Diplomatic Security.

"If you replace Simpson, we'll have each other's back. And frankly, Alex, you'll be in line to replace me when I retire one day. Plus, if it isn't already obvious, I'm pretty sure you'll get promoted this fall, so staying in town and filling the second most senior job in DS wouldn't be a stretch."

"Gosh, Jim, this is unexpected." Until now, Alex had spent the majority of his career abroad, and that's how he liked it. But if he became Riley's official deputy, he would have the authority to make, or at least to recommend, important innovations within Diplomatic Security. He liked *that* idea a lot.

"I've thought about this from every angle," Riley continued. "You've served with distinction as a senior RSO at many posts, including two major ones, Islamabad and Rome. In both cases, you overcame powerful internal and external threats. You've also been the Director of International Operations here in DC. I've spoken to many people who have worked for you, and they all agree you're an excellent leader, mentor, and also fearless in doing the right thing."

"Wow, maybe we should turn my career story into a movie?" "I failed to mention, you're also a wiseass." They both smiled.

"Seriously, how could I say 'no' to your offer?" Alex said. "Thank you."

"Okay, then. Keep this conversation between us, although you can tell Rachel. This opportunity may not arise for several months. Naturally, the State Department senior assignments panel will have to approve it, including that prick, Dennis Hager."

"Got it, Jim," Alex said. "By the way, are you and Caroline still going to Watson's house tonight for dinner?"

"Yes, we are. Assistant Secretary Archibald Watson is one guy I really like. We'll see you and Rachel there at eight."

They shook hands on their secret deal, and Alex returned to his office excited about the opportunity. In his gut, he knew he could do the job, although others might feel he hadn't put in enough 'bureaucratic time' in Washington to take on such responsibility.

Perhaps, it's time to leave my action-man image behind and take on senior executive responsibilities. No one stays young forever, he thought. *I'll tell Rachel about the offer after dinner tonight at Watson's house. That will give her some time to plan her next assignment in Washington.*

As he settled back into his leather office chair, he didn't realize he had totally forgotten the old adage about not counting chickens . . .

4

STAYING FOCUSED

Oxfordshire, England

Lars Nilsson bolted through the heavy rain from the hotel entrance to his car, tossing his leather weekend bag onto the passenger seat, and jumped behind the wheel. He wiped rainwater off his face and breathed in the aroma of a fresh spring rain.

Crap, my rendezvous with April was a disaster, he thought while leaning back against the headrest; he closed his eyes and tried to think about his next move. *I can't possibly contact my controller now because I've been drinking heavily. Whatever I say might sound unprofessional. Tomorrow will be better.* Lars reached into the center console and pulled out cigarettes that he kept there for April. He lit one and took a few drags before cracking the window and flicking it onto the gravel parking lot.

Should I return to the room, tell her I want to get married and apologize for not saying so immediately? Should I tell her the truth and admit that my name isn't Lars Nilsson at all?

He dwelled on it for a moment, turning it over in his mind,

then rejected the plans.To explain that his real name was Dimitri Vasiliev would require approval from Moscow. That would mean his bosses in the SVR would conclude there was no other way to control April Scott other than to reveal the truth, with the expectation of turning her into a willing accomplice. Or in the worst case, blackmailing her into cooperating. Lars knew blackmail was the least favored method. The SVR would be far better off if April voluntarily agreed to continue to pass secrets.

Another reason against revealing his true name was that Moscow had invested years of time and money setting him up under the alias of *Lars Nilsson*, and they would be reluctant to compromise that legend. They had carefully created an artificial background for him to operate as an "illegal." In other words, a Russian spy who used a false flag approach as a Swede to recruit or influence sources of value.

He sighed, knowing he could do nothing until after he had sobered up. Lars started the car and drove out of the hotel's parking lot. *I need to think about what to do, but for now, I'm just going back to London to sleep it off.* Nevertheless, his tradecraft kicked in. Although he assumed he was operating below the radar of both Scotland Yard's Special Branch and MI-5, he decided to take a different route home just to make potential surveillance more difficult. He avoided the bypass road he had taken earlier and drove directly into the heart of Oxford City. Hating all the one-way streets, he had long accepted the fact that he had to be cautious. After making a few turns, he didn't see anyone following him.

Not that it was easy to spot a professional tail in a downpour.

The sound of the rain hitting the roof of the car was like listening to a percussion orchestra. He cursed the weather and looked forward to the warm embrace of his flat in London's West End. As he drove down a narrow residential street with parked cars on one side, he decided he wanted to enjoy another cigarette, a rare treat for him. Reaching into the console with one hand, he managed to extract one. When he raised it to his mouth, it slipped through his fingers onto the floor. He cursed, slowed the car by a few miles per hour and reached down to pick it up.

Bam!

He heard it first, then felt a thump against the left side of his Volvo. Lars braked and looked into his rear-view mirror. Nothing was there.

What the hell?! Checking the left side mirror, he realized it was hanging by a wire. The rain continued to hammer down, making it hard to see much of anything. Although he wasn't wearing rain gear, he felt an obligation to see what he had hit. Getting out, he walked a few yards back to a horrific sight. A young man lay immobile between parked cars, his right arm bent at a hideous angle, his head bleeding into a pool of water next to the curb. Lars bent over him and shook the man's shoulder. No response.

Oh my God! What have I done?

He rushed back into the warmth of his car. Cold water dripped off his head and down the back of his shirt. *Should I remain or leave? Could I be arrested or survive to continue my work?* He gripped his head with his hands to think. Then he pushed the manual shift into first gear and slowly drove off. He tried to focus on the road ahead, feeling terrible about leaving as the windshield wipers worked overtime to carry the water away. Lars had always considered himself a good man, so leaving the accident victim on the ground was dishonorable, but it was the only viable option. Now his thoughts changed to how he could get away with his crime.

He wanted to call for an ambulance and anonymously report an injured man lying in the road but guessed the cops would trace the cellphone to his account. As he drove, he spotted a gas station with a phone booth, but when he pulled into the station, he saw a CCTV camera mounted on the building. No way could he allow himself to be caught on camera, so he drove back onto the road without making a call.

An hour or so later, he was back at his apartment building in West London and parked in the underground garage. As he inspected his car, he saw the left side mirror still dangling loose. That side of the car had a medium-sized dent in the front door, but no other damage. He walked over to his individual unit's storage room, unlocked it, and took out a black auto cover, then draped it entirely over his vehicle. At least it would look like he was protecting it from dirt and dust. He would figure out a way to get it repaired without alerting authorities.

Suddenly, he felt ill and ran to a garage support column and threw up twice. Once recovered, he went inside his three-bedroom apartment and stripped off his wet clothes, taking a hot shower. He put on pajamas, took an aspirin, and made a cup of steaming Earl Grey tea. Lars then sat at his desk and pulled out pages from his espionage one-time pad given to him by the SVR. He prepared to write a secret cypher with five letter groups to his contact in London. Upon completing the message about April's reluctance to continue their relationship, he would take a photo of it with a burner phone, used only for espionage purposes, and text the photo to his contact's own burner phone. Then he would await further instructions.

This type of secret transmission was incredibly hard to break. The major flaw in the system was that the SVR insisted on a complicated password to open his secret cell phone. Therefore, they gave him a 27-character log-in which was impossible to remember. So, he secretly wrote in down, thereby circumventing the entire point of its security. As he started the cypher, he realized April Scott had never given him the SD card with the latest batch of embassy secret telegrams.

God damn it, he thought. *What else could go wrong?*

5

THE DINNER

Bethesda, Maryland

Archibald Watson's Maryland house off of Massachusetts Avenue was just beyond the Maryland state line from the District of Colombia, also not far from The American University. It was a typical red brick colonial built in the 1930s which he had enlarged a decade earlier by adding a spacious family room on the back with a study/bedroom above on the second floor of the newly constructed extension. Tall, leafy oak trees were interspersed among all the houses on the lovely, tranquil street, adding elegance to the neighborhood.

Bethesda was an expensive part of town, yet not flashy. Solid upper-middle class would best describe the area. As Assistant Secretary of State for European Affairs and a couple of ambassadorships under his belt, Watson fit right in with this prestige address.

Alex arrived for dinner and parked his "British racing green" Ford Mustang GT on the street in front of Watson's home. He loved the powerful sound of the V-8 engine when he accelerated.

Not very environmentally friendly, I know, but considering I've almost died for my country on several occasions, it's no one's goddamn business what I drive.

He looked for Jim Riley's car which hadn't apparently arrived yet. Rachel had left her deep navy-blue BMW at the State Department and ridden with Watson to his house. Alex walked up to the front door and pushed the bell. A moment later, Watson opened the door, all grins, and offered a hearty handshake. He matched Alex's six feet, two-inch-tall height, and two-hundred-pound weight. Despite being over sixty years old, Watson still appeared athletic, even though his hair was mostly grey.

Alex recalled the first time he had met Watson years ago in Rome and first shook his hand. He'd been impressed with the strength of Watson's grip. Only later did Watson tell him he'd been a former Marine Infantry Officer who had gone to war in Vietnam. In other words, his background was different from your run-of-the-mill senior Foreign Service officer.

"Alex, Welcome! You've been here before, so please come in and make yourself comfortable."

"Thank you, Archie. Here's a present for you." Alex handed him a bottle of Santorini Assyrtiko, a unique white wine from Greece that complimented grilled fish extremely well. He had remembered Watson once told him that when he had been the US Ambassador to Greece, he was partial to this wine.

"What a nice surprise! Thank you very much. Your taste in wine matches your taste in women."

They both watched as Jim Riley's car pulled up across the street. "Alex, I'll stay here and greet Jim and Caroline. Why don't you join Allison and Rachel in the family room?"

Alex walked to the back room and greeted the women. Allison rose from the sofa and they briefly embraced. She was a few years younger than Archie and an excellent part-time book editor when she wasn't playing tennis or golf to keep her figure trim.

He looked over at Rachel, who was still sitting on the sofa and appeared to be pleased with something by a half-smile on her face, looking relaxed. She winked at him and blew him a kiss. He returned it.

"Can I get you something to drink, Alex?" Allison asked. "What would go well with dinner?"

"I think white wine. We're having fish." "Okay. White wine it is for me."

She left the room, walking with a slight limp, still recovering from an ankle sprain after tripping on the tennis court a day earlier. Alex strolled over to the bookcase and glanced at the titles. A few books were in Greek or Portuguese, languages from where Archie had been the US Ambassador, while others were in French. He noticed, however, quite a few in English about the Vietnam War.

"Are you going to join me?" Rachel asked.

"Yeah, sorry. I thought I'd just peek at his reading preferences." He sat down next to her, held her hand, and looked into her green eyes. "When are you going to tell me your secret?"

"How do you know I have a secret?" Rachel grinned as she swung her long wavy brown hair to one side.

"Conosco tutto la mia bellezza!"

She laughed knowing the Italian phrase meant: 'I know every-thing, my beauty.'

Jim and Caroline Riley entered the room with Archie, just as Allison returned from the kitchen with Alex's glass of white wine. All the men took off their suit jackets and the group chatted for thirty minutes in the family room over drinks and a few Greek hors d'oeuvres of dolmades, olives, and flaming Saganaki, a tradi-tional Greek cheese.

"Alex, I've been meaning to ask you, has your gunshot injury from last year bothered you lately?" Archie asked.

"No . . . the only pain in my side has been Rachel."

Everyone laughed while Rachel pretended to pout momentarily, then laughed as well.

"I can't wait to get you alone tonight," Rachel said while making a terrible face at him in jest.

"Funny you should mention that my dear, I was thinking the same!" More chuckles around the room.

"Archie, to answer your question seriously," Alex said, "I'm fine. It's been six months since I was shot in Cairo and while my side is still sore occasionally, it's no longer *painful*. The State Department doctors have given me full clearance to serve overseas again."

Of course, he was painting a perfectly macho picture of himself, and while he *did* have medical clearance to go abroad, he really felt much more discomfort than he would freely admit. Rachel knew this but remained silent.

"That's great! Glad to hear it." Archibald popped a piece of Greek cheese into his mouth, chewing while continuing to talk. "By the way, have you spoken to Ellen lately?"

"We had lunch with her a few days ago," Alex replied.

Rachel jumped in. "She was really excited with her new confirmation as Assistant Secretary of State for the Middle East. Considering she was almost killed by the terrorist attack in Cairo when she was serving as ambassador there, things have worked out pretty well. Even though I know she misses being there."

"I know," Archibald said. "She's a great officer and a good friend. I invited her tonight, but she begged off because by the end of the day her back is sore and she's tired. Hopefully, she'll continue to recover. It's only been a few months since the operation that fused some of her vertebrae."

"Here's to Ellen," Alex said, raising his glass in a toast.

Everyone did the same.

"I understand the Egyptian authorities are still looking for the terrorist responsible for the attack on Ellen," Archibald said.

"You mean Ammon Mansour?" Alex replied. "Yes, they are. He went into hiding immediately after we killed most of his men. My guess is that he may not even be in Egypt now." Alex stared at nothing in particular while thoughts of Ammon Mansour raced through his head. *I have a hard time coming to terms with the notion that Mansour and I were once junior high schoolmates, even friends at the International School in Cairo.*

After more banter, Allison announced they should move into the dining room.

Halfway through the main course of sea bass, topped with slivers of almonds, accompanied by medallions of eggplant as a side dish, Alex noticed Archie making eye contact with Rachel who nodded back at him.

"This afternoon," Archie addressed the group, "I read two interesting cables from our embassy in London. Let me say, Jim, I apologize for not discussing this with you earlier, but I did call, but you were out of the office. Besides, I knew we'd be seeing each other this evening." Riley acknowledged the comment, not upset in the least.

Hmmmm, something's up, Alex thought and assumed the matter would link to Rachel's cheerful persona which had been apparent throughout the evening.

"The first cable asked if we could provide a representative for a two-week symposium on 'Foreign Policy and Public Relations,' hosted this summer at Oxford University," Archie said. "Several other foreign embassies have been approached as well to support this program. Additionally, there will be senior staff from a few top British newspapers and possibly from their TV networks. Frankly, it didn't take me long to decide who we should send as the American representative. I am, of course, referring to Rachel. In the past, she's been the Department's deputy spokeswoman, and she has a keen grasp of US foreign policy dealing with both Europe and Asia."

Alex looked at Rachel and gave her a thumbs up. Her wide smile lit up the room as if strobe lights had just been turned on. Alex had a brief image of himself sitting at an outdoor table at an Oxford pub, soaking up the summer sun, while drinking a pint of British ale and munching on Stilton cheese. *Now, that would be a great vacation,* he thought.

"What makes sending Rachel even *more* enticing," Watson continued, "is that we still haven't filled the upcoming vacancy for the position of political counselor in our London Embassy. By July, we'll need an outstanding officer in that job."

Alex froze. He immediately sensed what Archie was implying and glanced at Riley. Apparently, Jim had reached the same conclusion as he only raised his eyebrows and gave Alex a small shrug.

"I know by now you've all guessed where I'm heading with this news. Late this afternoon, I discussed this with Rachel, and she will consider taking the political counselor opening in London . . . of course, pending a chat with Alex."

Rachel looked at Alex with apparent delight and anticipation nearly holding her breath.

"You mentioned there was a second cable of interest," Alex said, trying to sound enthusiastic.

"Yes, and here's where you could enter the picture, Alex."

"Again, I recognize this is totally up to you, Jim. You're the director of Diplomatic Security and you'll decide if this offer is even of value to DS."

"The British Foreign Office would like a DS officer to advise them on setting up an appropriate, but very small unit comparable to DS. They have nothing in place at present, and currently rely on MI6 to offer guidance on security. While a few British police officers are currently assigned to their embassies, apparently that is only to handle police liaison on criminal cases, much like our FBI does at some of our embassies. They'd like to pick our brains and even have a DS officer help get the program up and running. He or she would be in an advisory capacity only. I thought that with Rachel living in Oxford for a few weeks, this might be a perfect opportunity for Alex to handle the Foreign Office tasking in London. The locations are only an hour apart and connected by a direct train ride."

Rachel smiled at Alex, clearly hoping for a positive reply, but Jim Riley responded first.

"This does, indeed, sound like an interesting opportunity for DS. But what happens to Alex once he finishes his short-term task with

the Foreign office?" Riley looked over at Alex but continued speaking. "I doubt he and Rachel want to be separated for the next three years while she takes the political counselor position in London."

Alex guessed Riley was probably miffed that this matter hadn't been discussed privately between Watson and himself. Fortunately, everyone at the table were good friends, so Watson's enthusiasm could be forgiven. These were, after-all, last minute and unexpected sets of opportunities.

"I completely agree," Archie replied. "I hoped you might assign Alex to London as the RSO. Bainbridge Wellington, our deputy chief of mission in London, told me that his current RSO is transferring this summer, and while a replacement has been named, Bainbridge made some inquiries and doesn't think the nominated officer has Alex's star power."

Alex laughed. "I'm sorry, Archie, but did you say Bainbridge *Wellington*? And does *he* think I have star power?"

"Apparently he does," Archie replied. "Why do you ask? Is there something I'm not aware of?"

Rachel smirked and said, "It's just that six months ago, Alex and Bainbridge had a somewhat uncomfortable chat in London about Bainbridge's bold selection of striped shirts. There was also an awkward discussion of how to add security at our embassy in Cairo." She and Alex exchanged glances and smiles which said there was probably more to the story.

"Ah, I think I recall what you mean about his shirts, and Cairo," Archie said, "But seriously, Bainbridge told me late this afternoon that he would welcome Alex being assigned as the RSO."

"I hope you'll understand that Rachel and I need time to discuss all of this. It's a lot to consider." Alex said. "And, of course, Jim must decide on changing the RSO assignment for London. I imagine he'll have to sweeten the pot considerably for the guy who is being bumped."

"Of course, of course. I just wanted you and Jim to know that the European bureau will fully support you and Rachel should you decide to move forward with these offers."

The rest of the evening was charming. Alex thought about Riley's original plan to nominate him as a deputy assistant secretary for Diplomatic Security. Archie's alternative suggestion of the London assignments would kill that plan. He watched Rachel's expression during dessert and after-dinner drinks, recognizing that her transition from being a press officer to being a political counselor at a major embassy was something she wanted very badly. It would mean further promotion and could even open the door for onward assignments as Deputy Chief of Mission, or perhaps, even getting an ambassadorship one day.

How can I not be on board with that idea? he thought. *Her happiness is far more important than achieving higher positions for myself. I'm already in the Senior Foreign Service. That has to be enough if the alternative is to support Rachel's career.*

The real issue is not long-term advancement versus living in the moment abroad. Alex thought. *Rather, it's about loyalty to both Jim and Rachel. I'll do the right thing for her and support Rachel in any way I can. Somehow, I'll square it with Jim later.*

6

INVESTIGATION

Oxford, England

By 6:00 am, the overnight rain had stopped, and Sheila Abercrombie left her brick townhouse with her small wired-hair terrier for their morning walk. One block into the journey, the dog began tugging on its leash, determined to leave the sidewalk and lunge into the road. Trying to pull the dog back, Sheila spotted the body laying between two parked cars. She gave a short scream and picked up her little fur ball. Because much of the man's blood had been washed away during the night's rainstorm, she thought he had only passed out, and wondered if he had overdosed on drugs or was comatose from alcohol. Either guess would be dead wrong.

"Hello?" she ventured aloud. "Hello . . . are you awake?" No reply. She moved closer to the body, nudging it with her foot, then looked around for help but no one was on the street this early. Reaching into her pocket, she took out her mobile and called the police emergency number. The operator instructed her not to

touch the body and asked her to wait nearby since she had told
the police operator that the body couldn't easily be seen between
the parked cars.

Within five minutes, the first patrol car arrived, lights flashing but
with no siren. The officers quickly determined the man was dead
and noted he had what appeared to be a fatal head injury. They
radioed their report in and moments later more police arrived
from the Thames Valley Constabulary. After the police listened to
her explanation of what she knew, Sheila Abercrombie was
allowed to return to her house down the street and was told to stay
at home where they would take a formal statement from her soon.

The cops ran yellow tape around the area and placed a small
portable tent over the body, pending the arrival of the medical
examiner. Detectives arrived shortly after the medical examiner,
who gave them his preliminary assessment of the cause of death -
blunt force trauma to the head. By 7:30 am, police constables were
knocking on the doors in the neighborhood to make inquiries, but
no one had seen or heard anything.

After the body was taken to the morgue, detectives continued to
search the immediate area and found several small pieces of shat-
tered blue plastic on the ground near the body. The lab would eventually examine these under a microscope, but the lead detective at
the scene, Sergeant David Taylor was reasonably certain the plastic
had broken off a vehicle. He also assumed the body had been the
victim of a hit and run. Taylor, twenty-eight years old, had been a
plainclothes detective for four years and had investigated several
such incidents in the past. Before that he'd been a uniformed cop
for six years in Oxford. He had seen such things before.

Once Sgt. Taylor was finished at the crime scene, he returned
to the police station to examine items from the victim's pockets. He
opened the man's wallet and found an Oxford University student
photo ID card in the name of "James Fletcher," along with a

matching driver's license which showed his address on the street where the body had been found. Eighty-seven pounds sterling in cash was in the wallet, and there were a few credit cards and receipts from purchases. Finally, there was a set of house keys and a mobile phone.

"Did anyone check his address?" Sgt. Taylor asked Bill Walker, the uniformed constable standing next to him.

"Someone must have, we hit all the houses on the street. Maybe no one was home."

"Let's drive over there and see what develops. Bring his house keys," Taylor said. Taylor turned to a young police constable, Lizzy Jacobson.

"Lizzy, please check any CCTV cameras in the area. Maybe we can identify the vehicle that hit this student. First, speak with Dr. Harding in the medical examiner's office and get an approximate time of death.

"Yes, Sgt. Taylor." She left the office. Taylor was impressed with young Lizzy Jacobson. She was hard-working and paid meticulous attention to detail in any task given to her.

Taylor and Constable Walker drove back to the street where the body had been found, parked their car, and went to the address on the victim's license. Taylor knocked on the front door, then glanced at the time, it was 9:30 am.

After knocking a few more times, an unshaven man of around 20-years-old opened the door. He was dressed in a sweatshirt with "Oxford University" emblazoned on the front, blue jeans, and sandals. His thick brown hair was uncombed, and he looked like he had just gotten out of bed. He was, however, holding a steaming cup of coffee.

"Yes, may I help you?" he asked in a rather posh accent.

Oh no, Sgt. Taylor thought, *just what I need, another Oxford University heir to the landed gentry.*

"I'm Detective Sgt. Taylor and this is Constable Walker. We're investigating a possible hit and run down the street."

"Was that you lot knocking on my door about an hour ago?" "It probably was another police officer."

"I was sleeping and didn't get out of bed. I only recently got up."

"Do you know a Mr. James Fletcher?"

"Yes, he's my roommate. Do you wish to speak with him?"

Taylor was shocked by the comment. "Are you saying he's in the house?"

"I think so. I didn't get home until two in the morning. I assumed he was sleeping, and still is."

Taylor reached into his jacket pocket and took out the driver's license of James Fletcher, showing it to the man. "Is this your roommate?"

The man looked confused. "Yes, that's him. What are you saying? Is he all right?"

"I didn't catch your name," Sgt. Taylor asked. "It's Ben . . . Ben Atkinson. What's happened?"

"I'm afraid your roommate is dead. I think it was a hit-and-run accident. May we come in and talk?"

Ben Atkinson's townhouse rental was referred to as a two-up, two-down, meaning there was a kitchen and living room-dining room combo downstairs, and two bedrooms plus a bathroom upstairs. The furniture was all inexpensive, basic student accommodation that had seen better days. Scattered around the living room was the normal assortment of student garbage - empty beer cans and bottles of wine, crumpled bags of crisps, or "potato chips" as the Americans called them, as well as fast food wrappers.

"When was the last time you saw James Fletcher?" Sgt. Taylor asked.

"I guess about 9:00 pm last night. We had a beer together in the kitchen, then I left for a party. He was still here, but said he was going out later." Atkinson looked stunned by the turn of events. He slumped down onto the sofa, stared at the tattered and stained brown carpet, and shook his head in disbelief.

"Did he have any enemies, or had he argued with anyone recently?" Walker asked.

"No, he's a really nice guy. Sorry, . . . he *was* a nice guy. Everyone liked him."

"Do you know where his family lives?" Sgt. Taylor asked. "Kind of. They're from Derbyshire, but I don't know where exactly."

"We'd like to see his bedroom," Sgt. Taylor continued.

Atkinson led them upstairs where they searched for fifteen minutes but found nothing of interest. The three returned to the living room.

"One last question, did he say where he was going last night?" Walker asked.

"No, he didn't. He's two years older than me and has friends he made before I moved in with him last fall. So, I don't always hang with his group."

Sgt. Taylor gave him his business card and told him to call if he thought of anything that might help the investigation.

After Sgt. Taylor and Constable Walker returned to the station, Constable Lizzy Jacobson arrived and reported that Dr. Harding estimated the time of death at around 10:30 pm the previous evening.

"He was also of the opinion that Fletcher had been hit on his side by a vehicle which is how his arm was broken," Lizzy said. "When he fell backward, he most probably hit his head hard on the concrete curb. Dr. Harding said the cause of death was probably from the head injury but he would know more after the autopsy."

As for the CCTV images, Constable Jacobson said she had a team of constables scouring the neighborhood collecting this info, but so far, camera coverage of the immediate area was negligible.

"I'll tell you more if they find anything," she said.

7

TWO MONTHS LATER

Washington DC

Alex accepted the offer of the London RSO assignment with delight. In the last two month interim, he had also collected supporting material in preparation for his short gig with the British Foreign Office also known as the Foreign and Commonwealth Office or FCO. He had spoken on several occasions with Gary Jones, the US Embassy's current regional security officer. It seemed the only problem with his embassy assignment would be convincing most employees that London *could* be a dangerous place, especially if one let his or her guard down.

This afternoon, Alex's going away office party had ended ten minutes earlier when Riley asked Alex to join him in his office for a final chat.

"Here's to you, Alex," Riley said, raising his wine glass, "and here's to your next assignment in London. I'm happy for you and Rachel. But I can't lie, you'll be missed."

"I deeply appreciate that you agreed to Archie Watson's plan of putting Rachel and me in London. It's absolutely the best thing for her career."

"Did you ever tell her about our discussion of making you the number two man in Diplomatic Security here in DC?"

"No, I didn't want her to feel guilty about what *could* have been. Besides, who wouldn't want London as an assignment?"

Riley nodded. In truth, Alex felt bad about leaving Riley while Under Secretary Dennis Hager was still on the warpath against Diplomatic Security. Hager had recently proposed eliminating fifty percent of all embassy RSO positions worldwide and using the money that would be saved for other so-called "substantive" areas like political or economic functions. Fortunately, Riley had let this idea slip out – albeit intentionally - when he was testifying before Congress on the annual State Department budget. The congressmen were outraged upon hearing the suggestion that America's embassies would have half their DS forces removed, thereby becoming more vulnerable. It resulted in quick bi-partisan support to trash Hager's plan.

Nevertheless, Hager was a man on a mission and his arrogance matched his political naiveté, because he then offered most RSO positions abroad to the FBI, thereby enabling them to expand their presence overseas. The FBI had long wanted the slots for their own agents but when they discovered such appointments would include the responsibility of doing embassy security work, that plan died as well.

"Jim, do you think Hager is dreaming up all these schemes on his own?" Alex asked.

"I tend to doubt it," Jim answered. "I still think that he could be an agent of influence for another country."

"Maybe he's just sucking up to Deputy Secretary Wakefield Summers or trying to please the Secretary of State."

"That's a good point about Hager sucking up," Jim said. "It's in his nature, but I don't know. As far as I've observed, Summers focuses on arms control, relations with Russia, and a few multilateral issues. I have little idea what he thinks of Diplomatic Security. As for the new Secretary of State, he likes his DS protective detail, but then he still seems to be getting his policy agenda set up."

The sixty-year-old Deputy Secretary Summers was a political appointee who had been easily confirmed by the Senate following a highly successful investment banking career in New York. Early in life, he had briefly served as a very junior CIA case officer in Buenos Aires.

Alex looked at his watch, reluctant to cut short this farewell with Riley. "I have to meet Rachel at a restaurant for dinner." He stepped forward and firmly shook Riley's hand. "Thanks for everything, boss, I mean it. Without your support, I would have been in deep shit years ago. You and Caroline are always welcome to stay with us in London, if you need a break."

"I'll keep that in mind. Meanwhile, I'll figure out how to get you back to Washington someday."

ONE WEEK LATER, Gary Jones, the RSO from the US Embassy in London, spotted Alex and Rachel as they deplaned from the United Airlines red-eye flight from Dulles airport to Heathrow. Each carried an overnight bag and briefcase and wore blue jeans, blue blazers, and comfortable black walking shoes, essentially the traveling attire for any man or woman traveling on business.

Gary waved to them, and they returned the gesture until they were close enough to shake hands. Alex noticed Gary was wearing a British government-issued VIP airport pass around his neck which was standard for diplomats, especially from the US Embassy.

Nor was Alex too surprised that Gary would make the journey to Heathrow to meet him at 6:30 a.m. Diplomatic Security special agents felt they were part of a brother or sisterhood. He and Rachel had met Gary last year when they had overnighted in London following the failed Middle East Peace conference in Cairo. Alex liked him, and thought he was competent with great contacts. He humorously recalled Gary having 'the hots' for Rachel before he found out that Rachel and Alex were married. That wouldn't make him the first man to think Rachel was a real-life "goddess."

"Of all the DS officers who could have replaced me, I'm glad they selected you," Gary said as the three of them walked to the immigration control area.

"When you were here last year, I thought you bonded amazingly well with Assistant Commissioner Davies and the other guys." The "other guys" referred to Ray Penner, head of the Metropolitan Police Special Branch, and Colonel Mark Thompson-Parker from 22 SAS.

"Thanks, I feel this is going to be an extraordinary tour of duty."

"Rachel, the political section has assumed you'll stop by the embassy tomorrow or the next day before heading on to Oxford. Is this right?" Gary asked.

"Yes, that's what I thought I'd do," she replied.

"I also want to go to the embassy before heading to the FCO for my gig," Alex said. "Although it will be a few weeks before you leave London, Gary, I think I should meet your team and familiarize myself with some other sections in the embassy. I especially want to meet Erica Evans, the management counselor. She was really helpful answering our inquiries on housing, buying cars here, etc. Oh, yeah, and I want to meet the CIA station chief and the FBI Legal Attaché."

"Not to worry, I'll line this all up tomorrow. What about meeting DCM Bainbridge Wellington?"

"I guess I should see the DCM sooner than later," Alex said. "I *definitely* want to talk to him," Rachel quickly interjected. "And the current political counselor, Nelson Ramsay."

"Regarding Wellington," Alex added, "better make separate appointments for each of us."

Within a short time, Gary had whisked them through immigration; they collected their luggage, passed through customs, and drove toward London on the M-4 motorway. Forty minutes later, they pulled up to their new home on Walton Place in Knightsbridge. Much of the block had white three or four-story townhouses, all with adjoining walls to other townhouses.

"Wow, this street is gorgeous!" Rachel said, looking up and down the block.

"You're not kidding," Gary replied. "You're in the postal code SW3. It's probably the poshest and most expensive neighborhood in London. Technically, it's the Borough of Kensington and Chelsea. But this part is usually called Knightsbridge."

"How the hell did we rate *this* place?" Alex asked.

"That was Rachel's doing. I had recommended you should live north of the embassy in the areas where many of us live; it's called St. Johns Wood, nice, but not this upscale. However, it's rumored that the European bureau's Assistant Secretary, Archibald Watson, called the DCM and said because both of you are in the *Senior* Foreign Service, he wanted Rachel to have an appropriate residence for entertaining senior UK government officials."

"Gosh, Rachel," Alex said with a smile, "I think you're a 'keeper' after all."

She chuckled. "You better believe it, big boy. But don't worry, if you feel this residence is out of your league, you can take 'posh' lessons from a tutor."

Alex shook his head with a grimace. "Okay, Gary, let's go inside."

Getting out of the car, they carried the luggage into their new digs. As soon as they entered, however, Alex stopped for a moment. The smell of fresh paint mixed with Lysol brought back memories of his recovery in the hospital in Cairo. It wasn't a happy smell, and momentarily sent a chill down his spine.

The townhouse had large living and dining rooms. The kitchen was modern with a modest-sized breakfast table and four chairs. The master bedroom with ensuite bath was one floor up, on the top floor were two further guest bedrooms with a shared bath. Finally, there was a finished basement which was used as a TV lounge area. The embassy management section had already filled the place with American-made furniture since the Department expected its officers to "hit the ground running," a silly phrase that both Alex and Rachel detested.

"Gary, aren't we near the Special Forces Club that you took us to last year? This neighborhood looks really familiar."

"Very observant. Yes, it's close. To help you get your bearings, when you leave the front door, walk to the right, and take a left at the next street. You'll end up on Brompton Road, where Harrods is located. There's a map and two sets of house keys on the kitchen counter, along with info about the neighborhood. We put some food in the fridge, and you'll see on the info sheet there are a few small grocery stores within walking distance."

"This has exceeded our expectations," Rachel beamed. "Thank you."

"Well, in addition to thanking Archibald Watson, you can also thank Erica Evans. She went to bat for you guys with the embassy inter-agency housing board.

"I assume you're bushed from the overnight flight, so I'll leave you on your own. My cell phone number is on the info sheet, along with other numbers for key contacts in the embassy. Oh, and there's info on public buses that you can take to get around. There are two Embassy provided cell phones on the kitchen counter, pre-loaded with contact numbers. I'll call you later this afternoon to see how you're doing."

As the front door closed behind Gary, Rachel and Alex smiled at their incredibly good fortune. He wrapped his arms around her firm upper body, playfully nibbled on her ear, then lowered his hands to grab her tight ass, pulling her against him. They kissed with moist lips lingering together. When they parted, he stared into her sparkling green eyes and gently ran his hands through her thick, wavy brown hair.

"Shall we christen our new bedroom, then take a shower and walk around the neighborhood?" Alex asked.

"Exactly what I had in mind." Rachel looked down at the front of his pants. "In fact, I think a part of you is already pointing the way."

8

TWO COUPLES

London

For the past two months, Lars Nilsson had avoided being investigated for killing James Fletcher in the hit-and-run accident in Oxford. However, he was ever vigilant when police officers crossed his path. Lars was also perplexed that the police had apparently never identified his car's license plate number from the Oxford citywide CCTV camera system; perhaps, he was on a lookout list somewhere and they were waiting to close in on him. This made him a bit anxious.

In the immediate aftermath of the accident, he had found a shady garage operator who had agreed to replace his Volvo's broken side mirror and fix the dent in the bodywork. Lars had lied and told the operator that he had run into a support column in his underground car park and didn't want his insurance company, or anyone else, to know about it because he had been drunk at the time. A large additional fee to the garage operator had insured his silence.

Also, immediately after the accident, SVR intelligence headquarters in Moscow had responded to his query concerning how to handle April Scott. Via covert communications, they told him to continue his Swedish cover name of Lars Nilsson and to agree to marry the American embassy political officer. Moreover, he should momentarily refrain from asking her to copy any more classified material. They reasoned that she had years of service left before retirement and might make an excellent long-term asset. Lars' SVR handlers felt it was vital to keep her happy. After London, they would figure out a way to have her assigned to another NATO country, or to NATO headquarters in Brussels. Yes, they had more work planned for her.

Now, this Sunday morning, Lars stood in front of the mirror and ran a comb through his blond hair one last time. He wore a well-tailored, Harris Tweed brown sports coat with brown dress slacks, along with a tattersall button-down shirt. To complete his country-casual look, he wore brown brogues with suede uppers. He was satisfied with his appearance, even though he knew it was stereotypical attire for an English country gentleman. Lars left his apartment to pick up April for their visit to the British Museum to be followed later by a casual Chinese meal near Leicester Square.

Two months earlier, after he had proposed to April, he had noticed her attitude improve markedly. They had set a wedding date for September, which at that time was six months away, giving them an opportunity to pick a church for the service and time to invite relatives. As her fiancé, he was subsequently introduced to Nelson Ramsay, April's immediate boss at the time, who was the Embassy's political counselor, and also to Bainbridge Wellington, who had become the charge d' affairs, or acting ambassador, because the US Senate had yet to confirm the new president's ambassadorial nominee. Lars' access to the inner circle at the US embassy was growing with each passing week.

Meanwhile, he had filled out paperwork for his US government security background check, hoping his legend was solid

enough to pass muster. He knew that long ago the SVR had clan-
destinely inserted a birth certificate in the name of Lars Nilsson
into official Swedish government records. And Lars, himself, had
actually graduated from Sweden's Uppsala University. So, that
university record correctly existed along with his student ID
photo. His former Swedish employment records were also real
since he had really held those jobs; the same applied to former
residences where he had lived. He recognized there were a few
tiny gaps in his legend but he doubted investigators would take the
time to notice. For example, while he did have the requisite
Swedish government's social security and medical insurance
coverage, the data had been inserted into the system years later
than it should have been and reflected the time when his legend
was created, rather than at birth. Would anyone notice the actual
entry date? Or would they merely verify he had the coverage?
Time would tell.

He grabbed a taxi to take him from his apartment to April's
townhouse in Chelsea. As the number two officer in the US
Embassy's political section, she was entitled to a nice, but not too
large home in one of the better areas of the city. During the ten-
minute drive, Lars reflected upon his fortuitous passage to this
comfortable point in his life.

Because his parents had been minor Communist Party
members and government officials in the former Soviet Union, the
young Lars (then going by his birth name Dimitri Vasiliev) had
been eligible to attend one of the prestigious primary schools
reserved for families with impeccable loyalty to the Soviet State.
By the time he was nine years old, he was showing exceptional
intellectual superiority over other students. His scores in mathe-
matics and grammar were at the top of his class. But what caught
the attention of the then-KGB was his grasp of foreign languages.
After only two years of instruction in English and German, he was
approaching fluency for his age group.

At that point, the KGB interviewed his parents and asked permission to further test his skills. They had agreed, and the KGB soon discovered that the child was truly gifted in understanding foreign languages; moreover, he had a natural ability to role play and could adopt different personalities when challenged to do so as part of his playtime. A deal was struck between the KGB and his parents. In exchange for allowing the state to control their son's special education and to train him professionally at an early age, the parents were rewarded with a much larger apartment in Moscow, a new car, access to special government stores, and promotions at their workplaces.

As for Lars, he was treated as a prodigy, and was enrolled into "The Institute," part of Directorate S of the KGB. There he was given intense language training and, even at a young age, provided with introductory courses in espionage tradecraft. His handsome Nordic appearance made him a natural to assume an identity of a Scandinavian boy. The KGB decided to focus on Sweden, and by age fifteen, he was packed off to Stockholm and inserted into a family of Russian deep-cover operatives. That's when the KGB forged his background and Dimitri Vasiliev transformed into Lars Nilsson.

During school breaks throughout high school and university, Lars' new family would travel through Europe, but in reality, they would also covertly make their way to Moscow so Lars could be back in the bosom of his real parents for a time and also receive more training in espionage techniques.

When the Soviet Union collapsed in the early 1990s, the KGB morphed into the SVR, but nothing changed for Lars. He continued to be fully trained, indoctrinated, and readied to further the interests of Mother Russia.

~

THE TAXI PULLED up to April Scott's house, Lars paid the driver, and knocked on April's door. When it opened, she was standing there dressed in an attractive blue blazer with a scarf of red, white, and blue wrapped around her neck. She had on grey slacks and looked fantastic. Since his wedding proposal, April had started exercising and had trimmed her figure. She also had stopped smoking and had cut down on her excessive drinking. In short, her transformation was like a caterpillar blossoming into a beautiful butterfly. Lars felt she was now a sexy and loving woman, clearly devoted to him.

They embraced and she took his arm to guide him inside. As with his previous visits to her townhouse, he was impressed with the quality of the furnishings provided by the American embassy. Because of his deep cover, he never visited Russian diplomatic homes in London, so he wasn't certain what their digs looked like. He imagined they were not comparable to what the Americans had.

"Are you ready for our outing to the museum?" He asked.

"I am, but first I want to ask if you've had time to look at my ideas for our wedding reception?"

"I did. Your plan seems perfect." April smiled and hugged him.

Other than having his fake parents from Sweden attend, Lars wasn't sure how the SVR would populate the reception with other fake relatives. But he was confident something would be arranged and he'd be notified in advance.

"Okay then," April said. "Shall we go?"

They strolled out of the house and down the street to King's Road where they were able to wave down an empty taxi. From there, they went to the British Museum located in Bloomsbury, Central London, where they stayed for two and a half hours, marveling at the Egyptian and Oriental exhibits. Afterward, they took a taxi to Leicester Square with the intent of finding a Chinese restaurant for lunch in adjacent Chinatown.

ON THIS SUNDAY MORNING, Alex and Rachel had more than christened their new bed. Their physicality had created a bit of drama during their lovemaking and they began to be concerned about the non- stop creaking and movement of the bed frame. Alex later inspected the frame and found it had not been screwed together tightly enough by the embassy workers who had installed the furniture.

I'll take care of that later, he thought, *if I can find a screwdriver and pliers in the house.* Slipping back into bed, he held Rachel tightly, feeling the warmth of her body pressed against his, a feeling he could only describe as "divine."

"Rachel, I love your muscles and strength, but I guess the embassy workers couldn't possibly know how wild their new 'posh' political counselor usually gets when aroused."

He laughed at his own joke and drew the anticipated response from her. She rolled on top of his muscular six-foot-two body and twice thrust her pelvis against his with considerable force. Holding down his wrists, she sensually rubbed herself against him. Their eyes locked in a mutual understanding of the enjoyment that was coming next.

From their very first lovemaking, years ago, he had enjoyed every moment of her naturally aggressive nature made even more exciting by the recognition that she fully intended to fulfill her sexual desires.

"Oh, no! I've unleashed the beast!" he laughed as she pressed her body down against his. "I thought political counselors were skilled in the art of *nuance,* not brute force. Apparently, that's a myth."

"You've been listening to the wrong people, big man."

Her smile was electric. She planted a long kiss firmly on his lips and explored his mouth with her tongue until he started laughing. Rachel broke off the kiss and released his wrists but continued to rub her pelvis against his a few minutes longer. Then she wrapped her arms around him and squeezed his upper body against hers. Since she was at least one hundred-sixty pounds of muscle, her strength commanded respect, and she damned-well knew it.

"So, what do you think about brute force *now*, buddy?" she asked while continuing to squeeze.

Still in her tight grasp, he rolled her onto her back and passionately kissing her neck. Slowly, she relaxed her grip as he continued to kiss her neck and nibble on her ear. She moved her hands to his upper back and felt his strong, rippling muscles. Alex's right hand sensually caressed one breast, his fingers gently running circles around her nipple. Then, slowly, he placed a hand between her legs and massaged her without penetration for several minutes.

"Oh, Alex! That's so *damn* erotic." Her body quivered with excitement. She reached down and put him inside her. Alex heard moans of pleasure as she did so. They moved in synch, slowly at first, then more rapidly. All inhibitions were tossed aside in the heat of their passion. Then, just as they climaxed together . . . *Boom!*

The bed collapsed, crashing onto the floor. They burst out laughing yet continued to milk every last second out of their mutual enjoyment and movements.

When they finally stopped from exhaustion, Alex slid off her and they lay side by side, breathing heavily.

"Well, you certainly live up to your nickname, 'Hunk Man,' but perhaps that's not an entirely accurate nickname for you. You're much more skilled than being just hunky." She reached between his legs and squeezed with moderate pressure.

Alex turned toward her, smiling, and looked into her eyes. "I'm glad you have a 'handle on the situation.' But as much as I'd like to stay in bed with you *all* day, maybe it's time to shower and go out sightseeing. We could also find a place for lunch."

"Only if you promise to fix the bed after we return. I think we have unfinished business," Rachel said.

"I love you Rach." He planted a long kiss on her lips. "Seriously, I'm so proud of you and everything you've accomplished."

"You're the best, Alex."

"Time to shower, Honey Bunch."

She got out of bed first and walked naked toward the bathroom. He watched her go, admiring her lean muscular physique and her tall athletic frame. *Rach has the beauty and sleekness of a panther, combined with the muscular squeezing power of a python.*

He chuckled to himself. *Did I just mix my metaphors? To hell with English 101, Rachel is what she is,* he thought, *and the most amazing part about her is that she's really, really smart and witty. I couldn't find another woman like her in a million years.*

A minute later, she yelled out from the bathroom: "Alex, I can't seem to figure out how to put soap on my back. Can you come help?"

He laughed. "I'll be right there."

9

CHINATOWN

Main Street

After attending to every inch of the goddess's body in the shower, Alex shaved and put on casual khaki pants and a blue button-down shirt. Rachel applied minimal makeup and opted for a pair of designer jeans and a blue and white striped blouse. Both chose comfortable leather walking shoes.

"When we finish exploring our neighborhood, do you want to take a taxi or use the tube to go to lunch?" Alex asked.

"Since we've already agreed to go to Chinatown, which isn't far, let's stay above ground so we can see the city."

They walked toward Brompton Road, exploring shop windows as they walked. Being Sunday, some stores were closed while others were just opening such as jewelry or women's dress stores. "Oh my God, I can't wait to do some serious buying," she said.

"Oh, poor baby, you have nothing to wear," Alex brought her hand up to his lips and kissed it. She laughed.

"Don't be silly. A girl can never have too much to wear," she said, giving him a peck on the cheek.

They arrived at Harrods and decided to grab a taxi which was waiting in front. The drive out of Knightsbridge, past Hyde Park Corner and the Wellington Arch toward Piccadilly Circus, was magnificent. There were hotels and clubs on the left, with Green Park on the right. When they passed the Ritz Hotel, they were in an area of more high-end stores.

As planned, they exited the taxi at Piccadilly Circus and walked to Leicester Square, again looking into shop windows along the way. Leicester Square was huge with two large movie theaters, American fast-food restaurants, and a few shops.

Even though the area was jammed with people enjoying a rather warm and sunny day in May, Alex didn't see the big deal of being in Leicester Square. It seemed quite ordinary to him.

"Hungry yet?" Rachel asked.

"Only for your body. Is it time to go back to the bedroom yet?" Rachel ignored his quip with a smile.

"Where's Chinatown?" she asked, knowing Alex had an uncanny sense of navigation as if he had a GPS chip embedded in his head. He took her hand and steered her out of the square. Two blocks later, they saw the large red Chinese arch at the corner of Wardour and Gerrard Streets. When they passed under it and looked beyond, they saw every restaurant on the street was Chinese.

"Gosh, how can we choose?" Alex asked.

"That's my territory. Dim Sum, or spicy?"

"Spicy," he replied.

"Okay, let's look at the menus in the windows."

After ten minutes, she made her choice, and they entered a restaurant with red lanterns hanging in the window with displays of artificial food on colorful plates. There was also a selection of ducks hanging inside the window. *Hmmm, no doubt for a meal of*

Peking duck, Alex thought. *I wonder if the ducks are real or plastic imitations?*

As they approached the hostess, a middle-aged Chinese woman wearing a red jacket and pants in traditional Chinese design asked in perfect English, "Do you have a reservation?" It seemed more of a perfunctory question since there were several available tables.

Rachel replied in Chinese. Alex watched as the woman's eyes grew large and a broad smile swept across her face. They chatted for a moment in Chinese, the woman gave a mini-bow, and led them toward an available table. But their progress was stopped by a well-dressed, somewhat attractive western woman standing in their path.

"Excuse me, aren't you Rachel Smith?"

Alex whispered close to Rachel's ear, "Hollywood, you're a star, even in London." Rachel usually liked it when he reverted to using her Middle Eastern call sign that she had been given at last year's Peace Conference in Cairo, but at this moment, she didn't hear him while focused on the mystery woman.

"Yes, I'm Rachel Smith. Have we met?"

"I'm sorry, I should have introduced myself. I'm April Scott and I'll be working for you in the Embassy's political section."

It took only a moment for it to register. "Of course, April! I remember reading your bio in the material sent to me in Washington. What a coincidence to meet in this restaurant."

"It certainly is. When did you arrive in London?" April asked.

"About seven hours ago," Rachel said.

"Well, you don't waste time getting out and about." Then she looked at him. "And you must be Alex Boyd, our new RSO?"

"The very same," he replied. "We would have gotten here even earlier, but . . ." He stopped speaking mid-sentence as Rachel subtly grasped his wrist and applied a pressure point using her thumb, one of her martial arts techniques. He smiled, trying not to grimace.

"Why don't the two of you join my fiancé and me at our table?" April said. They agreed and followed her to a corner of the room where Lars Nilsson stood. He nodded as April introduced them.

"Congratulations on your engagement," Alex said, having done his homework on Rachel's co-workers. Lars and April thanked him, and everyone sat down.

"Are you with our embassy, Lars?" Alex asked.

"No, I'm a businessman living in London. And I'm not American, I'm Swedish."

"How did you two meet?" Alex asked.

"We meet at RUSI, the Royal United Services Institute for Defense and Security Studies."

April smiled and joined in. "The Foreign Secretary was giving a speech on British Foreign Policy and I happened to take a seat right next to Lars."

The waiter arrived and Rachel asked him in Chinese for two more place settings and menus. He stared at her momentarily, so she repeated herself and the guy's eyes lit up. He scurried away, looking happy.

"What was that about?" Lars asked.

"I asked him for place settings and menus, but in Cantonese. I assumed he might be from Hong Kong, but I was wrong. So, I repeated myself in Mandarin."

Lars and April looked at each other, then April said, "You're not kidding, are you?"

"No, I'm not," she smiled. "My first tour in the Foreign Service was Hong Kong and my second was in Beijing. But I had already studied Mandarin Chinese in college." Alex watched their expressions and could tell they were highly impressed.

"April, I assume you recognized me from my bio-material the European Bureau sent to post," Rachel asked. "Correct?"

"Yes. There was a photo included, besides, I've seen you on TV during State Department press briefings." The waiter returned with menus and place settings, putting them down, then leaving again.

"Have you guys ordered yet?" Rachel asked. April replied they had, so Rachel and Alex opened their menus. The list of food items was huge and written in both Chinese and English.

After looking over the menu for a few minutes, Alex asked Rachel, "Anything jump out at you?"

"You bet. Do you trust me to order for both of us?" "Absolutely. Did I ever have a choice?"

"Now, you're catching on."

The waiter returned and seemed thrilled when Rachel again spoke in Mandarin.

"What type of business are you in?" Alex asked Lars. "Electronics. I distribute mostly Swedish manufactured products throughout Europe."

"Have you set a wedding date yet?"

"September, here in London. Of course, April is waiting for the State Department to complete my background investigation."

"Has there been a glitch?"

"Not that we know of," April replied.

"It can take a while to complete that type of investigation," Alex said. "But don't worry, there's still plenty of time before the wedding. Although I won't start working in the embassy for a few weeks, I can look into the status of the investigation now, if you'd like?"

"That's most kind. We would appreciate that," Lars replied. "Why aren't you starting work in the embassy before then?"

"I have a task to complete at the British Foreign Office, first." Alex chose not to elaborate since he didn't really know Lars, and thankfully, Lars didn't press the matter.

Then April jumped back into the conversation. "Rachel, I

know you'll be busy with the symposium at Oxford, but will we see you in the political section before you replace Nelson Ramsey?"

"Yes, you will. I'll stop in from time to time, but I'll try not to step on anyone's toes. In fact, you'll probably see me in the next day or two before I head to Oxford."

"Terrific . . .if there's anything you'll need from us, just ask."

They spoke a few minutes longer before the food began to arrive. First up for Alex and Rachel was a soup with things floating in it. Alex stared at it suspiciously. He could eat almost anything, regardless of the culture, and he was familiar with Chinese food, but this looked . . . different.

"What's this, Rach?"

"It's a flavorful broth with some soybeans and a few vegetables. And, oh yes, breaded eyeballs."

There was a long pause. "Eyeballs?" What type?" "Tibetan Llama, I think."

"You're pulling my leg, right? Why can't we just have regular, old hot and sour soup?"

"Don't be so pedestrian. Try it, it's good," she urged enthusiastically. To set an example, she dipped her spoon into the soup and drew out some broth with what appeared to be an eyeball, swallowing it whole. Alex grimaced, and a shudder shook his shoulders.

"Yummy," Rachel said, smiling.

"You're just playing games because when we were in Cairo last year, you couldn't read the Arabic menus and I could. I don't believe those are eyeballs."

She put down her spoon and placed a hand on his. "Really? Do you think I would tease you about something so serious?"

Everyone laughed, and Alex ate the soup, fake eyeballs and all. Following came dishes of spicy chicken, beef in garlic sauce, and a side dish of fried seaweed; the latter was thin, crispy, and delicious. It was a marvelous meal, including the fake eyeballs, which tasted like olives that had been cut in half and stuffed with something.

Over dessert, Lars casually asked Alex about his background. While a friendship with Alex might prove beneficial, it also could be dangerous, if he or April let slip some indiscretion. April thought Lars was Swedish, and Moscow wanted to keep it that way. It was up to Lars to balance collection of intelligence with his need for safety.

10

POWER BROKERS

Washington, D.C.

The following day, DS Director Jim Riley sat at one end of a State Department conference table looking directly at Secretary of State Charles Martin at the opposite end. Seated around the table were Deputy Secretary Wakefield Summers, Assistant Secretary for Europe Archibald Watson, Director of the FBI Henson Williams, and the Director of the CIA Lynda Cooper. This was typical of the level at which Riley operated, especially when the stakes were deadly. Sitting in a row of chairs against the wall were the assistant directors of Counter Intelligence for the CIA and FBI, and Undersecretary Dennis Hager from State, along with one of Secretary Martin's special assistants.

Now, why is that son-of-a-bitch, Hager, included in this meeting? Riley wondered. *Since it has nothing to do with financial or personnel resources, he needn't be here, yet, there he is.*

A cursory glance around the room would easily lead someone to think it was like any other conference room with cream-colored walls and a dark mahogany conference table with cushioned chairs. Otherwise, the room looked Spartan, without artwork or superfluous furniture. But it was different, special. While there were no windows, behind the ordinary walls were special screening materials to thwart electronic surveillance. Every item in the room had been carefully examined by DS security engineers to ensure the room was not bugged. Without any other offices nearby, *this* room had been constructed to ensure conversations could not be overheard anywhere outside.

Previously, Riley had interacted with all the players in the room at one time or another, though none were close friends. However, this group reflected the top-secret nature of today's discussion. While the topic they had gathered to discuss today had already been taken up at prior meetings, those meetings had ended each time without successful resolution of the issues. Maybe this time would be different.

Secretary of State Martin made an opening comment. "Since our last session, we've tried a few strategies attempting to identify just *who* is leaking critical classified information, and how it's being done. I'd like Lynda Cooper to open the meeting with a recap of her efforts at CIA."

"Thank you, Charles. So far, our special investigative unit has done an extensive review of the leaked information, as well as pinpointing who had access to the identities of our spies working within SVR in Moscow. We have cross-referenced data on employees with access to critical information against significant lifestyle changes such as the purchase of a new house or car, luxury travel, and so forth. We've looked at the past assignments of employees of possible interest. We've also created a complex matrix of anomalies, trying to tie together known facts with unexplained events that might link a specific employee to the leaks. That is still a work in progress.

"Finally, our team has used several ploys to search for the traitor, or traitors. We've created a number of false, yet highly plausible and unique intelligence stories with the expectation that one or more of them would be reported to the Russians. Each fabricated story has been shared with only one senior player at the CIA. If we find out that the Russians have picked up on one or more of these stories, then we'll have a better idea of where the story originated, and therefore, *who* is leaking it. So far, either the Russians haven't taken the bait or their collection technique is better than we expected. The last conclusion would be that the leak is *not* coming from within the CIA.

Secretary Martin interrupted. "Am I correct in understanding that the real leaked information was shared within several US government agencies?"

"Yes, and no," Cooper replied. "The names of our spies in Moscow, who were caught and imprisoned, or executed, were known *only* within the CIA, and among an extremely small number of people. But the information regarding Russian war plans and NATO defense measures was known to a much wider group, including our NATO allies."

"What are we doing to coordinate with other NATO countries?" Jim Riley asked. He liked Director Lynda Cooper; her background as a career CIA operations officer gave her an excellent perspective on the issue.

"That's a good question," she replied. "We're working with various NATO intelligence agencies to examine who had access to both the raw data and the assessments. But the number of people involved is larger than I would like. As for the identities of our spies, none of the NATO countries would be in a position to leak that information because they never knew names in the first place. Let me add that we have coordinated much of this intel in detail with the British. This is because MI-6 also has Russian assets at risk, either in Moscow or elsewhere in Europe."

"Thank you, Lynda," Secretary Martin said. "I'd like to ask the FBI for an update on their efforts."

FBI Director Henson Williams cleared his throat and glanced down at his briefing paper. Riley saw this and wondered whether Director Williams, a former federal judge, was ill-prepared for the meeting. In Riley's experience, it was best to neither underestimate nor overestimate the ability of the FBI. He had worked with both smart and rather dimwitted agents in the past. *I think the culture of conformity within the FBI keeps their agents well-focused on fulfilling their orders,* he thought, *but it comes at the expense of healthy speculation and curiosity.*

"We've gotten approval from the FISA court for electronic surveillance of all potential subjects of investigation. The list is long, but our technology and algorithms are sifting through a massive amount of data," Williams was saying, as Riley refocused his attention. He assumed that long list included everyone in the room.

Henson Williams continued. "In our partnership with the National Security Agency, our surveillance efforts are comprehensive."

Riley scanned the room, but no one moved or seemed about to comment. So, *he* spoke. "We should consider that our American traitor might not have direct knowledge of *who* the CIA has recruited as spies in Moscow. I speak of the imprisoned SVR agents or those who have been executed and have worked for the CIA. It might, however, have been sufficient for the Russians just to know *what* information was being passed to the CIA, then to focus on who had such access within their own country. This is, of course, exactly what *we* are doing to find the Russian spy or spies here within the US government. The Russians are totally capable of putting two and two together and laying their own trap." Heads nodded around the table.

"In other words," Riley continued, "we could be dealing with two separate issues. First, for the SVR to identify the CIA spies with certainty, they need *not* have been given the information directly from a CIA case officer or analyst. They may have deduced who their traitors are from analysis of the information provided to us. Secondly, the number of people having access to the Russian war plans spans several agencies and countries and could easily be unrelated to direct knowledge of who the CIA spies are in Moscow."

Archibald Watson, Assistant Secretary of State for Europe, spoke up. "Is it still the case that only top-secret information involving Europe has been leaked?"

"As far as we know, that's true," Lynda Cooper said, "None of our personnel have reported leaks of information to the Russians concerning other regions of the world."

"So, we may assume," Watson continued, "that our spy is either in Europe, deals with Europe, or has been tasked by the Russians with collecting *only* European information. If that's true, why would it be the latter?"

Deputy Secretary Wakefield Summers replied. "If it is the latter, the Russians may want to limit their spy's exposure and risk, so their tasking is limited."

"Lynda, the CIA, and the NSA, have the best technology in the world," Secretary Martin stated. "Is it possible for the Russians to be using electronic communications with their spy or spies and for us not to be capable of intercepting their transmissions?"

"It is possible due to the enormous volume of electronic transmissions to scan. But it is equally likely that the Russians fully understand our capabilities, and therefore, have reverted to using old-school methods to pass on information. Indeed, this is exactly what Al-Qaeda did in the early 2,000s after the US media leaked our capability to intercept their communications."

Secretary Martin leaned back in his seat and rubbed the bridge of his nose. His background in foreign policy stretched for decades, but his involvement in intelligence methods was far less comprehensive. The point was equally true for FBI Director Henson Williams, whose legal expertise was solid, but not his understanding of spy tradecraft.

"Okay, let's continue to search for the leak and use whatever methods we can under the law," Secretary Martin said. "The Russians are extraordinary in the field of intelligence, and we'll have to up our game if we are to thwart them."

Riley had been watching Dennis Hager taking copious notes during the discussion. He knew the man was irresponsible with classified information, so he spoke up. "Gentlemen, and madam, let me make a gentle reminder that *everything* discussed in this room is not only top secret, but subject to special category clearances. For those who have been taking notes, you will need to secure your notes in a safe within an office or facility approved for top secret storage." He looked over at Hager who flashed daggers back at Riley.

"Okay, thank you for attending. Meeting adjourned," Secretary Martin said.

On his way out, Riley literally bumped into Hager at the doorway. "Don't worry, Riley, my notes will be securely locked up tonight," Hager said.

Riley watched him leave the room and shook his head. *Talking to Hager about security precautions is like talking to a bag of hammers and expecting an intelligent response.*

He, again, considered mentioning his suspicions to the FBI about Hager's loyalties, but then, took a deep breath, and decided it would be unwise without concrete facts.

Jesus, I miss not having Alex here to toss around ideas, Riley thought as he walked back to his office.

11

FIRST IMPRESSIONS

US Embassy, London

Alex and Rachel were dressed to kill. Today, they were giving a first impression to embassy officials and intended to impress. He wore a dark blue pinstripe suit with a light blue shirt and red tie; she wore a similar dark blue pantsuit with a cream-colored blouse and three-inch high heels by Salvatore Ferragamo. Earlier, they had examined the morning bus schedule and subsequently took a bus that dropped them at a stop on Park Lane, only a two-block walk to the US Embassy at Grosvenor Square. The BBC's morning television weather report had said that temperatures would be a little cooler than on Sunday, but skies would remain clear and sunny.

Gary Jones had confirmed their separate appointments the previous afternoon. Now, as they approached the embassy, Alex noted the armed Metropolitan Police officers patrolling around the building. Each was carrying an H & K MP-5 sub-machine gun and a Glock 9 mm pistol. London might be one of the safer capitals in Europe, but many terrorist groups knew that the US

Embassy was in Grosvenor Square, so armed protection was absolutely required.

Once inside the front doors, after presenting diplomatic passports to the local embassy guard for entry, they saw a US Marine
Security Guard standing behind the bulletproof glass enclosure.
For a second, Alex thought he saw recognition in the man's eyes.
The Marine briefly looked down, no doubt checking a photo array
of today's known visitors given to him by RSO Gary Jones. Then
he snapped a smart salute to Alex, who returned it. It was a nice
gesture for his new boss on the first day which the Marine would
never need to repeat again. As they progressed through the heavy
access door electronically controlled by the Marine, Alex caught
him staring at Rachel from the corner of his eye. He couldn't help
but smile when the Marine silently mouthed the word, 'Wow.'

London had the best U.S. Embassy lobby he had ever seen. It
was a huge open area of marble soaring at least two stories high,
often used for diplomatic receptions. Large portraits of former
ambassadors hung around the four sides of the room. Almost all
were political appointees and included men and women of
substantial wealth, and political connections. Of course, as political appointees, not all had seriously concerned themselves with
the details of America's foreign policy. That's why the State
Department selected its Deputy Chief of Mission very carefully,
for he or she would have to carry the load when a specific ambassador was more interested in the social aspects of the job. In this
case, the DCM was Bainbridge Wellington, who had been in
London for many years. He would be the direct boss of both Alex
and Rachel.

After Rachel and Alex parted ways and went to separate floors,
she sat in the political section with the officer she would replace
within a few weeks, Nelson Ramsey, while Alex sat in another
office opposite Gary Jones, who would depart post at about the
same time as Ramsey.

"Well, your office is large; the furniture looks really nice," Alex complimented.

"Thanks, it's just luck of the draw," Jones said, "as well as having Erica Evans as a great management counselor. She likes security and supports us, a real asset to this job. Are you ready to be introduced to the staff?"

"Indeed, I am."

Gary's office management specialist was Diana Carrington; the two assistant RSOs were Tom Lopez and Frank Stevens. Tom had experience at two prior posts abroad and Frank was on his first overseas tour of duty. Alex chatted with each of them and said how much he was looking forward to speaking in-depth with them soon.

A minute later, the Security Engineering Officer, Billy Caldwell arrived and was introduced. Alex chatted with him as Tom and Frank returned to their previous work. Billy's responsibilities covered the Embassy in London, the Consulates in Edinburgh and Belfast, and the Embassy in Dublin, as did the RSOs. His expertise was in focusing on technical security countermeasures and ensuring that all security equipment was operational.

"Okay, Alex, our next stop is with Erica Evans, our management counselor," Gary said. "Her office is just across our shared reception area."

As they approached her office, she came out by coincidence, with an empty coffee cup in hand. "Erica, I want you to meet my replacement, Alex Boyd."

She immediately smiled and put out a hand. Alex shook it, noting that her grip was solid. "I'm delighted to be working with you, Erica."

"The pleasure is mine," she said. "Last week I spoke with Jeff Tolson in Cairo. He sends his regards and said some really nice things about you."

"Jeff's a great guy. And by the way, thank you for all your

support in answering our questions before we arrived. I understand you went to bat for us with the Embassy housing board,
thank you. Our townhouse is lovely."

She nodded. "Would you like a cup of coffee? I was about to
get a refill?"

"Yes, thanks, I would." The three of them grabbed some java
and entered her office which was like Gary's, overlooking
Grosvenor Square with its large garden in the middle. Alex liked
Erica Evans. She was warm, bubbly, and attractive with short
brown hair and an athletic figure. Being the management counselor in London implied she was very well thought of in the State
Department. The three of them spoke for twenty minutes about
past postings, problems, and budgets, before Alex and Gary
returned to his office.

"If you're going to be around after lunch," Gary said, "I can
introduce you to First Sgt. Ken Waters. He's in Hyde Park now,
exercising some of our Marines who need to improve their fitness
scores."

"Really? Young Marines who are below standard?" Alex asked.
"I know. That's crazy, right? But the last detachment commander
was, shall I say, a little slack in some of his duties. But now we have
First Sgt. Waters who joined us from the MSG school at Quantico.
He was the senior enlisted instructor. He's great, and a terrific
leader."

Gary let a moment pass to let Alex take it all in. He wasn't one
to crowd a situation. "Next subject: I couldn't get you on the
DCM's schedule until 2:30 pm, but Anna Battles, the CIA station
chief is available now. Are you ready?"

"Yeah, that's fine. By the way, when is Rachel seeing the
DCM?" Alex asked.

"Bainbridge Wellington is having lunch with her today at his
club." "His *club*? My, my, how very British!"

"Oh, yes, last year you may have noticed his hand-made British shirts and suits? Well, he's completely bought into the whole British scene. That's just who he is, I guess. But he's a good guy and extremely competent. While he's a stickler for protocol, he likes security as long as we can keep things low key."

"Is he such an anglophile that when I see him this afternoon, he'll offer me traditional British tea and crumpets? Or perhaps a glass of sherry?"

Gary laughed and shook his head. "Could be, we'll see! Let's go."

ANNA BATTLES STOOD AROUND 5'8," not quite as tall as Rachel, and looked to be in her late fifties. She wore wire-rimmed glasses and had a magnificent head of thick, white hair, well coifed. She also had a pleasant smile and piercing hazel eyes complimented by a businesslike long-sleeve blue and white patterned dress, and modest heels.

Before he left Washington, Alex had called on Carter Ambrose, the CIA head of western European operations. He was the former Station Chief in Rome when Alex had been the RSO; they had worked closely together for several years.

According to his friend Carter, Anna Battles had a distinguished record; she had served once in Africa but had spent most of her time in Europe --- Paris, Budapest, Frankfurt, Stockholm, and Berlin. In Washington, she had held some challenging jobs focused on countering the threats from the Russian KGB (now the SVR,) as well as countering the old East German Stasi. Carter had mentioned that Anna spoke French, German, Hungarian, and Swedish. Her impressive background was worthy of being the station chief in London.

"If you're not replacing Gary for a few weeks, why have you arrived early?" Anna asked.

She was sitting behind her desk with Alex and Gary opposite in two chairs. Behind her, on a low-level cabinet, was a photo of Anna standing next to a man and two young adults. Alex assumed it was her family, but decided to explore that at another time.

"I'm on loan to the British Foreign Office. They're considering setting up a mini-DS, and they wanted some advice.

"Really, that's interesting because currently MI-6 provides advice to the Foreign Office. Do they need a mini-DS?"

"I'll find out when I start talking with them. But I gather they don't want anything approaching our size or authority. I imagine much of what DS does will not be required by the FCO."

Anna looked as if she was analyzing this info in her head. "Can you keep me updated on what develops? It would be useful for me to know when I speak with officials from the FCO and MI6."

"Sure, Anna, I think we should work closely."

"Agreed. By the way, you probably don't know this, but I worked for your father in Paris and, of course, I know your mother."

"Really, I didn't know."

"Yes, it was my first tour overseas as a case officer and your father was the station chief." She paused for a moment as if remembering something. "Jack was a great mentor, especially back then when women were frowned upon in the clandestine service."

"You don't look old enough to have worked for my father in Paris."

Her smile turned into a laugh. "I see you inherited Jack's wit *and* sense of humor. But I appreciate the compliment, neverthe-less." She paused and stared at Alex. "Because you are Jack's son, you're practically part of my team here in London."

"Or, it could be the other way around, you're practically part of *my* team." He smiled and Anna chuckled. After about ten-seconds, her smile disappeared, and she looked deadly serious. Her quick metamorphosis was a trifle disconcerting.

"I have something I'm comfortable raising with you and Gary, but I'd like to do so in our SCIF," which stood for Sensitive Compartmented Information Facility." She nodded toward the door.

"Lead the way, Anna," Gary said. They walked down the hall within the CIA's secure office space and into a special room within a room. Anna secured the door after all three had entered, then they took seats in leather cushioned chairs.

"Are either of you aware of the arrests and imprisonment, or executions of our agents in Moscow over the past six months?"

"Yes," Gary said. "You've lost two agents who were our spies in the SVR."

"It's actually four now, but the press has only learned of the first two," she replied.

"Before I left Washington," Alex said, "Director Riley briefed me that the Russians know we've obtained their war plans for Europe, and also that the Russians stole our NATO defensive strategies."

"Good, I'm glad you're up to speed. This issue has recently heated up. We're working closely with the Brits to figure out how this is happening. The problem is that too many officials in Europe seem to have top-secret security clearances these days, so access to the military information is widespread. Knowledge of our specific agents who were compromised, however, was always held close to the vest within the CIA."

"Has the CIA narrowed down the possible location for the war plan leaks?" Alex asked.

"Not by much, I'm afraid. I don't even have a view on whether the leak is coming from the military or the civilian world."

"What about hacking? The Russians are really good at that. Could they have penetrated your computer networks?"

"That's always possible," Anna replied. "And that might account for the war plan leaks, but not the unmasking of our SVR agents in Moscow. That info is simply not included on a data base that can be accessed." She leaned back in her chair and clasped her hands together. "Just yesterday, your director, Jim Riley, speculated that the Russians may not even have had inside information about our SVR agents. Rather, they might have been clever enough to put together pieces of the puzzle and figured out by deduction who may have given us their war plans. He may be right. What's Riley's background, by the way?"

"He served in Moscow and Warsaw as the senior RSO during the cold war," Alex said. "After that, he was director of our office of counterintelligence. He served in other overseas posts as well. And before he joined DS, he was an Air Force officer in the Office of Special Investigations (OSI)."

"Okay. Seems that he's steeped in counterintelligence work," she said. "Well, we need to collaborate on this problem. The leak may be within the CIA, or at State, or in the military. Equally possible, it could be in another NATO country."

"Has MI6 taken the lead on this matter for the Brits?" Alex asked.

"Yes, they have. MI5, their domestic security service, has a big role as well."

"What about our FBI Legal Attaché in the embassy? Are they players in this?"

At this question, Anna Battles took a deep breath, rested her elbows on the arms of the chair she was sitting in and brought her hands together in a little pyramid. She looked from Gary to Alex and said, "What I'm about to say must stay between us, agreed?" Alex and Gary nodded.

"Seriously, I don't want to regret having said this."

"Agreed, Anna," Alex reconfirmed. "You should be aware that my history with the FBI has not been positive."

"Okay, then. In my view, the FBI's main role will be to escort the American traitor back to the U.S., if the traitor is an American working here in the UK. They can charge the traitor and complete their criminal investigation afterward. Naturally, they have no powers of arrest outside of the United States; so, if by chance, we find someone in the U.S. diplomatic, military, or intelligence community who has committed espionage, we'll need the Brits to at least detain, if not arrest, the suspect."

"Clearly understood, Anna. Is there a dispute over this?"

"Not so much of a dispute, as a *desire* by the FBI to exceed both their abilities and responsibilities. Our FBI Legal Attaché, who is personally a nice guy, is following directions from Washington and wants to play a greater role. That would be fine, and indeed would be welcome, if they had the wherewithal to do so. But they do not."

"How is this matter coordinated within the Embassy?"

She looked over at Gary. "Sorry, Gary. You are not aware of this, but there is a group that meets regularly to discuss the leaks."

"I didn't know," Gary replied. He looked surprised and slightly irritated at having been left out of the loop.

"As I said, sorry. The FBI convinced the DCM to keep the group as small as possible. In addition to the CIA, the others included are the Defense Attaché, NSA, OSI, and NCIS. But don't worry, Gary. The group has not made progress."

"What about contacts outside of the Embassy?" Alex asked. "We are in close contact with both MI5 and MI6," Anna Battles explained.

"Does the FBI contact MI5 directly?" Alex asked.

"Good heavens, no," Anna replied. "We chaperone them to MI5 meetings. I might add, that's at the request of MI5. But that wouldn't seem apparent if you listened to the FBI speak at country team meetings. They give the impression they have more access than they really do. I could set the record straight, but it's better to avoid a pissing contest in front of the other agencies. So, I let the FBI play their game of inflating their level of contacts. Besides, Bainbridge Wellington knows the real score." Anna glanced at her watch.

"This has been a great chat, but unfortunately, I have a meeting at MI6," Anna said. "I've enjoyed our first exchange, Alex. I know we'll stay in touch, and please let me know when your vacation at the Foreign Office is over."

"Vacation?"

12

NIGHT OPERATIONS

Washington, DC

Nickolai Petrov and his wife, Ludmilla, sat at their kitchen table in their upper-class home in northwest Washington, DC. One of the great perks of being a Russian diplomat was that the Russian Embassy paid for the Petrov's housing which was vastly superior to anything they could personally afford back in Moscow.

As the so-called Russian "cultural attaché," Nickolai was expected to entertain in a style commensurate with his rank, therefore, this lovely four-bedroom, two-story red brick home was assigned to him for the duration of his four-year tour of duty in Washington. They loved it here and loved the location in the heart of America's capital. It pained them to admit that the standard of American housing was vastly superior to what they might buy in Russia.

As they discussed an operational plan for this evening to defeat FBI surveillance, they sipped a second cup of mild Colombian coffee purchased at a boutique on M Street in Georgetown. Nickolai was not really a cultural attaché. He was the second-ranking SVR officer in the embassy; a spy, and a very good one. Ludmilla was a lower-ranked SVR employee who was expected to support her husband in any way that would help advance the embassy's espionage. Married for twenty years, they had served at several Russian embassies abroad and had two teenagers, both now attending a private boarding school in Switzerland.

Tonight, Nickolai needed to clear a dead drop, meaning collect secret information placed in a certain spot by a high-level American traitor. It was risky because the FBI was always present around the Petrov house, and always ready to follow them when they left the house. This human FBI surveillance was supplemented with technical tracking means, such as devices hidden on the Petrovs' vehicles, when possible, or cameras and sensors at strategic locations that picked up the movement of the Petrov vehicles. This was the nature of counterespionage worldwide and was not unexpected by Nickolai and Ludmilla. They knew they would be tracked by the FBI.

The Petrovs were skilled operators, having worked successfully in Washington for three years, and before that, they had operated out of Russian embassies in Ottawa and Oslo. Nickolai was forty-two years old, five feet nine inches tall, with short blond hair. While he had attained a black belt in judo, his work required intelligence and tradecraft, not physical force. Ludmilla was forty years old and five feet seven inches tall, with short brown hair and a lean physique since she went to the gym as often as possible.

"What are you thinking?" Ludmilla asked while reaching out to hold his hand.

"I believe our plan will go well. But I am prepared to abort if the FBI is not fooled."

"As always, that's wise, my dear. Don't take unnecessary risks.

The stakes are too high." Nickolai nodded and leaned toward her to kiss her gently. She smiled and squeezed his hand tighter.

They were ready for the evening. She tucked her short hair into one of Nickolai's favorite eye-catching red American baseball hats with the Washington Nationals logo and put on a dark blue windbreaker that matched one of his own. As a final touch, she slipped a small wedge into each of her tennis shoes to make herself appear taller. Her baggy dark sweatpants hid her thin legs.

Shortly, thereafter, she left the house alone and walked out to their silver Mercedes S-class parked in the unlit driveway. Then, Ludmilla drove off at a moderate pace; the plan was not to lose the FBI surveillance team but the opposite, it was to draw their attention away from Nickolai's own departure later.

He watched from behind a sheer curtain in the darkened upstairs bedroom. *It worked*, Nickolai thought as he watched a four-door sedan pull away from the curb behind his wife. He also knew there would be another FBI unmarked car waiting at the end of the block and hoped they would also follow Ludmilla, assuming it was he who was driving away.

He sat in a bedroom chair, looked at his watch, and waited. It was 8:00 p.m. They had assumed that the FBI's team on duty was not their first string. Rank and experience had its privilege, even in the FBI. So working the night shift to track Russian diplomats, would be relegated to less experienced agents.

While Ludmilla drove to one of her gym locations further out in Bethesda, Maryland, he would leave the house at 8:15 p.m. His assumption was that another FBI surveillance car was somewhere on the block, which he would have to evade it at some point. But this was certainly easier than operating against a team of three cars which he hoped was not the case tonight.

Finally, it was time to leave. He entered the garage from the kitchen door and slid into Ludmilla's black VW Golf GT. Two hours beforehand, he had checked out every inch of her car, looking for electronic tracking devices that may have been planted by the FBI. He found nothing. After he placed one of her floppy hats on his head, he slouched a little further down in the seat to approximate her height. A year before this time, he had removed the garage overhead light as a precaution. Now, when he raised the remotely operated garage door, he hoped the darkness would conceal him until he left the driveway. As he drove away from the house, he saw headlights turn on from a parked car down the street. His plan was to lose this tail before he could proceed to the dead drop.

Ten minutes later, after making a few changes in direction, the tail car was still with him. It appeared only one FBI car was following him, although he knew it was possible another surveillance car was moving parallel to them on a nearby road. Nickolai was familiar with the area's street grid and had a plan. He intended to seek out heavy traffic on Wisconsin Avenue near a congested shopping area.

Approaching a traffic light, he saw in his rearview mirror that the FBI car was not *directly* behind him, but had purposefully allowed another car to get in between, no doubt trying to mask the surveillance. As the light turned yellow, Nickolai slowed in the left lane, making the in-between car stop behind him. Then when the light turned red, he made a leisurely left through the light, effectively trapping the FBI car behind another vehicle that wouldn't follow him. Then, Nickolai accelerated at a normal pace as if there was nothing special about this journey. As soon as he was away from the scene, he made a righthand turn and picked up speed, disappearing from the FBI's view.

Still, Nickolai drove a circuitous route, often making turns and watching for surveillance behind him. On two occasions, he pulled up against the curb and waited five minutes each time, yet no one drove past. He smiled, knowing he had lost the FBI tail.

Finally, he drove to the dead drop, being careful never to exceed the speed limit.

Tonight's dead drop was in Georgetown, not far from the university. He slowed as he passed a specific telephone pole and spotted the chalk mark - a long vertical mark with a short cross above the middle. That meant the American had left new information. He parked the car around the corner and walked to a specific spot on the street, looking for his target, a hollowed-out plastic rock resting on the ground at the agreed-upon location. Inside the fake rock, an SD card was hidden. Since this location would never be used a second time, Nickolai spied the rock and openly walked to it, quickly picking it up and pocketing it before walking back around the corner of this residential neighborhood. He continued looking for surveillance as he returned to his VW Golf.

Rather than go directly home, he drove to the Russian Embassy, deposited the rock in his office safe, before heading back home. Leaving the rock and its contents at the embassy was a precaution in case the FBI stopped him in front of his house. Such a stop would be illegal, of course, because he had diplomatic immunity. Nevertheless, he couldn't risk the information being compromised, not to mention the danger of exposing his American asset.

As he approached his house, he saw the FBI surveillance cars back in place. They had no doubt discovered their mistake in following Ludmilla to the gym. He also assumed they realized he had left in the VW Golf. *So what!* he thought. *What can they do?* They could only accept the fact they had been out-smarted once again. Tomorrow he would examine the encrypted SD card at the office and see what tantalizing information awaited his perusal.

∼

Arriving the next morning at his Russian embassy office, Nickolai Petrov, opened his safe and took out the plastic rock. He popped it open and pulled out the SD card which had been left by the American. Plugging it into a stand-alone computer, he downloaded the information. As he read the documents on the SD card, he heard his door open, and was greeted by a deep voice. "Good morning, Nickolai. It went well last night?" The figure of Andrei Balakin, senior SVR resident in the Russian Embassy in Washington, filled the doorway.

"Yes, it did, Andrei, almost too easy."

The answer disturbed Balakin, somewhat. It made him nervous when things were "too easy." He had been in the espionage business his entire adult life, having served in New Delhi, Havana, Caracas, Bonn, Vienna, and now, Washington. When things were "too easy" either the opposition was incompetent . . . or sly as a fox.

"Have you had a chance to examine the material?" Balakin asked, pointing at the computer.

"A little. I only began looking at it five minutes ago. But, so far, it appears to be of very high quality. There are classified telegrams sent between American embassies in a variety of NATO countries. There also appear to be messages between various NATO commands. Plus, there are a sprinkling of CIA messages, as well. I can give you a report later today."

"Excellent. This source may be the best American asset we have had since Robert Hanssen of the FBI, Aldrich Ames at the CIA, or the Walker family in U.S. Naval communications."

"Agreed," Nickolai replied. "But this source is providing valuable strategic, top secret policy information, while the others gave us specific details of who was spying against us, and the general location of America's nuclear submarines on patrol. A different kettle of fish altogether."

Nickolai smiled. "I gave our source the new Nagra CCR card,

along with a docking station and charger. I believe that will make a difference. Has the Nagra's battery and microphone lived up to it's reputation elsewhere?"

"The card is exceptional," Balakin replied. "Moscow says the microphone can pick up clear conversations from everyone in a room, and the wafer-thin lithium battery is lasting longer than we anticipated. Also, the imbedded circuit board is working flawlessly. All this from a device the size of a credit card." Balkin sat down in a nearby chair, wanting to extend the conversation. "Let's review again how your source is using the card."

"Actually, it's two cards. The first one is his State Department ID card. It even grants him access into the State Department building because we replicated the security features of the real card. He wears the Nagra card clipped to his pocket. When he is about to have a meeting, he presses the card's covert on/off sensor to activate it. Since the card doesn't transmit, only records, it cannot be detected by intercept technology. So far, I've only received one download of information from him, but the material is exceptional and highly classified."

"And the second card?" Balkin asked.

"It is a credit card. We knew there would be times when he would be talking to important people, but the situation would be inappropriate to wear his State Department ID. Therefore, he can place the credit card in his shirt pocket and record the conversation."

"And duplicating his photo on the ID card was successful?"

"It was difficult," Nickolai replied, "but since we had experience operating against other countries, our technical geniuses made it work." Balkin nodded in appreciation.

"All right, let me know later today about this recent material. When is your next dead drop scheduled for?"

"I have not set a date yet. Perhaps in two or three weeks."

"Very well. You have done a marvelous job, Nickolai. Maybe

you and Ludmilla should stay on in Washington beyond next year to handle this source."

"I would like that very much, Andrei."

Knowing their meeting was over, Nickolai focused on the latest batch of documents from his American traitor. *If I can keep this source active for a few years, America's defenses will be severely degraded.* Nickolai was very pleased.

13

BAINBRIDGE WELLINGTON

US Embassy London

Alex's first round of morning meetings and greetings had exceeded his expectations. Then it was time to meet with the DCM Bainbridge Wellington. He would be Alex's direct supervisor and it was vital that Bainbridge became a supporter of Alex's security program.

"Hi, I'm Alex Boyd, and have a two-thirty appointment with the DCM," Alex said to the gatekeeper of Wellington's office. Ruth Yellen was in her mid-forties, a heavy-set and stern-looking woman who appeared to be in charge of *everything* as far as the horizon, or at least, who seemed to want to leave that impression. She looked him up and down, perhaps, deciding whether he should be burned at the stake, or stretched on a rack. To Alex's surprise, she broke into a smile.

"I believe you know my friend and counterpart in Cairo, Donna Vaughn."

"Yes, indeed, I do," Alex smiled back. "She worked for Ambas-

sador Ellen Hunt. Donna's a gem and a great professional," Alex
replied.

"Well, she told me all about *you*, Alex. By the way, I met your
charming wife this morning."

"It's great that we'll all be on the same team," he said. *What a
scary thought if Ruth was an opponent,* he thought. *I certainly
wouldn't want that.*

"The DCM is expecting you, Alex, I'll notify him that you're
here." She picked up the phone and buzzed Bainbridge Wellington. "Alex Boyd is here to see you now."

"Please go on in," she told him while hanging up the receiver.
"Thank you."

Wellington was sitting at his desk and dropped a folder into
his outbox as Alex walked in. He stood, flashed an electric smile
with *blindingly* white teeth, and walked around the desk as Alex
approached. They shook hands in the middle of the room. His
grip was firm, and he made good eye contact. *Very promising*, Alex
thought.

"Let's sit over here." Wellington pointed to a sofa and chairs
near the long bank of windows overlooking Grosvenor Square. As
they sat, Alex figured Wellington must be near sixty yet looked in
good shape. *Maybe he plays tennis or golf*, Alex thought while
assessing the man. The DCM's attire fulfilled an image Alex
recalled from six months earlier when he had flown in from Cairo.
Today, Wellington's shirt had white French cuffs, bold stripes of
purple and grey fabric matched with a solid grey tie. Alex hoped
that Wellington had forgotten his joking remark about getting the
name of Wellington's tailor.

"Here are business cards with the names of my tailors as you
requested last year," Wellington said as he reached over and
handed them to Alex.

He hasn't forgotten, Alex thought while smiling, uncertain if

Wellington was actually being helpful or had understood that Alex had been joking at the time and was now calling his bluff.

"Thank you." Alex placed the cards in his pocket. "And thank you for your support for my assignment."

"After what you've done at prior embassies, we're lucky to have you. I mean it. I know London doesn't conjure up images of anti-American terrorism, riots, or serious threats, but every place is vulnerable these days. Besides, London is one of the busiest posts in the Foreign Service."

"How so?" Alex asked.

"To begin with, we have congressional group visits about every two weeks. They're a pain in the ass and phony as hell, but that's life in the modern Foreign Service. The Secretary of State visits almost monthly and the President annually. Then we've got endless diplomatic or business receptions, held either at my house, at the ambassador's residence in Regent's Park, or in the U.S. Embassy lobby. All of this requires security preparation and liaison with Scotland Yard. Gary Jones told me that you've already met Assistant Commissioner Davies and the Commander of Special Branch."

"Yes, I have. I believe we'll continue our offices' great relationships."

"That's excellent. The police are vital for our protection, but as you know, both they and the Foreign Office can be touchy about weapons and the amount of police coverage that we want for events."

"We have an advantage there," Alex replied. Wellington didn't grasp the point at first and cocked his head to the side.

"You see," Alex continued, "Diplomatic Security protects almost all British government VIPs when they visit the U.S. including Prince Charles, other royals, the foreign minister and other cabinet members, along wiht anyone else designated by the White House. Only the Queen and Prime Minister are protected by the Secret Service. So, it's a busy schedule in Washington, New York, and a few other cities. In short, it's a two-way street where both DS and Scotland Yard benefit from cooperation."

"Of course. I forgot that. I assume you'll be subtle in pointing that out to the Brits, if necessary."

"Naturally. The Brits are our allies in so many fields. It's in our mutual interest to work things out in a low-key manner."

Wellington nodded his head and smiled. "I'm glad you understand. By the way, I'm truly delighted that you and Rachel will be part of our team. But let's first talk about your brief assignment to the FCO. Do they really need a mini-DS?"

"That's hard to say with certainty. I've spoken on the phone to the FCO's Permanent Secretary, Sir Nigel Sharpton, and got mixed signals."

"Wait, you already know Sir Nigel? You realize he's the most senior civil servant at the FCO."

"Yes, I know that. We spoke twice on the phone. My other calls were with lower officials. I'm scheduled to meet Sir Nigel personally tomorrow."

"Alex, I'm impressed. Of course, an RSO wouldn't normally speak to a senior British official of Sir Nigel's rank, but I guess if you'll be working with him, then it makes sense. But once you're back in the Embassy, I'd like you to check with me first before seeing someone that high up."

Alex recalled hearing that Bainbridge Wellington was a stickler for protocol, which definitely included rank, and decided to deal with the issue head-on.

"I know that protocol is vital. In fact, it holds relationships together and ensures that officials of equal experience carry the weight of the relationship."

Wellington nodded and seemed to like what Alex was saying.

"But I also feel it's *vital* for officials who are charged with carrying out specific aspects of America's foreign policy, who are experts in their respective fields, are encouraged to make as many contacts as possible. After-all, we want the best possible outcome for American interests."

Wellington leaned back in his seat, apparently digesting Alex's comment. The pause lasted for maybe five seconds. "You are exactly right, Alex. However, I have to ensure that our official discussions held at the highest levels reflect our employee's understanding of the broadest interests of America."

"How about we reach an agreement," Alex said. "I'll keep you informed of my conversations with senior British officials, and you agree to allow me a free hand to seek out the most appropriate officials to achieve our Embassy's goals. If issues can be solved at lower levels in the British government, that's great. But if I need to go higher, we shouldn't be overly concerned with specific ranks or job titles as long as the Brits don't mind. I'd also like to point out that I'm the first RSO assigned to London who's already in the Senior Foreign Service. That implies I have the broad experience and judgment you expect your senior staff to have."

That's a little pompous of me, Alex thought, *but I'll be damned if I'll be treated like some junior clerk.*

A long silence ensued before Wellington smiled and reached across the opening between them to shake Alex's hand. "It's not every day that someone in the Embassy has the *balls* or skill to argue with me, Alex. But I think we've got a deal. Call me 'Bainbridge,' by the way." Alex briefly relaxed, feeling he had summited an important mountain.

"Now, I've got something else I'd like to talk about," Bainbridge said. "I believe you've been briefed about our espionage problem."

"Yes, I have. I know what material was leaked and I know about the CIA's compromised human assets in Moscow. This morning I spoke with Anna Battles about this. Before leaving Washington, Carter Ambrose and I had a few long chats on the subject as well."

"You spoke to Ambrose directly? He's the CIA Director of European operations."

"Yes, Carter and I are friends."

The silence was deafening. Then Wellington held up both hands. "Okay, okay . . . apparently, I have seriously *under*estimated your circle of contacts.

"Well, of major concern is that much of the leaked material was seen in this embassy. Naturally, that doesn't mean the leak had to

have come from here. Probably fifteen US embassies in Europe were on distribution for the same information, not to mention US military commands, and a host of other NATO countries. But I want to ensure that we are doing everything possible to make our security as airtight as necessary. I'd welcome your thoughts on this."

"MICE," Alex simply said.

"I beg your pardon. What are you talking about?"

"MICE is an acronym that stands for money, ideology, compromise, and ego. I might also add, love. MICE means that we must search for the motivation of the leaker. There's no guarantee of success, but we have to inquire into *why* someone would betray America. Do they need money? Do they have political sympathies for Russia or with communist ideology in general? Have they been compromised, perhaps sexually, and fear they'll lose their job if they don't cooperate with the Russians? Or perhaps their ego requires them to show how important they are. Do they feel slighted by our government, or do they feel they should have been promoted more rapidly? And finally, the Russians are famous for setting honey-traps. They use both females and male agents to ensnare western officials, hoping that the foreigner will fall in love with their agent."

"Jesus, Alex. You really know your business."

Alex smiled. "I made it sound easier than it will be to catch the traitor. The State Department should immediately update the security clearances of all those who have handled this information. We'll have to check financial records, question co-workers and friends, probably have the Embassy IT section check who was looking at which documents and downloading them, etc. This will not only take time, it will only cover the State Department. What about the CIA and the DOD. Will the NATO countries be doing the same thing with their personnel? Who knows? At any rate, that's just a few thoughts off the top of my head."

Wellington slumped back in his chair. "How do we begin? Where do we begin?"

"I'll cable Director Riley and reference our conversation. I'll suggest that Washington start the security update project immediately at each of our European embassies. And I'll ask Riley to urge other US intelligence agencies to do the same. The commitment in time and manpower will be significant but necessary. One last thing. Because of the sensitive nature of the issue, I want to send this cable 'top secret' and I'll need you to approve it."

"Absolutely, Alex. When can you get this cable to me?"

Alex looked at his watch. It was 3:15 pm. "How about around 5:30 this afternoon?"

"Really! Okay then. I'll see you at 5:30."

ALEX COMPLETED his cable by the allotted time and gave it to Wellington, who signed off without changes. It would arrive in Washington within minutes, giving Riley half his day to get the ball rolling, assuming he would agree to the plan.

Before leaving his office, Alex thought back to earlier this morning on his first day: The security program was running smoothly, and his staff seemed excited that Alex would be on-board shortly. CIA station chief Anna Battles appeared easy to work with and Erica Evans in management was a delight, and a supporter as well.

The only downside seemed to be a few political and economic officers he had joined over a cup of coffee. He felt they were naïve concerning intelligence and terrorist threats. After lunch, Alex had held his first meeting with the Marine Security Guard Detachment Commander, First Sergeant. Ken Waters.

The first sergeant was in charge of twenty-five Marines, four of whom were women. About half the Marines were on their second tour of embassy duty, having transferred here from hardship posts in the third world. However, only the most senior NCOs had seen combat, the remainder hadn't been Marines long enough to experience that excitement and terror of such a deployment. Alex hoped, for their sake, they never would.

He and Waters had spoken one on one for thirty minutes before he met with the large group of Marines. Clearly, Waters was a leader, a Marine who understood the full scope of his responsibilities for the welfare, training, and operational effectiveness of the men and women under his command. On the personal side, he was married with three children who were happily enrolled in the American School of London. The meeting with Waters ended on a high note, with Alex affirming that once he took over, he and his ARSOs would participate in *every* embassy drill with the Marines. Waters was also delighted to hear that Alex intended to increase the number of drills from one to two per week. Despite a commitment to drills being expected, Alex knew some of his RSO colleagues around the world blew off such drills. *Not acceptable*, was the mild version of Alex's thoughts about those colleagues.

Checking his watch, it was time to head home. Turning off the lights, his thoughts shifted to Rachel and looking forward to their evening at home.

14

RACHEL

London

By the time Rachel arrived home to their London townhouse, Alex had changed into jeans and tennis shoes. She quickly threw on a pair of shorts and canvas boat shoes. He leaned back in his chair and propped his feet up on the living room coffee table, sipping a Glenlivet single malt scotch with light splash of water. It felt wonderful to be in London and diving into the thick of overseas business. Tomorrow, he would be at the FCO and in another two weeks would take over security in the U.S. Embassy.

"How did your lunch go with Bainbridge?" he asked Rachel. She was sitting opposite him in a living room chair, drinking Grey Goose vodka on the rocks. They were sharing a plate of thinly sliced Italian salami, prosciutto, Stilton cheese, and marinated black Kalamata olives he had picked up in the Harrod's Food Court.

"*Bainbridge*, is it? My, my, aren't you getting chummy?" she replied. "Didn't you deride him just last year as faux American aristocracy?"

"Yeah, yeah, you got me there. But you're saying that as if Bainbridge isn't *your* new best friend as well."

She smiled. "The lunch went extremely well. He took me to the RAC, the Royal Auto Club for the uninitiated."

"You drove *cars* while you ate?"

"Of course not, silly. The club dates back to 1897 when 'motorcars' were just being developed. Now it's a grand building on Pall Mall with elegant dining rooms for meetings, meals, or drinks; there's an indoor swimming pool and squash courts, and it operates as a hotel so members can stay overnight. Naturally, the club is still involved with automobiles."

"Naturally. Are you going to join?"

"I am. I picked up a membership application after lunch. You know I *love* to swim, and I can learn squash since it's sort of like tennis. You should join too. Think of all your contacts you could take there."

"Sounds like a good idea. Gary Jones told me that I'll also be eligible to join the Special Forces Club around the corner from here. That might be even better for me." They sipped their drinks and munched on more snacks. "Did Bainbridge say anything surprising at lunch that you don't already know?" Alex asked.

"No, we only spoke about security business this afternoon."

"Okay. Because we don't have an ambassador here, yet, since he's delayed in Washington trying to get through the Senate confirmation process, someone has to step into the deputy chief of mission role temporarily. Bainbridge is operating as the acting ambassador or 'Charge d'Affairs,' as the French say."

"Honey bunch, I know what Charge d'Affairs means. Do I really look *that* 'uninitiated?'"

She chuckled and stuck her tongue out at him. "As I was

saying, the Embassy economic counselor is currently acting as the DCM. But he transfers out very soon."

"Wait a minute . . . did Bainbridge say that if the new ambassador is further delayed, he'll ask *you* to be the acting DCM?"

"Precisely, Hunk Man. You're a lot brighter than you look." She cracked up.

"Oh, Rach, that's *incredible* news." Alex paused. She was waiting for him to think one step further while grinning at him. "Hold on, that means . . . *you'll* become my *boss*!" he said.

"Bingo!" she delighted in the moment. "But only temporarily. Besides, why should life at the office be any different from life at home? It's only right that I should tell you what to do at work." She saw the mischievous look in his eyes and put down her drink. As soon as he started to move, she leapt out of her chair, laughing, and backed up into an open area. Her hands were up in a defensive position, her muscular legs bent at the knees for balance with her left foot slightly forward. Rachel's grin was wide, and she looked up for the challenge.

"You think you can take me down, big man?"

Rachel's jiu-jitsu and pressure point skills were formidable. But now they were only playing. He moved in and pretended to grab her head, she raised her arms to block it and that's when he lunged for her sides and started tickling her.

"No, no, stop!" She squealed and protested. Her body squirmed and she laughed hysterically, twisting to get free.

"Who's the boss *now*, Hollywood?"

"Not fair, not fair!" she gasped with unabated laughter. Finally, she managed to grab him between his legs and squeeze. His tickling slowed down and eventually they embraced, long kisses interrupted only by laughter.

Finally, he said, "Shall we finish our drinks and snacks first, or...? He raised his eyebrows twice. She laughed again.

"It's still early in the evening," she replied. "As your future boss, I order you to prepare more snacks and drinks." He smiled, then kissed her before heading toward the kitchen.Watching him leave to get refills of everything, she sat back in the living room chair, crossed her long, shapely legs, and admired his physique.

"This is going to be a great tour of duty, Hunk Man." A few minutes later, she yelled out to him in the kitchen, "Did you fix the bed frame yet?"

15

TEMPORARY DUTY BEGINS

The Foreign and Commonwealth Office

The next morning Alex took a taxi to Whitehall, the main street for British government institutions. Arriving at his destination, he marveled at the array of office buildings, each one a large and impressive grey stone edifice representing an empire and heritage of power going back centuries. To his right was the narrow one-block long roadway that led to 10 Downing Street, the Prime Minister's residence and office. Further down Whitehall was the Horse Guards' Parade Ground, its arched entrance symbolically protected by a pair of horse-mounted British Army guardsmen in formal uniform with swords, shiny breastplates, and regimental helmets. To his left, stood the mighty Treasury building that controlled the finances of the entire United Kingdom. Further down the street were Big Ben and the Houses of Parliament.

It's show time, he thought while walking straight ahead through the main door of the impressive Foreign and Commonwealth Office.

"Good morning," he said to the civilian guard in the lobby. "I'm Alex Boyd and I have an appointment with Sir Nigel Sharpton."

"Yes, sir. Please put your briefcase on the conveyor belt for screening, along with any metal items such as coins or pens, then walk through the metal detector."

He did so, collecting his one-pound coins and fountain pen afterward. The view inside the FCO lobby was spectacular. There was an enormous double staircase with grand carved banisters in the center and a large open area that might be used for receptions. Historic portraits and landscapes hung on the walls. Clearly, the FCO had been built to impress and intimidate; Alex felt it achieved its purposes. Five minutes later, a staff aide to Sir Nigel greeted him and took him up the staircase to Sir Nigel's office.

Alex waited in the outer office for Sir Nigel's secretary to hang up the phone. Several somberly dressed men and women came and went. Black, dark blue, or grey suits or dresses seemed to be the expected civilian uniform. Alex was glad he had worn his solid dark blue suit and muted maroon foulard tie which he had purchased a few years ago in Rome.

Sir Nigel was the FCO's Permanent Secretary, meaning he was the top civil servant in the Foreign Office. America didn't have an equivalent position in its government departments. Sir Nigel had risen through the ranks of Britain's diplomatic service and had been an ambassador on more than one occasion. As Permanent Secretary, he was the most powerful career figure in the FCO and directly advised the Foreign Secretary, and other political appointees, all of whom were Members of Parliament rather than experienced diplomats.

"Yes, may I help you?" the secretary asked when she ended her call.

"I'm Alex Boyd and . . ."

"Of *course,* Mr. Boyd, I'm terribly sorry to have kept you waiting." She flashed a nice smile and stood. "Please follow me." They headed into Sir Nigel's office.

As Alex entered, Sir Nigel was taking off his reading glasses. He left them on the document he was examining and walked around his desk to greet Alex. His handshake was firm and smile engaging. His eyebrows, however, were the bushiest brows Alex had ever seen, much like an out-of-control English garden.

"Let's sit over here," he said, pointing to two comfortable-looking chairs placed on top of a large red patterned carpet; the design reminded Alex of a carpet from Afghanistan.

The room was huge, with two sitting areas filled with a mix of leather and fabric sofas, an assortment of leather chairs, and a mahogany coffee table for each sitting area. In another part of the room was a long conference table surrounded by leather chairs. A sizeable fireplace was in one corner of the room, more for decoration now, since the days of coal-fired heating were long over. On the walls between tall windows, hung immense portraits of distinguished-looking men. Alex assumed these were former foreign secretaries.

"Would you like a coffee, Mr. Boyd?" Sir Nigel asked. "If you're having one, I will. And please call me 'Alex.'"

"If you could, two coffees please, Harriett," Sir Nigel said. His secretary acknowledged the request and left the room, returning a moment later with a silver tray on which sat two bone china cups of coffee, a small silver cream holder, and another for sugar.

"I'm grateful to the State Department for sending you to provide advice, Alex. Not everyone in the FCO believes we need to create even a modest-sized security unit. But I do. I've seen Diplomatic Security operate abroad, and I think its good value for the money."

"Where have you served, Sir Nigel?"

"Several places, but most recently as Ambassador to Poland.

Before that, Ambassador to Jordan. I also served at the British mission to the UN in New York which gave me opportunities to see your security chaps in action during the annual UN General Assembly meeting in September. They were very impressive. In fact, I wonder if we didn't meet there many years ago. You look familiar."

"It's possible, but it would have been a long time ago."

Sir Nigel took a sip of hot coffee. "We'll be joined shortly by David Cromwell. He's our top administrative man at the FCO. We think he should supervise the new security unit. You'll be working with him on the project.I'm curious, Alex, in your opinion, would the administrative area be a good place to house the unit?"

Alex wasn't going to get between any internal power battles within the FCO, so he cautiously said, "I think it depends upon what you want the unit to do. Let's see how my recommendations are received."

"Sounds like a solid approach. By the way, Alex, how do you perceive your job in an American embassy?"

"That's an important question, and the answer is multifaceted. It's vital to convince the Foreign Service career professionals that security awareness is part of their own job and will actually support their mission. Unless classified information is protected, and they feel safe doing their jobs and actually remain safe, then their work will suffer and their mission may even be impossible to accomplish."

"How is that message being received?"

"The results are mixed. In historically dangerous places like the Middle East or Africa, the employees pay attention and follow Diplomatic Security guidance. In places like Western Europe, employees don't feel the threat and often become complacent."

"I understand completely. We have the same issue. How else do you see your job?"

"I have to ensure that the embassy or consulates have realistic emergency plans that employees understand. To accomplish this, we update our plans annually and hold regular drills." Sir Nigel nodded; Alex continued.

"Another vital concern is that our defenders, I mean our U.S. Marines, Diplomatic security officers, and armed local police are fully trained to protect our embassies and consulates in a worst-case scenario. They must drill constantly. The senior Americans must understand the internal defense chain of command and know exactly what we are trying to achieve in any scenario. Equally important, our defenders must have the flexibility and individual leadership skills to adapt to changing threats," he briefly paused, then continued. "There are other important areas such as physical security and supporting the American business community, but perhaps we can discuss that later."

Harriett re-entered the office and announced that David Cromwell had arrived. Cromwell was introduced and joined in a three-way conversation. He was short and bald and appeared to be in his late forties. Alex found that although Cromwell had served in British embassies abroad, most of his time had been spent in London, primarily in the budget field. After ten minutes of niceties, Cromwell's true colors emerged when he spoke.

"I want to emphasize, Alex, that we aren't interested in creating a 'heavy mob.' By that, I mean whoever handles security must fit comfortably within the FCO traditional culture."

"That's exactly what I thought," Alex replied. Cromwell and Sir Nigel glanced at each other, but Alex didn't wait for a reply.

"Since the intended unit is to be small, and to serve in an *advisory* capacity," Alex said, "I thought it best they should have sufficient diplomatic skills to operate successfully within the existing environment. They will, however, need to have specialized knowledge of certain fields. This is my preliminary thinking. You might consider drawing upon retired senior metropolitan police officers or British military retirees, or perhaps even private sector experts in some areas."

"I like what I'm hearing so far, Alex, go on." Sir Nigel said. "Okay. Let's start with several areas where I believe you'll want assistance. My ideas are based upon telephone conversations I've had with FCO staff while I was still in Washington." He looked from one to the other, but neither man commented, so he continued.

"I've broken this down into seven areas." He spoke without notes and shifted in his comfortable leather chair facing the other two men. "The first area concerns threat assessment and response."

"We already liaise with MI-6 for threat assessments," David Cromwell said. "This includes terrorism, espionage, or political instability."

"That's a good thing, David, and should continue. I also know you sometimes draw upon the SAS for emergency response if you need to counter a terrorism threat."

"How do you know that? It's very sensitive information," Cromwell replied.

"I believe Alex already has friends in high places," Sir Nigel answered with a small smile.

"I do," Alex said, returning the smile. "But addressing the issue at hand, do you have a central location *within* the FCO to consider regional or worldwide patterns of threats? I am *not* suggesting you develop an internal staff to compete with MI-6, rather it would be useful, for example, for a *few* people in the FCO to examine what is happening in, let's say, Saudi Arabia or Yemen, and compare that information with what is going on in nearby African countries.

"Terrorists will attack embassies that are relatively easy targets, and they're very mobile these days. You may recall that the Al-

Qaeda terrorists who attacked our embassies in Kenya and Tanzania had arrived from outside of those countries.

"Ah, I understand," Cromwell replied.

"I don't know the extent of what you already have in the FCO, but these are merely ideas to consider for discussion," Alex said.

"Secondly, perhaps it would be useful to hire a few people to monitor physical security at your embassies, consulates, and high commissions. The idea is to ensure that 'best practice' is used whenever feasible. The background of these people might be in engineering or construction. I have visited several of your embassies and their security is impressive. But having a few internal advisors to assist your overseas staff when planning a modification of an existing building or when beginning new construction could be useful."

"Third point, and let me be very honest . . ."

"I think we're in trouble now," Sir Nigel interrupted, but didn't seem upset.

"You can relax, Sir Nigel, because the third issue is easy. Wherever I have served abroad as a regional security officer, I have been frequently visited by British businessmen who asked about local security conditions, or they wanted to know *who* to contact with the local police for help."

"Ah, that's more of a commercial function and we have people in our embassies to address their concerns," Cromwell replied, somewhat smugly.

"Actually, David, they aren't doing their job. These British businessmen I mentioned, told me they had already visited the British embassy, which gave them little or no advice at all. That's why they came to the US Embassy because they know Diplomatic Security has an active and large program to support American business abroad."

"So, what's the answer?" Cromwell asked. "We don't intend to create a cadre of security staff overseas."

"I realize that, but the solution is less complicated. The FCO needs to inform each of its overseas missions that supporting the security needs of British businesses is a mandatory requirement. Next, ask each mission to formally designate an existing officer to be responsible for creating a list of local law enforcement officials, along with their phone numbers and address that can be given to British business as appropriate. This isn't really a commercial function. It has more to do with the political and law enforcement environment. Here, in London, hire a few people to track and update this information. I am certain that every American embassy will be glad to help you with identifying local contacts in law enforcement."

Crowell said nothing, but Sir Nigel spoke. "I like that idea very much, Alex."

Harriet knocked on the door and entered before Alex could continue speaking on additional subjects of internal security and countering espionage, fraud investigations, security inspections, and security training.

"Sir Nigel," Harriet said, "the Prime Minister's office just called and asked that you go to Number 10 now to brief him on the latest threat from China in the South China Sea. Apparently, the American President will be calling the PM later today to discuss this."

"Thank you, Harriet." Sir Nigel turned to Alex.

"I don't suppose you know anything about the South China Sea dispute?"

"Afraid not, Sir David, but my wife is the new Political Counselor at our Embassy, and she served in Hong Kong and Beijing. She speaks excellent Chinese and probably follows that issue."

"Extraordinary. I imagine that she and I will meet in the near future. This issue isn't going to disappear, I'm afraid. However, we'll have to continue this discussion later. David, I'd appreciate it if you could show Alex to his new office and see that he gets an ID card for building access."

After shaking Sir Nigel's hand, Alex left the room with David Cromwell. He was thoroughly pleased with Sir Nigel's preliminary reaction to his briefing. If Cromwell's initial comments were reflective of the views of the FCO bureaucracy, however, Alex knew the road ahead was not going to be without its pitfalls.

16

THE SYMPOSIUM

Oxford, England

Rachel envied Alex's temporary assignment at the FCO because he could spend the entire time in London while settling into the townhouse they would have for the next three years. Plus, his schedule was his own. She, on the other hand, had to travel back and forth on weekends between London and Oxford. Her work schedule was set up by the university and would be based on the demands of the symposium.

It was a little before 9:00 a.m. when she boarded the train at London's Paddington Station. She pulled a medium-sized roller bag at her side. The satchel over one shoulder contained her computer. She took a seat for the approximate one-hour journey; there would be four stops along the way.

She stared out the window and watched the suburbs of each town passing by until the train arrived at a local station stop; then they were off again for more of the same. No glorious vistas of vineyards, or hilltop villages, as was the case between cities in

Italy, nor the exhilaration of a high-speed Eurostar train as in France.

Oh well, she thought, *the city of Oxford should more than make up for the mediocre transport experience.*

Eventually, the train crept into Oxford's station and Rachel exited her carriage, hoping that her contact, Professor Hilda Humphries, Ph.D. in modern history, would spot her. Rachel stood on the platform waiting until she saw a heavy-set woman in her mid-forties approach.

"I believe you are Rachel Smith," the woman said, hand extended. Rachel shook it, feeling the woman's chubby fingers.

"I am. You must be Professor Hilda Humphries."

"Correct on the first try, but please call me just 'Hilda.' All my friends do."

She had a nice smile and piercing blue eyes. Although overweight, she offset her size by dressing attractively with a colorful red scarf around her neck and an expensive-looking long dress. Rachel's own attire was a pale cream shirt-waist dress, knee length, with a black belt and two-inch heels. She had purchased the outfit during one of her visits to Milan.

"Hilda, thank you for all your advice when I was still in the D.C. area."

"I should thank *you.* You're going to be the star of the symposium. We appreciate your commitment. Let's go to your apartment so you can drop off your bags."

They walked out of the station and into a parking lot. The first thing that caught Rachel's attention was the huge number of bicycles in the lot.

"Golly, I thought school was out of session. Why all the bikes?"
"The student population is not as heavy as during the normal school year, but we still have a lot of students here for the summer, and this is how they get around."

Professor Humphries' car was a white Renault sedan. They headed toward Rachel's furnished one-bedroom corporate apartment provided by the U.S. Embassy. It was only a five-minute drive away from the station and located in the Centre City. Luckily, it was a short walk from there to where the symposium would be held at Pembroke College, part of Oxford University.

She used the keys provided by the Embassy Management section, and the two women entered the apartment. At first glance, she felt it was perfectly suitable for her. There was a comfortable sofa and two chairs in the living room, and the open-plan dining area had a small table with four chairs adjacent to the petite kitchen. She checked the bedroom and found it a little austere. *But what the heck*, she thought, *it's only for two or three weeks.*

Hilda suggested Rachel take a few minutes to unpack her clothes, afterward, they would walk to the college for a discussion about the symposium.

PEMBROKE COLLEGE WAS VINTAGE OXFORD: Four hundred years old, constructed of sand-colored limestone, with a central courtyard surrounded by the main building. Each room that faced the courtyard had a window box filled with flowers.

Hilda walked Rachel through the arched dining room with high ceilings that held long communal tables for students. They went up to Hilda's office which was cluttered with books, newspapers in several languages, and her large, dark wooden desk set off to one end. There was a sitting area at the other end with a plush sofa and two comfortable-looking chairs.

Almost immediately, they were joined by Professor Malcolm Weatherspoon who ran a program on contemporary Asian political studies.

"Welcome to Oxford, Miss Smith," he said smoothly after Hilda made introductions. They shook hands, but when he was slow to let go, Rachel increased the pressure of her handshake to an uncomfortable level. He let go while still maintaining his smile.

"We hope to pick your brain extensively with regard to the media's role via-a-vis foreign policy."

"That's what I understand."

Malcolm Weatherspoon was handsome and looked to be about forty-five years old. He was fit and solid looking, six feet tall, had a full head of dark hair, and even had a slight tan.

"Have you just returned from a vacation, Malcolm?" Rachel asked.

"No, why do you assume that?"

"It's your tan. I thought perhaps you went to the beach or were on holiday in southern Europe."

Hilda Humphries laughed. "Oh, no, Malcolm is our resident *athlete*. He plays tennis, and also rows."

"*I* play tennis," Rachel said. "Are there courts nearby?" "Not far from here," Malcom replied. "Do you play well?"

"Better than average. I've played most of my life." Rachel was being modest since she was a former PAC-10 singles champion when she attended UCLA.

"Once you get settled in, I'll show you the courts. Perhaps we can have a few matches. I don't suppose you brought your racket with you?"

Rachel noticed him staring at her legs while he spoke. "No, but it's coming in my air freight shipment and should arrive next week." Rachel looked over at Hilda. She was standing somewhat oddly with one arm across her body and the other resting against her chin. Rachel detected an ever so slight sideways nod of Hilda's head. *Is that a warning of sorts?*

"Excellent," he said. "I have to run now to a meeting, but I hope we'll soon have time to discuss the symposium," he paused, "in-depth." They shook hands again; this time he knew when to let go. Rachel had a sixth sense that the distinguished Malcolm Weatherspoon was somewhat of a sleaze ball.

Not the first time I've have to fend off a man who thinks he's God's gift to women. As he walked out of the office, Rachel looked at Hilda who was shaking her head negatively. Rachel grinned. University politics and testosterone, both sides of the Atlantic had some things in common.

"Let's go to early lunch," Hilda suggested. "We can discuss the symposium." She took Rachel to a nearby Greek restaurant where they both ordered lamb shank with eggplant and a small Greek salad.

"I hope your tennis ability is good, Rachel, because Malcolm is an excellent player. By the way, he's also a terrific rower and even got a 'blue' when he was a student here."

"A blue?"

"Sorry, it's a British phrase, meaning he was a champion rower and won medals."

"I take it you've heard his pick-up lines before."

"Oh, god, yes. I've known Malcolm for twenty years. Ever since he became a professor at the college, he's been notorious for cheating on his wife with female faculty and graduate students. Finally his wife left him after he failed to control his sexual appetites."

"I see. Well, I'm not on the menu. I'm happily married, and if he becomes too irritating, neither I nor my husband will put up with that type of behavior."

"Good for you. Shall we discuss the symposium now?"

"Absolutely. I can't wait to get into the program. By the way, thanks for sending me the syllabus and list of attendees. It appears we'll have strong participation from the media and good support from other professors at Oxford. But it seems there are people enrolled in the program who are not students. They appear to work either in the government or corporate world."

"Yes, that's correct. By the way, I should tell you that I liked what you suggested regarding your own presentations. Nothing compares with real world experience to bring a subject to life. For example, there's a lot of interest here in how you handled the American Ambassador's kidnapping in Italy. It couldn't have been easy navigating the crosscurrents of the State Department, FBI, and Italian agencies."

"That's for sure. Although it was easier working with the Italian Foreign Office than advising the FBI."

"Interesting comment."

Hilda paused as she swallowed some lamb. "So, I know you speak excellent Italian because I watched your old news clips, and your curriculum vitae indicated you also speak Chinese?"

"Yes, I also speak French. What about you, Hilda? If you don't mind me asking, have you worked outside of academia?"

"I worked at the FCO for five years, but resigned because I find academia more appealing than government bureaucracy. The FCO had assigned me to the British Mission to the European Union in Brussels, but I was only a small cog in a big wheel there. It was exciting, though. I speak French, German, and Russian. By the way, Malcolm speaks Chinese, so don't be surprised when tries to impress you on that score."

"Thanks for the warning. I'll try not to embarrass him in public."Hilda responded with a broad smile. "This might be fun watching you two fence with your abilities.'

They spoke for another two hours. Rachel liked Hilda's keen mind and political sense and felt they would make a good team for the symposium. She couldn't wait to meet the other speakers during the next few days.

After lunch, Rachel was free for the rest of the afternoon, so she walked around the city on her own, exploring shops, before returning to her apartment and calling Alex to tell him about how her first day went in her new role.

"Oxford could be a wonderful break," she told him as she recalled the tension she had experienced at her other embassy assignments, even in Washington. "After all, Alex, what could possibly go wrong in academia?"

17

ESPIONAGE ON THE MENU

London

Lars Nilsson put down the lunch menu when he saw April Scott walking toward his outdoor table at the Sofra restaurant in Shepherd's Market, Mayfair. She wore a knee-length light blue dress and a blue blazer with a matching scarf. To Lars, she looked great. He stood and they lightly embraced before both sitting down in the table side chairs. "Did you get a new hairstyle?"

"I did, yesterday. Do you like it?"

"It's terrific." He meant it. It framed her face perfectly and drew onlookers to her brown eyes and prominent cheekbones. Her total appearance had improved from a few months ago. When they were in bed together, he could tell that she had lost around ten pounds; her body was firmer now, plus her energy level had noticeably picked up. He couldn't stop staring at her. *Am I really falling for her,* he wondered.

"Is everything okay?"

"I'm just enjoying the view."

She reached over and took his hand. "That's a wonderful compliment. Thank you."

They looked at the menus and were ready to order when the waitress brought glasses of water. She asked for a *mezza,* a mixture of middle eastern appetizers, and he asked for *turbot* with basmati rice. April glanced around the pedestrianized street on which they were seated. "I love this area. Restaurants, pubs, and small shops are all here."

"It's charming, isn't it?" he replied.

"Lars, did you see the article in the paper about the French wanting to create a separate European military force paralleling NATO?"

"I did, and my Swedish friends are very interested in this issue." "Interested . . . or concerned?"

"Both. They worry it will undermine the American commitment to defend Europe."

"In Washington, we're also worried because without America's strength and leadership, Europe doesn't seem prepared to spend enough money to defend itself."

"That is exactly our concern as well. I imagine Russia will love this idea. What do the Germans think of it?" he asked.

"Not much, thank goodness. So, it won't go anywhere with the current government in Berlin."

They spoke for another ten minutes before the waitress brought their meal. Of course, Lars wasn't consulting his "Swedish friends" about anything, but April didn't know that. His masters were headquartered in Moscow and extremely keen on any French idea which had the potential to split NATO in half. Completely unaware, April continued on the subject.

"We think France wants to re-establish the importance of its own military and be considered, once again, as a first-tier political player, *a la* the Charles De Gaulle era. But we feel it's more important for NATO to worry about the resurgence of the Russian Navy on the northern flank of the Alliance. Moscow wants to rebuild their submarine force to sink our ballistic missile subs if war begins, and afterward, they'll interdict our reinforcement convoys."

"I'm always impressed with your understanding of political-military affairs, April. You're really knowledgeable."

"It's what I do for a living. I should know a few things, don't you think?" He reached out and held her hand. She responded by squeezing his.

"How is your new boss working out? What's her name . . . Rachel Smith?"

"Rachel's not working in the Embassy, yet. She's involved in a symposium at Oxford University at this time."

"Oh, I forgot."

"But I can tell you this, she's brilliant. And get this, Bainbridge Wellington told me that if he has to continue acting as the ambassador, he'll move her up to be temporary deputy chief of mission."

"Won't that leave you short-handed in the political section?" "It will, but Wellington said that I'll take over as acting political counselor until Rachel returns to her regular duties. So, who cares if we'll be short-handed?"

"Congratulations, my dear, that's wonderful."

"Yes, it is."

They talked until the wait staff removed their plates, then ordered Turkish coffee. He also had a *baklava*, loaded with tons of honey. Twenty minutes later, Lars excused himself to use the toilet, and rose to walk inside the restaurant.

"I need the restroom, too," April said. They leisurely walked inside, past tables full of patrons, then down a narrow hallway toward the bathrooms. That's when April grabbed Lars' arm, forcing him to stop. With no one in sight, she reached into her purse and pulled out an SD card, discreetly placing it in the palm of his hand. He looked down with surprise as she folded her hand over his.

"Consider this a nice gift for your Swedish friends. I appreciate that you haven't asked me to do this in months, but I want to help. I *love* you, Lars. You mean more to me than anything in the world."

"Thank you, my love," he said, hugging her tightly and placed the SD card in his suit coat pocket before entering the men's room.

AFTER THEIR MEETING, April walked back to the Embassy at Grosvenor Square, enjoying the afternoon sunshine. Now sitting behind her desk in the political section, she felt upbeat, doubts no longer lingered about passing classified information to her fiancé. She trusted Lars completely. He was the kindest man she had ever known. And although he claimed little knowledge of global political matters, she interpreted his frequent silence as agreement with her professional views. She believed their stars were finally aligned, and in a few months, she and Lars would be married.

Before I met Lars, I had almost given up on finding a partner in life. Now, my world is different; it's shared with the man I love. I'm truly happy for the first time in years. She smiled at the thought as a small tear of happiness dribbled down her cheek. Not troubling to wipe it off, she wanted to feel the joy of this moment for as long as possible.

THREE WEEKS LATER IN LONDON, Alex and Rachel were about to finish their interim projects and begin their three-year assignments at the American Embassy. Summer was in full bloom.

The Foreign Office task had not been strenuous for Alex; after his daily interactions at the FCO, he would return to the US

Embassy and read highly classified files and briefing memos on the latest disasters concerning Russian penetration of American and NATO intelligence, diplomatic, and military operations. For him, it was like business as usual.

More CIA spies within the Russian government had been arrested, and even one British spy in Moscow. Furthermore, he found the Russians seemed to have the American and NATO playbooks as negotiations occurred on issues such as arms control, dealing with China, or the latest Middle East flare-up. The West was bleeding agents and classified material at an alarming rate.

So far, the combined counter-intelligence forces within NATO had theoretically narrowed down the likely source - or sources - of the leaks to a few locations, based upon a detailed examination of all known facts and the type of information being leaked. Prominent on the list of locations were both Washington, D.C. and London. Alex was glad that Anna had repeatedly shared both her concerns, and her detailed analysis of the situation.

Since Anna was in regular contact with the British intelligence services, MI-5 and MI-6, Alex's job was to focus on the Special Branch of the Metropolitan Police. The latter had a long history of countering both foreign intelligence operations and fighting Irish Republican Army terrorism.

In the waning days of Gary Jones' role as RSO, before Alex took over, he and Alex took a taxi from the American Embassy to Metropolitan Police headquarters, now called New Scotland Yard since the location had changed. Exiting the cab in front of the glass and steel building, Alex looked up at the structure where they had an appointment with Gerald Davies, Assistant Commissioner for Specialist Operations. After signing in, they were escorted up to his office.

"Alex, it's good to see you again. And Gary, as I recently told you, we're going to miss you," Davies greeted them.

"It's been a great three years, Gerald. I want to thank you for all your help."

"Nonsense, that's what allies are for. Now, Alex, I understand you'll be taking over from Gary in a few days, correct."

"That's right. I know you and I will be working closely together and I'm looking forward to it."

"When does Rachel return from Oxford?"

"This is her last day there. Although we've seen each other on weekends, it will be great to be together again full time. In fact, she'll be with me this evening in London."

"I'm sure it will be good to have her back. I haven't told you yet, but a week ago the Commissioner sent our public affairs officer up to Oxford to participate in the symposium. The topic was working with the press during a terrorist incident. She thought Rachel did a smashing job of addressing the issue. Apparently, there were kudos all around for Rachel's performance."

"Thank you. I'll pass that on to her. She mentioned becoming friends with someone from the Met named 'Deidre.' Is that the right person?"

"Indeed, it is, Deidre Plummer. Whenever we have a terrorist attack or some other major incident in London, she must be involved. Deidre is one of the busiest people in the Met."

There was a knock on the door and Ray Penner came in. During the last two weeks, Alex and Penner had lunch together twice to chat about work and get to know one another better.

Gerald Davies looked at his watch, "I believe it's almost 6:00 pm, and it's Friday. Can I interest you gentlemen in a whiskey?" They all agreed. He reached into a cabinet and took out a bottle of Glenlivet single malt and four glasses. Although the shots were small, the hospitality was enormous.

"Can we discuss a little business while we drink?" Alex asked.

"Absolutely," Davies replied.

"Have you been briefed on the intelligence compromises involving the Russians?"

"Christ almighty, we certainly have," Ray Penner replied. "The cold war never really went away, did it?"

"No surprise there. Putin continues to operate like he's still in the KGB and he's determined to restore Russian power," Alex said. "My question is how involved is the Met in dealing with this problem?"

"MI-5 and MI-6 share the lead for us," Penner stated, "but in Special Branch we're using a lot of resources to support the investigation. Unfortunately, the range of possible culprits is large. It's almost certainly an inside job within the intelligence service, diplomatic corps, or the military."

"That's how we see it as well," Alex said. "The CIA is talking with MI-5 and MI-6, and I'll liaise with you concerning any potential Embassy leak."

Penner and Davies glanced at each other. Then Davies spoke. "What about the Embassy's FBI office? They told us *they* have the American lead on the case."

"Yes, well, this is a bit touchy, and I know you'll do what is best for Britain," Alex replied. "Technically, the FBI has the overall lead on *domestic* counter-intelligence cases and the CIA has the lead abroad. You should indeed talk to the FBI. But inside the Embassy, Diplomatic Security has primacy until such time as a suspect is found. Then we're obligated to notify the FBI. They will have the lead after *that*, and we'll support them."

"So, it's not complicated, then," Davies gave a hearty laugh. "I'm glad you have a sense of humor, Gerald. Let's all try to make it work and keep each other informed. I find personal relationships are always more important than written agreements that were executed years ago."

Davies agreed. "What are you doing for Rachel's first weekend in London, now that her symposium is over?"

"Rachel and I are getting out of town and going to Hereford,"
"Oh, yes, Colonel Thompson-Parker of 22 SAS told me he had
invited you for a show-and-tell. Have you been there before?"

"No, I haven't."

"I've been there several times," Jones said. You'll enjoy it."

"I'm sure you will. His men are good chaps," Davies said.

"I know that's true. I've seen them in action in Cairo."

"Since Rachel is coming home tonight, I don't want to keep
you," Davies said. They all shook hands. Gary took a taxi back to
the Embassy and Alex grabbed one to his townhouse in Knights-
bridge.He couldn't wait to ask her about her symposium at Oxford
and to discuss tomorrow's adventure with the SAS.

18

THE REGIMENT

Hereford

On Saturday morning, Alex and Rachel sped along the M-4 motorway in their red Jaguar two-door F-type on their way to Hereford, its powerful V-8 engine growling as if telling other cars: "Outta the way . . . coming through!" Rachel had said she really wanted to drive, so Alex agreed. Every time she depressed the accelerator on the sports car and the engine roared, it filled her with delight.

"I love it!" she raised her voice over the roar of the engine. She looked stylish in her aviator sunglasses, often turning her head toward Alex for confirmation of the amazing experience. He grinned back and had to admit she was an excellent driver, effortlessly shifting gears when needed, and changing lanes with gusto, yet always in control.

"This car is made for you, Hollywood. Sleek, fast, and with great wheels, just like you."

She laughed. "But I think I need more practice using the gear shift." She reached over and touched Alex between his legs, then began "shifting" in slow movements. After a few seconds, he was groaning in pleasure.

"On second thought, I don't need more practice," Rachel laughed. "I believe I've already mastered the technique. Who knew?" She gently let go of his manhood and gave a fist pump. He swallowed hard and looked over at her. They locked eyes and she laughed before quickly returning to watching the road ahead. He smiled, knowing there was more to come later.

The M-4 motorway was flat and straight for more than two hours of their journey west. After they crossed the Severn River, Rachel took the exit at Chepstow north toward Monmouth and then onto Hereford. Immediately after the exit, they entered the Wye Valley and had to reduce speed as the road became windy and more dangerous, allowing Rachel to shift gears often. Alex watched her face, with its perpetual smile.

God, she's exciting, he thought.

When they arrived at the SAS base in Hereford, she said, "Let's do this every weekend."

The guard on duty checked both their IDs, comparing them to his weekend access list, then directed them to a parking lot a few blocks away where they were met by Warrant Officer Bill Turpin. The previous year, he had been in Cairo protecting the British Ambassador when the terrorists attacked the US Ambassador's motorcade at a hospital location. Turpin and his small team of SAS troopers had helped DS agents and two Navy SEALs defeat the attack.

Alex and Turpin shook hands, but Turpin disregarded Rachel's outstretched hand and said, "I think I need a hug."

"That's the most transparent pickup line I've ever heard, Bill," yet she willingly embraced him.

Looking at the Jag, Turpin said. "That's a great set of wheels you've got."

"I know, the car's nice too," Alex replied, looking at Rachel. The joke slipped past Turpin, but Rachel smiled and wagged a finger at him when Turpin wasn't looking.

"Come on into the office and I'll tell you about our weekend program."

The inside of the red brick building looked like many other military locations Alex had seen. Probably constructed in the 1950s, it was in decent condition but could use some freshening up. They passed a few troopers, some wearing civilian clothes, either jeans or cargo pants, tennis shoes or hiking boots, with casual shirts or tee-shirts. A few others wore the traditional British Army camouflage uniform. No one was openly wearing a gun. Alex felt he could be on any British Army base.

"You remember Patty Dempsey from Cairo?" Turpin said as they entered the office.

"Of course, I do," Alex and Rachel replied simultaneously. Dempsey stood and they exchanged firm handshakes.

"Everything's already lined up; here's what I thought we'd do," Turpin said. "Let's start with a brief on the training and missions of the SAS. Then we'll go to your rooms and you can check-in. Afterward, we'll grab lunch in the mess, which is in the same building where you're staying. Then we'll go to our shoot-house for a demonstration. Finally, I'll take you to see our hand-to-hand fighting instructor working with some new troopers. Tonight, we'll go out to dinner at a local restaurant."

"Sounds like an excellent plan, Bill," Alex said.

"I see you followed my instructions about what to wear," Bill said, referring to their attire of blue jeans and hiking shoes. "That's excellent because we planned to let you participate in the fun."

FOLLOWING THE OUTSTANDING BRIEFING, Turpin drove out of the lot in a green Army Land Rover Defender. They followed him to the combined barracks and mess hall. Rachel parked their Jag, and they grabbed their overnight bags from the trunk.

At the check-in desk, Turpin said, "I'm sorry I can't give you one room with a double bed because we use the barracks for single soldiers or individuals who are here for training. Also, everything is spartan by civilian standards. So, you'll each have a room with a bed and a wash basin. The toilets and showers are down the hall, one for men, the other for women."

Turpin turned and spoke to the civilian behind the check-in desk to get their keys. Alex whispered to Rachel, "I guess there won't be any gear shifting tonight."

"Not unless you use a self-drive model."

"Oh, God, Rach, I can't believe you said that?" Rachel burst out laughing.

Turpin led them down a hallway until they came to Rachel's room. "Here's your key. And Alex, your room is next door." He handed him another key. "We passed the mess walking down here. Why don't I meet you there after you drop off your bags in the rooms? The toilets and showers are across the hall."

Turpin headed toward the mess. In their respective rooms, Alex and Rachel unpacked clothes and toiletries for the next day, then joined Turpin. Not only was Turpin waiting for them, but so was Colonel Mark Thompson-Parker, who they had dined with a year earlier at the Special Forces Club in London. There were six other uniformed troopers in the mess, clustered in two groups at the long dining table.

When Rachel entered, every one of them stopped what they were doing to stare at her, but not because she was a woman. Alex figured they had seen females in the mess from other British military units. No, it was because Rachel was, well, Rachel. Just your common Miss Universe contestant with a great physique, long flowing hair, and standing taller than some of the men at the table.

"I see you have a new fan club, sweetheart," Alex said, noting she was smiling at the gaggle of men.

"Silly me," she replied. "I had assumed it was your natural command presence that caught their attention."

"Sure."

"Rachel, Alex, I'm delighted you could visit us in Hereford," Colonel Thompson-Parker said, shaking their hands.

"We wouldn't miss this opportunity for anything," Alex replied.

They sat down, examined the menu, and one of the staff came out from the kitchen to take their orders.

"Darling, I know you wanted to eat quiche or escargot, but I'm afraid they're not on the menu," Rachel said.

"Rach, you're in rare form today . . . way too much humor."

She looked at Turpin, who was grinning. Alex turned to the kitchen staffer and said, "I'll take the fish and chips, thank you."

Rachel ordered the same, and Turpin and the Colonel had steak and chips. As they waited for the meals to arrive, they chatted.

"Colonel, have you ever had a woman in the SAS?" Rachel asked.

"No, they're not even permitted to take the selection course. A few women from undercover units in the Army, however, are assigned here for short duration courses."

"Do you think a woman could pass SAS selection?"

"I doubt it. But even if one or two could pass the course, it wouldn't be worth the expenditure of time and money to weed out the other ninety-nine percent, just to be politically correct. As you've been briefed, the role of the SAS is often for surveillance deep inside enemy territory then, to attack the enemy and kill them or destroy targets. Afterward, successfully evade capture. It may be the stuff of legends, but it's not glamorous nor is it for those who want to make a political statement. I should add that the same applies to your Delta Force and Navy SEALs. Let me ask you a question. Are you an athlete, Rachel?"

"Yes, I was a varsity tennis champion at a major U.S. university, and still play a lot. Plus, I have black belts in two martial arts."

"I see. That's quite impressive. But could you beat the men's tennis champion?"

"I would like to try. But I understand your point."

"Look, you know from our dinner last year in London that I greatly admire what our women did during the Second World War. Some operated behind German lines in occupied Europe to run espionage networks and disrupt enemy supply lines. It was incredibly dangerous work, and the women were extraordinarily brave. The nature of their work, however, required brains, linguistic ability, and judgment. No one asked them to overpower German sentries or to carry one-hundred-pound rucksacks filled with explosives and ammunition for twenty miles to attack a target. The jobs and capabilities of men and women are simply different."

Alex decided he needed to lighten the conversation. "I understand. The jobs requiring brains and cunning were given to the women." Everyone smiled.

"I couldn't have said it better myself," Colonel Thompson-Parker replied. Their food arrived and conversation went on to other topics. As they finished, Turpin suggested their next stop.

"It's time we look at the training facilities. Let's begin with the shooting house," he said.

"Good choice; I'll see you later today," the colonel replied.

As Rachel and Alex walked toward Turpin's green Land Rover, she looked at Alex. "Well, I guess it's nice to know that if I had been a Brit in the early 1940s, I could have contributed to the war effort by parachuting behind enemy lines because of my French language ability and brains."

"Exactly, Hollywood, but don't minimize your ability to drive and shift gears."

She laughed. "I love you, but sometimes you're too silly."

19

SHOW AND TELL

Hereford

Everything at the shoot house was done with live fire rounds and, therefore, dangerous, so attention to detail was vital. As Alex, Rachel, and Bill Turpin entered the facility, Turpin pointed out what they could expect.

"This is one of several such facilities on the base for use by SAS. The exercise we're going to see is designed to maintain the shooting skills of our on-call hostage rescue squadron. The first scenario involves a cardboard hostage being held at gunpoint. The hostage will be sitting in a chair and there will be one or more cardboard terrorists in the room with the hostage. Depending upon the 'situation,' one or two SAS troopers will have to find the hostage in the building and kill the terrorists. All walls within the shoot house have ballistic absorbing material so we can use live ammunition.

"For today's scenario, the lights will be turned off and a single trooper will use his night-vision goggles to find and shoot a single terrorist. The three of us will be observing in the dark, standing behind a ballistic glass window and wall which will keep us safe. Are you ready?"

Alex and Rachel nodded and accompanied Turpin farther inside. Awaiting their arrival was a trooper ready to make his entry into the operational part of the shoot house. He was wearing an all-black outfit with black boots, a ballistic vest, a gas mask, and helmet with night-vision goggles flipped up until needed. He held a Heckler and Koch MP-5 9 mm sub-machine gun in his hands, and a Sig Sauer 9 mm pistol strapped to his right leg. Turpin nodded to the trooper, then led Alex and Rachel down a corridor toward the viewing window.

In the room on the other side of their ballistic glass barrier was a cardboard cutout of a hostage seated in a chair and a cardboard cutout of a terrorist standing behind and slightly to the side of the hostage. The terrorist was pointing a gun at the head of the hostage. Only the terrorist's head and right shoulder would be visible to the SAS trooper once he entered the room.

When they were ready, Turpin hit a switch to turn off the lights in the building and radioed to the trooper to begin. Alex and Rachel tried to see, but it was pitch black. Turpin wore night vision goggles so he could monitor the training. Alex knew Rachel was excited because she reached over and squeezed his hand periodically whenever there was a small sound. About a minute passed. Alex assumed the trooper was clearing other rooms before reaching the target. A burst from a sub-machine gun erupted, announcing the trooper's presence. There had been no hint of it until the long flashes of flame shot out from the barrel of his gun, momentarily lighting up the darkness as if a searchlight had been turned on. Rachel jumped and gasped at the unexpected action. Turpin abruptly turned the lights on.

"Follow me."

They went through a connecting ballistic door and walked up to the cardboard hostage and terrorist. The trooper had fired a burst of three shots, all of which had hit the "terrorist" in the forehead. Had it been for real, the terrorist would have died immediately before he could have pulled the trigger on his own pistol.

"Oh, my God, that was amazing!" Rachel said.

"Thanks," the trooper acknowledged. "All in a day's work."

Time passed, and after witnessing a number of drills, Turpin looked at his guests. Knowing Alex already had the skills, he offered a surprise.

"Rachel, would you like to try?" he asked. "Really? Can I? Yes, I'd love to."

"Have you fired a weapon before?"

"I have, but I don't know about this type. Alex, have I?"

"No, she hasn't. But she has used an Uzi submachine gun."

"Okay then. Here's what we'll do," Turpin said. "You will have to wear the ballistic vest, gas mask, helmet, and night vision goggles. I'll put you outside the door to this room and you just enter and shoot the terrorist when you're comfortable. If you can control it, fire a three-round burst, then let go of the trigger. Got it?"

"Got it." She looked both nervous and excited.

"Good, the sergeant will be with you outside the door. He'll switch the gun from safe to full-auto just before you enter. Then after you shoot, take your finger off the trigger, and keep the weapon pointed at the terrorist. We'll take the gun from you."

She looked at Alex. "This is so cool."

He could tell she was getting more super-hyped with each passing second. Alex and Turpin returned to the viewing window while Rachel waited with the sergeant outside the door to the killing room. When the trooper radioed that Rachel was ready, Turpin turned the light switch off and a few seconds later Alex saw a long continuous blast from her sub-machine gun firing at the target. When the lights were turned back on, the trooper took possession of the weapon, put it back on safe mode, and the group inspected the target.

"Well, sorry to say you missed the terrorist with all six of your shots. Judging from the wall behind the target, you fired too high, not to mention too many shots. But, still, this is just your first attempt."

"Damn. It's harder than I thought," she said. "Guess I'm not ready to be a ninja yet."

"That's okay, Rachel, no one is ready until they've practiced a lot," Turpin replied. "Alex, what about you? Want a try?"

"I thought you'd never ask."

They repeated the same scenario. Minutes later, when Alex saw the target through the green glow of his night vision goggles; he leaned forward in the dark to fire, but got a stabbing pain in his left side, precisely where his bullet wound from Cairo had been operated on. He fired anyway. Afterward, when they inspected the targets, they saw he had hit the terrorist twice in the forehead, but to his horror, he had also drilled the hostage once in the right side of his face.

"I saw you flinch just as you fired," Turpin said. "What happened?"

Alex paused, absorbing the disaster. He had always been an amazingly accurate shooter, especially in real combat in Pakistan, Egypt, Italy, and in the Libyan desert. Now that this happened, he was more than merely upset with himself, he was embarrassed.

"I guess my wound isn't completely healed. I didn't expect to feel a sharp pain in my side; it surprised me."

"Don't worry. That's why we practice until we get it right," Turpin said. Rachel moved closer to him and held his hand.

"It's only cardboard targets, sweetheart."

"*This* time, it's only cardboard."

"Let's go to our last stop for the day and watch the hand-to-hand fighting," Turpin said.

Alex remained quiet on the drive to the next area. *My only consolation*, he thought, *is that my next job as regional security officer at the embassy in London probably won't require me to shoot anyone in self-defense.* That was his expectation, but he'd been wrong before.

The three of them drove a short distance before arriving at the gymnasium on the base. Inside, floors were covered in blue mats and an instructor was holding court in front of six big troopers.

"These six men have recently passed the SAS selection course and are beginning their advanced training," Turpin told Alex and Rachel.

"Today, the training will involve unarmed hand-to-hand combat. In the next stage, they'll move on to disarming someone with a knife, and in the third stage, they'll practice taking away a gun from an enemy. Naturally, all these men are already highly qualified soldiers; each one probably has about five years of Army service under their belt. Four of them are from the Parachute Regiment and the other two are from the Coldstream Guards."

Colonel Thompson-Parker entered the gym and walked over to Alex. They all watched the training together. It was intense, full speed, and with full contact. Alex glanced at Rachel, who appeared to be studying the instructor's moves, perhaps trying to figure out which style of fighting he was using.

Finally, the instructor told the troopers they could take a break and he walked over to the colonel.

"I think we have an exceptional group, sir," the instructor said. "Alex, Rachel, let me introduce Bob Simpson," the colonel said. "He's our lead hand-to-hand combat instructor and a former paratrooper himself." His handshake had a very firm grip.

"So, you're not on active duty anymore?" Alex asked.

"That's right. I retired five years ago to run my own fighting academy."

"What style of martial arts are you using?" Rachel asked. "I couldn't identify it." He smiled.

"That's because it's a mixture of what works on the street, or in the jungle, or in the desert." He paused and looked at Rachel. "You said you couldn't identify it. Do you know a lot about martial arts?"

"I know a little," she replied modestly. He nodded, then looked over at the men.

"Okay, break time's over!" Bob Simpson returned to the mat.

"Who's up next?" Alex asked.

"I think it's Sgt. Castle," the colonel replied. He pointed to a burly man with ginger hair now facing off with Simpson.

"Attack me," Simpson said. Castle charged and swung his right fist at the instructor's head. Simpson partially blocked it with his left forearm while at the same time driving the heel of his right hand into Castle's chin, knocking him back on his ass. Blood dribbled out of Castle's mouth as he lay on the ground, partially stunned.

"As you can see," Simpson spoke to the other five troopers, "you're going to get hit in a serious fight. Don't let him land a solid blow, and counter with superior speed and force at the same time. Remember, you may have to fight off several men. So, don't dick around, and don't let them take you to the ground. Your objective is to the end the fight as quickly as possible and get out of there."

Rachel and Alex watched for another ten minutes, very impressed. "You're the martial arts expert, what do you think?" he asked.

"I like it. The instructor is excellent."

The colonel had been listening and stepped forward. "Would you like to have a go, Rachel?"

"Me? Oh, no. I think watching has been informative enough," she replied.

"Okay, then. I just thought since you have two black belts, you might want to test yourself."

It was a direct challenge, and she couldn't let it pass. "Well, since you put it *that* way, I guess so. But only if it's full contact."

Bob Simpson has been listening and replied, "That's the only way we train, Miss."

"Rachel?" Alex was about to caution her, but she put a finger on his lips.

"Don't worry, big guy. What could possibly go wrong?"

"Not funny."

Rachel had an aggressive streak and loved competition. Usually, her brain countered her impetuous emotions, but not this time. She put her hair into a long ponytail and walked to the mat. She and Bob respectfully nodded to each other and shook hands. Her nerves were edgy and she felt her heart beating faster, but it wasn't the first time she had fought a man with superior strength. It was Bob's skill that concerned her and, therefore, made him dangerous. She looked him over: While balding, Bob was solidly built, appeared to be in his mid-to-late forties, and looked as if he weighed maybe one hundred-eighty pounds.

Twenty pounds more than I carry, she thought, *but he's about my height.* He was also a combat veteran and highly trained.

Alex knew she couldn't back down now. Everyone was watching, including the six troopers who had overheard the conversation and stayed for the show.

"What do you think will happen?" Turpin asked Alex.

"My guess? Since she heard Bob tell the troopers not to take the fight to the ground, that's exactly what she'll try to do."

"Not going to happen," Turpin replied, shaking his head negatively. "Let's get real. Bob is one of the best and . . . she's a woman."

"Ha! You haven't seen 'the beast' in action. Oh, I'm sorry," Alex corrected himself. "You haven't seen *my wife* in action. She's incredibly fast and strong . . . for a woman."

On the mat, Rachel stood six feet away from Bob and moved cautiously to her right, then back to the left, assessing his reaction.

Bob stood his ground, merely pivoting to address her change of position. Both had their knees bent, left feet forward for balance, with open hands placed a little in front of their bodies, elbows bent.

I'll have to be quick, she thought, *he knows his stuff.* Moving closer, she began with a fake punch using her right hand, and, as she expected, he raised his left forearm to block it. Quickly, he stepped forward, attempting to strike her chin with an open palm heel of his right hand which left his fingers in an upward position. She grabbed his fingers with her left hand, bending them back towards his elbow completely taking him by surprise. Just as quickly, with her right hand, she pushed his elbow upwards from underneath and back toward his head.

With the element of surprise, now, she side-stepped to her left and grabbed his right wrist, quickly bringing his arm down and behind his back, then upward again as she wrapped her left arm around his neck from behind to anchor her position while thrusting her left knee into the back of his thigh. Bob's leg buckled and he collapsed onto the mat face downward. Getting on top of his back, she twisted his right arm further up between his shoulder blades while pressing her left knee on his upper back and her right knee on his neck.

"Okay, okay, I give," he called out and slapped the mat with his left hand. The swift takedown had surprised him; he never imagined she had such skills. Now loosening her grip, Rachel stood up with a confident smile, adjusting her ponytail.

She saw the troopers buzzing amongst themselves at the jaw-dropping moment. A few were mouthing something like "holy shit." She heard one of the troopers use the British expression, "I'm gobsmacked." Shaking his head, Turpin spoke to Alex. "I don't fuckin' believe it. I simply don't believe it. Back in Cairo, you told me she was a big girl who easily gets pissed off. But I never expected *this.*"

"Think of the fun we have in private," Alex said. Turpin laughed.

"Shall we go again?" Bob asked Rachel as he stood up. "I'd love to, but I have a train to catch."

"No, you don't. Come on. Just one more time. I want a rematch." At least, he was smiling.

"Okay, but play nice, Bob."

The colonel stared intently at the action, dead seriousness on his face. He looked over at Turpin, who could only shrug. The six troopers moved in closer to watch the action.

Again, Bob and Rachel faced off. It was obvious to her that Bob preferred to counter-attack so, once again, she had to use her guile. She feigned a thrust several times with either her shoulder, or hand, and each time, he reacted quickly and appropriately.

This won't be so easy the second time around, she thought. *If we weren't really allies in real life, I'd kick his knee or shin and strike him in the throat.* But she wasn't about to permanently disable him, as she knew she could do. *I only hope he feels the same.*

She stepped closer with speed, and considerable force, walloping the left side of his face with an open hand strike, followed quickly with her right hand to the other side of his face before she backed off. He blinked twice and shook his head, then unexpectedly moved in and grabbed her around her waist from a side angle. She slid her hips back and dropped her center of gravity to avoid being lifted off the ground. Then, just as rapidly, she changed tactics and stepped closer to trap him in a headlock. She thrust her right hip into his stomach and pulled him closer onto her back before flipping him onto the ground while maintaining her grip on his head.

But Bob was stronger than she anticipated and he forced her arms off his bald head, then pulled her down to the mat. While they scrambled on the ground, he was able to straddle her body with his legs on either side as she lay on her back, one forearm pressing against her throat. She couldn't allow that because he would control the fight from on top. So, raising her hips quickly, she bucked him higher onto her torso which allowed just enough room for her to raise her legs up and capture his neck between her powerful thighs. Now she locked her ankles and squeezed with full force.

There was a god-almighty groan from Bob as he flailed, trying to pry open her legs. She expected him to tap out or go unconscious within seconds, but to Rachel's surprise, even with her legs squeezing the life out of him, he somehow managed to twist to the side and get to his knees. Then, in a bent-over position, he got to his feet which forced her to release him.

Now, Bob grabbed her belt with one hand and using his other to grab her shirt, he lifted her off the ground almost to his waist level and body slammed her back down onto the mat with such force that the air exploded out of her lungs. It stunned her for a moment, and she fought to breathe.

At this point, Bob straddled her chest, his knees pinning her arms to the ground. Gasping, Rachel managed to say: "I give."

Being a gentleman, Bob rolled off her and raised her into a sitting position. Alex and the others came over to ask if she was all right. She nodded.

"I'm okay, really," she told the group. "Nice fight, Bob."

"Are you kidding," Bob replied. "You're remarkable. I mean it. If you ever want to change your line of work, you can have a full-time job at my fighting academy."

She smiled, but in truth, her back was too sore to contemplate a career of fighting.

Bob turned to the stunned troopers. "Okay men, nothing more to see here. We're done for the day." As everyone was walking away, one trooper caught Rachel's eye and gave her a thumbs up.

Rachel stood now and Bob warmly shook her hand with both

of his. Then she joined Alex and Turpin walking back to their vehicle.

"Rachel, you've got a few hours until I pick you guys up for dinner," Turpin said. "Get some rest; maybe Alex can massage your sore back. By the way, great fight. You have serious talents."

"Hmm, I don't know if she deserves a massage," Alex joked. "She can't hit the target when she shoots, and she got beat up by an old bald guy. Who knows what other deficiencies she might have?"

Rachel and Turpin laughed.

"I'll take the massage," she said, "but you're lucky we have separate rooms tonight. Otherwise, you'd be in *big* trouble and might not survive 'till dawn."

As soon as Turpin got in the vehicle, Alex whispered, "That's what I love about you, Rach. You're up for anything."

"Maybe not tonight, big boy. I'm really hurting."

20

RECEPTION AT THE WELLINGTONS

London

A few days later, Alex and Rachel were again in the familiar embrace of the American Embassy. Their temporary assignments at the Foreign Office and at Oxford University had ended, and DCM Bainbridge Wellington was hosting a buffet dinner at his house to welcome them into the London family while saying goodbye to their predecessors.

Alex and Gary Jones had asked Wellington to invite not only senior and mid-grade Metropolitan Police officers, but Alex's key contacts from the FCO, and a few American corporate security directors who were residents in London. The latter group was active in the local chapter of the DS Overseas Security Advisory Council. Unfortunately, Colonel Thompson-Parker and Bill Turpin of 22 SAS could not make the dinner since they were in the Middle East for a few days.

To welcome Rachel, Wellington invited Dr. Hilda Humphries from Oxford University, and several Foreign Office senior officials whom she would be dealing with during the next three years. He also invited a select number of British television commentators and newspaper columnists, or editors, that Rachel would need to know.

Considering the equal number of embassy officials in attendance, it was a large gathering and reflected well on Bainbridge Wellington's sense of duty, political acumen, and hospitality.

Among the guests were two senior MI5 and MI6 officials, April Scott, and her fiancé, Lars Nilsson. No one could possibly know how close the espionage threat was to the West this very evening.

On one side of the Wellingtons' beautifully appointed living room, Alex had just finished a chat with the Met's head of Organized Crime Unit and walked over to Roger Carpenter, the Embassy's FBI legal attaché.

"Here's to having an excellent working relationship," Alex said. They clinked wine glasses and after a sip, Carpenter cleared his throat.

"I wish the same thing, Alex. Frankly, I've heard about your difficulty in Rome with John Reynolds and Mark Terranova, but to be honest, most Bureau agents think Reynolds is a prick. As for my counterpart, Terranova, he was put in a difficult spot when Reynolds arrived from Washington and took charge of the FBI effort to help solve the Ambassador's kidnapping."

"I agree. When the kidnapping ended, Terranova and I did become friends, and we worked well together for the remainder of our tours."

"Good to know. Here's to working well together," Roger and Alex raised their glasses again.

I'll give Roger Carpenter an opportunity to demonstrate how cooperative he will be and how supportive of the broad US Embassy and foreign policy goals now in place, Alex thought. *After all, the mission of the FBI is important and deserves support from fellow law enforcement agencies. If, on the other hand, Carpenter proves untrustworthy, and only wants to screw the other agencies for short-term public relations to benefit the FBI, then I'll deal with it at that time.* He made a mental note to ask Gary Jones if he knew what the DCM thought about Carpenter. *I think everybody deserves a chance to show their cards.*

ACROSS THE LIVING ROOM, Anna Battles, CIA station chief, was chatting with April Scott and her fiancé Lars Nilsson. Alex excused himself from Carpenter and walked over to join the conversation. To his surprise, it was mostly a two-person conversation between Lars and Anna.

"I love Sweden," Anna was saying to Lars in fluent Swedish. "When I was a junior at Yale, I did a year abroad at Uppsala University. Later, I served at our embassy in Stockholm for three years."

"I don't believe 'Battles' is a Swedish name," Lars replied.

"You're correct. It's my married name. My family name is Lundquist and my parents are second-generation Americans. I grew up in Minnesota where we spoke some Swedish at home."

"Fantastic! Maybe we can all go to a Swedish restaurant that I know near the Baker Street tube station."

"I know that place. Great food. Let's plan on it," Anna smiled.

It was rare for Alex to be lost in a foreign language. He spoke Spanish, Italian, Arabic, and French, but had no experience in Swedish. He nodded to Anna and walked away, going in search of Sir Nigel Sharpton from the Foreign office.

Anna continued talking to Lars but was surprised to detect small grammatical errors in his conversation. Her perceptive antenna immediately registered that perhaps Lars was not a native-born Swede after all.

"Tell me, again, where your family is from in Sweden? Perhaps I have visited nearby," she asked, setting a small trap that she hoped would tell her more about this man.

"We're from Malmo, but when I was young, we moved to Stockholm."

"I see." Anna said, then asked a few subtle questions about Swedish social and economic government policies in the past, focusing on when Sweden made the short-lived transition to socialism, and back again to capitalism, following the miserable failure of government control over the economy. *Considering that he was the owner of a Swedish electronics company, I think his answers are lacking in depth and reflect textbook narratives he could have memorized. He seems to lack the first-hand experience I would expect if growing up and working in Sweden,* she thought. *This is interesting.*

Knowing April Scott had access to highly classified information in the embassy, Anna made a mental note to make inquiries about her fiancé, Lars. She would confide in Alex Boyd about her reservations concerning Lars Nilsson.

THE DINNER ENDED at 9:30 in the evening, but Ray Penner, Commander of the Special Branch, suggested to Alex and Rachel that they join him and his wife, Maureen, for a drink at a nearby pub. It was an opportunity Alex couldn't pass up, so they walked two blocks and grabbed a corner table in the first pub they found. Alex and Ray each ordered a pint of lager, and the ladies had shandies, a mixture of beer and lemonade.

"I've been meaning to ask you, Ray, what's happening with the proposal to combine Special Branch with the Counter-Terrorism Branch," Alex asked quietly.

"The mandarins are doing their final assessment right now. In my view, it will come down to saving money. They want to cut the budget without *appearing* to cut the budget. Since the government has reached agreement with the IRA to end terrorism, and because communism collapsed some time ago in Eastern Europe, there are fewer terrorists and spies running around. Whitehall, therefore, believes that by combining the two branches, they can eliminate redundancies and save money."

"You're referring mostly to senior positions?" Alex replied. "Exactly, but they also plan on returning some line officers

to regular uniformed police duties. So, our ranks will be thinned out, to say nothing about being demoralized. I think it's extremely short-sighted, but the mandarins are not worried."

Rachel listened to the conversation. "I assume 'mandarins' refers to senior Whitehall officials?" Rachel asked.

"Indeed, it does," Ray replied. "They're both career civil servants and politicians, and they have the authority to recommend to Parliament a new police structure. It doesn't help that MI-5, our domestic Security Service, is chomping at the bit to take-over the lead in all counter-intelligence cases. So, they'll probably grow at our expense."

"What will happen to you if the merger goes through?" Alex asked Roger.

"I think I'll retire. I'm still young enough to go into the private sector for another ten years."

"Gosh, I'll miss you," Alex said.

"Thanks. But I'm not gone yet. Do you know the Commander of the Counterterrorism Branch?"

"Not yet."

"I can introduce you, or you can ask Roger Carpenter to do it. He, or his FBI assistants, are there a few times a week."

It would be easy to have Ray Penner make the introduction, but this may be an opportunity to test my new relationship with Carpenter, he thought. "I'll ask Carpenter first and see what happens."

Ray Penner smiled. "You may want to re-phrase that statement." Alex was blank for a second, then appreciated the implication.

"You're right, Ray. I want to find out if Carpenter is a team player."

They finished their drinks and left the pub. As he and Rachel looked for a taxi, his cell phone vibrated in his pocket. It was an incoming text message from Anna Battles:

See me first thing tomorrow morning, I have something important to discuss, it said.

21

RED FLAG

London

The following morning, Alex reached out and turned off the alarm clock before it sounded. Rolling over in bed, he slid a hand under Rachel's pajama top to cup her firm breast, loving the feel of her body. Her eyes fluttered open, and she asked if it was six o'clock already.

"Indeed, it is, boss."

That brought a grin to her face realizing Alex recognized this was the first day in her temporary position of acting deputy chief of mission, the second most powerful position in the embassy. She lay on her back as he slid on top of her, resting his elbows on the bed with his pelvis pressed against hers. He kissed her deeply on the lips, arousing by her sensuality.

"Your Majesty, may I bring you something this morning from the kitchen?"

She laughed. "For God's sake, I'm only the acting DCM, not the *Queen*."

"Ah ha! But you're royalty to me."

"Jesus, what *bull*shit. Are you going to do this *every* morning?"

"That depends on what type of temporary boss you are."

He moved his hips back and forth over hers. Rachel wrapped her arms around his body, caressing his back muscles and shoulders.

"I'd like to spend the morning making love to you, Alex. But we both know we've got to go to work."

"I know, I know. But a fella can dream, right?"

"Absolutely, hunk man. Dream of *this* throughout the day." She locked her long muscular legs around his waist, gave a tight squeeze, and grinned at the sight of his face scrunching up in discomfort. Demonstrating her strength was a turn-on for both of them, and a routine part of their foreplay. He ran his hands over one of her thighs, feeling the large muscles as she constricted him for a moment. Then, she abruptly let go.

"Time to shower."

"Together? Is that an invitation?"

"You're such a bad boy this morning. Let's make a date for tonight."

"You've got a deal."

They showered separately, dressed, and ate breakfast. As he drove to the Embassy in their Jaguar, she asked Alex what he had planned for the day.

"I going to talk to my staff about what security improvements, or changes if any, they'd like to see. Also, Anna Battles texted me last night and wants to talk this morning. Maybe something arose at the reception that caught her attention."

"She spent a lot of time speaking to Lars and April. Do you think it has something to do with them?" Rachel asked.

"Perhaps, I'll find out soon. What will you do today, oh mighty, Princess?"

"I thought I was a queen earlier this morning. Have I been demoted already?" Not waiting for an answer, she continued.

"Honestly, I'm worried that I'm not up to speed on the DCM job. After all, I'm just starting out as the political counselor, but now I have to know about the entire embassy, and I didn't even go through the DCM course in Washington. So, I thought I'd begin by having each section brief me on what they're working on."

"Sounds like a good plan. Listen, I have total confidence in your ability to deal with anything that comes up. I mean it. You're one of the brightest people I know, and a good manager. If anyone can handle the job, you can."

"Wow, that's so nice of you to say. Let's turn the car around and go back to the house to finish what you started this morning."

"I know you don't mean that."

"That's why I married you. You're the smartest hunk man in the West."

He pulled into the Embassy underground garage, they kissed goodbye and headed toward their respective offices.

"Thanks for coming in so early," Anna Battles said as Alex took a seat in front of her desk.

"If you feel something is important, then it's important to me as well," he replied.

"Okay. Did you have a chance to talk to Lars Nilsson last night?"

"Just a little. But we've spoken before. Why do you ask?"

"I feel there's something off with Lars. Not mentally," she smiled. "But when we were speaking in Swedish, he made a few grammatical mistakes. Considering his education level, it seemed odd. So, I decided to talk about Swedish government policies going back decades and I felt his responses were perfunctory, not personal. It was like he was repeating a script. I don't want to sound an alarm unnecessarily, but . . ."

"I assume you're worried because of his engagement to April Scott."

"Exactly. You know everyone talks about work in bed, regardless of their denials."

"So, you want Lars checked out in more detail."

"I think we should. Has his State Department security clearance been approved yet, you know, for when he marries April?"

"No. The investigation is still pending completion by our embassy in Stockholm. I can send an email to the RSO asking them to comb through every aspect of his background in as much detail as possible."

Anna tapped her fingers on the desk a moment. "That's good. But I ask that you not share the specifics of my concern with the RSO in Stockholm. I'd prefer they conduct a normal background investigation. If something is fishy with Lars Nilsson, there's no sense in alerting him or someone he may know. I'll ask British Intelligence to examine him covertly. Normally, they wouldn't be keen to do so without further justification. But I can emphasize that April has considerable access to classified material, including some British material which is shared with us."

"What time frame are we looking at?" Alex asked.

"That's not clear. I'll press the Brits and perhaps we can have results within two weeks. Also, I know senior officials in SAPO, that's the Swedish intelligence service. I'll personally talk to them after I notify the CIA station in Stockholm. In both cases, I'll emphasize the urgency of the matter."

"Excellent," Alex replied. "Is there anyone else in the embassy you plan to talk with about this?"

"I think I better mention it to Bainbridge Wellington."

"I agree. Anyone else?"

They stared at each other. Anna said nothing. Alex crossed his arms and waited. Finally, he said what he knew was on her mind.

"You do realize we talk in bed."

Anna chuckled. "Touché. But only because Rachel is April's boss, and she's married to you."

"But not because she's acting DCM?"

"Hell, no. But I'd be interested in hearing Rachel's opinion if April has been seeking an unusual amount of classified material since she met Lars. Can Rachel find out?"

"That would be impossible for Rachel to know; she's only started working here a week ago."

"True. Okay. In any event, I'll talk to Rachel today and share my concern with her as well as tell her that we've spoken."

"It's a pleasure doing business with you, Anna," Alex said, rising to leave and return to his office.

22

DEPUTY CHIEF OF MISSION

London

Rachel's first morning as acting Deputy Chief of Mission went swiftly, but in her estimation, it could have gone even faster if some Embassy officers had been able to explain their issues concisely. Nevertheless, she felt it was best to hear them out in full to demonstrate her interest and support, as well as to master as many details as possible.

None of the issues raised throughout the morning were new to her, but it was the first time she had the responsibility for helping solve problems from multiple agencies. She was certain Alex would find something humorous to say about her ability to multitask.

Her last meeting before lunch was with Anna Battles. Up to this point in Rachel's career, she only had been on the periphery of CIA matters. Alex, on the other hand, had routine issues of mutual concern with them. Now, as long as she was acting DCM, she would be thrust into a loose oversight role of the CIA station. It would give her a new perspective

Rachel's office management specialist buzzed her on the phone to let her know that Anna had arrived. She greeted Anna warmly and they sat in two comfortable chairs in Rachel's office. "It was nice to have met you last night, Anna."

"The same here. And congrats on taking over the DCM job while Bainbridge is acting ambassador. How long do you think you'll be the DCM?"

"I'm not certain, but we hope the Senate Foreign Relations Committee will schedule a hearing for our new ambassador after their summer break, if not sooner."

"Oh my, so it could be a few months before you return to the political section."

"I'm afraid so. You'll have to put up with me until then." "Nonsense. It's good to have you on-board. I think you and Bainbridge will make a good team running the embassy. By the way, my view has always been that the more the ambassador and DCM understand what the CIA station is trying to achieve, the more effective we'll all be. So, I intend to share as much information as possible. Naturally, I can't divulge our sources and methods, but I'm sure you understand."

"Of course, Anna. You know where I've served abroad, so you can assume I have high regard for the Agency and what it has accomplished. Now, what would you like to talk about?"

"I'll skip the routine explanation of CIA mission and how we're organized. You know that stuff. I need to mention a specific issue that came to my attention last night."

"Okay. Alex told me you texted him and that he planned to see you this morning. Did you two meet already?"

"Yes, we met a few hours ago. The issue involves your deputy in the political section, April Scott." Rachel was surprised but showed no reaction. "Specifically, her fiancé, Lars Nilsson, is my concern. This may take a while to explain. Do you have the time?"

Over the next twenty minutes, the two professionals discussed

Anna's suspicions that Lars might not be who he claimed to be. Anna detailed how she and Alex were proceeding to check on Lars' *bona fides.*

"Tell me about April's access to classified material," Anna asked. "Specifically about her access to NATO's defense plans."

"In the political section, we don't work with detailed military unit movements or equipment issues. We do, however, deal with individual country commitments within the overall NATO defensive plan, and we're aware of reinforcement scenarios. Naturally, April Scott has access to all of this classified material. She can also see cable traffic involving US discussions with European countries that are *not* NATO members, such as Sweden and Finland."

"That last point might be significant since Lars Nilsson claims to be Swedish," Anna speculated.

"What can I do to help?" Rachel asked.

"In general terms, just note any special NATO interests that April mentions. To be honest, we're grasping at straws at this point. The leaks we're trying to counter could be occurring elsewhere. But until we can confirm Lars' background, he's a legitimate person of interest."

As talk moved on to personal chatting, the two women rose, shook hands, and Anna departed. Rachel looked at her watch . . . lunchtime. She called Alex.

"Are you free for lunch?" She asked. "I am. Where do you want to go?"

"I thought we'd just get a bite in the cafeteria. It's quick." "You mean you're not taking me to your posh club on Pall Mall?"

She laughed. "I haven't joined yet. And besides, you haven't taken your lessons in posh behavior. So, let's just eat downstairs where we can talk."

"As your Majesty desires. I'll meet you there in five minutes."

AFTER LUNCH, Rachel had a general meeting with her political section staff. There were eight officers and two office management specialists. Relations between the US and UK were so close and extensive that even issues concerning other countries or continents were monitored by her office and subsequently discussed with either the British Foreign Office or other appropriate UK agencies.

But after her conversation earlier with Anna Battles, and further talk with Alex at lunch, she believed it would be best to have a one-on-one with April Scott before speaking with the rest of the political team. She wanted to gain a better sense of who April was, and what motivated her, then observe her demeanor during the discussion. She called April to come to her office for a chat. Before long, they were sitting face-to-face.

"April, are you enjoying running the political section as much as I am working as DCM?"

"Very much so. Thank you for the opportunity. Since I've been here for two years, it's not like any issues are new to me. But I'm sure you've been thrown into an entirely new arena with all the additional agencies you have to supervise."

"That's true," Rachel admitted. "But it's only short term, and let's face it, the other agencies basically run themselves. I'm here to coordinate among agencies and settle any turf disputes. It's not like they don't all know the embassy's goals and objectives."

"That's very realistic. I'm glad you're acting DCM," April smiled, "but I'm also looking forward to your return to the political section. Can I ask you a personal question?"

"Sure, go ahead?"

"As you know, Lars and I will be married in late September. I haven't had many boyfriends in my life, but now at thirty-eight years old, I believe I've made the right decision. How did you know Alex was the guy for you?"

Now Rachel smiled. A million ideas flooded her mind at once.

"It's impossible to settle on one particular reason. We met in Pakistan a week before the terrorist attack on the American Embassy. In that short week, I was amazed at how our personalities clicked." She debated how much to reveal to April about her feelings and their intimate relationship. But April appeared to need reassurance.

"Before we even went out, there was first, a physical attraction. I thought he was handsome, and after the first day at the office, we ran into each other at the embassy swimming pool, and while this may sound shallow, I thought he looked really good wearing only swim trunks. But his looks were just one factor. We quickly found out we had a lot in common. We were both athletic, spoke difficult languages, and love to explore new countries. I love his sense of humor and wit; he makes me laugh. While he's intentionally modest about his intellectual abilities, Alex is very smart and could easily be a political officer, a lawyer, or just about anything he wanted to be."

"Well, he sounds like a great package."

"There is something more, April, and this is vital: Everyone who's around Alex in a crisis feels safe in his hands. He's calm, unflappable, and exudes a sense of confidence that comes from some combination of intuition, knowledge, and experience. I trust him with my life." She looked at the younger woman.

"If you don't mind me asking, April, how did *you* know Lars was the right man for you?"

"Oh my," she looked out the window, then back at Rachel. "Well, he's great to be with. He's considerate, cultured, and loving. He's also smart and respects other people, even with those who are far less than his equal."

Hmm, Rachel thought, *it's not what she's saying, but how she's saying it. I don't think she's all that experienced with men. Her description of Lars' qualities, while flattering, are generic, not personal.*

"It sounds like he's never made you feel uncomfortable?" she said probing a little. There was a slight delay in April's answer, but just enough for Rachel to pick up on.

"Oh, no. He's a delight," April replied.

They spoke another twenty minutes about Lars, and April's work; it was obvious to Rachel that April was deeply in love with him. Would that be sufficient for April to compromise her professional judgment and be indiscreet with classified material? Rachel considered it a possibility. *A woman like this could be grateful for a man's attention; she might do anything to keep it. This is a situation that needs to be watched,* she decided.

AROUND 6:00 PM, April Scott walked through the political section and saw only one officer at his desk at the far end of the room. The rest of the staff had gone home and she knew it was time.

Closing her office door, she pulled out a few highly classified telegrams from her safe which she had printed out earlier in the day. Now she laid the first document on her desk. Reaching into her purse, she took out the encrypted cell phone Lars had given her, typed in her password, and snapped a photo of each page.

The document, classified Top Secret, was a report from Swedish authorities which had already been shared with the American Embassy in Stockholm. It stated that the Swedish Navy had detected, and successfully tracked, a Russian diesel-electric submarine the previous month in Swedish sovereign waters off their southern coast.

Just having this cell phone in her possession was a violation. All cell phones were forbidden in classified areas, but she had carried this one in an inner pocket not easily seen by the casual viewer when she opened her purse. This act alone was premeditation.

April quickly moved on to two other telegrams and

photographed them. One dealt with an upgrade of air-to air missiles for Swedish fighter planes, and the other with an upcoming UN vote on a thorny arms-control issue. When done, she placed the cell phone back into her purse and paused while her heartbeat returned to normal. She collected the documents and walked out of her office to the shredder down the hall. Within seconds, all three documents were destroyed, removing the paper trail.

She was terrified every time she did this for Lars. Originally, she had merely put the documents into her briefcase and took them home to copy. But there was always a risk, however small, of being stopped by the Marine Guard when exiting the embassy. So, Lars had suggested it would be safer to just photograph the documents in her office. Once at home, she would transfer the cell phone photos to an SD card, eventually giving a collection of documents to Lars. She understood very well what she was doing was treason, but rationalized that it was *only* for Sweden, not an enemy nation.

Taking a few moments before leaving, April sat in her office chair, focusing on where she had arrived at this point in her life: While she'd had several lovers in the past, most of her life had been without serious male companionship. This situation had finally changed her life for the better, and soon, she and Lars would be married. No more coming home to an empty house. She would have someone to share her life with, to talk to about her intimate thoughts, and someone who cared about her.

As far as any negatives, she didn't know what would happen to her career once she married Lars. Would he accompany her when she was transferred out of London? Would they have to live apart from time to time? She couldn't work it all out in her head, so she pushed the problems aside.

As for her work, she hoped Rachel Smith stayed on as DCM for many months, because then she could claim that she, April, ran the political section for a long stretch. That could help with future promotions.

Realizing it was late, she packed up her briefcase, grabbed her purse, and left the embassy, knowing that life was full of uncertainties and dangers.

Sometimes, you can only play the game one day at a time, she thought.

23

COUNTER MOVES

London

"I didn't know you wore glasses," Management Counselor Erica Evans said, walking into Alex's office the next morning and taking a seat in front of his desk. She looked at him while smiling.

"Yeah, well, these are my super-power x-ray reading glasses from the drugstore. Besides, the light's not very good in here." He took them off and placed them on his desk, just a little self-conscious.

"Well, they make you look distinguished," Erica smiled, brushing her medium-length grey hair back behind her ears. "Besides, I never noticed any poor lighting."

"Okay, you got me. What's up? How can I help?"

Erica's expression changed to one of concern. "This conversation has to be off the record."

"Sounds serious."

"I received a private email from Under Secretary Dennis Hager concerning RSOs. He's secretly contacting Management Counselors at every major embassy asking us about the feasibility of cutting assistant RSO positions."

"Erica, I thought that plan of his was *dead* because Congress had shot it down."

"Not exactly. Previously, Hager wanted to eliminate single RSO positions at small and medium-sized posts. *That's* what Congress put the kibosh on. This is a new idea to reduce the number of *assistant* RSOs at large posts. Hager can argue there will still be a security presence at these embassies, just with reduced numbers."

"That asshole."

Erica smirked. "I assumed you would disagree."

"What do you intend to tell him?"

"I haven't decided exactly *how* to say 'no,' but I think his idea is stupid. Hager, however, wants all management counselors to raise this idea with their DCMs and convince them it will save money. We're not supposed to discuss this email with anyone *other* than the DCM or ambassador. So, you can see why I shouldn't be telling you this." They sat in silence.

"I also heard Hager wants to use the money saved from cutting ARSO positions to expand other areas of the State Department," she said. "But I don't agree that's the way to accomplish anything. He needs to ask Congress for more funding. You just came from Washington, Alex. Do you have any idea why he would focus on cutting DS, again?"

Alex tapped his fingers on the desk, debating whether to mention Riley's idea that Hager might be working for the Russians. But the implications of revealing Riley's thoughts at this time could be catastrophic if word spread about these uncon-firmed allegations. Alex chose to ignore the question.

"I appreciate that you shared this with me. Hell, we're already fully occupied here in London. Although I have two assistant RSOs, we also have to cover the embassy in Dublin, and our two consulates in Belfast and Edinburgh. Plus, the Secretary of State overnights in London monthly to consult with the Brits. Add to that, we need support staff for weekly congressional visits. And I run the largest chapter in the world of the Overseas Advisory Security Committee. I can tell you that American corporations won't be happy if I don't have time to give them security advice."

"I know. Believe me, I know. I'm on your side."

"Now that I think about it, speaking to DCMs might be a good idea," Alex said. "I assume the RSOs at these other major posts have been doing a good job and won't have a problem gaining DCM support to push back on Hager's idea. Here in London, convincing our DCM to deep-six the proposal will be easy. After all, I'm sleeping with the acting DCM."

Erica Evans laughed. "I think the other embassies will need a different strategy." Alex smiled.

"You think so? How about this then: I'll draft an email to Director Riley, tell him of Hager's secret plan, and ask Riley to counter with an email to RSOs at these large posts. I'll even draft Riley's email to the field, focusing on why the embassies need to retain a full complement of assistant RSOs. I'd like you to look at it before I send it."

"Sounds excellent."

"Oh, and here's another idea: We should counter-attack. Director Riley is currently focused on the Russian espionage threat, as is the Secretary of State, the CIA, NSA, and DOD. Do you recall a few years ago when DS loaned out a number of special agents to consular sections worldwide to deal with the growing visa fraud problem?"

"You bet I do. Those DS positions are still located in consular sections. We have one here in London. Are you suggesting we do the same thing with the espionage threat?"

"Yes, how about if you tell Hager that due to the increased espionage threat from Russia and China, large embassies should have an *additional* assistant RSO dedicated to handling counterintelligence? That officer would report to the senior RSO. Even if Hager and HR won't buy that notion, at least Hager will have to defend his position instead of being on the attack."

"I like that, Alex. First, let me fly the idea past Wellington."

"Absolutely. His support will carry great weight in Washington." Erica crossed her arms and gave an appreciative smile.

"What?" he asked after noticing her expression.

"I think your talents are under-utilized in security. You should be the designated embassy negotiator in the political section. Your analytical skills aren't shabby either."

"Thanks. But you haven't seen Rachel in action. She has all those skills, plus more. So, I think the political section is in good hands already."

She grinned and seemed impressed that Alex supported his wife so strongly. "I hope Rachel knows how highly you think of her."

"I hope so, too, otherwise I'm in deep shit. But let's get back to our problem. When do you have to respond to Hager's email?" Alex asked.

"The good news is that he's given a week for all management counselors to respond."

"Great, that's more than enough time. Now, I'll have to focus on pleasing our DCM for another seven days. It's hard work, but someone has to do it for the benefit of the country and the free world."

"We should all be so lucky," Erica said with a hearty chuckle before returning to her office.

A FEW HOURS LATER, the workday ended and Alex and Rachel met in the embassy lobby for the short walk to the Audley Pub on Mount Street. Some embassy staff had highly recommended it.

When they entered, Alex thought the Audley was a great choice. There was a smell of savory food being cooked, and of course, the aroma of beer.

An extremely long bar was on the left where patrons sat with drinks in hand. The large double room also had clusters of semi-circular booths with round tables, plus there were other square tables with solid wooden chairs in the center of the room. The place was busy, always a good sign. Then Alex heard a ruckus from one corner and saw a group of darts players enjoying themselves.

"What would you like to drink, Rach?"

"I'll take that thing with beer and lemonade."

"A shandy?"

"Yeah, that's it."

"Do you want to eat anything? Remember, I'm hanging around the embassy tonight to have my first internal defense drill with the Marines."

"I better order some food then, because afterward, I need to look at some briefing papers back at the embassy."

Alex went to the bar and placed their orders: Steak and kidney pie for him and shepherd's pie for Rachel. He also asked for a half-pint of Carlsberg lager and a shandy. He really wanted a full pint but he had the Marine drill to deal with, plus he wasn't sure which one of them would be driving the Jag home. He returned to the table with their drinks and wait for the food.

"How was your day, Rach?"

"So busy. This afternoon, I made my first visit to the Foreign Office. By the way, Sir Nigel Sharpton sends his regards."

"Excellent. He's a nice guy and not as stuffy as I had expected for a permanent secretary."

"He said the same thing about you," Rachel waited a moment, then smiled.

"What'd you talk about? Or can't you tell me in the pub?" "Just preliminary plans for a U.S. presidential visit."

"I guess that's to be expected with a new president. I didn't see any cable traffic on this yet."

"No, you wouldn't have," she replied. "The White House just wanted to know if the time frame was acceptable."

"Have I told you how impressed I am with how you're handling your new role?"

Rachel smiled. "Am I the best DCM you've ever had?"

"I've never made love to my past DCMs, so I can't compare."

She shoved his arm.

"But you do have the best legs."

"If I didn't know you better, I'd think you were exceedingly shallow. By the way, I spoke with Erica this afternoon and she told me what you said about my skills. Thank you. It means a lot to me that you said that to her."

He grabbed her hand and kissed the back of it. "I've been impressed with you since the moment we met. I hope you know that."

She removed her hand from his, placed it behind his neck, and drew him toward her for a lingering kiss. They stared into each other's eyes until a waitress interrupted with their food.

Twenty minutes later, after finishing dinner, Rachel asked, "How long will your drill take with the Marines?"

"Good question. I imagine it will be only one hour, maybe a max of ninety minutes. I'll ask First Sgt. Waters to run the drill so I can see what they're practicing. If I want improvements, I'll speak with Waters separately tomorrow."

"Okay, I'll be in my office. Afterward, let's drive home together."

They left the pub, clasped hands, and walked back to the embassy.

24

FALSE FLAG

London

The sign read "Nilsson Electronics" in large, bold red letters on the front of the two-story brick building, the company's home office. It also served as a storage and distribution warehouse for all its products.

Lars sat behind his desk on the second floor, looking through his large window toward a school playing field. Devoid of students now, he knew children would be filling the field and screaming their heads off with delight in a few hours. In the distance, below a bank of puffy white clouds, a small corporate jet flew at low level, making its final approach to the Northolt Airfield, the former RAF base once used by a Polish fighter squadron during the Battle of Britain in 1940.

He stood and walked to the window, opening it to freshen the air inside his office. He stretched his back, then looked at his watch to confirm he had a few hours yet before leaving to meet April. He couldn't recall being this happy in years. Their relationship had started as antiseptic as a hospital surgery room, but recently had blossomed into deep love. April's transformation, both physically and mentally, had been miraculous, matching his own increased passion for her. What's more, his SVR handlers in Moscow were extremely pleased with the quality of classified information April had provided him to pass on. It reflected well on him.

As he walked into the hallway, and strolled by each office, he hoped to chat with a few of his employees. Passing the accounting and receivables office, he strolled by the planning section, and finally the marketing and advertising room. All his employees were busy, either on the phone, meeting with someone, or working on their computer. The business was humming.

Deciding he could talk later, Lars took the stairs down to the ground floor and watched one white van drive off from inside the garage, while another was being loaded with equipment for a job somewhere in the London metro area.

"Everything okay, boss? Need anything?" George Harding, his deputy, asked.

"No, thank you, George. I'm just taking a break. How are things going?"

"Fantastic, boss. We've almost completed the job to rewire and install new lighting at the manufacturing facility outside of Reading, and we're gearing up for the new contract at the industrial park in Essex. I expect we'll hear back this week about our bid to support the mobile phone tower system in Budapest."

"You're doing a great job, George. I couldn't run this company without you."

"Thanks, boss."

"If you need me, George, I'll be walking around the outside of the building."

Lars thought of April as he strolled. He wished he was located closer to central London so he could see her more often, but this location off the A-40, about 11 miles west of London, was too convenient to consider moving.

Funny how things can change, he thought. *Months ago, I felt she was always nagging, always wanting to see me. Now, I can't get enough of her.*

At least he lived in London's West End, which was convenient to see her in the evenings. He stopped walking to look at his office building. *What will happen when April transfers to another country? Will I have to sell my business to be with her? Can we commute, if she is assigned somewhere on the continent? Damn. Life has become much more complicated than I had expected.*

Of major concern to him now was how she would react if, and when, he had to explain that he wasn't Swedish at all, but really a spy . . . for Russia. If she accepted this, then life would continue as they knew it. But if she was appalled, and decided to report him, then he would have to flee back to Russia. No more April, no more electronics business, and no more freedom to live in the West. He shuttered at the thought and resolved to avoid revealing who he was for a long as possible.

MEANWHILE, earlier that day, Alex had telephoned Commander Ray Penner of Special Branch to meet mid-afternoon in Penner's office at New Scotland Yard. In the short time he had known Ray, Alex had grown to like him, not only because he was professional, but because he had an excellent sense of humor and was down to earth. Penner's office, located on a high floor within police head-quarters, had an amazing view of Buckingham Palace and St. James Park.

"I thought I had a good view overlooking Grosvenor Square," Alex said when he arrived. "But *this* is incredible."

"Yeah, it is spectacular, isn't it? Reminds me of home."

"Of course, it does," Alex said. "Listen, I have an idea, and I'd like your opinion and your support."

"Anything for our trans-Atlantic cousins, Alex."

"I know you're aware of the London Chapter of the Overseas Security Advisory Committee that I run from the Embassy. Not only is it the largest chapter in the world, but half the members are corporate security directors from British companies which own significant-sized American subsidiaries."

'I know. OSAC is a marvelous concept," Penner said. "Special Branch has lectured about crime and terrorism at some of your embassy meetings in the past."

"Yes, I read that in our files; that's why I'm coming to you with this idea. I'd like to explore a new area for our next meeting. I'm thinking of 'Espionage and How to Counterattack' as a topic. Russia and China not only recruit human spies in our corporations, but their illegal electronic surveillance hacking operations are phenomenal."

"Right," Penner replied. "They steal everything they can get their hands on, then duplicate it in both countries. The Chinese are especially aggressive and good at spy craft."

"Exactly. So, my plan is to have an officer from the Metropolitan Police give a presentation on the espionage threat here in the UK. But I'd like concrete examples. I'll ask Diplomatic Security to send someone here from Washington and have them brief everyone on historical efforts to steal our technology. I'll also ask the FBI to do something related. Perhaps I can convince the CIA to send a non- covert analyst to provide a briefing as well. What do you think?"

"Is this focused only on the corporate sector?"

"Not necessarily. I'd like most of our embassy staff to attend, and if you have additional ideas for the audience, I'd welcome your thoughts. We could have briefings for several hours, broken up by a simple lunch of sandwiches at the Embassy."

"Splendid idea. Let me discuss it with Assistant Commissioner Davies and I'll get back to you."

"That's a deal." Alex paused for a moment. "On the personal front, I have a question for you. Rachel and I are thinking of visiting the Cotswolds this weekend. Do you know the area? I'd appreciate any recommendations for villages, pubs, and restaurants, if you do."

"Indeed, I do. I'll send you a note with some suggestions. Maybe my wife and I can meet you somewhere in the Cotswolds for a meal."

"That would be wonderful. So, I assume, as Commander of Special Branch, the government lets you escape from London upon occasion."

"Not often, but don't worry about that. Terry can always drive us back if there's an emergency."

"Who's Terry?"

"He's my police driver."

"Your driver? You're kidding. You have an *official* car?"

"Yes, I do. It's a perk of my rank and helps make up for the decade of grungy undercover work I did from twenty years ago when I joined Special Branch."

"Holy shit . . . I'm working for the wrong government." Ray laughed. "I imagine you're doing okay."

Alex smiled. "Yeah, not bad."

As he left the Metropolitan Police headquarters, Alex was feeling that this London assignment was turning out to be his most enjoyable career posting yet. But before he could kick back and enjoy his new life, he needed to speak with Anna Battles and see what she had learned regarding Lars Nilsson's background.

≈

WHEN ALEX ENTERED HIS OFFICE, Diana Carrington, his office management specialist, handed him a file on her desk.

"Is this what I think it is?"

"Yes, it's the RSO's report from Stockholm on Lars Nilsson. It just arrived."

"Thanks, Diana. Anything else I should know about?"

"Yes, Anna Battles called and said you could come up to her office to talk. I assumed you would know about what."

"Right, as always, Diana. I'll read this report first, then go see Anna."

Alex grabbed a cup of coffee and walked into his office to read the RSO's report from Stockholm. Ten minutes later, he laid the file on his desk and leaned back to think.

This is disappointing, he thought. *There's nothing much here. I wonder if Anna is right about Lars being questionable.*

Everything in Lars' background checked out - birth records, employment, neighborhoods, and required Swedish government paperwork. He was vanilla. Alex buzzed Tom Lopez, his deputy, and asked Tom to join him. With Tom's two prior ARSO assignments, one in Mexico City, and the other in Madrid, he might see another angle on this Lars.

"TOM, you've done as many background investigations as I have. Would you look at this report and tell me if you see anything unusual, anything I could be missing. I'd appreciate it if you took a seat and did it right now."

While Tom read, Alex refilled his coffee and returned to look at new incoming telegrams on his computer. Fifteen minutes later, Tom looked up. "Everything seems in order. Why did you ask?"

Now Alex realized that things had moved so quickly he hadn't briefed Tom on Anna's concerns on Lars Nilsson. He took the next few moments to do so.

"Okay, I understand," Tom said. "But I still don't see anything unusual in the report."

"Exactly, what I thought, but I wanted fresh eyes on it. I appreciate your view, thanks."

"What's next?"

"I'm about to speak with Anna Battles, but unless she has something from her intelligence sources, I guess Lars will be cleared to marry April Scott."

Tom rose, but Alex spoke before he left the room. "By the way, you did well in the drill with the Marines last night. But I'd like to do more to encourage tactical leadership from the sergeants. After all, if we're ever assaulted, we can expect to lose some key personnel which could include you or me. The sergeants need to be ready. Let's talk to First Sgt. Waters this week about extra measures."

"You got it, boss."

Alex picked up the file and went to see Anna Battles.

ANNA WAS JUST FINISHING a meeting with several people in her office suite when Alex arrived. He hadn't met any of them, yet, but everyone nodded at Alex as they left the room. He assumed they were part of her stable of case officers.

I figure I'll get to know them in time, he thought.

"Come in, Alex," Anna said. "I've had some success from our inquiries. What about you?"

"The RSO's report revealed nothing suspect. Everything seems in order. Do you want to look at the report?"

"No, thanks. If you say it's okay, I'll accept that. However, we have an interesting development from our station in Stockholm.

Our chief there asked SAPO, the Swedish intelligence agency, to look into Lars' background. SAPO even gave our chief their full investigative report to examine. SAPO came back with the same results as your RSO."

"So, I don't understand, what's interesting?"

"Our station chief asked a new case officer to read the SAPO report. This officer happened to have done her master's thesis in college on the Swedish welfare state, and is very familiar with Swedish government bureaucracy. She noted that SAPO's investigation had anomalies regarding the dates of Nilsson's social security and medical insurance registration. Specifically, instead of Nilsson being registered into the system at birth, it didn't occur until he was about fifteen years old."

"Really?" Alex said. "Could that have been a clerical error, or a mistake by SAPO?"

"Possibly, but I've learned that even a tiny detail like this one can unravel a big lead. I'd like to pursue it further."

Then a funny thing happened during their momentary silence. Both Alex and Anna called out simultaneously: "*False flag!*"

Could it be possible that Lars Nilsson was not Swedish at all, but could be working for a hostile intelligence service from another country? At that moment, Anna's secretary interrupted the conversation by walking into the office with two cups of steaming hot coffee.

"You must be telepathic." Alex said, gratefully accepting a cup. "Anna always likes coffee about this time," she replied with a smile, and left the room.

"Weren't you also checking with British MI-5?" Alex asked.

"Yes. They said he's legit in the UK. Pays his taxes, runs a profitable electronics business, and his Swedish passport is authentic with the requisite British visa. He seems to be who he claims to be.

But I would expect no less, if he's really part of a false flag operation."

"Yes, indeed. Now that you have this additional information from Sweden, will MI-5 reopen their inquiry? Perhaps run surveillance on him, search his home, or tap his phones?"

"I doubt it, not without something more suspicious than anomalies from Sweden."

"We may be making a big deal out of nothing," Alex said, "but I'll talk to Special Branch and see if they're interested in getting involved."

"That would be nice."

"One more thing, Anna, have you briefed Bainbridge Wellington on this matter?"

"No, I assumed you had. Rachel knows, but are you asking me to brief Bainbridge now?"

"Let's do it together after I speak with Special Branch,"

"If they agree to help, I'll want Bainbridge onboard with our strategy."

"Fine. It's your call. I hope you've also thought about informing Roger Carpenter, our FBI Legal Attaché. You've met him, right."

"Yes, we met at Bainbridge's reception, but I haven't talked shop with him yet. When we have concrete evidence that an American employee is involved with a foreign intelligence agent, I'll bring in to the FBI. But only at the right time."

"Okay, just so long as you've considered it."

ALEX DECIDED that Director Riley had to be brought up to speed on this potential situation. He sat at his office computer and began typing the entire saga, starting with Anna Battles' suspicions over Lars Nilsson's grammatical errors in Swedish, and finishing with the inconsistencies in his registration dates in Sweden for social security and medical insurance.

Then, Alex further laid out the plan for what he and Anna intended to do next. After checking the message several times, he typed in the words, "DS Channel" meaning only Diplomatic Security in Washington would receive the telegram. He also added the words, "FOR DS DIRECTOR RILEY ONLY."

Finally satisfied, he hit the send key. Considering the time zone differences between London and Washington, Riley would get the telegram by mid-morning. He anticipated Director Riley would jump on this information immediately, therefore, could expect either a return telegram, or a phone call, soon after that. He intended to be ready.

25

WHEELS OF DECEPTION

Washington DC

Nickolai Petrov and Andrei Balakin sat together in the Russian Embassy's secure communications vault listening to audio tapes from the Nagra card just returned to them from their high-level source in the US government. Balakin couldn't stop smiling as he listened to the conversations in English.

"This is pure gold, Nickolai. We're actually listening to top-secret conversations between the Secretary of State, Director of CIA, and Director of the FBI. Moscow will be impressed when they hear what we have captured."

Nickolai had his arms crossed, watching Balakin with satisfaction, knowing this espionage operation was among the best Russia ever had accomplished. It *almost* ranked up there with the theft of America's nuclear secrets in the 1940s, the compromise of several CIA and FBI agents in the past.

This is as valuable as Russia's contemporary operations to cultivate agents of influence in the American media, academia, and among a few US politicians and staff, Nickolai thought.

"How old is this particular recording, Nickolai?"

"The meeting was held two days ago. The other recordings on the tape are a little older. I cleared our dead drop last night and retrieved these recordings, along with some other documents."

Balakin shook his head with glee. "I'm going to have our courier –no – wait a minute! I think *two* couriers will carry duplicates back to Moscow tomorrow. I cannot risk sending this electronically just in case the NSA has broken our codes again. It is too valuable."

"Tell me, how is our agent holding up? How is he handling the pressure?"

Nickolai chose his words carefully. "Since we haven't met face to face in almost a year, I cannot say with certainty. But he knows how to contact us if he feels under threat, or if he is psychologically stressed. So far, he seems fine. Besides, he's an old hand in the espionage game. He made his commitment to us decades ago. I think he is solid."

"Has he asked for anything? Money, women, some other type of reward?"

"No, he has enough money. As for anything else, well, he hasn't asked. He is doing this for ideological reasons, which is rare for American traitors."

"Good. After listening to these conversations, do you think the Americans are any closer to identifying their leaks than before?"

"No, I believe we are safe. But I'm sure you noticed that the Director of the CIA mentioned the US government is aware of what information is being stolen from *them*. That can only mean that someone else is still operating in Moscow as a spy working on their behalf."

"I *did* notice. But tell me, who is this spy actually working for? The Americans or the British? Maybe even the Poles or the

French. We must be careful what we tell Moscow. Sharing information is one thing, but we can never reveal who *our* State Department source is."

Nickolai didn't like to disagree with Balakin, but had to state the obvious. "But he was not originally *our* spy, Andrei. We inherited him when we were assigned to Washington. There are other SVR officers in Moscow who have worked with him in the past."

"True. Hopefully, they are professional enough not to brag about who they've recruited. In the meantime, let me know when you have copied the tapes and written your report for our files. Then I'll schedule the couriers." Balakin left the vault and returned to his office.

A few minutes later, Nickolai's wife, Ludmilla, arrived. She was allowed to enter the vault only because she and Nickolai worked as a team to clear the dead drops, and therefore, she knew about the operation.

"How did it go with Balakin?"

"Well. We share a view on the importance of the information, as well as our concern that someone else is a traitor in Moscow. Sometimes, I wonder if all this espionage just cancels itself out," he said.

"What do you mean, Nickolai?"

"We spy on the West, and they spy on us. Most of the secrets we obtain give us a short-term advantage, but does it change the balance of power?"

"Why are you depressed, darling? You're having remarkable success with this latest operation."

"I know. But when I hear the Director of CIA say on tape that he knows what secrets they are losing to us, it makes me wonder if this 'great game' between the superpowers actually makes a difference."

"It makes a difference if we can shut down *their* spies. That way we could gain a huge advantage. And surely, our *agents of influence* in the West make an immense long-term difference in how their public perceives us, as well as how their public underestimates their own need for national defense. These 'useful idiots' also help undermine the American rule of law in American society. It diminishes the need to reward success with government spending rather than wasting resources on social and corrupt experiments. This is incredibly valuable to us in the long run."

Nickolai leaned back in his chair and clasped his hands behind his head. "You're right, Ludmilla, perhaps I am just tired."

"I know Russia isn't as dominant as it was during the height of the Cold War," Ludmilla said. "But we are still a world power, while America divides itself along ideological lines, in part, thanks to our historic efforts to spread propaganda about socialism among their political elite and educators. Personally, I am more concerned with the rise of China. They are everywhere, creating military bases overseas, influencing American universities, buying up companies in the entertainment and media industries, gaining power in international organizations, and stealing technology from the West at an astonishing rate."

"You're right again, Ludmilla. Listen, I have a few more hours of work to do," he said. "When I'm done, let's grab lunch outside the embassy."

She smiled and kissed him on the forehead. "I'll like that, Nickolai. We can even play our game of trying to spot the number of FBI agents tailing us."

ONE WEEK LATER, in Washington, D.C., DS Director Jim Riley happily perused yet another incoming telegram from a major US embassy criticizing Under Secretary Hager's plan to cut assistant RSO positions. Thanks to Alex's earlier initiative in alerting Riley to the impending threat, as well as to his excellent draft pointing

out the weak points of Under Secretary Dennis Hagar's argu-
ments, Riley was able to force the issue out of the shadows and
bring it to the attention of Secretary of State. He also made sure
key supporters of DS in Congress became aware of the foul plan,
too. For the last two days, one post after another had said they
wanted to retain their full complement of security staff. Furthermore, each commented that to eliminate positions, only to save
money, was foolhardy. This correctly implied that Hager did not
see the big picture, nor recognize the threats. His position was
weakening.

Riley was immensely proud of the senior RSOs who had
marshaled their facts and made crucial counter-arguments to
their deputy chiefs of mission and ambassadors in a very timely
manner.

He was, however, disappointed in a very few senior RSOs who
had opted to sit on the sidelines, not joining the battle, perhaps
simply marking time until either retirement or their next assignment. Riley noted which ones had laid low by failing to rise to the
occasion. In his view, one was either part of the solution, or part of
the problem.

The main question about Hager's plan was whether it
concerned saving money at all. Or was it merely another attempt
by Hager to knowingly reduce the effectiveness of DS. Again, Riley
felt that Hager's unnatural hatred of DS must stem from something other than balancing the budget.

Riley's phone buzzed, he picked it up, and his secretary told
him Secretary of State Charles Martin had just requested his presence for a meeting. Riley had been expecting this, especially after
he heard that Martin was angry that the entire issue of downsizing
security had been handled without his knowledge, and without
proper inter-agency consultation in Washington. Riley put on his
suit jacket and left for Martin's office.

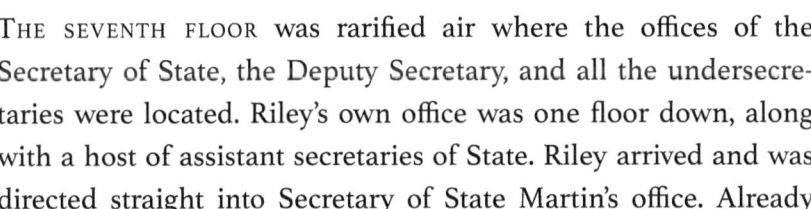

THE SEVENTH FLOOR was rarified air where the offices of the Secretary of State, the Deputy Secretary, and all the undersecretaries were located. Riley's own office was one floor down, along with a host of assistant secretaries of State. Riley arrived and was directed straight into Secretary of State Martin's office. Already present were Deputy Secretary Wakefield Summers, and Under Secretary for Management Dennis Hager.

Martin and Summers were laughing about something when Riley walked in. Hager appeared to be the odd man out, standing a little off to the side, not engaged in the discussion.

Hager doesn't seem to be enjoying himself, Riley noted. *Well, he doesn't have much of a sense of humor . . . never did.*

All took seats while Riley was directed to sit in a burgundy chesterfield sofa.

Secretary Charles Martin was an old hand at foreign policy. He had served in two prior administrations, first as the Legal Advisor for the State Department, and later as the Deputy Secretary of State. Moreover, his former Wall Street law firm had some of the world's most powerful clients, comprised of corporations, wealthy individuals, and even sovereign nations.

In fact, Riley had recently learned that the families of Secretary Martin and Deputy Secretary Summers had been friends for decades, dating back to when their fathers had served together in World War II in the Office of Strategic Services, known as the OSS, the forerunner of the CIA. Martin's father had fought in Italy supporting

U.S. forces, while Summers' father had fought with the partisans in Yugoslavia. It was typical of their father's generation that the two Ivy League graduates, both working on Wall Street, had been recruited by General Wild Bill Donovan to join the OSS.

"I want to discuss the relationship between the two of you,"

Martin said, glancing between Riley and Hager. "There is no doubt you are both skilled in your areas, but it's obvious there is a lack of respect and lack of coordination. Your clashes have risen to a level of concern that has become divisive for the work of this Department."

Oh my God, Riley thought. *Am I about to get sacked? Will this be the end of Diplomatic Security as I know it? Not on my watch, if I have something to say about it!*

"I would like each of you to comment on this matter?" Secretary Martin said.

Dennis Hager spoke first. "DS has grown out of proportion to the needs of the Department. It wants to operate independently from the chain of command. Basically, it has become bloated, and needs to be reined in. We can start by making cuts to non-essential programs that don't support core functions of the State Department."

Martin and Summers looked at Riley for a response. Riley knew his answer had to be on point, as much about the future as the past. He needed to show he was a team player.

"Gentlemen. Diplomatic Security has grown because worldwide threats have grown exponentially. DS has done the work *requested* by every administration and *authorized* by Congress who agreed with the needs. Our physical security programs, which have been accomplished with the full support of other cabinet agencies and which have representation overseas, are a response to the *destruction of our embassies by terrorists* in Africa and the Middle East.

"The growth of our bodyguard protective operations, both domestically and abroad, is a result of being continually requested by the White House and the State Department. The expansion of our training programs is a direct result of added resources *requested* by the Department, *supported* by Congress, and *reflects* the continued professionalization of our efforts to provide the best service possible.

"Our criminal investigations have resulted in the arrests of countless human trafficking smugglers, visa and passport fraudsters, terrorists, and criminals wanted for a variety of other felonies. These investigations are often done in coordination with other federal law enforcement agencies. I would add that the investigations have been under the direction of US prosecutors at the Justice Department, who have praised the high quality of our work. Our conviction rates are among the best in federal law enforcement.

"So, I can agree with Under Secretary Hager on the fact that we have grown substantially. We are now located at 250 locations around the globe. We are the most widespread law enforcement and security organization *on the planet*. And, most important of all, we clearly work under the direction of the Department of State.

"If State wants *less* physical security, *less* protection of its employees around the world, and *less* protection of foreign government VIPs visiting America, then you can order it. But I am certain that is not what you want.

"Dennis Hager wants you to believe DS can fulfill the missions mandated by the Department, the White House, *and* Congress with *fewer* regional security officers, *fewer* special agents, and *fewer* support personnel. This is not possible, not realistic, and not a desirable goal."

There was silence in the room.

Deputy Secretary Summers looked at Charles Martin. "We wanted to hear both of you make your case. The question in our minds was not really *whether* we wanted to support the current size of Diplomatic Security, but whether *the two of you* could work together going forward."

Summers turned to Secretary Martin, who signaled he would take over. "Director Riley, we are delighted with the work of Diplomatic Security, and we wish for it to continue its high level of support, not only for our State Department programs, but to continue its support of other US government agencies as well. As Wakefield said, the issue for us is whether both of you can work together. It is apparent, that this is not the case. So here is our solution.

"We will ask Congress to authorize a partial reorganization of the Department so that Diplomatic Security can be moved out from under management and placed directly under the supervision of the Deputy Secretary's office. Obviously, DS will have to continue coordination with management for administrative procedures concerning both procurement of items and budgetary matters. We assume this is acceptable to you, Director Riley." Riley detected a small uptick of Martin's mouth. He knew he had won.

"Yes, sir, it is completely acceptable."

"Under Secretary Hager, we realize this may be difficult for you to swallow."

Hager paused, but not for long. "*Sir.* I serve at your pleasure, and I accept your decision."

"Excellent. Dennis, you can now focus all your attention on the vital issues of managing the Department of State's *non-security* functions, which is a massive and important worldwide task."

Riley was elated. He hadn't felt this good in months; a tremendous weight had been lifted off his shoulders. In fact, he felt as if he had just been reborn. When he would return to his office, he'd give his wife, Caroline, the good news. The next person he would call would be Alex Boyd. He recognized he owed both Alex and Erica Evans a huge debt of gratitude for bringing this battle to a successful conclusion.

"Dennis, thank you for coming," Secretary Martin said. "Jim, I'd like you to stay and the three of us can discuss your new relationship with Wakefield."

That was it. Jim Riley felt his entire body tingle with energy.

He and DS had survived, had prevailed against the odds. Now it was time to move forward to meet new challenges and demonstrate they were worthy of the trust bestowed on them by Secretary of State Martin.

How sweet it is, Jim thought.

26

SPECIAL BRANCH HELP

London

It was pouring rain when Alex left the American Embassy amid rumbles of thunder and dark clouds blotting out the sun. He had agreed to meet Commander Ray Penner at Special Branch to pursue suspicions about Lars Nilsson. It would fulfill the pledge he had made to Anna Battles. Lucky enough to get an embassy motor pool car and driver to drop him off, he arrived at Metropolitan Police headquarters and was escorted up to Penner's office by a police constable. Penner was talking with a tall, stunningly beautiful woman dressed in a dark blue pants suit.

"Alex! Welcome," Penner said. "let me introduce Deidre Plummer."

"Hello, I'm Alex Boyd," he nodded and reached out to shake her hand. "Your name is familiar," Alex said.

"Perhaps your wife mentioned me. I participated in the Oxford symposium."

"Of course! Now, I remember. She enjoyed meeting you."

"The same here. Your wife put on quite a show. I was very impressed with her skill and experience."

"I'll mention you said so. Thank you."

"Do you come to Special Branch often, Alex?"

"Ray and I talk routinely."

"Well, it was nice meeting you. Perhaps the four of us can meet for a drink after work sometime?"

"That would be nice," Alex replied. Both men watched as Deidre left the office, then took seats in Penner's office.

"Did she mean *you* to be the fourth in the group, Ray?"

"Unfortunately, not; I think she meant her *husband*. He's a successful solicitor in the city."

"And she's a stunningly beautiful woman," Alex noted. "Too bad for you, buddy."

"I noticed. She reminds me of *your* wife . . . beautiful, you know. Now, what did you want to talk about?"

"Okay. We have a major concern about a London resident who's a Swedish national, and has a relationship with one of our embassy's political officers. They're engaged to get married."

"Ah, Swedish women are beautiful."

"That's true," Alex smiled, "but you have the situation backward. Our *officer* is the female, and the Swede is a guy."

"Sorry. Guess I'm just a male chauvinist."

"That's what Deidre Plummer told me about you."

"Yeah, yeah, I had that coming," Ray laughed. "Do go on."

Alex detailed the entire story. He knew that Penner was familiar with leaks of NATO information, as well as stories of several CIA-recruited Russian SVR agents who had been arrested in Moscow, put in jail, or since executed.

"MI-5 recently told Anna Battles that they were *un*willing to do anything beyond some record checks on this Swede, Lars Nilsson. So, I was hoping that Special Branch might take it on as a matter of interest."

Commander Penner leaned back in his chair and clasped his hands behind his head to think. Then he rose and walked over to a coat rack near the door, took off his jacket, and hung it up before returning to sit down again.

He's thinking about it, Alex thought. *That's good.*

"I might be interested, but it depends on what you'd like us to do." "Surveillance on Nilsson to start with, then surreptitiously make a visit to his house and see what's in it."

"You don't waste time coming to the point, do you? Is that all? No water boarding or pulling out fingernails?" Penner smiled.

"Perhaps, later. But seriously, anything you're willing to do to verify that Nilsson is legit will be appreciated, or if you uncover anything we see as a problem."

"The good news for *you* is that Special Branch has this capability; we've been doing this sort of thing for decades. The bad news is that this decision is a little more complicated these days. What about your embassy employee? Do you want us to break into her residence, too? That will be very touchy to our legal staff."

"I realize that. Frankly, I still need to discuss the idea with our acting ambassador, Bainbridge Wellington, I just wanted to check with you first that it was a possibility. I doubt he'll be keen on the idea, but I wanted to be prepared."

"Why don't you just go into her residence yourself? I imagine the embassy has a spare key."

"We do, but I'd need legal clearance from Washington since we're talking about a potential criminal investigation. This would not be some type of administrative inspection of the property."

"I'll tell you what, Alex. I'll run this idea past our people, while you get back to me on what Wellington says."

"Deal. Thanks, Ray."

Not totally sure whether the plan would work, Alex believed it was a reasonable option.

THE RAIN HAD STOPPED, leaving a wet shine on sidewalks; the air was filled with a wonderful aroma following the summer rain. Riding in a taxi, Alex listened to its tires splashing through puddles, and debated whether it was time to bring Roger Carpenter into the picture from the embassy's FBI office.

If not now, it'll have to be soon, he thought, *perhaps it's best to do after I meet with Bainbridge Wellington. After all, I have no evidence, yet, of April Scott doing anything illegal.*

Before seeing Wellington, Alex still needed to speak with Rachel since she was both the acting DCM and April Scott's direct boss. So, arriving back at the embassy, he went directly to her office, entered, and closed the door behind him. "Wow, that's some stack of papers you have on your desk," he said.

"Yeah, and this is the second round today," she added, seeing him enter. "The pile was even higher earlier this morning." No one else was in the room, so he walked around her desk and kissed her lips.

"Thanks, I needed that," she said.

"What did Shakespeare say about crowns being heavy on the head? Paperwork is the price of stardom, Hollywood."

"I need a break." She rose and stretched her arms straight up. "Gosh, I had no idea how much crap a DCM has to look at."

"Maybe that's because you're a stickler for things being done correctly. I admire your concern, fortitude, and attention to detail."

She chuckled. "Stop sucking up. Besides, I know your technique. When you have this much paperwork you give it to your deputies and claim it will be a good learning experience for them."

"Ah, you've noticed," Alex laughed, "You always *were* too quick for me. But listen, I'm here on business. I need to talk with you about the latest developments on April and Lars." He described his chat at Special Branch and asked Rachel to join him in meeting with Bainbridge.

"Okay. I've already briefed him on everything up to this point," Rachel said, "so he's up to speed, but I will tell you that he's concerned."

"Terrific." Alex looked at his watch; it was time for his appointment with Wellington. "Let's go give him the latest update. But he may not like one of my suggestions."

WELLINGTON WAS on the phone when Alex and Rachel entered. He waved them into his office, and they sat in brown leather chairs in front of his large antique desk.

". . .sounds like a marvelous time," Wellington was saying to someone on the other end of the line. "I'm looking forward to it, Chummy."

Alex and Rachel looked at each other. Alex whispered, "Chummy?" She lifted both her eyebrows and shrugged.

After another minute of conversation, Wellington hung up, all smiles. He pulled on the sleeves of his ghastly looking bold blue and white striped custom shirt.

"That was Lord Chumsford."

"Ah, I thought so," Alex replied. Rachel glared at Alex and gave a slight negative shake of her head.

"He invited me to his estate in Scotland to go grouse shooting in September."

"I didn't know you were a shooter," Alex said.

"Frankly, I'm not very good, but it's a chance to mingle with some of the aristocracy and maybe talk some government business. Lord Chumsford has just been named to a commission that will study national defense in an age of artificial intelligence."

"Like fifth generation fighter aircraft and drone ships and submarines," Rachel said.

"Precisely," Wellington replied. Alex turned to Rachel and gave her an appreciative nod. She smiled back.

"Do you have your own shotguns?" Alex asked.

"Good heavens, no. Chummy will lend me two of his. He said they are both Purdy double-barreled."

"Aren't Purdy guns custom made for each client, based upon the person's unique build and arm length?"

"Well, Alex, I see you know your weapons. Indeed, they are. But who cares if I hit anything. It's only blowing up a kind of duck. This is a social and *business* event as far as I'm concerned."

The more Alex found out about Wellington, the more he liked the man. *He might have his eccentricities,* Alex thought, *but he knows his business.*

"I gather you want to give me an update on the situation with April and her fiancé," Alex said.

"Yes, I've just returned from Special Branch, and they'll consider searching Nilsson's home to see if he has anything linked to espionage. They wanted to know if we wish them to do the same with April's house. I told them I'd check with you because searching a US diplomat's house could a problem."

"Very wise of you," Alex said. "I'm against it. It's a question of diplomatic immunity. We can't allow the precedent of local authorities searching our residences without *damn* good reason. As concerned as I am about these leaks of classified information, I don't see a verified link to April Scott. Do you?"

"No, not a verified link. But Nilsson has some discrepancies in his background that need to be addressed. And he and April will be married soon."

"Fine. Then Special Branch can search *his* place. He's a private citizen, April is *not.*"

"Alex, didn't you tell me about an old precedent involving the police and one of our former employees?" Rachel asked. Wellington glanced back and forth between them and looked curious.

"Yes, actually, back in the late 1980s, one of our consular officers was murdered in her apartment in London. The State Department allowed the police to search her place and to interview several of our employees."

"*Really* . . . " Wellington replied slowly while thinking. "I didn't know that . . . I assume Washington was asked in advance for their counsel on this matter." It was mostly a question.

"We did, and they approved both the search and interviews. Of course, a murder inquiry is extremely serious business, and, admittedly, we had a dead body as proof of the crime. However, this issue with April Scott is different . . . and unproven."

Wellington played with one of his gold cufflinks. "How about if *you* just search her house instead of the police?"

"I'd still need to ask Washington's approval and get a search warrant. All employees have the same rights abroad as if they were in the States."

"They do? That seems nonsensical. They live on US government property."

"Yes, but they don't waive their rights, simply because Uncle Sam is paying for their digs. This is different from having management inspect their property for damage or, for example, to ensure the smoke detectors are working in their house."

Rachel added more food for thought. "Bainbridge, what Alex said is based upon a federal court *ruling* in a past case. This is more than a State Department *guideline*."

"Who knew?" Wellington responded. "However, because of that precedent from the 1980s, I suppose I could ask our legal advisor's office in D.C. for their viewpoint."

"That would be a good idea, Bainbridge. I'm not saying April is guilty of anything, but we should explore all our options."

"Okay, I'll make a call to D.C."

AN HOUR LATER, Wellington spoke to the State Department's legal advisor in Washington and received a negative response. They didn't want British police entering American residences unless there were extraordinary circumstances, and so far, the situation did not meet that parameter. Wellington passed this information on to Alex, who in turn notified Commander Ray Penner. Alex accepted this decision while starting to think of other options.

The next call Alex made was to Roger Carpenter in the FBI office about needing to brief him on an important matter. Roger came to see Alex, and after the briefing, never expressed irritation at not being brought into the picture earlier on. This impressed Alex. Roger also claimed he looked forward to working with Alex and Anna Battles in the future. *Interesting guy*, Alex thought.

THAT EVENING at their townhouse in Knightsbridge, Alex and Rachel were finishing their light dinner of a *Salad Nicoise* accompanied by a large glass of Cote Du Rhone burgundy.

"Thanks, Rach, for mentioning the 1980s murder case to Bainbridge. It broadened his perspective."

"She reached across the table and squeezed his hand. "As your new boss, it was the least I could do."

He smiled. "You really like reminding me of your *temporary* status."

"I do. It's fun. Can you handle it?"

"Sure, I can see you're enjoying yourself. I've got to say, I was really impressed that you knew about artificial intelligence and national defense."

"You mean you didn't think that a California girl-jock like me would know about such things."

"No, no, not at all. You're *way* better than merely a California girl-jock, Hollywood. Now that you've become an *elder* stateswoman, while still retaining your astonishingly good looks and muscles, I have to take my hat off to your brain power and grasp of complex issues." Her eyes turned squinty, and her jawline tightened, yet a mini smile remained.

"Would you like to take this conversation up to the bedroom and test your theory about me being an '*elder* stateswoman?' I think you've overstated my status and *under*estimated my endurance and strength."

Alex laughed. "Oh, God, I hope so. But seriously, I'm so proud of you and I'm lucky you're my wife." She reached out and clasped his hand, blowing him an air kiss.

While he still had the night to look forward to with this gorgeous woman, he couldn't help but plan ahead. *Tomorrow I'll get back to Ray Penner in Special Branch. Hopefully they can push ahead with surveillance of Lars Nilsson.*

27

LARS MEETS HIS FAMILY

Stockholm

The flight from Heathrow to Stockholm's Arlanda International Airport arrived on schedule after a two-and-a-half-hour flight. The trip offered Lars Nilsson an opportunity to meet his "Swedish relatives" for the first time, the ones who would be attending his wedding. With his bulging canvas weekend bag slung over his shoulder, he spotted the Russian operatives acting as his surrogate Swedish parents; they were waiting for him just beyond the security checkpoint. He had known them since the age of fifteen and actually loved them as deeply as his own real parents back in Russia. Although his last trip to Stockholm wasn't that long ago, it was always good to be back "home."

They all embraced and walked out of the terminal to their parked car. On the ride into town, his Swedish father said, "You will be meeting two of your 'cousins' who will attend your wedding - Linda Hendrickson and Johan Nilsson. Like you, they are in their mid-forties and were 'officially' born in Stockholm, although Linda now lives near Berga and Johan resides in Gothenburg."

"Did they also arrive here as teenagers as I did?"

"We should not talk of such matters, ever," his "mother" replied sternly, "but yes, they did."

"Will anyone else from my 'family' attend the wedding?"

"Well, of course, *we* will, darling," she replied in a much softer tone of voice. Lars smiled. He had instinctively liked his faux parents upon his first arrival in Sweden years ago while using the covert name of "Lars Nilsson." His real name, Dimitri Vasiliev, was now confined to secret files in Moscow.

I am saddened, however, that my birth parents will not be attending the wedding because they live in Moscow, speak no Swedish, and have no cover story to explain their relationship to me, he thought. He assumed that one day the SVR might arrange for them to meet April Scott, but that was not even under consideration yet, and in any event, could only be in the far distant future.

The car pulled into the driveway of a comfortable-looking two-story, four-bedroom house with a typical Swedish red tiled roof and flower boxes in every window. There was a small yard in front and a larger one in the back. This is where Lars had lived for several years before going to Uppsala University.

His new "cousins," Linda Hendrickson and Johan Nilsson, came out of the house. In case neighbors were observing, they exchanged hugs with Lars as if they had known each other their entire lives. Although both were Russian-born, no one would ever doubt that Linda and Johan were Swedish to the core. Linda was tall with straight blond hair hanging to her shoulders, blue eyes, and had the slender physique of an athlete. Johan had brown hair with Nordic good looks and was the tallest of the three with a solid frame. Everyone entered the Nilsson home together.

Once inside, his parents went into the kitchen and returned with a tray of snacks and a bottle of vodka. Drinks were poured and all had their first shot of the day. For the next four hours, Lars memorized the legends of both Linda and Johan during the conversation. They exchanged common memories that all would be expected to know and recite without hesitation. Linda and Johan had already been briefed on Lars' background and cover story.

His parents brought out a photo album with doctored photos, showing them all together decades ago. Lars examined the photos carefully and had to admit that the SVR technical wizards had done a remarkable job of not only creating these images but of aging the photographic paper so that it appeared authentic.

As the afternoon wore on, Lars' father said, "I have a surprise for you. Your old friend, Stanislaw Wojcik has arrived in Stockholm on vacation, and wants to meet you."

Lars' mind focused with absolute clarity on what his "father" had just said. Yet, he paused a bit too long. Now his father asked: "Is something wrong? Surely you remember Stanislaw."

"Of course, I do," Lars laughed. "I just haven't seen him in a few years, and I didn't expect he would be in Stockholm."

"He is looking forward to talking with you again, and wonders if you will be free this evening."

"Yes, yes, I will."

"Good. He has asked that you meet him at his hotel. It's the Radisson Blu Royal Viking in Vasagartan."

"I know it. It has a great central location. What time and what is his room number?"

"He said you should come at 8:00 p.m. and that you can find him by his room number 536."

"Please tell him I'll be there."

~

LARS EXITED the taxi he had taken from his Swedish parent's suburban house and entered the Radisson Blu in Vasagartan. It was a modern hotel, surrounded by department stores, bars, and restaurants. People were out walking, eating and drinking, going to discos, and a lot more; he missed the vibe of downtown Stockholm at night. Had this been a year ago, he might have searched for a one-night stand with an impossibly beautiful Swedish woman. But in the last few months, that urge to roam had dwindled as April Scott had blossomed into an attractive woman with a fabulous overall appeal to Lars.

Stanislaw Wojcik, a senior SVR officer, had helped train Lars many years ago and had stayed on as one of Lars' handlers over the past twenty years. Even Lars didn't know his true Russian name, although he did know that Stanislaw has been born somewhere on the Polish/Russian border and may have had at least one Polish parent, which explained his fluency in the Polish language. He also traveled using a Polish passport, claiming to be a businessman.

Lars took the elevator up to the fifth floor and knocked on Stanislaw Wojcik's door.

"Lars, my old friend!" Stanislaw said, grabbing him in a big bear hug, then inviting him in. He was a large man, but not as powerful as he once had been. When they sat, Lars noticed the liver spots on Stanislaw's hands and scars on his face from what might have been the results of minor surgeries for skin cancer.

How old was Stanislaw? Lars wondered, *seventy-five years old, or more?* First, they spoke of inconsequential things - tourism, the weather, and travel in general. Lars thought Stanislaw had already been drinking quite a lot because his speech was slightly slurred and his balance seemed a little tipsy. Indeed, when he offered Lars a glass of Vodka, the bottle from which he poured was not quite half empty. Stanislaw reminisced about old times, then finally, they got down to business.

"You have done incredibly well in London. All our friends are deeply impressed."

"Thank you."

"I want to talk about your future. Can April Scott select where she is assigned next?"

Stanislaw poured them each another glass of vodka as he spoke. When he turned to grab nuts from the can provided by the hotel, Lars reached over and poured half of his drink into Stanislaw's glass.

"She can request assignments from a list of vacancies, but the final decision rests with Washington," Lars replied.

"Okay, I thought so. We would like her to seek out jobs in either the U.S. Mission to NATO headquarters in Brussels, or if that is not possible, then something in Germany, Poland, or Ukraine."

"I will talk to her about that, but it is still early for her to make formal selections."

"Okay. Just try to influence her selection list. I should add that as secondary choices we would be happy with any of the countries in the Baltics." Stanislaw swallowed most of his drink and belched loudly.

This is not the old Stanislaw I knew, Lars thought, *maybe it is old age, or maybe he has a problem.*

"I assume you have found my reports worthwhile," Lars asked.

"They have been excellent" Stanislaw replied. He finished off his glass and poured another. "When we compare her material with that from other sources, it has given us a clear and comprehensive view of what the Americans and NATO have in mind." Lars was delighted.

"I probably should not mention this," Stanislaw said before he swallowed more vodka, "but since we are old friends, indeed, *very* old friends, I will." Lars waited for Stanislaw to focus.

"I have *personally* heard recordings from the highest level of

Washington officials discussing our successes in intelligence, diplomacy, and military matters. Imagine that? Recognition from the Americans of *our* success!"

"Maybe we shouldn't talk about this here," Lars cautioned.

"Nonsense. Don't worry," he replied unsteadily. "I tell you, our deep penetration agents are doing a wonderful job . . . *every*where."

Lars was becoming uncomfortable talking about this in a hotel room and thought for a moment before asking: "Where are those recordings made that you mentioned?"

Stanislaw grimaced, swallowed hard, then gave a crooked smile as only a very drunk man would do. "From *inside* the State Department. We have a very high-level spy in the State Department." His words were now slurring together.

At first, Lars had assumed that the spy had planted a microphone within a State Department conference room, until Stanislaw said, " . . . and the best part is that the guy can carry around his recording device *wherever* he goes."

"What? And no one suspects him?"

"He is too important and too powerful. I tell you the guy is at the *very top*."

Lars wanted to talk more but noticed that Stanislaw's eyes were beginning to close and he was now slouching in his chair. Lars had to act quickly.

"Who else is on these recordings?"

Stanislaw's eyes popped open. "H-Heads of their intelligence services, like the FBI . . . and C-C -CIA . . . you get the idea." Stanislaw started to wobble in his chair. Lars thought he would fall over and need to be caught. In that moment, he realized that was all he could expect from his drunk old friend.

"Well, it has been great seeing you again, Stanislaw. You should get some rest. Do you want to talk tomorrow?"

"No, I told you what I needed to say . . . about your future wife's next assignment. . . It was n-nice meeting again-n-n-n. Next time, let's make it further . . . east."

Stanislaw rose unsteadily and they embraced. Lars left the room, far more enlightened than when he had arrived. But he felt sorry for his old mentor and friend, doubting he would be in the business much longer.

Nevertheless, he filed away his memory of what Stanislaw had told him. The story seemed remarkable. A high-level resource inside the State Department. Someone at the *top*!

Then, he recalled an old saying from his training days: *Never underestimate what an intelligence service can do. We are only limited by our imagination.*

28

BREAK-IN

London

J immy "The Rabbit" Jones and his Special Branch team of three more trained "search specialists" sat in their cream-colored van parked in front of Lars Nilsson's apartment on Lennox Gardens. The van had a blue sign painted on each side that read: "Pearce Renovations." This cover afforded them a reason to enter any place with equipment needed to thoroughly look around such as today at Lars' apartment.

Earlier, when Commander Ray Penner had discovered that Nilsson was in Sweden, it was a no-brainer that this was the perfect time to search his apartment in detail. His staff had pulled city property records and made note that Nilsson's unit consisted of three bedrooms, a living room, a separate dining room, a kitchen, and a study. Considering it was located in the heart of Brompton, a very upscale London neighborhood adjoining both Belgravia and Knightsbridge, Penner knew this apartment had cost Nilsson a small fortune. Indeed, the property records revealed it had cost him a few million pounds to buy.

"Okay, guys, let's do it now," Jimmy said.

The team opened the rear double doors and retrieved cases holding their equipment. They casually walked to the building's front door where Billy, one of the team members, pulled out a set of master keys that could fit any lock in the UK. He opened the door and the team walked up to the first-floor landing, then opened Lars' security locks on his apartment door. A third member of the team, Charlie, walked into the study, found the alarm system in a wall cabinet, and quickly disabled it. Charlie would reset the alarm before they left.

"Okay, guys. I'll start in the living room and dining room," Jimmy said. "Charlie, you might as well handle the study, and Billy and Richie, you two do the bedrooms."

Jimmy had always been fast, hence, his nickname, "The Rabbit." He was a veteran of the secret war against the IRA, who had been masters at hiding weapons and explosives in ordinary places. His success in uncovering caches of material was legendary. In the old days, Billy and Richie had focused more on countering espionage threats from communist bloc intelligence services when they had operated in London. Charlie was an electronics wiz but also a jack-of-all-trades. Among the four of them, the key would be to examine every inch of the apartment without leaving a trace that they had ever visited at all.

Jimmy started by checking baseboards in the living room, tapping here, gently prying there, always looking for a hidden compartment. Next, he moved on to floorboards, seeing if any of the boards were loose or if the floor seemed to have a void underneath. After moving small carpets and tables, he carefully returned everything to its original place. He also checked furniture, looking for false bottoms underneath, or secret drawers.

Meanwhile, Charlie methodically examined Lars' study. It was filled with bookcases and file cabinets. Knowing it would take a while, he pulled every book off the shelves and thumbed through each one, looking for loose papers or pages that had been marked in a coded manner. Some books were in Swedish, but the vast majority were in English, including many thrillers, or action-adventure novels written by Patterson, McLean, Murray-Smith, LeCarre, and Follett. He then went through every file in the cabinets but found nothing out of the ordinary. Charlie pulled out all desk drawers, sifting through their contents, and examining the back and bottom of each drawer for anything taped to it.

Billy and Richie took separate bedrooms. While Billy searched the guest bedroom, Richie focused on the master. He used the same technique as the others: Baseboards, floorboards, dressers, the armoire, and nightstands. Nothing. They were all searched without success.

In addition to the armoire, there was a medium-sized closet. Although he found nothing suspicious inside, he noted there was a step stool folded against one wall. So, he looked up, expecting to find a storage area, or perhaps a trap door where Lars could place excess items. But still, there was nothing.

Now, why would he have a step stool in the bedroom? Ritchie thought to himself. He realized the stool could have been used anywhere in the apartment and was merely being stored in the closet, but still...

He moved back into the room and looked around. The only things high enough to require a step stool was either the top of the curtains, or top of the armoire. He chose the latter and opened the step stool in front of the wooden piece to take a look. Taking two steps up, he felt around on top. Then he tapped. The wood jiggled. He stood on the third step and was able to lift a section of the top off the armoire. Then he called out: "Billy! I've found treasure."

Billy appeared and Richie handed down a narrow box, a thin laptop, a cell phone, and an 8" x 11" notebook. Once he was certain nothing else remained, he got off the step stool and the two men spread the material out on the bed.

"I'm getting Jimmy," Richie said. Moments later Ritchie and Jimmy returned followed by Charlie.

The box wasn't locked and inside was a "one-time use" espionage pad of letters and numbers that formed a grid. It was used to send and receive encrypted messages. There were also a half dozen SD cards loose in the box.

Charlie turned on the laptop, but not knowing the password, found no success there. The paper notebook appeared to have random writing on some pages which made no sense to him. He reached into his own case and pulled out his Special Branch laptop. One at a time, Charlie inserted each of the SD cards. Most of the images were encrypted, but, regardless, he tried to download each one. "Jimmy, look at this," he called out. "I think it's material from the American Embassy."

"Download it, Charlie."

After photographing everything, Jimmy said, "Okay, guys, the job was to find 'tools of the trade.' We were successful. I'll call Commander Penner."

RAY PENNER and Alex were talking when Penner's encrypted mobile vibrated on his office desk. Both he and Alex Boyd stared at it for a moment before Penner picked it up. "

"Penner here." He knew the call was from Jimmy and put it on speaker.

"Sir, we found treasure." Jimmy said and went on to describe their haul, including materials from the embassy.

"Since Charlie can't open Nilsson's laptop files," Penner told Jimmy, "I think we should leave everything in place and start intense surveillance of the targets."

"Yes, sir, that's what we assumed," Jimmy replied. "Hang on a second, Jimmy." Penner looked at Alex. "Do you have any thoughts?"

"I need to see the material from the SD card concerning our embassy documents, first."

"You can count on it."

"Ray, we've already discussed this as a possible outcome," Alex said. "So, I'm comfortable with your plan." Ray nodded and turned back to the phone call.

"Alright, Jimmy, photograph the find, put everything back in its place, and continue searching the apartment. I'll see you later."

"We're almost done, Sir. See you back at the office."

Alex was rubbing the back of his neck when Penner returned his gaze. "You realize this situation has just taken an enormous leap forward, don't you," Alex said, "at least from the American perspective."

"You think?" They both chuckled.

"I'm obliged to report it to Washington. The FBI and CIA will be heavily involved, as well as my headquarters," Alex said.

"That's to be expected. When Jimmy gets back, and after we look at the American material, I'll brief Assistant Commissioner Davies. I'm sure he'll want to bring in MI-5 and MI-6."

"Ray, I can't thank you enough for carrying the ball on this operation. You did what others were reluctant to do."

"I'm just happy the Branch could provide good value for money."

Alex knew it was a traditional British phrase, but, in this case, it truly understated Penner's contribution.

"Alex, what are you going to do now?"

"Can I wait here until Jimmy and his team return?"

"Absolutely. Would you like to go to the cafeteria for a bite?" Alex paused. "Is today when the French chef is on duty?"

Penner laughed. "Afraid not, but you're in luck. This is Reggie's first day back from leave, and he makes a superb leek and celery soup, and a traditional beet salad."

Alex was silent for a half-second. "I recall seeing a MacDonald's down the street."

"You, *yanks,* are such picky eaters."

"Are *you* going to have the leek and celery soup with beet salad?"

"Hell, no, Alex, that stuff is rubbish. On second thought, I'll join you for a burger and fries."

"Excellent! I'll make an American out of you yet."

Despite his levity, Alex realized that finding material from the U.S. Embassy confirmed their suspicion: Someone on the inside was a traitor. *And that someone is April Scott,* he thought.

29

EVIDENCE

London

After everything was returned to its original place in Lars Nilsson's apartment, the search team drove their van back to the parking lot in the police undercover building. There, they printed copies of all the photos they had taken at Nilsson's apartment. Then, Jimmy "The Rabbit" and his team used a different car to drive to Special Branch and brief Commander Ray Penner on their find. Jimmy spread the photos out in separate piles on Penner's conference table.

"May I examine these?" Alex asked. "Do I need gloves?" He wasn't sure if these might be used in court.

"It's okay. We have a separate set for the courtroom," Jimmy replied. Alex went directly to the pile with the secret U.S. Embassy telegrams that had been downloaded from the unencrypted SD card. The first document was four pages long. He saw it was a recent outgoing telegram from London. The drafting officer was listed as April Scott. Penner recognized it, too.

"Alex, does this mean this specific document came from her office?"

"I wish it were that easy, but I'm afraid it only means that someone who had *access* to this document printed it out. It may have been April Scott, but look here, other offices are on the distribution list, too." He pointed to a short list of acronyms, indicating which offices had received a copy including the ambassador, DCM, and defense attaché.

"Each office has multiple employees who might also have handled this document," he said.The text of the telegram concerned a conversation between April and an official at the British Foreign Office concerning British attempts to sell defense equipment to Sweden. The stumbling block was that Sweden was a manufacturer of an entire range of excellent defense items such as aircraft and electronics, and therefore, did not need to purchase such goods from abroad.

There were additional secret cables on other political subjects, some originating from the U.S. Embassy in London while other messages were from U.S. embassies in other European countries. Fortunately, all pre-dated Rachel's arrival in London. Therefore, no one could challenge sharing the status of the investigation with her.

"Can I have copies to take back to the embassy?" Alex asked.

"Of course," Penner replied as Assistant Commissioner Gerald Davies entered the room.

"What have we got here?" He looked in no mood for idle chitchat. As Penner explained the piles of separate photo arrays, Davies stood next to him looking over the cache.

Next, Alex and Penner examined a pile containing Jimmy's photos of every page of the code book, known as the "one-time pad," which was used to encrypt secret communications using just one sheet of paper for each separate message. The next sheet was used for the subsequent message, and so on.

"I assume this is pure gold," Alex said.

"You're not kidding," Penner replied. "But we have to be able to intercept Nilsson's transmissions for it to be useful."

"I've got good news for you," Jimmy said. He pointed to another pile. "You'll see we photographed every page of a ruled notebook that we found. The scribbles don't seem to mean a lot, but you can see there is a telephone number written on one of the pages. We thought it might be a reminder of Nilsson's mobile number for the secret phone we found above the armoire. So, when we were in his apartment, we called the number and his screen lit up, He had the ringer and vibrator turned off. However, the phone is encrypted, so we'll need his password to gain access."

"Nilsson probably uses his laptop to transmit most documents," Alex said. "But since the phone was found together with the 'one time pad,' he may use the phone on occasion to transmit his coded messages, or perhaps, images of the telegrams. He may not have erased all his transmissions which will be great *if* we can break into it."

"You're probably right," Davies replied. "At least now we know his mobile number. We can monitor it." He turned to Penner and Jimmy. "You left the phone in place, right?"

"Yes,"

"As much as I want our tech wizards to examine it, it's too early to make the seizure without alerting Nilsson. If and when we arrest him, we'll ask MI-5 and MI-6 to help with the electronic wizardry on his phone."

"Since you just alluded to a joint operation, what's your protocol for bringing in the U.S. Embassy?" Alex asked.

"We'll contact Roger Carpenter in the FBI office," Penner replied.

"Good. When I get back to the embassy, I also want to bring in the CIA and NSA. As you implied, this must be a joint technical operation. Is there a standing UK-US group, formal or informal, that already exists to handle this type of situation?"

"Yes, but in the past, your office wasn't directly involved," Commission Davies said. "It will be now, though, at least as far as I'm concerned."

"Thank you."

"I'm afraid I can't give you copies of *all* the materials we found," Ray Penner said.

"That's okay. The Embassy telegrams will be sufficient to get the ball rolling at the American end. I'll let the other agencies know you'll be contacting them. I assume at some point they'll all have access to the total haul of goodies."

"Yes," Davies replied.

"Anything else I need to know?" Alex asked. "That's it for now," Davies said.

"We'll be in touch."

Alex left Scotland Yard and returned to the embassy in a police vehicle with a driver to help ensure the safety of the materials he was carrying. In the back of his mind, he was troubled by one thought, and unsure of how to deal with the problem.

Should I inform Bainbridge Wellington of events? Technically, it's possible he could be the top-level spy, in view of his long tenure in London, Alex thought, *especially with his comprehensive access to all classified information at the American Embassy. This is unlikely,* he finally decided, *but so is the very notion that a foreign service officer is a spy among us.*

~

ALEX GATHERED his office staff to brief them on the situation. Billy Caldwell, his security engineering officer, offered the most useful idea. "We can place a covert surveillance camera in April Scott's office," Caldwell suggested.

"That's a great idea, Billy," Alex replied, "but first we'll need Washington's approval. Furthermore, by the end of the day, the FBI will be in the lead. So, let's keep your idea in mind for later. Besides, we shouldn't rule out other potential suspects in the embassy."

ALEX MADE copies of the embassy telegrams found on the SD card at Nilsson's apartment, then called a meeting with Anna Battles, Roger Carpenter, and the embassy representative of the National Security Agency. Since all were aware that Lars Nilsson and April

Scott were suspects, Alex only needed to give them an update on the Special Branch search of Lars' apartment and pass out copies of the telegrams that were found.

"I want to emphasize," Alex said at the meeting, "that your counterparts in the British government will provide to you photographic copies of both the 'one time pad,' and the notebook. I know you will contact your Washington agencies and report this new information.

"Anna, I have a specific request for you," he said. "Since it appears our embassy spy is in the State Department and is, most likely, April Scott, I want to limit what I send back to D.C. through State Department communication channels. This is just in case there are other State Department spies unaccounted for."

"I agree," Anna replied, "but I shudder at the thought."

"Yeah, I agree, so please have your telegram passed to DS Director Riley from CIA headquarters with a note saying the information is being shared with Riley at my request. I will call Riley on my secure phone and tell him to expect the telegram from you through the CIA communique channels."

"Consider it done," Anna replied.

Everyone looked at Roger Carpenter. He drew a deep breath. "I guess the ball is in our court since we now suspect an American citizen."

Alex nodded. "As soon as you speak with Washington, I would like the FBI's agreement for me to brief Bainbridge Wellington. I've thought about this, and while technically he can't be ruled out as our spy, it also applies to the entire embassy communications section, the Defense Attaché office, and even Anna's shop. It's tough while suspecting everyone, but we have to draw the line *some*where, and work with people we believe are on the right side."

"Hell, I've worked with Bainbridge for a few years, and I'm comfortable briefing him now," Carpenter replied. Anna agreed, as did the NSA representative.

"One last thing," Alex said. "Rachel is acting Deputy Chief of Mission for the entire embassy. Her arrival at post occurred *after* the material was leaked, so she is in the clear. So, Rachel needs to know whatever Wellington knows. Do you all agree?" The answer was a resounding agreement.

"Okay then. Let's go upstairs and clue them in."

BY CLOSE OF the business day, Bainbridge and Rachel had been briefed, and the FBI had formally taken charge of the investigation. Technical experts from both the FBI and CIA were being sent to London in anticipation of assisting the Brits in examining Lars' tools of the trade: SD cards, cellphone, and laptop, whenever the decision to finally arrest him and seize his technology was finally made.

The FBI was also sending a small team of agents from their counterintelligence division to help work the case. DS Director

Riley called Alex to inform him that he had received the information from Anna Battles that had been passed by the CIA. Efforts were moving in the right direction. Coordination among US agencies, and between the US and Britain was good.

There was only one remaining question: How long would it take to snap the cuffs on Lars and April Scott?

30

SETTING THE TRAP

London

During the next two days, political pressure from both the White House and Downing Street mounted, calling for immediate results in the espionage investigation.

Alex sat with a small U.S. team in MI-5 headquarters at Millbank Street, adjacent to the Thames River in London, near Parliament. The room was a secure inner sanctum for holding the most sensitive conversations. No mobiles or other electronic devices were permitted inside this conference room.

Geoffrey Carver, an assistant director of MI-5, spoke to the group. "Now that Lars Nilsson has just returned from Stockholm, we have placed him under 24-hour surveillance. While we have enough to arrest him, we want to know more about his operation before we take him off the grid. Let's see what develops."

When Alex had first met Carver, he noted his lankiness, standing at a considerable height of maybe six and a half feet tall. Also, Carver's hair was uncombed, standing up in some places, uncertain which direction to go in others. It gave him the appearance of a mad scientist.

"We agree, Geoff," replied Roger Carpenter, "but, the FBI's view is that we should infiltrate their inner circle in the hopes that Nilsson and Scott will reveal themselves as early as possible while still under surveillance."

Anna Battles was sitting next to Alex. He felt her knee nudge his leg under the table and understood. Earlier in private, they had discussed this very topic and both had hoped the FBI would *neither* press for an unduly speedy arrest *nor* seek to insert their own people into the operation. Each believed a reasonable delay might lead to a fuller understanding of the Russian network and depth of the espionage operation being run by Lars and April. If the opportunity arose to nail them in the act of passing classified information, however, the Brits would have no choice but to arrest them.

"What do you mean precisely when you say, 'infiltrate their inner circle?'" Geoffrey Carver asked.

"Perhaps we could insert an 'agent-provocateur.' The FBI has a cadre of undercover personnel skilled in this type of operation," Carpenter replied.

"To do what, exactly?" Carver asked. "I don't understand your point. From the evidence we obtained at Nilsson's flat, we already assume April Scott is passing secrets to Nilsson. And it certainly appears Nilsson is in contact with a Russian SVR handler. At this point, how could inserting a third party advance our investigation?"

Carpenter didn't respond.

"I must emphasize," Carver continued, "there is a difference between arresting suspects with actual evidence of espionage, versus arresting them because we inserted a bogus Russian spy into the mix. The latter borders on entrapment. Besides, Nilsson can easily verify the *bona fides* of your pseudo-Russian agent-provocateur with his real SVR contacts. Alternatively, if you intend for your FBI agent-provocateur to be an American or a third party-national with access to classified material, then to gain Nilsson's trust, this could take months, or years. Again, I ask for what purpose should we agree to this, considering what we already know?"

"It was just a thought by Washington," Carpenter replied. It sounded as if he didn't buy into this strategy himself.

"I see."

It was clear Geoffrey Carver also thought this would be a counter-productive tactic. Alex was concerned that without access to Nilsson's encrypted electronic equipment, the Brits and Americans would be unable to gain *additional* evidence for prosecution or to develop a better understanding of the network. He was about to introduce an alternative plan.

"I have a suggestion," Alex said. "It might split the difference between conducting a long surveillance operation versus taking more immediate action." All eyes in the room turned toward him.

"As you suggested, Geoffrey, let's give the surveillance operation a few more days, although, I believe we would be extremely lucky to uncover information about Lars' network in so short a time. Rather than inserting in a third party, as the FBI suggests, let's create a phony document that will seem so valuable to Lars that April will almost certainly pass it to him. It will be April initiating the action, without the need to insert a third party. Then, we can arrest them with the handoff of material. By catching them in the act, we can squeeze them for information, play one against the other, and perhaps, persuade Nilsson to give us access codes to his electronics.

"The document must contain at least some classified material so that it can be used later in court as evidence of espionage," Carver added.

Alex sat back and surveyed the group. *Did the room just get brighter or were lightbulbs turned on in everyone's head?*

"Did you have something in mind? Carver asked.

"Not exactly, but it should be along the line of new political or military thinking. It must also be plausible."

"How about if we imply that Sweden wants to aggressively challenge Russian warships sailing near Sweden's coastline?" one of the FBI agents from Washington offered. "Even sink them, if they do not cease and desist. *That* would capture their attention."

"It certainly would," Anna Battles said as if speaking to a child. "But perhaps Nilsson would suspect that story as being a bit over the top since that type of provocative action by Sweden is very unlikely and could easily lead to World War III."

A representative from MI-6, the British Intelligence Service, spoke in support of Anna's comment. His name was Reginald something-or-other, Alex didn't catch his name but could see that he had awkward- looking teeth with a large gap in the center of the upper row.

Alex had another idea, but hesitated, not wanting to overplay his hand. After all, Diplomatic Security was supposed to be a defensive organization rather than an initiator of intelligence operations. But he couldn't hold back, so . . . "Here's a thought," Alex said. "It might be more believable if Sweden would want to move toward eventual full integration with NATO, if circumstances in Europe were to change. For example: if the perceived threat from Russia were to increase. Why not create a secret report, allegedly from the U.S. Embassy in Stockholm, reporting that Sweden's Prime Minister has approached us with an offer to locate one squadron of U.S. fighter aircraft at a Swedish base?

"Admittedly, this would be unprecedented, but that's the point. Our group can create the bogus classified report and insert it into April Scott's incoming Embassy messages. Our own embassy senior communications officer in London can help pull this off.

The report will need to have all the realistic markings expected on such an incoming document.

"Since Lars is under 24-hour surveillance," Alex continued, "I suggest we put April under similar surveillance. We should be able to observe her passing this information on to him. Then we can make the arrests. If, on the other hand, we miss the exchange between them, there is another possibility."

Alex looked over at Mr. British-bad-teeth who subtly shifted his position and looked uncomfortable. Alex assumed this guy was really smart and understood what he was about to suggest.

Then he went on. "We all know the CIA has lost several assets in Moscow recently and, therefore, has reduced capability. But what about MI-6? If Nilsson does manage to transmit the bogus Swedish request back to Moscow, would your MI-6 assets in Moscow know of this? Could they inform us? That's another way of confirming that April Scott had passed the info on to Nilsson."

"I like that idea," Geoffrey Carver said. "Reginald, let's talk after this meeting. In the interim, perhaps you and Anna Battles can jointly create this bogus document, say, in the next day or two."

Everyone agreed and the meeting adjourned. On the way out of the grey stone building, Anna asked Alex to ride in her office sedan back to the embassy.

"HONESTLY, Alex, you've got a sneaky and creative mind," she said while they were riding back. "You remind me a lot of your father's operational skills and your mother's analytical abilities. You should work for us in Langley. We could put you to good use."

"First, tell me about the perks; perhaps an Aston Martin, custom-made tuxedo, expensive watch with hidden lasers, and free martinis?"

"Sorry, that would be MI-6. We'll just give you a free metal office desk and government ballpoint pens."

"Thanks for the offer, Anna, but I'm almost happy where I am now," he said.

"Almost?"

"It is the State Department, after all."

"Well, the opportunity is there if you're interested in pursuing a career change," she said.

"I never want to slam shut any doors, but for now, things are working out fine. But seriously, Anna, *thank* you. I mean it."

RACHEL HAD SPENT her lunchtime at the Royal Automobile Club turning in her membership application. She couldn't wait to use their squash courts and swimming pool. Her new embassy job meant she had to spend a lot of time sitting at her desk and increasingly felt the need for more exercise.

Earlier, she had mentioned her need to work out to Alex. He had joked that she was turning into a pudgy weakling. While she usually enjoyed his wit, she had to admit to gaining an extra five pounds since arriving in London. At least her weight was evenly distributed over her height of five feet, ten inches, so she wasn't too concerned . . . yet. As for her muscles, they weren't going to disappear anytime soon.

Leaving the Royal Automobile Club, she decided to walk back to the embassy which meant walking to the end of Pall Mall, taking a right on St. James Street toward Piccadilly. After that, she continued up New Bond Street while window shopping. The Salvatore Ferragamo and Gucci windows caught her eye first, then Alexander McQueen, Givenchy, and Versace, to name a few. *Pure heaven*, she thought. *I'll con Alex into buying something for himself, then say it's only fair we visit New Bond Street to balance out our purchases. Because he's so considerate, this ploy will work every time.*

BACK IN HER OFFICE, she saw a pile of memoranda and telegrams in her in-box. *Another typical day,* she thought. American embassies in Asia were closing now, so their end-of-day cable traffic had just been launched. Meanwhile, Washington had just opened for business, so their telegrams wouldn't bombard London for another few hours. The world was so interconnected that everyone sent info copies of reports to everyone else. Whether she was head of the political section or the acting DCM, she needed to see it all.

Oh well, Alex doesn't call me the 'multi-tasking Queen' for nothing. She smiled, then dove into the pile of material. Before reading her first document, she wondered how his meeting at MI5 had turned out. As she turned her attention to the document, her eyes grew wide.

31

CON JOB

London

Bainbridge Wellington looked intense as Alex briefed him and Rachel on the meeting at MI-5 headquarters. They had asked Roger Carpenter to join them, but he was tied up with his own Washington-based FBI visitors. Anna Battles, however, was able to attend and now sat next to Alex in one of the grey tic-weave-covered chairs. Listening to Alex's briefing, Anna commented only when she could add a twist from either the CIA or British intelligence perspective.

"It seems we're about to bring this issue to finality," Bainbridge said.

"Not completely, I'm afraid," Alex replied. Wellington looked confused.

Rachel added, "You mean the Nilsson-Scott connection doesn't completely explain the arrest and execution of the CIA sources in Moscow."

"Exactly," Anna replied. "There is no way that April Scott could have known about our sources. Exactly *who* disclosed their names or provided enough information for the SVR to figure it out is still unresolved. It appears there might be someone else to uncover. We may have *two* separate cases of spies among us." Anna gave Rachel a knowing nod of her head.

"Oh, yes, I see your point," Wellington said. "But at least we should be wrapping up our London end soon."

"Perhaps," Alex replied.

Wellington rubbed the back of his neck and said, "Maybe the State Department's legal advisor *should* have allowed Special Branch to search April's apartment. I guess I *could* have pressed them on it."

"Don't worry, it isn't too late," Alex replied. "The FBI mentioned that they'll be seeking a search warrant for her apartment this afternoon. The question is whether the court in Washington will agree that it has jurisdiction over an American government-owned apartment in a foreign country. It will depend upon the judge."

Bainbridge shook his head. "God, these legal issues are complicated. Let's change the subject. Anna, I want to see a draft copy of your bogus telegram about basing US aircraft in Sweden as soon as possible. I just want to ensure that it looks like a legitimate State Department cable."

"Understood. By the way, the bogus cable was Alex's idea, but I thought it was brilliant, and so do the Brits." Bainbridge and Rachel smiled.

"Well done, Alex!" Bainbridge said. "Is there anything else I should know?"

Alex and Anna exchanged glances. His look said that she should respond. "No, I don't think so," Anna answered.

∾

RACHEL AND ALEX returned to her office. "Oh my, it's already 7:00 p.m. Let's call it a day and go home for a drink and snacks," Rachel said.

"That works for me," he replied. She locked up her classified material in the safe, set the office alarm on the way out, and they headed down to the garage.

"Shall we flip for it?" Alex asked.

"Okay, do it. I'm calling tails."

Alex pulled a coin from his right pocket and tossed it into the air. When he caught it and slapped it onto the back of his other hand, it came up heads.

"Gosh darn it! You almost *always* win," she said. "Why is that?"

"I cheat."

"I don't see how; I was watching closely. But I'll figure it out."

As the winner, Alex got behind the wheel of their two-door Jaguar F-type, started it, and gunned the powerful V-8 engine a few times, watching her reaction.

"If you keep doing that, I'll have an orgasm."

"You always did have uncontrollable sexual urges."

"Funny, I didn't think you minded."

They laughed as he drove out of the garage, heading home to Knightsbridge.

ONCE INSIDE THEIR TOWNHOUSE, they changed into jeans and casual shirts. Alex headed down to the living room to fix their drinks and snacks. Rachel's eyes glanced over at Alex's nightstand where he had emptied his pockets of several coins.

Hmmm, why do I almost always lose the coin flip? She wondered. *I have to figure it out.* She walked around the bed and looked at his things. Lying among his stuff were two American quarters next to his wallet. *Look, he's still carrying American change. Why not British coins?* She picked one up, examined it, and turned it over.

Damn! No wonder he wins so much. The coin had heads on both sides. She picked up the other coin, it had tails on both sides. *That sneaky creep,* she thought. *Where did he get these coins?* Then she smiled. *Payback will be a bitch!*

Rachel put the coin with the double heads into her right jeans pocket and the other one into her left pocket, then went downstairs to join Alex for their drinks.

Quite the connoisseur, he had cut up salami and ham from the refrigerator and placed equal portions of food on two plates along with green olives, and a few slices of Taleggio, a soft and pungent Italian cheese. He had put her glass of vodka on ice with an olive on the coffee table in front of her chair. By the time she came down, Alex was already sipping his single malt whiskey with a light splash of water.

"I gather from your briefing that the meeting with the Brits fulfilled your expectations."

"It did," he said. "Anna was supportive, and the FBI guy was a team player although an idea of theirs wasn't too well-received. As for the Brits, they have a lot of experience in this type of business. Frankly, more than I have. But, overall, I thought it went well."

Alex took another sip of whiskey and continued. "Have I kept you in the loop enough? You're a key decision-maker now, and I want you to feel that I've shared everything with you."

Rachel smiled. "Don't worry, I have full confidence that you'll tell me whatever is appropriate." He returned the smile, feeling her phraseology was a little unusual.

It's probably nothing, he thought, and shrugged it off.

"I've been thinking, Hunk Man, London is a shoppers' paradise, and we haven't even begun to do our share of buying yet. How about if we go shopping this weekend, if we have time?"

"Sure, if that's what you want." He reached over and grabbed a chunk of salami.

"I do. Furthermore, you should upgrade your 'action-man' digital watch to something more suitable for sophisticated London living. It should be elegant, thin, expensive, and make a statement."

"Really?" Alex was surprised. "But I like my current watch, it's a useful tool, and I like its rugged looks. And besides, a few years ago you bought me an exquisite fountain pen in Italy, that's more than enough elegance for me."

"Nonsense, my dear, but, if you don't want a new watch, then we can spend that money on a half dozen designer dresses for me from Alexander McQueen, Givenchy, or Versace."

"Whoa, whoa! This is news to me," his eyes widened. "Aren't they very expensive?"

"Now that you mention it, yes, they are. But I'm willing to buy *you* a pricey watch."

There was a pause while she chewed on some ham and took a swallow of vodka. "I tell you what," she said. "Let's flip for it. If I win, we buy the dresses. If you win, you get your new watch."

"Well, ahh . . . okay. But hold on a minute, I don't have any change on me. I'll go up and get a coin."

"Don't worry about that. We're in luck! *I* have a coin in my pocket," she smiled at him.

Alex had a sinking feeling. "Okay, let's flip," he said, without enthusiasm.

"Call it, Alex."

"Tails."

Rachel reached into her right pocket, pulled out the coin, and tossed it high in the air. Catching it, she slapped it onto the back of her other hand and revealed it. She let out a satisfied chuckle. "Imagine *that*. It's *heads!*"

They locked eyes for a few seconds, each sporting a wide grin.

He rubbed one hand over his chin, realizing the con man had been conned.

"Congratulations, Honey Bunch. So, how much will these dresses cost?"

"Only a few thousand."

"Okay, that's not bad for six designer dresses."

"Oh, no, I think you've misunderstand, my sweet. That's the price for *each* one, and in British pounds."

He sat there for a moment with arms crossed, still smiling, and shook his head slowly. He then leaned toward her and took her hand, kissing the back of it tenderly, and said, "Well played, my dear, very well played, indeed."

Her smile was brilliant. "So, it seems from now on we'll be taking turns driving the Jag. Isn't the right, Hunk Man?"

"Absolutely. That seems fair to me." He paused, feeling his defeat. "You're not just a woman with magnificent hair, a gorgeous face, and spectacular legs. As I once said, in the competition between us for the biggest brain, I am always and hopelessly in second place."

She stood up and walked over, sat on his lap and planted a long and sensual kiss on his lips. "I prefer to think of our competition as a tag-team sport, rather than a one-on-one game."

"Agreed."

Her bright green eyes looked into his. "Let's go upstairs," she said with a wink.

32

SPRINGING THE TRAP

London

S hortly after 8:00 a.m. the next morning, Alex was sitting in his office talking with Billy Caldwell, his security engineer. Billy was a few years older than Alex and had a wealth of technical experience. His current assignment to London was a reward for his years of service on the front lines of technical security.

When serving in Moscow, Billy had uncovered a KGB-wired microphone system implanted in the walls of one of the embassy's political offices. The wiring had been cleverly hidden by placing it within hollowed-out rebar during a renovation project. Moreover, during the waning days of communism in Eastern Europe, Billy had made additional finds of electronic bugging by the Polish and East German government's hostile intelligence services.

Today, Billy wore blue jeans and a work shirt because he would spend the next few hours re-aligning the heavy access control doors in the lobby. Helping him would be a U.S. Navy Seabee also assigned to the London embassy.

As they talked, Alex asked, "Tell me, again, when did you speak to Roger Carpenter?"

"It was yesterday at about 6:30 p.m."

Alex would have preferred that Carpenter had approached him first before asking for Billy's help, but he had been busy briefing Bainbridge Wellington and Rachel, so he couldn't complain.

Billy continued. "Carpenter said the FBI had gotten a warrant from the federal court in D.C. to search April Scott's apartment, as well as her office. They also wanted to place a hidden camera above her desk in the political section to see what she was doing. Do you recall, I had the same idea earlier?"

"Indeed, I do recall. Did you see this warrant?"

"No, I guess I should have asked."

"That's okay, Billy. I just want to ensure that we're covered legally. I'll speak with Carpenter later. How long will it take to put in the camera?"

"Not long. The tedious part is running the wiring to the monitor."

"Where will that monitor be placed?"

"Carpenter didn't say," Billy said. "Where do you think it should be?"

"Since it's their warrant, I guess it should be in their office. Hold off until I speak with Carpenter and Wellington. Can you do the project in a night?"

"Sure, not a problem."

"Okay, Billy, thanks. I'll get back to you."

When Billy left, Alex walked out to look at Diane Carrington's desk, always left clean and tidy. He saw a pile of phone messages in one corner with his name on it, so he picked them up. Most appeared routine, but he spotted a message from Roger Carpenter who had called to speak with him. The time was 6:15 pm last night, before Carpenter had spoken to Billy Caldwell.

I'm pleased Carpenter is willing to cooperate, he thought. *That's professional, and the right thing to do. It's also, a little uncharacteristic for the FBI.* The door to the office suite opened and Tom Lopez entered, trailed by Frank Stevens.

"Good morning, guys," Alex said to his two deputies. He noted time on the wall clock showed 8:15 a.m., a full 45 minutes before the official opening hour of the embassy. Alex had never asked them to arrive early, but correctly figured that his own example would be followed.

"Good morning boss," Tom replied.

"There have been some developments overnight," Alex said. "Once you grab a coffee, I'll bring you up to speed."

After dropping their jackets off in their offices, they went down to the cafeteria and returned with coffee and muffins.

FRANK STEVENS WAS on his first DS tour overseas and had started as a special agent in the Los Angeles Field Office before going through RSO training in D.C. Alex saw him looking at the awards hanging on his walls and hoped it would inspire him to work hard and learn, rather than to become a "glory seeker."

"Have a seat, fellas," he said. Fifteen minutes later, Alex had completed the update on Lars and April.

"Thanks for the info," Stevens said. " I guess you've handled these types of espionage cases before, right?"

Alex smiled, this time, slightly embarrassed. "Actually, no I haven't. I'm happy to say the State Department hasn't had a lot of traitors. I've been involved in giving counter-intelligence training to employees, as well as following up on leads of *potential* espionage, but thank goodness, actual espionage cases are rare."Frank nodded and seemed to take the answer in stride. "What about you, Tom?" Alex asked.

"The closest thing I had to espionage in my prior posts was in Mexico City. We had a local employee taking money from one of the drug cartels in exchange for information on what DEA was working on at the embassy. In the end, we nailed him. When I was in Madrid there was nothing."

Alex liked Tom Lopez and found him personable, smart, and willing to listen before drawing conclusions.

"Here's what I intend to do: We'll support the FBI since they now have the official lead in the case. We'll stay close to them to ensure Bainbridge and Rachel are informed. Also, we need to make sure that Director Riley is kept in the loop. However, I want us to do one thing more."

"What's that?" Frank asked.

"I would like for Tom to give a counterintelligence briefing to the Marine Guards. If the Russians are bold enough to recruit an embassy political officer, we should expect them to try to recruit a young Marine as well."

"Sure, I can handle that. I won't mention our specific case."

"Excellent. And you, Frank, I want you to accompany Tom when he lectures the Marines to see how it's done."

The meeting ended and after the men left, Alex logged onto his classified computer. He saw the first message was an urgent transmission from the DS Counter-Intelligence Office in Washington, informing him that the FBI had obtained search warrants for both April Scott's office and her residence. He was instructed to cooperate. He acknowledged receipt of the telegram, glad that DS was ensuring he was kept up to speed. Then, he picked up the phone and called Rachel. A broad smile forming on his lips before he spoke.

"Your majesty, I have something important to tell you and Bainbridge. Are you free now?"

She laughed. "Indeed, we are." There was a pause before she

continued. "If you continue your good deeds within my kingdom, I shall grant you a knighthood one day."

"You are too gracious, My lady. But I only need the Jaguar bestowed upon me."

"How dare thee speak blasphemy? Remember, I still possess thy magic coins."

"Okay, okay. Your peasant husband shall arrive at your royal castle in a few minutes."

Gosh, she's quick witted, he thought, *only one of the things I love about her.*

AFTER BRIEFING Bainbridge and Rachel about the FBI search warrants, Alex walked downstairs to the FBI office where Roger Carpenter was listening to his agents from Washington explain how they intended to search both April Scott's residence and her office. When Alex heard their plan, he wasn't happy seeing how it could easily backfire, yet he waited for an opportunity to speak.

"Your search warrant authorizes you to confiscate her home computer and any other electronics, is this correct?" he finally asked.

"Yes," replied an agent who seemed about forty years old and looked to be the most senior of the four-person group. He had on silver-framed thin glasses, wore a white shirt, and a dark grey suit. His closely cropped hair made Alex think he had served in the Marines at a younger time, or perhaps had been a State Trooper.

"Have you coordinated these searches with MI-5 and Special Branch?" he asked.

"Not yet. We thought we would share information afterward."

Alex looked at Carpenter who appeared to understand where Alex was going. "Guys, maybe we need to re-think the timing of these searches," Carpenter said.

"Why?" the lone female FBI agent asked. The tone of her voice was a trifle too harsh for Alex's taste. Not only did Carpenter outrank her, therefore, she might have chosen a less confrontational tone, but it also implied that she and the rest of the team didn't like to be challenged.

"Alex, would you care to explain?" Carpenter said.

"Gladly. Gentlemen, and Madam, you should indeed search the two locations, but only *after* we give April Scott the phony telegram about Sweden wanting to base U.S. fighter aircraft there. The idea, previously agreed upon with MI-5, MI-6, Special Branch, the FBI, and the CIA, is to arrest Lars Nilsson *after* Scott hands the SD card over to him. We would detain her for interrogation at the same time. If you make your search to seize her equipment too early, then April will know the jig is up and she'll inform Lars who will probably flee the country as fast as possible. Therefore, we will lose the chance to catch them in the act of espionage."

"Okay, that wasn't made clear to us," the senior agent replied.

"No problem, we're coordinating now," Alex said, "So, if you agree, let's talk to Anna Battles, our CIA Station Chief, and find out if she's already drafted the bogus telegram we'll give to April. If so, then let's get *that* operation going first. Furthermore, either Special Branch or MI-5 is presently following Lars Nilsson 24/7. If you want to get involved in following April Scott, you should coordinate that with the Brits."

"What do you suggest?" the female agent asked.

Alex was pleased she had asked his opinion and was impressed with her apparent willingness to consider options. "I suggest you let the Brits handle street surveillance of April Scott because they know the city and the surrounding area much better than you. However, you can join the Brits in their command center. That way it's a legitimate joint operation and you'll be a full partner."

Carpenter looked at the DC agents who all nodded in agreement.

"Okay then, please stand down from immediately executing the search warrants and I'll see Anna Battles about the phony telegram," Alex said.

ANNA HAD JUST FINISHED TYPING a minor revision from Bainbridge Wellington, which he believed would make the telegram look more authentic, when Alex walked in. She handed it to him while Carpenter read it over Alex's shoulder; they both agreed it looked like the real deal.

"Okay, it's time to bring our senior embassy information management officer into the loop. His name is Phil Blanchard. He's both highly skilled and a great guy to work with. Phil will have to scan our bogus telegram into the embassy communications computer, then send it only to April's electronic inbox. He's aware this operation must be kept absolutely confidential."

"It's that easy?" Carpenter asked.

"More or less, but I'd like both of you to accompany me to our communications center to add gravitas to our meeting." Battles and Carpenter agreed.

Phil Blanchard had successfully worked with RSOs for decades. He willingly accepted the task but suggested he also send copies to Wellington and Rachel because it would add to the telegram's authenticity, otherwise April might realize she was the only recipient.

Within a minute after Phil hit the "send" button, the phony telegram arrived in the computer inboxes of all three people. However, no one knew when April might open it. Now, Alex had to notify Special Branch, while Anna Battles contacted MI-5. Carpenter returned to his office after Alex promised he would tell him which British agency would handle the surveillance operation on April Scott.

~

AT MID-AFTERNOON, April returned to her office from the embassy cafeteria with a coffee and a yogurt. In the old days, she would have gotten a pastry, but now she was concerned with her appearance and was delighted she had already lost ten pounds before her wedding.

She sat at her desk, pivoting her chair so she could look out the window onto Upper Grosvenor Street. A light-to-moderate rain was falling. Because the overcast sky was blocking the sun, some of the vehicles had their lights on as they drove past the embassy building. She watched pedestrians fighting against gusts of wind to keep their umbrellas from turning inside-out.

Ah, more lovely British weather, she thought turning her chair back toward her desk. Spread out on top were newspaper clippings, and a stack of previous telegrams the embassy had sent. The first telegram seemed difficult to read and she glanced up at the ceiling lights, noting the one directly above her head had gone out. She reached across her desk and turned on the lamp. *Now, that's better,* she thought.

Rachel had tasked her to report on the growing anti-Semitism in the British Labour Party, and to spell out implications for Britain's Middle East policy, specifically focusing on Israeli-Palestinian issues. April felt this was a great assignment and looked forward to writing a series of telegrams on the subject. *I can also seek interviews with key British politicians,* she planned. April was impressed with Rachel's background as a press officer and her sophisticated grasp of important issues. While she had expected Rachel would be aware of these things, April had not anticipated her depth of knowledge. *Because Rachel's last position had been the*

Director of Italian and Maltese Affairs in the State Department, she thought, *perhaps I've underestimated Rachel's ability. In any event, I'm delighted to be working for her.*

Finishing her coffee and tossing her empty yogurt cup into the trash, she logged onto her classified computer and after it booted up, clicked on her in-box. The title of an incoming telegram from the US Embassy in Stockholm immediately caught her eye: **"Swedes request U.S. to base fighter planes in Sweden."**She quickly opened the email and read it. Not having served in Sweden nor being an expert on Swedish affairs, still she believed they had never asked for a foreign military presence to be located within Sweden. Coordination was one thing, but actually having NATO military forces on their soil was another matter entirely.

I've got to get this to Lars, she thought. She assumed Wellington or Rachel intended to discuss this with the British Foreign Office as soon as possible so, decided she would talk to them about it later.

She printed out a copy of the telegram and laid all four pages on her desk. Then she closed her door, took out the mobile phone that Lars had given her, and quickly photographed each page. After putting her mobile back into her purse, she walked down the hall within the political section and shredded the document. Now she had to call Lars to set up a meeting for tonight.

Overhead, the camera was catching all her actions.

33

THE STING

London

Towheaded Constable Jill Wainright leaned back in her chair, feet propped on her desk, when she heard her computer give off a loud sound. The telephone number at Lars Nilsson's office she was monitoring had just come to life. Snapping to attention, she dropped her feet to the floor. Displayed on her computer was an incoming call from a number at the American Embassy.

This could be it, she thought, holding her breath and listening carefully through her headphones. Although the call was being taped, Jill adjusted her headphones to ensure she caught every word as she scribbled notes.

"Hi Lars, it's April."

"Hello, darling. How are you?" he replied

"I'm fine. I was wondering if you're free tonight. I have something for you."

Whoa! That's a pretty obvious opening line, Jill thought. April sounded excited.

"Yes, I'm free in the evening. I'm looking forward to seeing you. Your place or mine?"

"I'd like to go someplace new and have heard of an excellent pub called the Royal Standard."

"I don't know it," Lars said.

"I don't either, but it was highly recommended to me. It's in Forty Green, between High Wycombe and Beaconsfield. You take the A355 exit off the M-40 to get to it. But I thought I'd meet you at your office; we can drive there in one car."

"What time did you have in mind?"

"How about six-thirty?" April suggested.

"Sorry, I'll be at an appointment in High Wycombe that probably won't end until around then. Let's meet at this Royal Standard Pub at seven. Is that okay."

"Sure. I'll see you there, darling."

When the line went dead, Jill called the Special Branch extension number she used for urgent situations.

"Inspector Jenson speaking," a deep voice answered.

"Hello sir. It's Constable Wainright. I have something very important for you to hear."

"Good to hear your voice, Blondie."

Damn it. He always calls me 'Blondie.' One of these days I'm going to report him, she thought. "Thank you, sir. I'm serious, this is urgent. You know what I'm working on."

"Of course. I'll come to your office immediately."

AFTER LISTENING TO THE CALL, Inspector Jenson made a copy of the tape and returned upstairs taking it directly to Commander Ray Penner's office. Both Alex and Carpenter were with him having driven over earlier from the embassy to discuss the espionage case. Jenson played the tape.

"Yes, that's April Scott's voice," Alex confirmed. "Before she called Nilsson, she's had time to digest our bogus telegram. I believe she'll try to pass it to him on an SD card tonight."

"I agree with Alex," Carpenter said.

"Do you know this pub . . . The Royal Standard?" Penner asked them.

"I do," Alex replied. "Rachel and I told April Scott about the pub last month and recommended it, but it's not easy to find."

"How many pubs can there be in a place called 'Forty Green?'" Carpenter asked.

"Only one, but the problem is *finding* Forty Green."

"Inspector Jenson," Commander Penner ordered, "alert the surveillance teams about the meeting, and have a team of heavies in place at the pub by half past six."

"Yes, sir." Jenson left the room.

Carpenter whispered one word to Alex. "Heavies?"

"I think he means big guys. Maybe rugby players, boxers, you know the type."

Walking out to his reception area, Penner returned with a cup of coffee. "Help yourself, if you'd like some." Alex and Carpenter both declined.

"You know, this may be the last arrest Special Branch makes," Penner said.

"You're referring to the upcoming merger with the Counterterrorism branch?" Alex said.

"Precisely."

"How many men have you put on this surveillance job?" Carpenter asked.

"Fourteen on Nilsson, six more on Scott. In the old days, we'd have twice as many for an espionage case, but we're already reassigning officers to other duties in anticipation of the merger."

"Alex, can you show me the location of this pub on a map?"

"Sure." He waited while Penner pulled a map out of a drawer

and handed it over. The map had a thirty-mile radius from central London.

"You're lucky," Alex said. "Forty Green is right here on the edge of the map, about 28 miles from London. On a weekend, it takes about forty-five minutes to get there. With rush hour approaching, it's anyone's guess."

Penner noted the grid reference and called Jenson to give coordinates to the surveillance teams.

"Now we wait," Penner said.

COLLEEN AND HARRY had been on surveillance duty for the past two hours. They sat together in a dark blue mini parked half a block west from the U.S. Embassy's garage exit on Upper Grosvenor Street. Colleen had figured that for April Scott to drive to Forty Green, she would have to pass by that location. They knew the type of car April drove and had her license plate number.

Colleen, a Metropolitan police sergeant, was 28 years old with a jumble of black curly hair and plain face that seemed to blend in with any crowd. She was also team leader and designated navigator with a natural sense of direction in addition to her police training.

Harry was a 26-year-old constable and an obsessive Arsenal football fan. He loved to be the driver when they were out on surveillance. His hair was short with a prematurely receding hairline.

Both were average in height and build. On this day, they wore blue jeans and untucked casual shirts although their attire could be spiffed up with blue blazers they had stored in the boot of the car. But that wasn't tonight.

At five-forty p.m., they spotted April pulling out of the

embassy garage onto Upper Grosvenor Street. They knew where she was headed, so there was no rush to stay too close behind her. In fact, two other teams were waiting for Colleen's direction. One was a block away on a cross street; a third team was waiting about a mile further down at Westbourne Terrace. Colleen figured that Westbourne was most likely the road April would take to gain access to the M-40 heading west toward Forty Green.

Leaving the garage, April turned onto Park Lane heading north, drove around the Marble Arch and followed the road directly onto Edgeware Road for a few blocks before turning west onto Sussex Gardens. Then after a few blocks, she headed north again on Westbourne Terrace. The third surveillance car saw her coming and pulled out in front, taking the only logical route. A small jog to the left down a short street, then back to the right onto Gloucester Terrace led directly onto the A-40 west overpass. After a few miles, the A-40 would change designation into the M-40, a larger motorway.

During the one-hour trip, all three surveillance cars took turns staying within eyesight of April Scott's white Ford Focus. Sometimes one car would pull ahead of her and the other two would fall back. Finally, April took the exit off the M40 onto the A355 at Beaconsfield.

Looking around, the town looked interesting. Colleen commented to Harry on the pubs, restaurants, shops, as well as pointing out an old church. There was even a train station with a direct line to London.

"I bet people who live here have buckets of money," Harry said, passing an area of mini-mansions with sprawling lawns and long driveways.

"For sure."

Then April slowed down, appearing to be uncertain. She slowly took a left down a country lane, eventually going through a very narrow area surrounded by tall bushes, and when she came out the other end, she drove a little further on before turning right into a parking lot. A sign next to the entrance read: The Royal Standard Pub of England. Not wanting to be spotted, Harry waited for over a minute before driving into the lot. Colleen radioed the team waiting inside the pub, alerting them that April had arrived. Then Harry parked near a large sign next to the walkway announcing that an establishment had been at this location for over 900 years.

The pub, itself, was gorgeous. Made of wood, it had a dark slate roof. Outside, there were clusters of chairs and tables with open umbrellas, all of which were filled with people enjoying themselves on a mild evening in late summer. The rain had ended hours ago and a clean smell lingered in the air.

Once Colleen and Harry walked inside, they saw dark wood ceiling beams everywhere, a few cozy small rooms that could accommodate groups of six to eight people, and much larger rooms with numerous tables filled the spaces. All the rooms had fireplaces that could be used during the cold winters. Many of the exterior windows had stained glass, several adorned with designs of ancient ships from the Middle-Ages, or with coats of arms.

"This is the finest pub I have ever seen, and I've been to quite a few," Harry said.

"Let's find our 'friend.'"

"I see her in the corner of the large room," Harry replied.

Colleen and Harry found an available table reasonably nearby. They took seats so both had a view of April's table and the empty chair opposite her. As they looked around, Colleen spotted the four "heavies" from Special Branch. The three men, all known to her, were over six feet tall with broad shoulders and barrel chests. Colleen knew the woman in their group as Tara. She was no slouch in the strong-body department. Colleen had watched her play on England's national rugby team and felt sorry for whoever got tackled by the powerfully built Tara.

All cops were wearing highly discreet earpieces with well-concealed microphones. None of them were armed unless their substantial biceps and fists were counted as weapons. April was apparently receiving a text because she was looking at her phone and typing. She left her jacket on the chair, stood up, and went to the bar to order. She came back with two glasses of red wine and two menus. Colleen and Harry didn't want to stand out, so he also went to the bar and ordered sparkling water with lemon for himself and orange juice for Colleen.

Five minutes later, Lars Nilsson arrived, and after a hug and a kiss from April, sat in the chair opposite her at the table. Colleen whispered into her microphone for the vehicular surveillance teams on Lars to stay in the parking lot but called the other four members of her team inside to distribute themselves around the rooms. That made a total of ten cops within the pub, more than enough to make an arrest. The six from Lars' surveillance teams in the parking lot would remain there as backup.

Lars went to the bar and ordered food, but the cops did not. Ten minutes later, as Lars and April were talking, smiling, and laughing, their appetizers were delivered to their table. Colleen noticed that Lars had ordered garlic prawns while April had fried calamari, based on the menu she had perused earlier.

"I'm famished," Harry said. "Since there's no prohibition against eating while doing surveillance, how about we order some grub?"

"Hmm, I guess we'll be less conspicuous if we do."

Harry went to the bar and ordered fish and chips for himself while Colleen had asked him to order roasted pork belly with vegetables for her. When Colleen looked around the room, she saw the 'heavies' had already ordered and were eating.

Halfway through her meal, Colleen pulled out her phone and texted Inspector Jenson to give him an update. She knew he would pass it on to Commander Penner. Fifteen minutes later, Lars and

April got their main courses of roast lamb shoulder and something that resembled a game pie.

Colleen would have given anything to be able to hear the conversation, but she could only observe Lars and April mouthing words, touching each other affectionately, and smiling a lot. Then she noticed that they became serious.

Colleen whispered into her microphone. "Attention all team members. We may have some action." She glanced at the other cops and saw them observing Lars and April without being obvious. Then she watched as April reached into her purse and took out what seemed to be a small item — the SD card, perhaps? April palmed it and reached over to squeeze Lars' hand. Immediately afterward, he put his hand into his jacket pocket, then returned his empty hand to the table. Two Special Branch team members had videotaped the exchange with their mobiles.

It was time.

"All teams in the pub," Colleen whispered on the surveillance microphone, "let's move in without fanfare and quietly escort them to the parking lot."

The heavies moved first, casually walking over to the table and standing in front of Lars and April, who looked up, concern registering on their faces. Then Colleen and Harry approached, and the heavies parted to make room.

"I'm with the Metropolitan Police," Colleen said to Lars sternly in a low voice while flashing her warrant card and badge. "Follow my orders and give me what you put into your right jacket pocket."

He hesitated while slowly looking at all six policemen. The biggest heavy was ominously cracking his knuckles. The guy next to him flexed his pecs a few times under a tight shirt.

"Let's do this without violence, Mr. Nilsson," Colleen said.

He reached into his pocket and took out the SD card, handing it to her. Colleen looked triumphant. "Lars Nilsson, you are under arrest for espionage." She quoted the relevant passage of British law then looked at April.

"We know you are an American diplomat, Miss Scott. However, we have the authority to detain you until such time as your ambassador may invoke diplomatic immunity. I'm ordering both of you to walk with us to the parking lot without resisting arrest, or you will be dealt with physically. Have I been clear?"

Lars and April were in shock; they looked up at the four bulky heavies and nodded.

"I want to emphasize, if you attempt to flee, we have more police officers outside who will *not* let that happen. Again, have I been clear?"

Again, they nodded and stood up. By this time, some of the crowd in the pub were staring at the scene. Colleen took a brief glance and decided this was an upscale neighborhood crowd who probably weren't going to cause trouble.

"Let's go," she said to the heavies, who led the way. Lars and April were surrounded closely by the cops as they walked through the inside crowd, then past the outside tables, and into the parking lot where they were both handcuffed. Colleen read them their rights under British law:

"You do not have to say anything. But it may harm your defense if you do not mention when questioned something which you later rely on in court. Anything you do say may be given as evidence."

Bundled into separate vehicles, they were driven back to the Paddington Green police station off of Edgeware Road, in London where high-value or high-risk prisoners were detained. The station had seen better days and was about to be closed in favor of using Belmarsh Prison in southeast London for suspects involved in espionage or terrorism. But, not tonight.

On the drive into the city, Colleen had called Inspector Jensen, speaking cryptically to report the arrest. He went to Commander Penner's office to inform him, Alex and Carpenter.

Roger Carpenter then called his fellow FBI agents to initiate the search of April Scott's residence and office.

Alex's alerted his deputies, Tom Lopez, and Frank Stevens, who all assisted the FBI. Then Alex used his mobile again to call Wellington and Rachel with a pre-arranged phrase to report the arrest.

Despite the success of the operation, it was a sad day for the State Department. Wellington had to send an urgent telegram to the Secretary of State updating him on events. Serious interrogations would begin the following day. Although Wellington could have demanded that the British Foreign Office not incarcerate April overnight, he chose to let her stew in jail.

Let her assess her own situation for a while, he thought. *Maybe she'll understand just what she's done to herself.*

34

AFTERMATH

Washington, DC

J im Riley was waiting in his office for Alex's call from London. He felt like shit; it was his worst physical day in years. His stomach was making acid reflux like a volcano, probably because he had gobbled down a late afternoon sandwich plus a huge sour pickle at his desk while waiting for the call. He also suffered from a stress headache, so he had been popping aspirin more than usual. As he daydreamed of better days while massaging his temples, his secure voice telephone rang. He inserted the encrypted activation key into the phone and answered.

"Riley speaking."

"Jim, it's Alex. We did it! The trap worked and they're both arrested. April Scott gave Nilsson an SD card with the phony telegram at the pub. Special Branch not only saw the exchange, but they got it on camera. Moreover, we caught Scott on videotape from the camera in her office photographing the fake telegram."

"That's terrific," Riley said, feeling invigorated. "Were you able to access the SD card to ensure the goods were really there?"

"Yes. She carried the encrypted phone in her purse, and Special Branch used it to open up the drive."

"They didn't need a password?"

"Oh, yeah, they did. But she had it written down on a piece of paper she carried with her. Apparently, she has no memory for passwords. So typical, right?"

Riley looked at his watch. It was 5:00 pm in Washington. He did the time zone conversation in his head. It was 10:00 p.m. in London "What else have you got?

"Wellington just sent an urgent 'eyes only' telegram to the Secretary of State, then followed up with a secure phone call.

"I'm in Wellington's office now with Rachel. Nilsson and Scott's interrogations will begin tomorrow morning at Paddington Green police station."

"Is the FBI cooperating?"

"Yes, completely. Furthermore, when they searched April Scott's apartment, they found a supply of SD cards, but all were empty. Unfortunately, the volume of evidence is not as plentiful as we wanted. When they searched her office, they came up with nothing. It seems the extent of her involvement was to take photos of documents and pass them on to Nilsson."

Without missing a beat, Riley said, "Ask your Embassy IT office to check their archive for a list of Scott's downloads of classified telegrams. It may not be accepted as evidence in court to prove espionage, but it could provide leverage during her interrogation."

"Okay, will do. Speaking of interrogations, the Brits are letting the FBI participate in questioning Scott, with one or more of the British agencies in the lead. Do you want me to be in the interrogation room as well?"

Riley thought about it for a minute. "I'll leave that to your discretion. Just remember, we want her cooperation. See how the interrogation goes before you decide. By the way, how is her mental state?"

"When I saw her being booked at the police station, she looked devastated. I think she's a psychological basket case. As for Nilsson, he seemed to be handling it better, but still looked stressed."

"Okay. I know you'll send telegrams to Washington as things develop but call me if you need advice or if something extraordinary occurs."

"Right, Jim. We'll probably talk tomorrow. Thanks for your support."

They hung up just as Riley's regular phone rang. He answered and immediately recognized the voice of the Secretary of State.

RILEY ARRIVED at Secretary Martin's office after the others were already seated and took a chair next to Archibald Watson. Across the conference table sat Under Secretary for Management Dennis Hager, and Deputy Secretary Summers. The State Department Legal Advisor, Jameson Henry, was at the end of the table and Secretary of State Charles Martin filled the final chair at the head of the table.

'For the benefit of the others, Jim, you should describe what just happened in London," Secretary Martin said.

During the next fifteen minutes, Riley covered the arrests in detail. The latest information was new to everyone except Secretary Martin. Archibald Watson and Jameson Henry had been aware of the general situation, while Summers had previously received detailed information on some points, but not everything. Under Secretary Hager had been left out of the loop and knew nothing about it at all.

"When was the last time you updated April Scott's security clearance?" Hager asked in a sharp tone.

"Four years ago; she was due for a regularly scheduled update this coming year," Riley replied. Hager grunted. Then Summers spoke. "I assume we'll want to prosecute her in the United States."

"That will be up to the Justice Department, but I believe your view is correct," Jameson Henry replied.

Riley respected Henry, who had only recently taken over the Legal Advisor's office as a political appointee in the new administration. Previously, he had been a partner in Secretary Charles Martin's former law firm on Wall Street, focusing on corporate mergers involving companies based in different countries. To say he was exceptionally bright was an understatement.

"Important issues include: First, whether she will cooperate, and secondly, how much she can actually tell us about Lars Nilsson and his espionage network," Riley said.

"Jim, do you think this Lars Nilsson is linked to the arrest or execution of the CIA spies in Moscow?" Henry asked. "I don't mean personally responsible, but could he be part of a larger network?"

"We need to establish, with absolute certainty, exactly who he is working for. It's probably the Russians, but just to be professional, we'll need to rule out the Swedes or even another third party. If he is, in fact, working for the Russians, it would be unprofessional for the SVR to involve him in separate espionage operations on two continents."

"Or even a third party?" Dennis Hager asked sarcastically.

Riley leaned on the table with both arms and stared at Hager. The moment lasted long enough to make others see the bad blood between them. "How many espionage cases have you brought to a prosecutor, Dennis? How many *spies* have you caught?"

Secretary Martin interrupted the exchange. "Your point is well taken, Jim. Let's move on. I agree with Jim that we might have a second spy ring operating either in Washington or in one of the other NATO counties. It's clear from the volume of highly sensitive information that has been passed to the Russians, as well as the arrests of our CIA operatives in Moscow, that our adversary has made one or more high-level penetrations beyond April Scott.

"Jim, I want you to stay on top of the interrogations, both through your RSO in London and with the FBI in Washington," Secretary Martin said. "Jameson, talk with the Justice Department to determine what their course of action will be. And Wakefield, contact the British Embassy to learn whatever you can. It may duplicate what Jim is finding out, but perhaps they'll have an additional perspective. Okay, everyone, that's it for now."

"Is there anything I can do for you, Mr. Secretary?" Hager asked.

"Not at this stage, Dennis, but thank you for volunteering." After everyone had left the office, it was time for Riley to lay his cards on the table. He told Secretary Martin that he wanted to talk to him about Dennis Hager. His gut told him that Hager was disloyal. Although he didn't have proof that Hager was a spy, he wanted to caution Martin about Hager's past. After all, Hager was the one participant who had been at nearly every meeting concerning the original leaks of CIA information, and arrests in Moscow. Why Hager had even been involved in those meetings was a mystery to Riley. He understood that Hager wanted to worm his way into everything that was important at the State Department.

After all, information is power, Riley thought. *Just why was it that others agreed to include him?*

The Secretary listened to Riley's suspicions of Hager, asked several pertinent questions, and thanked him for bringing it to his attention. Somewhat disappointed, Riley wondered why Secretary Martin wasn't more upset with Hager.

I hope I hadn't blundered in revealing my concern, Riley thought.

Then he returned to his office and called the FBI to coordinate on the Nilsson and Scott arrests. Afterward, he leaned back in his chair and reflected upon the situation.

Being Director of Diplomatic Security had given him immense satisfaction. He enjoyed operating at this high level. Yet, like Alex, in his heart he wanted to be back in the field, making a difference on the front lines of crises. Riley wanted to know more, wanted to be in London involved in the interrogations, but knew he had to wait until late tonight or tomorrow to get the next update from Alex.

Rising in the ranks soothes one's ego, he thought. *Yet, it can never replace the adrenalin rush, the thrill of being in the center of action.* How he envied Alex's position, and wished he could go back in time.

35

GETTING TO THE TRUTH

London

Assistant Commissioner Davies of New Scotland Yard had telephoned Alex at the American Embassy and asked if he would come to New Scotland Yard for a meeting with MI-5. The latter had been designated as the lead British agency in interrogating Lars Nilsson and April Scott. Davies also said he was inviting the FBI to the meeting. Moreover, he understood that the CIA would be accompanying MI-5. Naturally, it was late at night, but Alex had agreed, and now he sat, an hour later, waiting.

He rubbed both his red eyes with the palms of his hands and wished he had taken aspirin before he left the embassy. His body was sore, but not from exertion. He would have welcomed that. It was sore from hours of sitting, waiting, and mentally considering "what ifs" such as "what if this" and "what if that." He looked at his watch, it was nearly midnight.

Shit, when are these guys from MI-5 going to arrive?

The phone rang on the secretary's desk outside of Davies'

office and a young police constable answered it. Then she stuck her head into the office. "Sir, MI-5 is on their way up now."

"Thank you," Davies replied. "Gentlemen, last call for coffee."

"I'll pass," Ray Penner said. Alex had lost count of how many cups he had consumed during the day but figured it must have been double digits, so he passed as well. Moments later, Geoffrey Carver arrived with two of his colleagues, one a male, perhaps in his thirties, and the other a female about fifty years old. Also accompanying them was Anna Battles. The newcomers took seats. Assistant Director of MI-5 Carver, saw Alex and they exchanged nods. Then Carver began.

"First, an hour ago, the Foreign Office informed me that the American government has waived diplomatic immunity for Miss Scott," Carver stated. "So, she will remain in jail and be interrogated jointly by MI-5 and the FBI. Nilsson will also be interrogated by MI-5, but we'll work in partnership with the CIA and Special Branch on Nilsson. There will be a nightly meeting at MI-5 headquarters to share all information."

"Gerald," Carver addressed Davies directly, "we want Special Branch included in all of our discussions. The offer applies to you as well, Mr. Boyd. You may observe Scott's interrogations as you wish."

Roger Carpenter spoke. "Your plan is sensible, Geoffrey. But the US Justice Department is appealing to the White House to bring Scott back to the States."

"Roger, within the last hour, that appeal was rejected by the President," Anna Battles said. "She'll be interrogated here."

Through his tiredness, Alex realized the CIA had prevailed over Justice and the FBI in how to handle Scott. Upon reflection, he felt that outcome might result in a better chance to extract information from both Scott and Nilsson. Moreover, it would eliminate the FBI's ability to block the sharing of information about the results of Scott's interrogation by claiming, "It is an ongoing investigation and too sensitive to share."

Geoffrey Carver was ignoring the Americans' internal battle over Scott's diplomatic immunity and said, "One goal is to get Nilsson to unlock his mobile and his computer so we can examine the total contents of his hard drive. We also need to see what he has on those SD cards stored at his home.

"Secondly, we want to find out everything about how he interacts with his handler, as well as a comprehensive understanding of Nilsson's background and training. This latter point will take time, so, for now, we'll focus on access to his electronics.

"Mr. Boyd, we would appreciate if you could give us complete background information on April Scott - where she has served and what she did, her education, her former residences, all of it."

"I know the drill. You'll have her entire file tomorrow morning." Luckily, he had anticipated this, and yesterday had asked DS for this information. It had arrived electronically shortly after his request.

"Thank you," Carver replied. "We'll begin the interrogations at 0800 tomorrow morning at Paddington Green police station. Any questions?"

"Do you have a list of contact phone numbers for us in case we need to reach someone quickly?" Alex asked.

"I do." He nodded to one of his officers, who passed a list out to everyone in the room.

The meeting broke up, and Carpenter and Alex shared a taxi back to the embassy. Anna Battles stayed to talk with Geoffrey Carver.

~

ONCE BACK AT THE EMBASSY, Alex saw that Rachel had taken the Jaguar home, so he took a taxi to Knightsbridge. She was sleeping when he entered their bedroom at half past one in the morning. She stirred as he slipped into bed.

"How was your meeting?" Rachel sounded groggy. "Excellent, I'll tell you about it in the morning."

"Okay. By the way, I won't be your boss much longer."

"Why is that . . . job too challenging?"

She rolled over to face him and smiled. "No, the Senate will finally hold a hearing to appoint our new ambassador. He should arrive in about two weeks; I'll be returning to just being the political counselor."

"You're not *just* a political counselor, Rach. You're *the* political counselor . . . the best one *ever*."

"You're so sweet," she said, rolling back over.

Within seconds, Alex heard heavy breathing and knew she was out for the night. He held her in his arms and soon fell asleep.

AFTER A FEW LONG days of interrogation, April Scott began opening up. While she had no meaningful physical evidence to give the FBI, she did recall every document she had copied for Lars Nilsson. That meant Alex could work with Phil Blanchard in the Embassy communications office to retrieve the full text of each telegram. The majority of information dealt with either NATO's northern flank, military deployments in the Baltic Sea, or political issues involving Sweden directly. The rest concerned overall strategy in Europe vis-a-vis Russia. If April Scott was convicted, it was enough to put her in prison well into her old age.

Lars Nilsson, on the other hand, was doing a reasonably good job of withholding specific information from MI-5. He admitted to receiving classified documents from April, but said it was only for his personal use. Everyone knew that was ridiculous, yet he never admitted he was anything other than a Swede until the CIA finally provided proof that his Swedish records were created when he was a teenager. He then reluctantly spun a story that he was a Russian refugee, but not a spy. Again, the story lacked plausibility.

On another front, MI-6 notified SAPO, the Swedish intelligence service that they wanted Lars' phony parents arrested in order to put pressure on Lars to cooperate. Swedish lawyers interceded on behalf of the parents, and they were released from jail. A day later, they disappeared; it was assumed they had returned to Russia with false identity papers.

Over half of every day, Alex spent observing interrogations from behind a one-way glass mirror and kept Director Riley informed of the events in London. Riley briefed the Secretary of State and others in Washington.

Alex briefed his two deputies daily on what was happening while they held down the embassy office with routine duties. Occasionally, he would write a note to be given to the lead interrogator, suggesting a question to be asked or a line of inquiry to pursue. Anna Battles or someone from the CIA office did the same. Finally, pressure to give April Scott legal counsel could not be resisted any more, and she was granted access to a British attorney. It didn't change anything.

On the morning of the seventh day of interrogations, Alex attended a morning meeting at MI-5 to review progress and discuss the upcoming day's line of questioning. Everyone was frustrated with Nilsson's lack of cooperation, although the group was pleased that Scott had admitted to what she had done. Now, the issue was how to convince Nilsson to tell all. Alex had been thinking of an idea for the last two days which he now brought up.

"So far, we've treated Nilsson and Scott as separate interrogations. Sure, they're in the same police station, but we haven't allowed them to see each other for a week. I'm sure I'm not the only one who has observed their love for each other during periods of questioning." The others nodded their heads in agreement.

"April has told us everything she knows, but Nilsson is holding out," Alex said. "What if we tell April about Nilsson's hardline attitude and that she will face the full brunt of the criminal justice system if Nilsson fails to cooperate. Let's further imply that she may get thirty years in jail. Then, we let them see each other. If she mentions this to Nilsson, he may decide to cooperate, if he gets assurances that Scott will be treated with leniency. Or she might surprise us with other information if she begins to think he doesn't care about her. I think it's worth a try."

The room was quiet and Alex wondered if he had explained his plan clearly. Then a half dozen separate chats began happening. Geoffrey Carver got everyone's attention by knocking on the table.

"In MI-5, we were contemplating this approach. We've used this technique successfully in the past with terrorists and other spies. Roger, will the FBI agree to this?"

Carpenter and his Washington colleagues whispered together before he spoke up. "Yes, as Alex said, it's worth a try."

"Ray? Anna?" Carver queried both Penner and Battles. They both agreed.

"Right. Roger, I suggest your people work this idea into today's interrogation of Scott. Then, we'll allow them to eat lunch together and observe what they say. Let's regroup early in the afternoon."

LATER, upon entering one of the interrogation rooms for lunch, Lars was shocked to find April sitting there. Immediately they ran into each other's arms. Their escorts left the room and locked the door. Alex and the rest of the UK/US team watched through the one-way mirror in the adjoining room, listening to their conversation via microphones planted in the interrogation room. Alex felt uncomfortable intruding on their private moments, but they were spies, and certainly knew they were being observed.

Both cried and were reluctant to let go of each other. Finally, they sat apart and began talking, ignoring the food which had been placed on the table. April's emotions were working overtime as she sobbed every other minute, while Lars appeared more analytical, he even looked at the mirror several times, showing he was aware of the situation, and their presence behind the glass.

"Lars," April cried, "Who are you, *really*? I don't mean your Russian name. I mean, who are *you* as a *person*? One minute you were my lover, but have you *always* been a Russian spy? Did you care about me at *all*, or only when it was convenient? Did you understand that you turned me into a traitor against my own country?" April wiped tears from her eyes and waited for Lars to respond.

Finally, he lifted his head up. "April, I admit that in the beginning you were merely a target to be exploited. But that phase ended a long time ago. I began to love you more than you can imagine. You're the best thing that ever happened to me, and I'm so sorry you've been caught up in my spying. Now, I wish our relationship had only been a personal one, but that isn't possible anymore. Please, forgive me."

Finally, April revealed the threat of her long-term incarceration, if Lars didn't cooperate. He hung his head.

Was he angry, frustrated, or accepting the inevitability of their predicament, Alex wondered. He was certain when Lars reached over to touch her hands that he heard him whisper: "I won't let that happen to you, my love."

Alex looked at Ray Penner, who had a smile on his face and gave Alex a big fist pump.

~

By mid-afternoon, Lars Nilsson admitted that he was really Dimitri Vasiliev, and he agreed that he would confess to espionage on behalf of Russia. He further stated he was prepared to reveal everything he knew about his spy network, his original training in Russia, and his placement in Stockholm under his false identity. But his cooperation was contingent upon the British and American authorities going lightly on April Scott. He accepted that she would have to serve a period of time in prison, but demanded that she serve no more than five years, with the possibility of time off for good behavior. As a gesture of good faith, he gave them the passwords to his electronics.

The British deferred to the Americans on this demand regarding April Scott, and the FBI stated they would immediately ask the Justice Department for guidance. Lars was told it would take a few days before they could give him an answer. He appeared relieved, and accepted the delay.

Both MI-5 and MI-6 were keen to find out everything possible about both Lars' training and Russian efforts to integrate him into Swedish society before he had moved to England. To encourage cooperation during his prolonged debriefing, MI-5 decided to move both Lars and April to a safe house in the countryside. The Americans agreed with the Brits that a relaxed setting might help loosen Lars' tongue.

Alex noted a subtle change in phrasing from "interrogation" to "debriefing." Now that Lars was willing to cooperate, the atmosphere seemed to improve, and while security was still in place to prevent their escape, Lars and April were being treated more as partners than adversaries. Alex was told that he could visit the country site with an escort, the same applied to the FBI and CIA, but only under strict rules of security since this site was covert.

By early evening, Alex had informed Bainbridge Wellington and Rachel about the situation and sent a long "eyes-only" classified telegram to Riley outlining the new arrangements and the expectation of full cooperation from Lars Nilsson.

As for April, her role was now to support and encourage Lars since she had already confessed and revealed everything she knew about the spy business. Alex had been told that the safe house for the ongoing debriefings was in Gloucestershire, though he didn't know the exact location of this country retreat. Still, he included the information in the telegram to Riley.

With the day at an end, Alex locked his office, set the alarm, and headed upstairs to see Rachel. She had spent her workdays during the past week without him as he endured long hours watching the interrogations.

Tonight, however, they would enjoy a nice Indian meal at one of their favorite London restaurants, and probably have a few beers. Later, as he and Rachel savored Chicken Jalfrezi with a sauce of chili peppers, tomatoes, and onions, he guessed April would probably be eating British sausages and baked beans with a glass of water. Talk about inhumane treatment!

Although he expected life would return to normal soon, Alex couldn't help but feel sad over April's situation. Yet, he reminded himself about the old saying about "Don't count your chickens . . ."

36

ANOTHER TRAITOR

London

With British plans underway to transfer Lars and April to a safe house in the countryside, Alex was free to catch up on embassy work, yet his mind continued to dwell on something Anna Battles had said a few days prior.

"There is no way April Scott could have identified the CIA sources in Moscow working within the SVR," she had said.

So, if not April, then who? Was there another American traitor secretly reporting to the Russians? He tapped his fingers on the desk. *That spy couldn't be in London because even the London CIA station hadn't known their names. No leak could have possibly come from them.*

He thought about all the angles, other embassies, other scenarios. Then a realization dawned that he didn't want to admit. *As hard as it was to believe, there was only one other logical place where another traitor could have gotten information on who was spying in Russia. It could only have come from someone in Washington D.C.!* The thought tightened his stomach as he reached for the phone.

Throughout this ordeal, Jim Riley had suspected Under Secretary of State Dennis Hager. But there was no specific information linking Hager to espionage.

Just because Hager is a jerk, Alex thought, *and enormously hostile to Diplomatic Security, doesn't mean he's disloyal to the country. Nor does whomever it is have to be in the State Department.* Alex's next call was to Anna Battles.

"Good morning, Alex, what can I do for you?" Anna said pleasantly.

"I need to pick your brain on something, Anna, are you free now?"

"Sure, come on up."

A few minutes later, Alex arrived at her office, carrying one of his coffee mugs filled to the brim. He took a seat in front of her desk.

"Is that a U.S. Navy emblem on your mug?" she asked.

"It is . . .four years of active duty; still serving in the reserves . . . lieutenant commander."

"Ah, yes, I heard about your last deployment in Libya."

"Really, but I shouldn't be surprised. Even though the mission was top secret, you have sources everywhere. Who told you about the mission?"

"Your father," she smiled. Alex nearly spilled coffee on his lap.

"I remember you telling me you had worked for him on your first CIA assignment abroad and considered him a great mentor. Did he tell you about the mission *before* I arrived in London?"

"I can't disclose secret methods."

Alex smiled and sipped at his coffee. "I suppose my father wanted you to be nice to me." For a moment, Anna paused, taping a pen on a pad of paper, apparently considering her next words carefully.

"Actually, he did not. Jack assumed that I would find out about you being his son, and wanted to ensure that I treated you like any other regional security officer. He was confident that you'd more than meet the challenge without special consideration."

Alex's throat choked a little thinking about his father's confidence in him. He cleared it, and took another sip.

"Enough chit-chat, what did you want to talk about?" she asked.

"I've been wondering if we're in a better position now to identify where our other Russian spy is operating. I am *assuming* the spy is in Washington. It's the only other logical place from where your SVR operatives in Russia could have been identified. We'd be incredibly lucky if Nilsson has useful information in that regard, so we'll have to work this out for ourselves."

"You're right, Alex, I spoke with Langley yesterday, but they're convinced the spy is not within CIA. But to be honest, that's always the thought just before we find that the spy *is* within CIA. In the past, we've had bad experiences that have only proven we were not as bright as we thought. For that matter, I doubt the spy is even in the military or overseas, or in another allied intelligence service.

"I really think Jim Riley was onto something months ago. He suggested that the SVR and FSB figured out who our operatives were by the reporting pattern of the US traitor. Neither the Department of State nor the National Security Council had the names of our Russian spies, but they did know what secret Russian information was being passed on to us. That fact was reported back to Moscow by the American traitor. So, the Russians figured out who had the right access for that info in Moscow. In other words, the Russians were never told the names of our spies. They simply figured it out for themselves.

"I must say," she continued, "it's not helpful that the State Department refuses to authorize its own employees to take polygraph tests, unlike every other intelligence agency in Washington. That hinders us from ferreting out any spies among our ranks."

"I'm sure the State Department believes Foreign Service officers are 'gentlemen and ladies of impeccable moral fiber,' and would never be disloyal."

"Yeah, I get your sarcasm, buddy," she said. "I'll grant you that the polygraph test is only as good as the machine operator. But they're useful tools, even if the test isn't foolproof."

"Anna, do you know who at State has routine access to the highest levels of your classified information?"

"We know who was *briefed,* but not whether they shared that info with someone on their staff."

"So, who are we talking about?"

"Routinely, it's the secretary of state, the deputy secretary, and in this case, the assistant secretary for Europe. Maybe the director of the Bureau of Intelligence and Research, but that's about it."

'Didn't Deputy Secretary Wakefield Summers once work for the CIA?" Alex asked.

"I was told that, but never met him back then."

"That's because you were too young," Alex said.

"Ahh, Alex, your father cautioned me about your bullshit, and flattery. So, I'm not responding to that compliment. By the way, you better not be hitting on me."

"Are you kidding? And risk the wrath of our acting DCM? No way! And no offense, ma'am."

They both smiled. "But humor aside," he continued. "I was thinking that Assistant Secretary Watson has been in the job for years, yet the arrests of your spies only occurred this past year. Based on *that,* I think we can rule him out, not to mention that I know him very well, and he seems an extremely unlikely candidate to be a traitor.

"As for the secretary of state, I believe some of the arrests were made *before* the Senate approved his nomination. Therefore, the leaks occurred before he had access to those specific CIA briefings."

"That pretty much narrows it down to Deputy Secretary Wakefield Summers," Anna said. "What do you know about him?"

"Successful investment banker on Wall Street. I read that his father also worked on Wall Street, and had served in the Office of Strategic Services during World War Two. But that's all I know. Can you query Langley and find out more about Wakefield Summers' brief service in the CIA?"

"I should. In fact, I'll do that immediately. I have another idea as well. Summers is of your father's generation. Maybe your dad can give us some advice. The CIA was smaller back then, so he may have some inside info for us."

"I have his secure telephone number where he works for a company with contracts for the Agency," Alex said.

"I'll tell you what. It's too early in D.C. to call him now but come back at two o'clock this afternoon and we'll call him together. Let's see if he can remember anything."

ALEX STOPPED by Rachel's office to chat. When he entered her office, she was standing in front of the window looking over Grosvenor Square. He stopped to admire the view. Rachel's brown wavy hair flowed gracefully down to her shoulder blades, partially covering her white blouse. Her straight pencil blue skirt came down to her knees, revealing spectacularly shaped calves. High heels accentuated her height and brought her to stand slightly over six feet tall. She was an impressive figure.

"Hey, sweetheart, how's it going?" He asked.

She turned with a smile on her lips. "Everything's fine, I was just admiring the view."

"Me, too."

"*And* I was thinking of poor April," Rachel said. "She was a fine officer, and compromised her loyalty for love."

"She must have been desperate. I imagine she suffered from competing loyalties. Her emotional need to hold onto Lars must have overwhelmed her judgment."

"Aww, sometimes, you're more sensitive and insightful than I realize." Rachel said, walking over to Alex and hugging him.

"Are you free for lunch in about two hours?" Alex asked.

"Sorry, I have a lunch date with a woman at the Foreign Office."

"Your club or hers?"

She smiled at the thought that Alex liked to tease her about her so-called posh club. "Neither, we're going to a restaurant or a pub near her office."

"What does she do?"

"She's in charge of China affairs. Like me, she served in Beijing and Hong Kong a few years ago."

"Well, enjoy your lunch, Rach. Don't worry about me. I'll get some gruel in the embassy cafeteria."

"That sounds fair. You're not getting any sympathy from me." He kissed her before he left.

AT TWO O'CLOCK, Alex sat in front of Anna Battles as she dialed Jack Boyd's secure corporate office number. When he answered, she said, "Jack, its Anna Battles. How are you?"

"Anna! It's good to hear from you," Jack Boyd said. "Shouldn't you be having 'high tea' at the Ritz at this time of day?"

"I'm afraid that's only for the old folks and tourists."

"You're right. You're much too young for that."

Alex laughed out loud, and Anna had to chuckle. "Is that Alex I hear in the background?"

"It is. I'll put him on." As she handed Alex the phone, she whispered, "Like father, like son."

"Hey, Dad!" The two men spoke for a few minutes before getting down to business. "Dad, Anna and I want to pick your brain on something serious. Do you know anything at all about Deputy Secretary Wakefield Summers? He worked briefly for the CIA."

Anna handed Alex a slip of paper with Summers' work dates written on it. He mentioned the dates to his father.

"Since you said it was serious, son, I'll tell you what I know. But its second-hand information. You and Anna will need to confirm it."

"We understand completely. Go ahead."

"Summers worked in Buenos Aires following his initial CIA training. I was serving in the Middle East at the time, but when I got back to Langley, this is what I remember hearing in the corridors: He was a first tour case officer, considered pretty smart by most people. Apparently, his work performance was very good, but he was suspected of having a serious personal problem. He ended up resigning from the CIA at the end of his three-year overseas tour of duty in Argentina."

"What kind of problem?"

"Before I tell you, I want to emphasize that I can't confirm this information. In fact, Summers was allowed to resign *before* a full investigation was conducted."

"Understood. Go ahead."

"Okay. He was suspected of pedophilia."

"Oh, my god," Anna blurted out.

"How did that come up?" Alex's voice resonated Anna's shock.

"An Argentine woman came to the embassy to complain. She and her family lived in the same apartment building as Summers. She had two young children who she claimed Summers molested. Of course, the woman didn't know he was a CIA employee, but she did know he worked for the embassy. When she found out about what happened, one or two years *after* the alleged molestations occurred, she reported it to us immediately."

"What happened next, Dad?"

"I don't know all the details, but I imagine he was confronted by the Station Chief. I heard that Summers denied it, but before the embassy could do a thorough investigation, he resigned and returned to the States. Don't tell me you're investigating that old charge?"

"I wish it was that simple," Alex replied. "I can't tell you anymore right now, but you've been a big help." The three of them spoke for another few minutes before ending the call.

"I bet we're thinking the same thing," Anna said.

"Yes, that Summers was, indeed, a pedophile, and the Russians found out, then blackmailed him into spying for them."

"Correct. You know who else had a major presence in Buenos Aires back then?" Anna said. "It was the East German intelligence service, the Stasi. When East Germany collapsed in 1990, the Stasi turned over as many sources as they could to the KGB."

"Holy shit. Summers may have been working for either the Stasi or the Russians for decades," Alex said. "Didn't the CIA gain access to the Stasi records when the Berlin Wall came down? How about if you ask Langley to search Stasi-Argentine records concerning who they had recruited when Summers worked there?"

Anna agreed although she mentioned that the CIA should already have searched those records when Summers was nominated for the position of Deputy Secretary of State.

Alex stared at the piece of paper listing Summers' service dates in Buenos Aires. *I think that's when Hager had an affair with a West German woman in Buenos Aires during that same time. Coincidence, or false flag operation, to entrap Hager as well?*

"You know, Anna, I think Summers was there at the same time as Undersecretary Dennis Hager. We should confirm this. Even though it was decades ago, I wonder if our embassy in Buenos Aires still has a computerized record of where Summers and Hager both resided at the time. The embassy may have owned their apartments, or had them under a long-term lease. Perhaps they still have those units in inventory. Can you send a query through your channels to find that out?

"Isn't it easier for you to do that through State channels?"

"It is, but it's also easy for someone in embassy management in Buenos Aires to report back to Hager that we're making inquiries. I think it's better for your guys in BA to use some tradecraft and obtain the records. Also, in my experience, properties are often passed down to the same agency over the years. You might be able to confirm everything through CIA records alone. At least as far as Summers is concerned."

Anna leaned her elbows on the desk, putting her fingers together to form a tent while smiling.

"What?" Alex asked.

"I never realized that being a spook was an inherited gene. I've said it before . . . you're working for the wrong agency."

Alex shrugged with a smile. "I'm just asking the same questions any good ol' DS special agent would."

"I'll get back to you once I get replies from our station in Argentina and our headquarters in Langley."

"Thanks. It's always a pleasure doing business with you," Alex said as he prepared to leave.

Later, Alex began to wonder if Riley was right about his suspicions that Hager was a spy. While it was most unlikely for two officers in the US Embassy in Argentina to be spies at the same time, who could know for certain, unless it was investigated.

Well, boys, he thought, *We're doing it now.*

37

WHERE THERE IS SMOKE

London

Twenty-four hours later, Anna told Alex that not only had the CIA station in Buenos Aires identified where Wakefield Summers had lived but that Hager had also lived in the same apartment building. Their apartments were in the wealthy Palermo district, an upscale area often used for embassy housing. Interestingly, the original record check revealed that a West German businessman named Gunther Braun had lived in the same building.

After learning this, Anna Battles sent an urgent follow-up request to Langley to expedite their search of East German Stasi intelligence records. A few hours later, her diligence was rewarded.

"Thank God that the Stasi was as exacting as the Nazis in keeping detailed records," Anna told Alex.

"You would have thought they would have learned their lesson after World War II," he replied. "I guess attention to detail is a German trait. So, what did you find out?"

"Okay, get this: Gunther Braun, the man who lived in Wakefield Summers' building, was an alias. The guy's real name was Heinrich Schmidt, and he worked for the East German Stasi. Long before that, in the last year of World War II, he served in the German Army as an intelligence officer. He died of cancer eight years ago."

"Is there confirmation as to whom Schmidt recruited in Argentina?"

"I'm afraid that would be too easy. While we found his personnel file in the Stasi records, Heinrich Schmidt's operational reporting files are missing. My guess is that those records were turned over to the Russians when the Berlin Wall fell."

'Damnit! But at least we have something to go on. So, we have a communist spy, masquerading as a West German businessman, living in the same building as Summers and Hager. If Schmidt knew about the allegations of pedophilia against Summers, he may have blackmailed him into espionage."

"Yes," Anna said. "By the way, I forgot to ask Langley for any records linked to Dennis Hager. If I recall correctly, you said he had an affair with a West German woman. Her name was unknown. Right?"

"That's right. If she was also Stasi, then maybe she was being run by Schmidt."

"That's what I think. Why don't you tell Riley what we know about Summers and Schmidt, while l follow-up with Langley on Hager and the mystery German woman?"

"Consider it done. We also have an obligation to brief Roger Carpenter. A State Department/FBI official Agreement requires it, and I know that the CIA and FBI have a similar agreement."

"You're right," Anna replied. "I think you should wait here while I ask him to come up to my office."

Forty-five minutes later, Roger Carpenter's briefing from Anna and Alex ended. All the agencies were cooperating with the same information. Carpenter said he would notify FBI headquarters about Deputy Secretary Summers. Both Alex and Anna insisted that the FBI in Washington should touch base with DS Director Jim Riley to coordinate efforts.

Alex returned to his office and rather than sending a telegram to Riley, decided to call Riley on the secure phone. He wanted to ensure that only Riley controlled this information at State.

~

Washington, DC

AFTER RILEY FINISHED his call with Alex, he could have jumped for joy. The potential espionage link to Summers was totally unexpected, but the possibility that Under Secretary for Management Hager had been in the same spy ring made him ecstatic. He was going to nail that son-of-of-a-bitch! Riley contacted his counterparts at FBI and CIA to ensure everyone was in the loop.

By the next day, Riley's euphoria came crashing down to earth when the CIA reported they had completed their Stasi record check on Dennis Hager. He had indeed been approached decades earlier in Buenos Aires by a German woman named, Hannah Weber, who worked for the Stasi. After they had a brief affair, she reported to Berlin that Hager had no meaningful access to classified material as a junior management officer in the embassy. Moreover, his future looked bereft of any type of information the Stasi wanted. In addition, she reported that Hager's personality appeared to be unstable: He was too self-absorbed and lacked a moral compass that even a spy would need.

Therefore, considering the Stasi's recent successful recruitment of an unnamed CIA officer in Buenos Aires, Hannah Weber recommended they not pursue Hager in order to avoid potential exposure of their other operation. Stasi headquarters agreed.

That was it. No indication that Hager had ever passed on intelligence, and no specific confirmation by name of Wakefield Summers having been recruited.

Oh well, Riley thought, *at least the Stasi confirmed that they had recruited a CIA officer in Buenos Aires.* His only joy came from the fact that they thought Hager's personality had severe deficiencies. So did he.

It was time for Riley to brief Secretary of State Charles Martin. It was essential that he know Summers was suspected of pedophilia in Buenos Aires, and that a Stasi agent, Heinrich Schmidt, had lived in Summers' apartment building and may have had knowledge of these events. The Secretary also needed to be aware of the Stasi's negative assessment of Hager along with the reference to the Stasi's recruitment of a CIA officer.

Riley made the appointment for the briefing and made a point of telling Martin's secretary the information was only for the ears of Charles Martin.

~

FBI DIRECTOR HENSON WILLIAMS, sat in his large office on Pennsylvania Avenue and listened to the briefing by FBI Assistant Director for Counter-Intelligence, Walt Prager.

"Based upon what Jim Riley has told me, we need to catch Wakefield Summers in the act of passing on classified information," Prager said, "otherwise our prosecution case will be circumstantial and probably fail."

Director Williams was in total agreement. Years as a prosecutor and as a federal judge left him no doubt of the importance of physical evidence in the Summers case.

"How you will proceed, Walt?"

"We'll assign a few dozen agents to watch Summers. Right now, I have no idea how long this will take. Naturally, we're also following Russian embassy diplomats, so that may bear fruit if their paths cross with Summers. We'll be on the ground everywhere Summers goes. We'll have electronic intercept capability with the teams. And of course, we'll be photographing and recording everything. We already have warrants to bug his home and car. We're working with DS about his office. Trust me, we're on top of this. It isn't our first rodeo."

Williams smiled. "I know it isn't. I was the presiding judge on a few of your cases. I'm worried, however, that if this takes a long time, Summers will have access to a lot of classified information to pass on. We can't remove his access without tipping him off. Frankly, I'm uncomfortable with the situation."

"I agree, but it's the only way forward."

"Okay, Walt. Can you start the surveillance immediately?"

"Yes. If you approve this now, we can begin in two hours," Prager said. FBI Director Henson Williams looked at him approvingly.

"Do it. Let's nail his ass."

38

GOTCHA

Washington, D.C.

On the first day of surveillance, FBI electronic wizards sent a phony email to Summers' personal email account on his home computer. It was allegedly from a well-known foreign policy think tank and contained an attachment. When Summers opened it, the attachment secretly downloaded a program that captured every keystroke that Summers would make thereafter and would send that data to an FBI office for analysis.

It worked successfully, but Summers' transmissions were innocuous. His office computer was even easier to deal with since everything ran through State Department servers and State was cooperating. The FBI was able to monitor all his cell phone and landline calls as well.

The following week of FBI surveillance on Deputy Secretary Wakefield Summers was without success. He maintained a normal schedule of leaving home at 7:30 a.m. for the State Department, driven by a government chauffeur, and if he didn't return directly home at the end of the workday, it was because he had a diplomatic reception to attend. It was, of course, always possible that he could have passed on information to a Russian contact during these receptions, but the FBI sat in their vehicles outside the two receptions he attended, and did not spot any guests or vehicles from the Russian embassy.

During this period, Alex was kept in the loop by talking with Jim Riley on secure voice calls, as well as meeting with Roger Carpenter at the FBI office in the embassy. But it was frustrating for Alex to just sit and wait. He felt the FBI was doing everything right, but it all depended upon Wakefield Summers inadvertently making a mistake. The guy was smart and had possibly been a spy for a long time. Nevertheless, he hoped the FBI was on top of the situation.

ON A SATURDAY EIGHT DAYS LATER, the FBI hit the jackpot. At midmorning, Summers drove himself in his Mercedes S class sedan to a nearby racquet and tennis club in Bethesda, Maryland. The FBI, in cooperation with Diplomatic Security, was aware of his usual Saturday morning squash game and had inserted several agents into the club as potential new members. All were dressed casually to blend in. However, nothing unusual occurred at the club.

After completing his match against his regular partner, Summers showered at the club, dressed, and drove to a local Starbucks. Summers entered the coffee shop carrying his personal laptop in a black leather soft briefcase. After collecting a latte, he walked over to a corner table, opened his computer, and started surfing.

All of his keystrokes were being monitored by an FBI technical support officer sitting in an SUV parked in front of the coffee shop.

Inside, six undercover FBI agents were dispersed in pairs around the room to observe Summers. The busy room had other customers, many working on their laptops. After ten minutes, Summers stopped surfing and begin typing a long document. The technical FBI support officer in the SUV immediately noted this on his monitor since every line Summers had typed became visible to the FBI officer.

Jim Radford, the FBI supervisor of the surveillance detail, sat in the back seat of the SUV and watched the monitoring screen. He picked up on Summers' handiwork.

"Radford to all agents," he spoke into the hidden surveillance microphone under his windbreaker lapel. "Look for a Russian embassy vehicle or embassy official in or near the coffee shop. They should have a laptop or cellphone in plain view."

Agent Radford was concerned that Summers might be using a modern espionage technique in which he didn't have to use the internet to send a message to another addressee. The Russians had equipped their foreign spies and SVR agents with a computer program that would transmit documents over very short range, perhaps 100 feet, as long as they had a line of sight. This was, of course, exactly what the FBI was doing in picking up Summers' typing.

Agent Radford watched the computer monitor in the vehicle as Summers typed a document about US and British secret diplomatic plans to counter Russian political or military attempts to reclaim territories from the former Warsaw Pact satellite territories, such as the Baltics or Ukraine.

"Agent Johnson to Radford, I've spotted a female Ruskie. She's at the back of the Starbucks sitting by herself with her laptop open." Earlier, FBI Special Agent Emily Johnson had entered the coffee shop with another agent and now whispered into her concealed microphone.

"Why do you think she's Russian?" Radford asked.

"I recognize her. She's that Petrov woman who works at the Russian Embassy and lives here," Johnson answered.

"Okay, all agents hold your position," Radford ordered.

Summers typed for twenty more minutes. Then waited while he re-read what he had typed and finally he hit the delete key for the entire document. It didn't matter because the FBI had captured everything on their computer. Summers leaned back in his chair and savored the last drop of his latte.

Meanwhile, Ludmilla Petrov closed her laptop, stood up, threw her coffee cup into the trash can and walked out of the Starbucks, headed toward a Metro station on Wisconsin Ave. Four FBI agents, two on each side of the street, followed her on foot, while two SUVs hung back with FBI agents until instructed to close the gap.

Agent Radford was frantically working the phone to get FBI headquarters' approval for the arrests. Permission took only one minute because the chain of command, operating in a joint counterintelligence center at FBI headquarters, had been awaiting this breakthrough all week.

"Radford to team Alfa, arrest Ludmilla Petrov immediately."

Team Alfa was comprised of the four agents following her on the street. As the order was received, they moved in, identified themselves, handcuffed her, and took her laptop. Petrov challenged them verbally, but did not physically resist. The two SUV's sped toward the group, and FBI agents bundled her into the back seat of one and drove to FBI headquarters for interrogation. The FBI knew she would declare diplomatic immunity, refuse to talk, and the State Department would soon be forced to confirm her immunity.

By that time, however, the FBI would have had an opportunity to attempt to clone her hard drive and see what other documents she might have. They hoped they could break her password encryption to do this, although, at least, they already had Summers' document in hand from Starbucks.

"Radford to team Bravo, arrest Summers when he leaves the Starbucks."

Summers strolled out of the coffee shop, looking very satisfied with himself, but as he turned toward his car, a gaggle of FBI agents surrounded him.

"You are under arrest for espionage, you have the right to remain silent . . ." Agent Springfield finished reading him his rights as other agents put him in handcuffs. He was taken to FBI headquarters.

Summers had no diplomatic immunity such as Ludmilla Petrov. He was merely a man who had committed treason against his own country.

39

FRIENDLY COLLABORATION

Washington DC

The interrogation of Ludmilla Petrov, as expected, was not successful. She refused to talk, except to say she had diplomatic immunity and demanded that the Russian Embassy be contacted. Six hours later, she was released after the State Department confirmed she did, indeed, have immunity. Her husband, Nickolai Petrov, picked her up and they drove home with the FBI following behind them. The next day, the State Department informed the Russian Embassy that both the Petrovs were declared 'persona non-grata.' Within the next forty-eight hours, they were expelled from the United States.

Wakefield Summers' interrogation was entirely different. At first, he objected to his arrest, stating he had done nothing wrong. Within minutes, the FBI showed him the electronic intercept of his communication to Ludmilla Petrov. He looked nervous. As the hours passed, additional deleted documents were uncovered on his laptop, each one appearing to be highly classified assessments of U.S. policy toward Russia.

"I guess you never realized that nothing is totally deleted from a person's computer," said FBI agent Harry Anderson, the lead interrogator. "It's only a matter of how many layers down we have to dig to uncover what's been typed. "You're going to be charged with so many counts of espionage and treason that you'll *never* get out of prison."

Summers looked stunned. He rubbed his hands over his face and took a deep breath. "I want to see my lawyer."

"As I said earlier, that's being arranged. Unfortunately, it's the weekend, and perhaps he's tied up for the moment. I'm sure he'll eventually respond to our calls."

"Listen, Agent Anderson," Summers said, "what you've seen are just drafts that I intended to transfer to my State Department computer. When I get an idea, I want to put it down in writing without having to go into the office."

"Good luck with that argument. I suppose it was a coincidence that we arrested a Russian Embassy SVR officer just after she left the same Starbucks where you typed today's document?"

"I don't control where the Russians buy their coffee."

"Cut the crap, Summers. When your lawyer gets here, I'm sure he or she will tell you that you're better off cooperating with us than spinning a ridiculous story."

"I'll wait for my lawyer."

TWO DAYS LATER, at the Monday morning courthouse hearing, Summers was refused bail by the judge and ordered to be held until his trial. Later that day, after considerable discussion with his lawyer, Summers surprised the FBI by agreeing to cooperate. Again, lead Special Agent Harry Anderson did most of the questioning, but was assisted by Diplomatic Security Special Agent Greta Jones, who had once been the senior regional security officer at the U.S. Embassy in Moscow. She was currently Chief of the DS Counter-Intelligence Office. Jones was in her mid-forties, and spoke good Russian and German.

Anderson's questions about current espionage activity were answered honestly by Summers upon advice from his lawyer present. He admitted he had used either the coffee shop or a library several times to pass information. He also explained his use of dead-drops when he needed to exchange SD cards filled with classified conversations or documents, and he outlined his use of the Nagra ID cards to record conversations. What was missing in the interrogation was his motivation. During a break, Greta Jones got permission from Anderson to lead the next round of questioning.

"Let's cover a different area in our chat," Jones said to Summers. "I want to know when you first decided to support Russia against America. What was your motivation? I'm trying to understand this from your perspective. As a wealthy man, you certainly didn't do this for money."

Summers whispered with his lawyer for a few seconds while Jones and Anderson waited. Then he began. "I started questioning the traditional values of American society at a young age. I was still in high school when I became aware of the poverty in the cities. I grew up on the Upper East Side in New York City, so we lived in luxury, but I could see the endemic crime and lack of opportunities in other parts of the city. I'd have long conversations with my parents about how to solve these problems."

"Your parents? Tell me about their views."

Greta Jones couldn't believe where this discussion was going because Summers sounded like a naïve high schooler, not a well-educated man who had succeeded on Wall Street.

"My father loved to earn money, but he donated a lot to charity. He told me that his own political views had been formed during the Second World War. He had served in the OSS, the

Office of Strategic Services, which was the forerunner of the CIA. His mission was to parachute into Yugoslavia and establish links with Tito's partisans in order to fight the Germans, who had occupied parts of their country. I guess my father was always a liberal, but once he hooked up with Tito's partisans to supply weapons and training, he learned about communism and it changed him."

"And when you discussed how to solve America's problems with your father, did you accept his communist views?"

"I did."

"You went to the University of California at Berkeley, correct?"

"That's right, I did." There was a pause, so he continued. "I selected it because it was very left-wing, and still is."

"Were you active in left-wing groups and causes in school?"

"I was, although I never officially joined any of the groups."

"Which groups?"

"The Communist Party USA and the Students for a Democratic Society. You might know them as the SDS."

"You said that you didn't officially join these groups. Is that because you were smart enough back then *not* to leave a paper trail on your political views?"

He hesitated for a moment. "I'm embarrassed to say that, yes, I was reluctant because I knew I wanted to work in government, or on Wall Street, and I thought that wouldn't happen if people knew I was a communist."

"Your file says that you majored in Economics and Business Administration. That sounds pretty middle-of-road politically."

He shrugged. "You can't change the system unless you understand how wealth is created. Besides, I figured if I could earn a lot of money, then I could donate a considerable amount to progressive causes and influence the direction of our country."

"So, when did you actually start working for the Russians?"

"It didn't begin with the Russians. I was recruited in Argentina by the East Germans. I would prefer not to say how that happened."

"Don't worry, Mr. Summers, we know about it," Greta Jones replied.

"How could you?"

She stared at him for a full ten seconds; he didn't say anything. Finally, she said one word: "Pedophilia."

Summer hung his head and rubbed both hands on his face before he looked up and continued. "It wasn't true, but that didn't matter. I looked guilty." Jones and Anderson exchanged a quick glance of disbelief. "In any event, I was approached by an East German man, a Stasi agent, who blackmailed me."

"You mean Gunther Braun. By the way, his real name was Heinrich Schmidt."

"Jesus, you know about *him*?"

"Of course, that's why we're Diplomatic Security."

Agent Harry Anderson looked at Greta Jones and gave a quick smile. She saw it, glad that he appreciated her competitive inter-agency sense of humor.

"How long did you spy for Braun?" She asked.

"About two years. Then the mother of the kids in the pedophilia allegation came to the embassy to report me, and I decided to resign. There was no way I would be trusted after that, and I didn't want the CIA to uncover my link to the Stasi."

Harry Anderson cleared his throat, signaling he wanted to take over the interrogation. Greta Jones leaned back in her chair to observe.

"Did you continue to spy over the years?"

"No, I returned to New York, got my MBA, and then worked on Wall Street for the next thirty years. I was never contacted by the East Germans or the Russians *until* I was nominated to be the Deputy Secretary of State. Of course, by that time, East Germany had collapsed and no longer existed. But the Russians never tried to reactivate me in the interim. Well, that's not entirely accurate. In the private sector, I joined several foreign policy organizations and served on a few committees. Occasionally, at meetings or receptions, I would run into Russian diplomats from their consulate in New York, or from their Mission to the UN. But, I swear, they never pitched me to spy for them. They only sought my opinions on various issues."

The interrogation continued for several hours, every day. At the end of each session, the FBI, DS, and the CIA compared notes and agreed on the next day's line of inquiry. Greta Jones reported back to Director Jim Riley every evening and Riley called Alex in London the next morning to keep him up to date.

Alex, in turn, briefed Bainbridge Wellington and Rachel on events, while Anna Battles and Roger Carpenter got their updates directly from their headquarters. The question, however, was what would the Russians do next?

40

RUSSIAN RESPONSE

Moscow

A week had passed since Lars and April were arrested at the Royal Standard Pub outside of London. Since Lars did not have a rigid schedule for contacting his SVR handler, his absence wasn't noticed in Moscow until Jim Riley shared Alex Boyd's telegram with Wakefield Summers. Summers then used a dead drop to inform Nickolai Petrov, his contact, an SVR operative in the Russian Embassy in Washington, D.C. Shortly thereafter, Summers, himself, was arrested by the FBI.

Moscow was shocked to learn that Lars Nilsson had decided to cooperate with the Brits and Americans. Now Russian wheels were being set in motion. Something needed to happen to Lars Nilsson. Wakefield Summers was another matter entirely. He would be missed, but the Russians decided not to tackle that situation at the moment.

For years, SVR Director of the Foreign Intelligence Service, Anton Kuznetsov had been in charge of Russia's overseas spy agency. Now, Summers arrest reflected badly on him after having served his country in covert capacities for over thirty years. Kuznetsov appeared polished, unlike some of his predecessors who had mostly looked like the Hollywood stereotype of a Slavic roughneck. No, Kuznetsov's facial features could blend in with a number of western countries, and his attire was typical of prominent businessmen throughout Europe. Despite his façade, opponents underestimated his ruthlessness . . . at their own peril.

Kuznetsov had personally ordered the execution of a few SVR traitors while they were living in the United Kingdom. But those killings had been carried out carefully through the use of poison or radioactive material, giving his killers an opportunity to escape. But now he faced a totally different situation, and he didn't like it.

"How was your meeting with President Putin?" Ilya Sokolov asked, as SVR Assistant Director of Operations. "Did he agree to wait before eliminating Nilsson?"

"No, he did not. Between us, Ilya, Putin is out of control. He's obsessed these days with traitors; he demands quick and vicious retaliation. I'm afraid subtlety is no longer in fashion."

"I wouldn't say that too loudly, Anton."

Kuznetsov crossed his arms and leaned back in his chair realizing he had made a mistake by saying this openly in his office. After all, even he couldn't be certain that Putin had not ordered the FSB, Russia's domestic spy agency, to bug his office. The only comrade he trusted was his deputy, Sokolov, but few others. *Not even Ilya always. I must be more careful.*

"President Putin wants the immediate execution of the traitor Nilsson. His cover is now destroyed, and according to Summers in the State Department before his arrest, Nilsson is cooperating with the British and the Americans."

Deputy Sokolov was an SVR veteran of many years, but unlike Kuznetsov, who was the face of the modern authoritarian state, Sokolov was a throwback to an earlier age when some in Russian intelligence looked like thugs. His face was flat, his nose had been broken much earlier in life, and reset badly; his prominent forehead made his features ideal for use in a museum to replicate a Neanderthal. He, however, was highly skilled in the black arts of espionage, and possessed a determination to accomplish whatever task he was given.

"I understand that Nilsson must be killed because Putin has ordered it," he said to Kuznetsov. "But if we cannot wait to carefully plan his assassination, how can we do it *and* get away successfully?"

"I asked that specific question to Putin," Kuznetsov answered. "His response was that it was our problem. He doesn't care if the British know we are responsible for killing Nilsson. Putin's concern is to send a powerful message to other spies that *death* is the consequence of cooperation with the enemy."

"Okay, but to begin with, where do we find Nilsson?"

"We are in luck. As I have said, we only found out about Nilsson's arrest through our Washington source. Luckily, he also saw a report from the American Embassy in London that Nilsson is being moved to Gloucestershire for long-term interrogation." Sokolov smiled.

"Excellent. Based on what we know, that narrows possible targets to three houses."

"Exactly. I have asked Putin to order satellite coverage of those targets; he has agreed. If we can observe activity at one house consistent with an operational UK government safe house, then that's our target. You should pick your assassins immediately; devise a plan to kill Nilsson as quickly as possible."

"I'll treat it as an urgent wartime mission. I will try for our men to safely get away."

"Let me know when they are ready to deploy."

"When the satellites identify the precise target, we will strike," Sokolov said.

~

SERGEI AND VIKTOR were chosen to kill Nilsson. Both were sergeants in an ultra-elite unit of the Russian army, called *Spetsnaz*. Technically, Spetsnaz belonged to the GRU, or army intelligence. In terms of training, they were equivalent to US Army Special Forces, Army Rangers, or Navy SEALs. Men like Sergei and Viktor were frequently loaned out to the SVR if they spoke foreign languages. In their case, both spoke passable English and fluent Lithuanian.

They would enter the UK as Lithuanian tourists with passports and supporting documents such as credit cards and drivers' licenses. Much to their disappointment, however, they would not be carrying any weapons. The plan was for them to acquire what they needed *after* their arrival in the UK, but because of the exhaustive training with Spetsnaz, they were also comfortable with improvisation.

Within three days of their selection, Russian intelligence had pinpointed the house in Gloucestershire where Nilsson was likely being kept based upon the number of cars that visited daily. The specific house was also chosen because of electronic interceptions from police radio transmissions.

"Look here, Viktor," Sergei said in Moscow as they poured over satellite imagines of the targeted large manor house.

"It is located off a main road and surrounded by some forest. I think we can approach through the trees and get reasonably close to the building."

"I agree. We can park on this secondary road, and once the job is done, quickly drive back to Heathrow. What do you think, nighttime or daytime attack?"

Sergei rubbed his chin and thought for a moment. "Either way, he'll be guarded. I'm not sure the time matters in terms of the number of guards on duty. But at night, there should be fewer people on the grounds overall."

"True. But if we strike at midday, there will be plenty of flights out of the country, either that afternoon or early evening. If we attack late at night, we may have to wait until morning for a flight. That will give British police more time to look for us." "Agreed. So, let's forget about entering through the trees,"

Viktor said. "Let's get a van and pretend to be workmen. We can drive up to the front door. It will be less suspicious. Besides, the wooded area around the house probably has ground sensors that will alert the guards." They both agreed upon the plan and informed their superiors.

TWO DAYS LATER, their plane from Vilnius, Lithuania, touched down at Heathrow Airport. Sergei and Viktor had no problem getting through British customs and immigration with their authentic Lithuanian passports. They each carried tour books and maps of several areas in southern England to support their cover story of being tourists and answered cursory immigration control questions without trouble.

To mask their level of physical fitness and muscles, they wore loose-fitting clothes, and since each was under six feet tall, they didn't particularly stand out among other travelers. Furthermore, because of their assignment in the elite Spetsnaz unit, they had already been allowed to grow their hair longer than regular Russian military personnel.

Once through airport controls, they took an express train into town and went to a modestly priced hotel near Paddington Station in the West End. After checking in, they went directly to a hardware store which they had found online before leaving Moscow.

At the "do-it yourself" store, they bought khaki coveralls that workmen wore, and which would keep blood splatter off their own clothes when they killed Lars Nilsson. They also picked up fully equipped tool belts and work shoes to look the part. Finally, they carefully selected sharp knives that would be their primary weapons for this assignment. Tomorrow they would rent a white van necessary to complete their cover story.

41

PLACES EVERYONE

Gloucestershire

The next morning, Sergei navigated while Viktor drove the white van. They had both been to the UK before, but neither was familiar with Gloucestershire nor Oxfordshire, so the road system was new to them. Besides, they were not fully comfortable driving on the left side of the road.

Earlier, they had made the mistake of driving into the city of Oxford, rather than taking the bypass road. But they finally managed to figure out the quickest way west from the City Centre.

Now it was mid-day, and their drive on the A40 took them to the charming village of Burford, known for its honey-colored limestone buildings, shops, and variety of restaurants.

"Let's have lunch, find a place for the night, and get a fresh start in the morning," Sergei said.

"I agree. That will also give us time to find a better route back to Heathrow. I'll be damned if I will be caught in Oxford traffic again after we pay a visit to Nilsson."

They found a pub on Burford's High Street that had an

upstairs bedroom available with twin beds. By sharing a room, they could pocket the extra money the SVR had allotted for two hotel rooms. After checking in, they went in search of food. Neither man had a sophisticated pallet, so they settled on pizzas and beers from a restaurant down the street.

Afterward, they browsed clothing shops like any tourists, not because they were enamored with British fashion. Any purchases they made would be useful on future trips to the West, enabling them to blend in. Sergei bought a tattersall shirt and pair of tan corduroy pants; Viktor found a lightweight Barbour jacket, the iconic image of the British country squire.

Then they returned to their room to study maps and GPS coordinates on their phones. Tomorrow was the big day and they couldn't make any more mistakes.

IN LONDON THE PREVIOUS AFTERNOON, Commander Ray Penner had called Alex at his office to urgently talk with him and Rachel. He offered to come to the American Embassy. Alex had agreed.

Arriving fifteen minutes later, Penner came directly to the point. "We're very worried about April Scott's mental condition. Special Branch had a psychiatrist talk with her and he fears she may be suicidal."

"What?" Rachel exclaimed. "But she's being held with Lars. They're together again. What did she say to make the shrink think she's suicidal?"

"It wasn't one specific thing. Rather, it's her overall attitude. We believe she realizes she'll be going to jail for years following the debriefing and a trial. She repeatedly mentioned that her career is over, her life is ruined, and her reputation disgraced."

"Geez, she should have thought about that earlier," Alex said, "but okay, how can we help?"

"We wondered if both of you could come to the safe house and talk to her. April has said several times how much she respects you, Rachel. If you could reassure her that her life is not in tatters, without promising anything concrete about her sentencing, she might be in a better mindset to support Nilsson."

"Of course, we'll come," Rachel replied.

"Excellent. Here's the plan. Drive to Chipping Campden, I believe you know where that is, correct?"

"Yes, we do," Alex said.

"We've already made a room reservation for you tonight at the Cotswolds House Hotel on the High Street."

"Whoa, that was very confident of you, Ray," Alex said. "That's why we're called Special Branch, instead of the Ordinary Branch."

Alex smiled. "Okay, go on. What happens next?"

"Tomorrow morning, one of my officers, Inspector Josh Rosen, will pick you up at 9:00 a.m. and take you to the safe house. It's more than a safe house, it's actually a manor house with extensive grounds. We'd like you to spend as much time as possible with April. If it takes more than a day, we'll continue to pick up the tab at the hotel for you."

"Okay, consider it done," Rachel replied. "We'll inform DCM Wellington now and then go home to pack our bags."

"Excellent . . . and thank you. Enjoy your evening in Chipping Campden." Penner left and they went to see Wellington, who agreed they should help out April and, of course, the Brits.

It was Alex who suggested they arm wrestle to determine who would drive the Jaguar to Chipping Campden, but Rachel would have none of that. She smiled and reminded him that even though they were the same grade in the Foreign Service, she was *still* the acting deputy chief of mission for one more week, so she playfully pulled rank.

"All right, but I drive home when the task is done," Alex said as if it was a compromise.During the two-hour drive, he watched

Rachel enjoying the thrill of shifting gears, tapping the steering wheel in sync with car radio music, and moving her body to the rhythm of the songs. Occasionally, she glanced at him through her large aviator sunglasses and smiled.

Luckiest man on earth, he told himself.

Arriving at Chipping Campden, Rachel drove down a lane behind the hotel and found the free parking area for hotel guests. They carried their weekend leather bags into the lobby, registered, and walked up one flight of stairs to a spacious room overlooking the High Street in front of the hotel. Their room had a king-size bed to the right and a large desk and chair to the left. The closet was surprisingly large, and the bathroom had a bathtub with a shower. It was perfect, as expected from one of the best hotels in town.

"It's only 5:00 p.m.," Rachel said, "let's explore the village before the shops close."

They visited a deli, and two women's clothing stores. They noticed a pharmacy, a small food market, a butcher, and a few restaurants and pubs, as well as other hotels. All were located on the magnificent High Street.

"Time for a drink," Alex suggested. They walked into the bar of the Noel Arms Hotel, directly across the street from their own hotel, and ordered two lagers on tap. The pub had a beamed ceiling, large fireplace opposite the bar and tables spread around the large room.

"This village is charming, so much beautiful stone architecture," Rachel said, as they claimed the last available table in the room.

"I could live in this village, forever," Alex replied. "Really?" she replied.

"I think I could. It's got most of what we need, and there are so many other villages in the area, not to mention Oxford isn't that far. What more could we want?"

An attractive British couple sitting next to them had overheard Alex and Rachel's comments. The man leaned their way and said, "It *is* a wonderful village, is it not? My wife and I come here often. By the way, we're Grant and Anne Keen."

Alex and Rachel introduced themselves, and Alex noticed a large golden dog sitting behind the couple. "What kind of dog is that?"

"It's a labradoodle. He's ten years old." Aware of some attention coming his way, the dog stood up and walked over to Alex, resting his head on Alex's knee. As Alex scratched the dog behind his ears, the animal leaned against Alex's leg. After that, a friendship was established, not only with the dog, but between the couples.

Alex and Rachel sipped their drinks, talked with Grant and Ann at length, and learned about living in the Cotswolds. The couple was well-traveled and, earlier in their lives, had even lived in Thailand for a decade. Finally, the Keens had to leave, but not before they exchanged contact information.

"What about dinner?" Rachel asked Alex. "Do you want to eat here in the Noel Arms? They have a separate dining room."

"Let's explore another place," Alex replied. "I read about an inn called the Eight Bells. It's just down the street."

They easily found the Eight Bells some two blocks away, and took seats at a table adjacent to the long wooden bar. As with the prior pub, the room had wooden floors, a fireplace, and an attractive beamed ceiling. The menu was very British, which suited them just fine. They both ordered fish and chips along with glasses of Pinot Grigio.

While they waited for their food to arrive, Alex said, "Tomorrow, I think I should leave you alone with April. She'll probably be more comfortable talking to you one-on-one."

"I agree. She might not open up if you're sitting with us. After-all, you represent law enforcement, and we already heard she's worried about what will happen to her. Besides, you have an aura that's very masculine, which might be off-putting to her in this situation."

"What if I show her my feminine side?"

Rachel laughed. "Hunk man, you don't *have* a feminine side. Do you think I would hang out with you if you did?"

"I wasn't sure." Although he pretended to be serious, he couldn't wipe the grin off his face. "A few weeks ago, I saw a BBC television show that polled London females; some said they prefer men who are "metro-sexual."

"What the hell is that?"

"I wasn't sure, but assumed it didn't refer to guys who play rugby, join the British Army, or the Royal Marines."

"You should have been a stand-up comic. Listen, Alex, I like you exactly the way you are. Your aura is what attracted me to you in the first place."

"You're just saying that because you want sex with me tonight."

She chuckled, "You're an astonishing mind-reader." Rachel paused for a second. "You know, there won't be too many more times in London for you to say that you had sex with a deputy chief of mission."

"That's really not a big deal, because I fully expect that one day I'll be making love to Madame Ambassador."

She felt an emotional lump rising in her throat, then took his hand in hers, kissing it softly.

42

THE SAFE HOUSE

Gloucestershire

Breakfast in the Cotswold House Hotel restaurant was an
elegant affair. They offered smoked salmon, eggs, yogurt,
and croissants, although the bacon was undercooked for
Alex's liking. The hotel also provided newspapers, which they
partially read; they even had some time to watch the morning TV
news. So far, the media had been silent about the arrests of Lars
and April.

Precisely at 9:00 am, Inspector Josh Rosen pulled up in front of
the hotel in an unmarked silver Range Rover. Alex wasn't sure
how British police departments could afford a fleet of expensive
Range Rovers but guessed they must have been offered a large
discount.

After morning greetings and settling into the SUV, Rosen
drove for fifteen minutes to the safe house. Along the way, Alex
noted that many properties were either surrounded by high brick
or stone walls or else trees and hedges providing privacy from the

road. Large gates blocked access to side lanes leading to the mansions, but he rarely saw any actual homes.

Finally, Inspector Rosen slowed and pulled into a driveway with double metal gates standing about fifteen feet high. There was a CCTV camera mounted on the adjoining wall and a speaker box with another camera on a stanchion next to the entrance. He pressed a remote control and both gates slowly opened; once inside, he waited for them to close behind him. Then he accelerated down the path. When they were beyond the tree line and other foliage, Alex and Rachel saw a large two-story manor house at the end of the long driveway.

"Holy smoke," Alex said. "U.S. government safe houses are *nothing* like this. Let's quit our jobs and enter the British witness protection program." Rosen chuckled.

The mansion was a Georgian-style red brick with a host of tall windows across its front. The lawn was immaculate, covering several acres until reaching the surrounding tree line.

"It reminds me of the U.S. Ambassador's residence in Regent's Park," Rachel said.

"I'll stop in front and take you inside," Inspector Rosen said. "But then I'll have to park around back. We're trying to keep this place out of the public eye, and we don't want a bunch of vehicles clustered in front."

Rosen pulled up to the front door, got out, and rang the doorbell. Alex noticed another CCTV camera off to the side. Moments later, an armed uniformed police constable opened the door and let them in. He was of average height and weight, wearing a protective ballistic vest, and carried a 9 mm MP-5 submachine gun with a strap slung across his chest. There was a Glock pistol on his belt, along with a flashlight, expandable baton, and radio with a wire running up to his collar where the speaker was attached.

"This is Constable John Everton," Rosen said. "He's part of a special unit that helps us protect people we bring to the safe house."

"What do you normally do, John?" Alex asked.

"I'm part of the Force Firearms Unit of the Metropolitan Police in London." Alex hadn't yet met the unit's commander, but was aware of the unit as one of the few in Scotland Yard authorized to carry firearms.

"Are you the only policeman on duty?"

"Yes, but I can call on an armed response unit from the Gloucestershire police, if necessary."

"What's their response time?"

"Perhaps fifteen to thirty minutes."

Alex didn't say anything because nothing he said would change the situation. However, he felt the response time was ridiculously long. *A lot can happen in fifteen to thirty minutes,* he thought. "I guess you're part of a rotating team?"

"Yes. My duty is an eight-hour shift. Relief comes at 4:00pm."

"Shall we go on upstairs so you can talk to April?" Inspector Rosen asked. The stairs were just off of the lobby; he led the way.

APRIL WAS SITTING in a well-decorated bedroom that she shared with Lars. A small sitting area was off to one side with two chairs covered in a yellow chintz pattern cloth. The staff had just brought up a pot of coffee and three cups and saucers, along with a few "biscuits," which Americans call cookies. Lars was a few doors down the hall in the upstairs library, at the moment, talking with an MI-6 officer, describing his teenage infiltration into Sweden.

April had been told that Rachel and Alex would be visiting her and was not surprised when Alex knocked on her door. When she opened it, she immediately stepped forward and embraced Rachel. April's eyes welled up with tears.

"I'm sorry Rachel, it's a difficult time for me."

"We completely understand. It's perfectly all right to get emotional, April. Let's go back inside and chat. Alex will find Lars."

April smiled at Alex, who gave her a reassuring touch on the shoulder, then left with Inspector Rosen. April and Rachel walked over to the sitting area and poured coffee before settling down to chat.

"It's hard for me to even know where to begin, Rachel. I've been so stupid. I've ruined my life. Everything I ever achieved in the Foreign Service is now flushed down the toilet. I guess I should have known Lars might have been working for someone other than his so-called 'Swedish friends', but I fell in love with him . . . God, how I love him."

For the next two hours, the conversation continued. Rachel intentionally avoided talking about any classified information that April had passed to Lars because she knew the interrogators had already dealt with it. Instead, she focused on April's feelings and her relationship with Lars. She allowed April to ramble on so she could assess her mental state. While not being a trained psychiatrist or psychologist, Rachel was a good listener. Her instincts told her that's what April needed; it might also guide her to understand just how April was doing mentally.

Earlier, when Alex and Inspector Rosen walked down the hall, they entered a bedroom that had been converted into an observation room. Inside was one of Roger Carpenter's FBI agents from Washington, and a case officer under Anna Battles in London. A large CCTV screen was in the room receiving an audio/video feed from the library where Lars was being debriefed. There was also a bank of recording devices against the wall, archiving the conversation with Lars, as well as capturing video images of the debriefing going on next door.

"This may be of great interest to you, Alex," Rosen whispered.

"They're discussing how Lars adapted to Swedish society at age fifteen, then developed his cover before finally moving to London as an adult."

"I appreciate the opportunity," Alex whispered back. They sat in two chairs behind the others and focused on the screen for the next ninety minutes. Finally, Rosen broke the monotony. "Alex, want coffee?" he asked.

"Yes, that would be great," he agreed. They walked down to the kitchen and began talking with Constable Everton in the lobby. Alex wanted Everton to explain the security operation at the safe house.

"So, what are your guidelines on the use of force?" Alex asked. He followed up with more questions on the number of visitors that might arrive on any given day and what kind of training did he have in self-defense. After their coffee and chat, Alex and Rosen returned upstairs.

By 11:30 a.m., the morning debriefing session with Lars was over. He told his MI-6 debriefing officer that he'd like to lie down and returned to the same bedroom where Rachel and April were talking. The interruption was just enough for April and Rachel to decide it was time to stretch their legs and they walked down the hall to the library while Lars took a nap.

At 12 noon, all the interrogation staff and observers left the safe house for lunch; some drove to Chipping Campden and others drove to the village of Broadway. Only Constable Everton, Rosen, Alex, and another female staff member in the kitchen remained in the house.

"The food isn't always good here, that's why most go out for lunch," Rosen said.

"I have an idea," Alex replied. "There was an interesting deli in Chipping Campden. Why don't we drive there for sandwiches and bring some back? I'll ask the girls what they would like. We can bring something back for Lars, too."

Rosen agreed and Alex spoke with Rachel and April. The constable said he'd eat what the kitchen staff had prepared. Rosen and Alex walked around to the rear parking lot of the manor house, got in the Range Rover, and drove off to Chipping Campden.

If they had only known how close danger lurked, they never would have gone. What was about to happen would be long over before they returned . . . and nobody would need sandwiches.

43

WHEN DESTINIES COLLIDE

The Safe House

S ergei and Viktor spent the morning going over their plans and, once again, examined the map and GPS phone app in detail. They knew the attack needed to be quick . . . and deadly. There was only one thing they wondered: Why had Moscow put them in a situation where they would likely have to kill one or more British citizens to gain access to Lars Nilsson? It seemed a rash decision, but they knew it had been personally sanctioned by President Putin, and they weren't about to openly question the wisdom of his decision with their masters in Moscow.

"I still can't believe we've been ordered to kill him within a British government safe house," Sergei said.

"We *can* do it, and we *will* get away," Viktor said adamantly. "Remember when Putin had the FSB traitor, Litvinenko, poisoned with radioactive polonium-210 in the Millennium Hotel? For God's sake, the hotel was right across the street from the American Embassy in London. And Litvinenko was *already* a British citizen following his defection. Yet the assassination plan worked, and our guys returned safely to Moscow."

"*Da*, but this will be more difficult," Sergei replied. "It's not just us versus Nilsson. He may be surrounded by intelligence types, some will most probably be armed."

"I know," Viktor acknowledged. "But if we're fast and *vicious*, we will win. The British will *never* expect such an attack, especially *inside* their Safe House. Besides, Putin doesn't care who dies. He had the journalist Anna Politkovskaya shot dead because of her opposition to his Chechnya war. There are even rumors the FSB was covertly behind the attack on the Moscow Theatre in 2002 that killed over one-hundred twenty Russians and fifty Chechen terrorists, only so that Putin could use it as a pretext to attack Chechnya, again."

"You're right, Viktor. We *can* do this. We are better trained than the British cops and certainly better trained than their intelligence types for this kind of battle."

Sergei and Viktor packed their contractors' uniforms into duffle bags. Their cover was simple, they had been hired by British Gas to inspect the Manor House's gas heating system. Allegedly, the last reading showed an abnormally high amount of consumption, possibly indicating a dangerous gas leak. Moreover, they would arrive at noontime, hoping some of the staff would be off the grounds taking a lunch break.

They left the hotel room in civilian clothes, carrying all their possessions, and walked to the parking lot to retrieve their van. Soon, they would stop at a remote location along the way and put on their khaki coveralls and tool belts. Each carried a British Gas ID card which had been fabricated by the SVR in Moscow.

Victor drove as they left Burford heading toward the safe house, Each carried a knife on his tool belt, and other items that could be used as weapons. The drive wasn't long and the road system was well enough marked for them to know where they were.

"I've rarely seen such an attractive area," Sergei said, as they meandered down winding country roads. "The rolling hills and agricultural fields are unlike anything I've seen in Russia. Everything back home seems so flat to me."

"Don't go soft on me, Sergei."

"How can you say that? You must be joking. Do you know how many people I've killed?"

"I *am* joking. I admit this area is beautiful. Let's get back to navigating."

Their route took them through the village of Chipping Campden, passed the stone-covered market in the center of the village. Neither Viktor nor Sergei could possibly know Alex and Josh Rosen were arriving at the deli at that moment to order luncheon sandwiches.

The two Russians drove on for another fifteen minutes, following the map and GPS on Sergei's mobile until they arrived at the gates of the estate. Viktor's English was pretty good, so he pressed the call button on the stone column and Constable John Everton answered.

"How can I help you?"

"We are from British Gas, and we are here to investigate a possible leak in the manor house."

"I don't know anything about that."

"Your gas usage has been extremely high. It could be a leak and very dangerous."

"Show me your ID card," Everton demanded.

Viktor pulled his card out and held it in front of the camera next to the speaker. The short delay made him nervous. Finally, after thirty l-o-n-g seconds, the double metal gates slowly swung open, and Viktor proceeded to drive up to the front of the house. When he parked by the front door, Viktor looked at his watch; it was a quarter past twelve. He and Sergei looked at each other and spoke simultaneously: "For Mother Russia!"

Climbing out of the van, Sergei rang the doorbell and waited for someone to open the door.

$$\sim$$

INSPECTOR ROSEN HAD PARKED his unmarked police Range Rover on the High Street of Chipping Campden, right next to the 16th century stone covered marketplace in the center of town. He and Alex walked up the slight grassy incline to the deli called Tokes. It was near where Alex and Rachel had spent the night before just a few doors down at the Cotswolds House Hotel.

"Josh, I love this village. It has everything anyone could possibly want - restaurants, convenience stores, pubs, small shops, and hotels. Plus, the honey-colored stone buildings are so picturesque."

"This is my first time here," Rosen replied. "I agree, this place is beautiful. I think I'll bring my wife here for her birthday."

They entered the deli and bought hand-made sandwiches of roast beef, chicken, or ham. Alex filled his shoulder bag with large plastic bottles of water.

A while later, upon returning to the manor house, Alex noticed a white van parked at the front door. It had no markings, which he thought was strange. It would, however, make sense if it was from MI5 or Special Branch

"What's this all about?" he asked Rosen, pointing to the van.

"I don't know. It's probably a maintenance company of some sort. I'll drop you off in front, then drive around back to park."

As Rosen drove off, Alex began to enter when he realized the front door was ajar. His instincts flared. *This isn't right,* he told himself, wishing he was armed, but this was Britain, and hand-guns were banned except for specialized police units. Alex cautiously pushed open the door and stepped inside. His eyes widened at the horrific sight before him.

Constable Everton lay on his back in a wide pool of blood, throat slit open. The front of his uniform and tactical vest were smeared bright red. Alex started moving toward him to check his jugular vein to see if he was alive, but out of the corner of his eye, he saw a man not fifteen feet away, holding a bloody knife in his right hand. The guy was wearing a khaki coverall, like a repairman, with a tool belt around his waist.

In a split second, Viktor rushed toward Alex who immediately dropped the bag of sandwiches and pulled his heavy shoulder bag off. He swung it as the Russian lunged with his knife. The heavy bag crashed into Viktor's wrist sending the knife flying across the room. With its impact, Alex lost his grip on the strap and the shoulder bag fell to the floor.

With the speed and aggressiveness of a tiger, the Russian unleashed a torrent of punches at Alex's head. With no time for anything other than defending himself, Alex put both arms up to block as many strikes as possible. A few got through his defenses, but by now, his adrenalin was pumping, and Alex felt nothing, until . . . Wham! The Russian connected with a powerful shot to Alex's left side, directly under his armpit and he staggered back against the wall. Excruciating pain shot through his body and he nearly collapsed. Viktor charged again. Although still in pain, Alex knew he had to kill this man or be killed.

Before the Russian could connect with another punch, this time to the head, Alex nailed him with a solid right to his chin. The solidly built Russian was momentarily knocked backward but remained upright.

Then Alex lunged forward, ignoring his own pain, and slammed a powerful left hook to the Russian's right side, hitting him just below the rib cage and directly on the unprotected part of his liver, a solid "liver shot." His vagus nerve was stunned, causing instant pain throughout his entire nervous system, but the Russian only went down to his knees. Alex immediately recognized the perfect lineup and kicked him hard in the face with his right foot. Viktor fell backwards onto the floor, completely stunned. But to Alex's disbelief, he staggered back up.

Now, he charged the Russian and got him into a rear choke hold. Standing behind the man, Alex put his right forearm across Victor's throat, locking his right hand onto the bicep of his own left arm. Alex's left hand was behind the Russian's head, pressing it forward as Alex choked the life out of him.

Viktor tried valiantly to fight Alex off, but was slightly shorter, even though his neck was thicker and his upper body more muscular. But Alex had the advantage with position. But try as Viktor might, he could not break away, and was now having trouble breathing. Still, this should have knocked Victor out in less than twenty-seconds; Alex was shocked that it wasn't happening.

Now Viktor tried pulling down on Alex's forearm, a natural instinct. But Alex's hold was locked in solidly under Viktor's chin. Viktor then took a short step to the right in order to swing his left leg behind Alex and trip him to the ground. But Alex anticipated the move and merely moved to the right as well. He could feel the Russian begin to panic.

Then Viktor used his legs to propel both of them backward, crashing into a wall. The air exploded from Alex's lungs, but he still wouldn't let go of the hold. The Russian tried unsuccessfully to reach behind him and gouge Alex's eyes, but the blood to his brain was being blocked by the choke hold and he began losing strength as the pressure continued.

Slowly, Viktor slid down to the ground. Alex dropped with him, maintaining pressure on the Russian's throat and carotid artery in his neck for another ten-seconds until Viktor stopped moving.

Even so, Alex maintained his hold for a while, finally releasing the Russian when he was sure there was no life left in the man. Then Alex stood up. His muscular arms were on fire, every fiber of his upper body ached. His left side hurt badly from the Russian's punch into the exact spot where he had been operated on last year in Cairo.

Viktor was now sprawled on his back. The entire fight with the Russian had lasted only a few minutes, but Alex was exhausted. He took a few deep breaths as he scurried over to the dead constable and pulled his 9 mm sub-machine gun off the body. When he pulled back the charging handle to see if a round had been chambered, he saw that it had not.

This poor cop never had a chance to defend himself from this assassin, Alex thought.

As he chambered a round, he heard a woman scream from the floor above. About to run upstairs, he saw Viktor twitching as blood returned to his brain. The big man rolled into a sitting position and supported himself with his arms on the ground.

Incredible! This guy won't die, Alex thought. The Russian would be fully alert in a moment and, again, be a deadly threat. Alex pointed the sub-machine gun at the top of Viktor's head and blew his brains out with one round.

44

LIFE OR DEATH

The Safe House

While Viktor and Alex were downstairs fighting for their lives, Sergei was upstairs searching for Lars Nilsson. Vaguely aware of noises coming from the lobby, Sergei quickly moved into two bedrooms, hoping to find and kill Lars without anyone else being present. Both bedrooms were empty.

He quickly walked down the hallway to the next door as April was coming out of the library. She screamed, coming face to face with this unknown man. It took one punch from Sergei's large fist to her face and she crumpled to the floor unconscious.

Rachel had been sitting in the library on one of the sofas and witnessed the attack through the open door. Immediately, she stood up as Sergei walked toward her.

Boom!

They both heard the shot from downstairs. The sub-machine gun had a distinct sound. Rachel immediately took a fighting stance, knees bent, hands up to protect herself. She watched Sergei's eyes boring into her. He had a rough, weathered face with an expression of pure evil. Her heart pounded as sweat ran down her body. She knew instantly this man was a Russian killer and, without a doubt, extremely well-trained. He took a step toward her and she moved away from the sofa to give herself maneuvering space. He motioned to her with his hands.

Son of bitch, she thought, *this guy wants me to attack him!* She prayed the gun sound below was from the police and not a second Russian. The man in front of her wasn't holding a weapon, except for his two fists, but her eyes glanced at his tool belt. There were plenty of potential weapons there.The large man in front of her took two more steps and closed the gap between them. She slid toward him as well.

Fuck, where's Alex? She realized her hands were shaking.

Sergei moved in and threw a right-hand punch at her head. Rachel blocked it with a rigid left side hand, took a step forward, and quickly slammed her right knee twice into his groin. She felt each hit solidly connect. Sergei gave a short yelp, backed up two steps and partially bent over. She saw pain on his face, but then he suddenly attacked, hitting her with a straight right to her solar plexus. She went crashing back into the fireplace, loudly knocking over all of the implements for stoking a fire. Crumpled on the ground in pain, she kept her eyes on the Russian.

He smiled as he walked over to her, grabbed her hair, and jerk her off the ground. When she was upright, Rachel slammed the heel of her right hand up hard under his nose, but it had little effect, other than to immediately splatter blood over the both of them. It stunned him momentarily, but he recovered quickly and spun her around, pulling her head back by her hair. She forced her head back down and saw the glint of a knife's blade in his right hand streaking toward her throat.

With no time to think, only react, she jammed the back of her left elbow into his solar plexus as hard as possible while twisting left. His grip on her hair loosened just enough to allow room for her to head-butt him again in the area where she figured his diaphragm must be. The knife raked across her back drawing blood. He said something in Russian she didn't understand before he gave a short, guttural growl. Bent low, her head was being held near his stomach and her face was to the floor. Now, with extraordinary power and speed, she brought her right fist up and into his groin, three times.

Where the hell are his balls? she thought. *Why doesn't he have anything hanging down there?*

With all her might, she tried standing up straight, bringing both arms up in front of her to create distance from him. Bringing her arms down again quickly, she tried trapping both his arms, but they were too thick, and he pulled away. At least she was free of him pulling her hair, but he still held the knife in his right hand.

Now he brought it at her from a top-down angle. She moved inward and blocked it with both forearms forming an "X" just above her own head. Then, stepping to her left side, she tried sliding her hand down his wrist to attempt and control the knife. But he had a death-grip on it and his thick wrist proved immoveable.

She backed up a few inches and slammed the flat of her left foot into the side of his right kneecap, hyperextending it. He bellowed in pain and tottered backwards a few steps, just enough to give her room to turn and aim her right foot at his left kneecap to try the same technique and cripple his movements.

Another bellow and he went down on his back. Now kneeling at his side, she dropped her right forearm onto his Adam's apple, attempting to apply downward pressure and strangle him. But she didn't realize the pain his Russian training had taught him to endure. She momentarily lost sight of the knife which he now used to lightly puncture her side. The surprise made her let up on the throat pressure and he rolled away, getting to his feet. She scrambled up, herself, and faced him again.

Am I losing? Am I going to die?

Flying upstairs, Alex heard the fireplace tools in the library crash onto the floor. *Something violent is happening there.* As he darted into the room, Sergei rushed next to Rachel, grabbing her and using her as a shield. Rachel yelled, "Kill him, Alex! Shoot him!"

Alex stood about thirty feet away. Quickly, he raised the sub-machine into firing position when a horrendous stab of sharp pain in his left side distracted him. Nevertheless, he fired. Two loud explosions sounded as the 9 mm bullets rocketed from his weapon and sped toward their target at over 1,300 feet per second. Sergei crashed backwards, onto the floor, but so did Rachel. Alex was stunned.

"Oh, no! Not *again*," he screamed, remembering the accident in the shooting house in Hereford. He raced across the room. Sergei had two bloody holes in the center of his forehead. Rachel lay quiet on the floor. Then, her eyes popped open.

"Dammit, did you get the bloody *fucker* ?"

"Rachel! Are you okay?"

"Yes, but goddamn it, help me up!"

"What a 'potty' mouth you have," he smiled, not being able to help himself. He knew there was nothing funny about the situation, but his nervous reaction was infectious. She smiled back. Alex bent over and picked her off the ground with his right arm. Tears flowed down her face. Then they heard April groaning on the floor by the library door. She appeared to have a bloody nose and seemed incapable of getting up.

Lars entered the room. "What the hell is going on? April!" He knelt beside her and helped her recover. Moments later, Inspector Josh Rosen arrived, Glock pistol in hand.

"Jesus, I heard shots fired! I've called for backup, but it looks like it's over," he said. Alex was holding the constable's submachine gun in his right hand.

"I better take this from you, or reinforcements might think you're one of the attackers."

Alex flipped the weapon on safe and handed it over, then embraced Rachel, again, squeezing her as tightly as he could without hurting her. He saw blood on her clothes but never wanted to let her go. Though fighting skills helped them survive, he knew they were damn lucky to be alive.

* * *

Later, Alex and Rachel were standing with Rosen in the downstairs hall waiting for the responders to arrive at the safe house. He had his arm protectively draped around Rachel's shoulder as they waited. She was holding her side where the knife had drawn blood.

So much for this being a low-key operation, Alex thought.

Ten minutes later, two police Land Rovers and two sedans arrived with eight armed cops, FBI, and CIA interrogators, and one each MI-5 and MI-6 officer respectively

Lars and April came down the stairs and walked over to Alex. "Thank you, Alex. You saved April's life, as well as mine. This attack certainly was the work of the SVR. My God, we all know what might happen to a Russian traitor, but the audacity to conduct an attack at a British *safe house*. It must have been personally ordered by Putin. I imagine the British will move us somewhere else now."

"Absolutely. I'm sorry. We'll have to figure out how this

happened, but I think the SVR has better information than we realized."

Rosen approached Alex and Rachel. "We'll need written statements from both of you. My guess is that after your roles in this interrogation are complete, you can return to life in London. Nilsson and Scott will be moved by MI-5 to another safe house. We'll never use this place again, that's for sure."

45

GETTING THE STORY OUT

London

Two days after the failed Russian assassination attempt on Lars Nilsson, MI-5 Assistant Director Geoffrey Carver asked Alex and Rachel to visit his office to discuss a problem. Ever cautious, he didn't reveal over the phone exactly what was on his agenda.

Arriving precisely at 11:00 a.m. as requested, they were escorted up to a conference room adjoining Carver's office. While the building was "seasoned," from past years, the décor in the conference room was modern with several large flat-screen TVs hanging on the walls. There were no windows in the room or artwork.

Carver rose from the conference table when they entered, and everyone shook hands. Commander Ray Penner was also present along with two women who had just filled their coffee cups from a large pot in the corner of the room. They walked over to greet Alex and Rachel. One woman, in her late twenties, was unknown to Alex, but the other one he recognized as Deidre Plummer, the police public affairs officer whom he had previously met in Commander Penner's office. Rachel and Deidre exchanged a brief peck on the cheek since they had become friends at the Oxford symposium back in June. Alex and Rachel declined an offer of coffee; everyone sat around the oval conference table.

"Thank you all for coming on short notice," Carver said.

"We've had time to review the statements you've made to the police about the attack, and your roles in thwarting it. I'm simply curious, but do all American diplomats have such survival training and fight as well as you do?"

Since Carver was smiling, Alex assumed this was just casual chit-chat. *So far, so good.* "The answer is no," he said, "but our backgrounds are a little different from most others at our embassy."

"I see. In any event, the reason I've asked you to come here today is because Special Branch and MI-5 have reviewed the video tapes of your fights."

"Video tapes?" Rachel asked.

"Yes, you may not have been aware of the CCTV cameras both outside and within the manor house."

"I did note the small lenses in most rooms," Alex said. "Are there inconsistencies between our statements and what appeared on tape?"

"No, everything is fully consistent."

"Then, what's the problem?" Alex asked. The direction of the conversation was beginning to make him feel uneasy.

"Ray, would you care to elaborate."

"Yes. Thank you, Geoffrey."

Alex reached over and squeezed Rachel's hand. With Ray Penner about to speak, he noticed Deidre Plummer staring intensely at him and Rachel.

"At issue, Alex, is *how* you killed the Russian in the lobby."

"I thought I was clear about that. I shot him in the head."

"Exactly the point," Deidre Plummer replied.

"I said this in my written statement."

"Yes, you did," she said.

"So, what's your concern?"

"Why don't we look at the videotape and you will see our dilemma." She nodded to the other woman at the table who had a laptop open in front of her. After she touched a few keys, one of the TV screens lit up. Rachel had heard Alex's side regarding the story of his fight, but this was the first time she was seeing film footage. There was no accompanying sound. The tape was cued to when the two Russians entered the lobby and produced ID cards. One of the Russians, Sergei, started walking further inside, but the police constable moved to stop him. That's when the second Russian, Viktor, pulled a knife and slit his throat.

Rachel's hand immediately went up to her mouth. "Oh my God!" The tape continued with Alex entering the lobby seconds after the first Russian had gone upstairs. His fight was relatively brief, but extremely violent. Rachel cringed watching the action; she grabbed Alex's arm when he got punched in the face a few times. When Viktor hit Alex in his side causing him to stagger backward, she lost it, and tears cascaded from her eyes. Yet, mesmerized by the action, she continued to watch. Alex subconsciously touched two places on his face that were still swollen.

When the video showed Alex choking Victor out, he could feel Rachel's arms get tense as if she was doing it to Victor herself. Finally, the moment came when Alex picked up the police officer's sub-machine gun and walked over to Viktor, who was in a sitting position, and fired a bullet into his head. Everyone could see Victor's brains blown out the back, splattering against the wall.

"Pause the tape, please," Penner asked. All motion stopped at that point.

"Are you all right Rachel?" Deidre Plummer asked.

"Yes, thank you. That was difficult to watch. I'm sorry for getting emotional."

"Then let's continue the tape."

The view changed to a different camera in the upstairs library. For the first time, Alex saw Rachel defend herself against Sergei. The men sitting around the oval table groaned when Rachel nailed him twice in the balls with her knee. Then the Russian punched Rachel in the solar plexus and she stumbled backward onto the ground. Alex's jaw tightened; he was furious. This extraordinary woman, normally so tough and confident, looked so fragile and helpless laying on the ground in a fetal position.

He whispered to Rachel, "I'm glad I killed that asshole." He held her free hand as she dried her eyes with a tissue. The tape ended after Alex entered the room and shot the Russian to death. There was silence for a moment. Alex collected his thoughts. Penner spoke.

"I have to point out that the Russian in the lobby was unarmed when you shot him, although he had used a knife earlier to kill the constable."

"I see your point, Ray. Did you notice that before I shot him, my head jerked upward? That's because I heard a female scream upstairs. I had to act, and as you can see in the video, the Russian I fought was coming around. He was still a serious threat. I didn't see any handcuffs or other restraints on the police officer's duty belt, which I might have used."

Deidre Plummer said, "Yes, we noticed your reaction to the scream. Rachel confirmed that April had screamed. We are not questioning the facts."

"Where is this going?" Alex replied testily. "The Russian had already murdered a policeman, he tried to kill me, and I thought Rachel, April, and Lars were in jeopardy. Moreover, Inspector Rosen was about to enter the lobby. He might have been killed, too, if I had just left the Russian alone."

"As Deidre said," Geoffrey Carver interjected, "we are not disputing the facts, nor the necessity of dispatching the Russian.

We are, however, concerned with the public's perception of the incident."

Alex leaned back in his chair somewhat relieved. *If that's the concern,* he thought, *I think we can come to some understanding on how to explain it.* Then Rachel spoke.

"I've spent my entire career in press relations and I'm now our embassy's acting deputy chief of mission. Since you are worried about the public's *reaction* to the incident, my experience tells me that we should agree on what exactly we'll disclose to the public."

Deidre Plummer smiled. "It's nice that your professional instincts are in-line with what we have in mind."

"The public will need assurances that the incident was handled completely within the framework of British law," Geoffrey Carver said. "They will also want to know that any security measures in place were adequate, and functioned properly."

Alex crossed his arms and sat up straight. He stared directly into Carver's eyes. Now he understood the game the Brits were playing. "God forbid the public should feel that having only one armed policeman on duty at the safe house was inadequate."

Both Carver and Penner cleared their throats and looked down at their hands, rather than reply.

"Let's cut to the chase," Alex said. "The solution is simple. Never mention to the media that I shot the first Russian. In fact, if you like, I never shot *either* Russian. They were killed by the policeman with his own sub-machine gun when they attacked him in the lobby. He will be the public hero of the event. As for the tape, what tape? Perhaps the taping system was out of action and needed repair."

Penner looked at Carver and Plummer. All nodded.

"So, if you are questioned under oath, you and Rachel will swear to that?" Carver asked.

"I will swear that the Russians must have been killed by the policeman since it was his weapon that forensics will confirm killed both Russians. After all, I wasn't there when the Russians arrived. Inspector Rosen can attest to that."

"Moreover," Rachel said, "I was upstairs with April and didn't know what was happening in the lobby. I didn't see anything downstairs. Furthermore, Lars was asleep in his bedroom. That leaves only April who saw one Russian upstairs before she was knocked out. She never saw Alex fire the gun."

"What have you told the State Department?" Plummer asked.

"Ah, good point," Alex replied. "I reported the truth. But because of the sensitive nature of Lars Nilsson's debriefing, my report is being filed as a classified secret. The State Department will never release that information to the public."

"I strongly suggest that you figure out how to channel all inquiries to Deidre," Rachel said. "I imagine you've had similar situations in the past involving police or army shootings in Northern Ireland which had to be handled with ... discretion."

"I have an alternative suggestion," Deidre said. "It always best to stay as close to the truth as possible. Let's not over-complicate the scenario. So, let's simply say the policeman killed the first Russian in the lobby, and then Alex killed the second one upstairs to save and protect the others, which is very close to what really happened. That way, we only have to say the tape recording malfunctioned in the lobby."

"Indeed," replied Carver. "I believe Deidre's suggestion should be the official story. I need to clear this idea with the Prime Minister and Foreign Office. I'll get back to both of you. Will you inform the State Department about what we agreed?" he asked Alex.

Alex looked at Rachel. "We will. I believe they will be delighted for the police to take as much credit as possible."

As they were walking out of the room, Deidre stopped Rachel by touching her arm. "I'm glad you're all right, Rachel. What you and Alex went through was incredible. Listen, I'll call you when we hear back from the Prime Minister and the FCO."

Walking on, Alex didn't realize for a moment that Rachel was no longer by his side. He stopped at the door and turned to look back at both women. A small smile grew on his face.

The women noticed him looking at them and returned their own smiles. Deidre turned to Rachel. "I bet you're as lucky as I think you are."

"I am," she said. "More than you can even imagine."

46

FRIENDS

London

Four weeks later, on a Saturday night, Alex and Rachel celebrated in the private Graham Greene dining room of Rules Restaurant in Covent Garden. Their London friends were all gathered: Bainbridge Wellington, Anna Battles, Erica Evans, Geoffrey Carver, Assistant Commissioner Gerald Davies, Deidre Plummer, Commander Ray Penner, and Sir Nigel Sharpton. Everyone had bought their spouse to this black-tie, evening gown dinner.

Rules was the oldest restaurant in London, dating back to 1798. It specialized in British cuisine, especially in-season game, and was known for its extensive wine list. The décor was upscale throughout - red carpets with a tan swirl pattern, attractive over-head chandeliers with fans, and red leather chairs on dark wooden frames. Prints and paintings of famous people or rural pursuits hung on walls throughout the old establishment. It had the feel of tradition, old money, and behind-the-scenes intrigue and deals.

"You look absolutely stunning," Alex whispered into Rachel's ear as they sat next to one another. She smiled and gently placed her hand over his thigh under the table, giving a gentle squeeze.

"You've cleaned up pretty well yourself. No black eyes or facial bruises. *Molto bello.*" It was high praise, meaning "very handsome" in Italian.

Alex was wearing a black tuxedo with traditional white dinner-shirt and black studs, cufflinks, and a black bow-tie. He also sported a new gift from Rachel, a rectangular and elegant Reverso model wristwatch by Jaeger LeCoultre.

Deidre sat across the table from Rachel. Although Rachel had known her for only a short time, the two women had quickly bonded over what the police would tell the press about the incident at the safe house. Tonight, Deidre had her hair pulled up elegantly on top of her head, unlike Rachel, who preferred to let her long wavy locks hang down, her part slightly off center. Around Rachel's neck was a gold necklace with a few inlaid green emeralds that matched her dangling earrings.

Deidre's husband, Oliver, sat across from Alex. He was a high-flying corporate attorney in London's financial district. He and Deidre had first met at Cambridge University twenty years earlier. Alex and Oliver had also hit it off and shared a common passion for British military history. The two couples were very happy getting to know each other.

"Rachel, your gown is exquisite," Deidre said. "I love the champagne color and those sequins are eye-catching. Did you buy it here? Who's the designer?"

Rachel's smile was instantaneous. "It's by Christian Dior. Alex gave me this gift two weeks ago. I'm delighted you like it."

"Alex, you certainly have good taste in evening gowns," Deidre said. "How did you decide on this one?"

"Oh, you might say that a flip of a coin influenced my final decision." Rachel chuckled quietly, enjoying the moment.

Bainbridge Wellington raised his glass of wine. "I propose a toast to Alex and Rachel. Without your presence at that manor house, not to mention your continued outstanding performance since your arrival, we would be dealing with a far different situation today."

All repeated the toast: "To Alex and Rachel." Everyone took a swallow of champagne.

"I have another toast," Alex said after he rose to address everyone. "Here's to all of our friends who have made success a team effort."

"To friends!" Everyone said in unison while slapping the table a few times, then all took another sip from their glasses.

The food began to arrive. Alex had ordered a Dorset crab salad as a starter and for his main course, a roast loin of venison. Rachel started with a half dozen raw rock oysters and moved on to a rump roast of lamb. Accompanying dishes were dauphinoise potatoes, and parsnip with pear puree. For dessert, Alex and Rachel shared dishes of stilton cheese, and a rhubarb and almond tart. Both washed it all down with glasses of Darius II, a magnificent and expensive Cabernet Sauvignon from California.

It was a wonderful evening filled with excellent conversation and good cheer. At one point, Rachel grasped Alex's hand. "You know, we've only been in London a few months, so we have almost three more years to go on our assignment here. I'm sure this will be a memorable one for both of us." She paused. "I love you so much, Alex. You saved my life at the manor house. I'll never forget it. You are a 'keeper.'"

He leaned toward her and kissed her slowly, sensually on the lips. "Does this mean I can drive the Jaguar *all* the time?" he asked.

"*Hell, no.* I didn't say I loved you *that* much." They both laughed easily. Everything seemed easy when they were together.

Bainbridge Wellington paid the bill for everyone, knowing he could charge it to the embassy representational fund since half the guests were British officials.

Late that evening, the group left Rules Restaurant well-nourished and sufficiently lubricated. Half of them took taxis home. For Alex and Rachel, and half the group, the next stop was the Savoy Hotel for an evening of ballroom dancing.

Neither Alex nor Rachel were great dancers, but that wasn't the point. It was more about further emotional bonding through the intimacy of holding one another and feeling the sensual touch of someone who meant the world to you.

Taking a wrong step on the dance floor didn't matter; what did, was moving in smooth unison with a partner one had chosen for life. And that's what they were doing.

EPILOGUE

Lars Nielsson continued to cooperate with his British interrogators after the Russians' failed attempt to murder him. They also granted his one firm condition: No jail time for April.

The FBI and **Justice Department**, however, never agreed to Nilsson's condition, but the **CIA** and **Brits** lobbied hard enough with the White House to strike a deal. Much to the chagrin of the law enforcement establishment, intelligence concerns about the long term Russian threat won out. Lars and April were relocated to an undisclosed place in the United Kingdom and given new identities. Lars Nielsson continues to advise the British on how to counter Russian espionage. April is expecting their first child.

Wakefield Summers, former Deputy Secretary of State in Washington, D.C., was convicted of espionage and is currently serving a life sentence in an American federal penitentiary. His lawyer tried to cut a deal, but because Summers' disclosures led to the death of several CIA operatives in Moscow, the U.S. government prevailed, and he will likely die in prison. Unless, of course, a prisoner swap of spies is arranged at some time in the future.

The FBI, using contacts in the press, took credit for the arrest of Deputy Secretary Wakefield Summers, downplaying the superb groundwork done by DS and the CIA.

Russian diplomats Nickolai Petrov and his wife, **Ludmilla**, were declared persona non grata in Washington and kicked out of the country.

Dennis Hager's short tenure as the Under Secretary for Management abruptly came to an end, and he was forced to retire. Secretary Martin finally realized that Hager's scheming against Diplomatic Security was endangering the lives of State Department employees overseas, so they gave him the boot. Hager subsequently found a job as an administrator at a small inconsequential college in the Midwest.

Jim Riley's health returned with the demise of Hager, and he continues to report directly to the new Deputy Secretary of State for the foreseeable future.

Alex and **Rachel** won the State Department's Award for Valor for fighting the two Russian assassins. Each award came with a financial amount, which they both donated to the 'Go Fund Me page' for the family of Constable John Everton, the police officer killed in the line of duty at the safe house in Gloucestershire.

They continue to serve in London, exploring antique markets, restaurants, small villages, and enjoying life with friends in one of the most cosmopolitan cities in the world.

And, they take turns driving the Jaguar, but he still owes her five more designer dresses as a result of Rachel's earlier 'magic' coin toss.

ABOUT THE AUTHOR

During Mel Harrison's twenty-eight year career with the U.S. Department of State, he won both the Department's Award for Valor and the worldwide Regional Security Officer of the Year award. Serving most of career in the Diplomatic Security Service, Mel was assigned  to embassies in Saigon, Quito, Rome, London, Seoul, and Islamabad.

Prior to joining the Foreign Service, he graduated from the University of Maryland with a degree in Economics, and he did post-graduate work at The American University. The Department of State assigned him to the NATO Defense College in Rome for political-military studies.

Following government retirement, Mel spent ten years in corporate security or consulting work, with assignments often taking him throughout Latin America and the Middle East.

OTHER NOVELS BY MEL HARRISON

BOOK ONE - DEATH IN PAKISTAN

In the early 1990s, America changed course and supported military and economic assistance to India at Pakistan's expense. As a result, Alex Boyd, deputy regional security officer at the US Embassy in Islamabad, Pakistan, must defend the Embassy, employees and a visiting US Senate delegation against vicious, heavily armed, fanatical terrorists who are supported by a rogue element within Pakistan's military intelligence service (ISI). Alex and his team fight for their lives.

Complicating the situation, Alex must overcome the staid traditionalists within the Foreign Service, itself, who believe nothing should be done to aggravate the locals even in self-defense.

The new Embassy press officer, Rachel Smith, an accomplished athlete and intellectual powerhouse, intimately bonds with Alex. She eventually battles the terrorist leader in ferocious hand-to-hand combat during the attack at the Embassy compound.

When you go to Pakistan, no one promises you'll return alive.

REVIEWS ON BOOK ONE

A true to life story of an Embassy under attack

The author is a veteran of the State Department and how it operates; the setting is our Embassy in Pakistan. His attention to detail of how Embassies work is right on the mark. I should know as I retired from State after 40+ years of service, Seventy-five percent of my time was abroad at Embassies around the world. He describes how his office (Diplomatic Security) fits in with the rest of the Embassy staff The story describes how

the Embassy security officers and the Marine Security Guards defend the Embassy when it's attacked by terrorists. This is an excellent story and well worth the readers time to devour it. - Jimmy D.

It takes a specialist to level the playing field.

Death in Pakistan is a fast based account of the working configuration of staff...top to bottom...in Islamabad during a crisis. well written by a retired Security Officer.Tom Clancy's Jack Ryan's and Vince Flynn;s Mitch Rapp need to make room for Mel Harrison's Alex Boyd!!The author supplies the reader with a great reference glossary of diplomatic personnel with acronyms.His insights into who is responsible for what during a crisis makes the reading uncomplicated and rewarding.The end of his story has the reader proud of Alex Boyd and wanting more novels featuring him.It is truly a "can't put it down story".

Exciting: Death in Pakistan

One of the most exciting novels I have ever read.

Anyone that wants to know anything about the US foreign service or what the ambassadors and their staff do while stationed in a foreign country will come away with a real knowledge that sometimes the cushy jobs can be more dangerous than you think they could ever be.

If reading this story doesn't get your heart pumping, nothing will. - Ben P.

BOOK TWO - THE AMBASSADOR IS MISSING

It's more nonstop action when RSO Alex Boyd arrives at the US Embassy in Rome. In the sequel to Death in Pakistan, Regional Security Officer Alex Boyd arrives in Rome expecting a comfortable assignment after the terrorist violence in Pakistan where he almost lost his life.

On his first day in Italy he's caught in the crossfire during a bank robbery where he saves the life of a grateful Italian VIP. Alex's new Embassy boss despises him for an old grievance, and his girlfriend, Rachel, is running hot and cold. When terrorists kidnap the Ambassador and his wife, Alex swings into full-on action. He must maneuver through a maze of State Department bureaucratic incompetence and interference from the FBI, dodge bullets during police raids, and confront lying officials within the Embassy staff.

After two weeks of being held in a filthy basement, the Ambassador is ill and running out of lifesaving medicine. With the FBI and State Department arguing with the Italians over how to deal with the crisis, Alex leads the way with the Italian police in a bold attempt to rescue the Ambassador and his wife while they are still alive.

REVIEWS ON BOOK TWO

Great read!

The second novel in the Alex Boyd series, The Ambassador is Missing, is a great follow-on to Death in Pakistan. Mel Harrison's descriptions of life working in an embassy are rich with detail and his characters are well drawn and interesting. The Ambassador is Missing is an especially fast-paced thriller that is hard to put down. The growing romance between Regional Security Officer Alex and Public Affairs Officer Rachel is a plus, as we follow these two talented and likeable characters on their professional and personal journeys. Looking forward to the next! - Ellen E.

Another Alex Boyd Thriller

Another thriller in the Alex Boyd series, can't put it down until finished. Having served in an Embassy and worked in security for many years, author Mel Harrison, I found it entertains while giving unique insights on Embassy workings and their unique cultures.

- D. W. CDR (Intelligence), USNR (Ret.).

Another Great Book

Another great book and can't wait for the next one. I told my wife and now she's getting into these books. I stayed up later than usual because I couldn't put it down. Fun to read but also very interesting as to the goings on of the state department. -Tom W.

❧

Another Fantastic Book

The second Alex Boyd thriller is even better than the first. This book brought me right back to Italy and inside the Embassy. Not usually a fan of nonfiction, I had to keep reminding myself this was a work of fiction. All around this was a great read. I finished the last page and downloaded the next book -Ryan L.

BOOK THREE - MOVING TARGET

Alex Boyd, restless at a desk job in Washington, D.C., hates bureaucracy and misses the excitement of an overseas assignment. When unexpected opportunities arise, he and Rachel Smith, his new wife, jump at the chance to work in Paris. But nothing goes as planned.

Soon their lives are at risk from a vicious Sicilian Mafia leader; their new bosses, Henri and Giselle Ducat, have disappeared. Were they kidnapped? Or did they run?

Moving Target is the third book in Mel Harrison's Alex Boyd thriller series after Death in Pakistan and The Ambassador is Missing. The Thrill continues!

REVIEWS ON BOOK THREE

Mel Harrison Has Done It Again

Just when you think Alex Boyd and his beloved Rachel Smith are settling in to long U.S. Government careers, they take a turn to the private sector with Paris as a background and working among the very wealthy. Mel captures the essence of greed in "Moving Target" that makes humans do foolish things that cost lives and destroy relationships.

Mel obviously has high profile, private sector experience to be able to depict the characters so realistically that the reader finds himself guessing what danger or action lies around the corner. Mel also portrays the network of contacts that he made and maintained in his exemplary Department of State career through Alex. Again, it is very tough to put the book down.

Congratulations again to Mr. Harrison. D.D. M.

His Best Book Yet

Reviewed in the United States on March 20, 2021
Verified Purchase - Ben P.

I was totally amazed at how the author put all the information together to make this storyline.His other books which I also have read were good and given 5 stars so I wish I could give this one SIX Stars.!

The cover says "An Alex Boyd Thriller" and indeed it is. - Ben P.

Mel at his best!

Mel has brought us into the international financial world with this well written book. My sister who was trapped at home in the blizzard with no power was delighted to have this book.We both enjoy Mel's writing, he brings us into the world international intrigue and it's a pleasure to enjoy his intelligent stories. -H.D. Bowers

∾

How does the author do it?

This book is so much fun , a page turner as they say. When I finish each book written by Mel Harrison, my first thought is when is the next one going to come out? For now, I'll just wait but I highly recommend Moving Target. - Tom M.

BOOK FOUR - TERROR IN CAIRO

Egyptian Islamic Jihad, (EIJ) a vicious terrorist organization determined to thwart peace with Israel, attacks an important Middle East Peace Conference in Cairo attempting to stop any chance of a successful conference outcome.

As special agent with the State Department Diplomatic Security Service (DS), Alex is responsible for the overall protection of

U.S. delegates, including the Secretary of State and several senior senators and congressmen attending the conference.

When it appears the peace conference may be resurrected, the terrorists seek to inflict a mortal wound against America with an unprecedented target. With superb Arabic language skills and military experience, Alex is tasked with identifying the leaders of EIJ before they strike again. A team of U.S. Navy SEALs leads the way into the harsh desert of Libya to terminate them.

Alex takes charge of Embassy security. Rachel Smith, now his wife, has assumed the role of Embassy Press Officer, risking her own life in the line of duty. Questions remain whether Alex, and his colleagues, can win this life and death struggle. Even more important, who is arming the terrorists?

REVIEWS ON BOOK FOUR

Gripping, fast-paced

From the very first page, this story is gripping and fast-paced. Alex & Rachel are the consummate high flyers. Their relationship and professionalism as career State Department employees is exemplary and yet realistic especially in light of their harrowing experiences. Anyone interested in embassy life will enjoy reading these books. With each book I become more invested in the characters. Thanks to Mel for his service and for writing these enjoyable thrillers.

This Is the Best One

This is the fourth book in the series about Alex Boyd and Rachel Smith. In my humble opinion, this was the best one. The story line from start to finish was presented in such a way that it was hard to put the book down once I started it. You could just picture the sights and sounds of Cairo as the story unfolded. The author was very accurate in his descriptions of the city, the people, the traffic and the food. I lived and worked at the Embassy in Cairo so I can attest to the authenticity of his descriptions.

The realism of the interworking's to combat these threats by the government and in particular by, Alex, Rachel, Ambassador Hunt, Marine Security Guards, Navy Seals, and Department of State Security advance team, etc., could not have been any more realistic.

Hats off to Mel for another great book. Can't wait for the next one!

Mel Has Hit His Stride

Having read the first three books in the series, I can confidently say that Mel Harrison has hit his stride. I found myself holding my breath as I read page after page of exciting prose. If you enjoy thrilling stories, then this book—and the earlier ones in the series—are for you. I hope that Mel will continue writing. His fifth book will be a blockbuster!

A Great Read

Really appreciated the character development, story of the inside life of U.S. Embassy employees and nature of foreign service life. Special salute to the Diplomatic Security mission and even though fiction. A great read.

www.ingramcontent.com/pod-product-compliance
Lightning Source LLC
Chambersburg PA
CBHW071514260626
47170CB00002B/362